Three Great Hardy Boys® Mysteries

The Hardy Boys®
in

The Masked Monkey

The Shattered Helmet

The Clue of the
Hissing Serpent

by
Franklin W. Dixon

This Hardy Boys Three-in-One
was first published in 1994 by Diamond Books,
77–85 Fulham Palace Road, Hammersmith,
London W6 8JB.

Published pursuant to agreement with
Grosset & Dunlap, Inc., New York USA.

Frank met the first attacker with a stiff right-hand punch.

THE MASKED MONKEY

·1·

A Puzzling Disappearance

"YOU mean your eighteen-year-old son drew fifty thousand dollars from his bank account and then disappeared?" dark-haired Frank Hardy asked incredulously. His blond brother Joe, sitting beside him on a sofa, also looked bewildered.

The two teenage investigators from Bayport were in the posh office of J. G. Retson, owner of a stone quarry near Granite City. He sat behind his desk, rocking nervously in a high-backed chair.

"Yes!" Retson answered Frank's question. "That's exactly what I mean. The fifty grand is gone, and so is Graham."

"And you want us to find him?"

"That's right!" Retson declared, striking the desk with his fist. "Find him and bring him back home. Tell him he can be anything he wants to be. He has my word on that."

"Sounds as if there's been a family quarrel," Joe observed.

Retson threw his hands in the air with a pained expression. "Graham and I didn't understand each other as a father and son should," he confessed. "He had some weird ideas I didn't go along with. But things will be different when he gets home. I won't try to change him any more."

The industrialist paused. All choked up, he pulled a handkerchief from his breast pocket and dabbed his eyes.

The Hardy boys felt embarrassed. They waited silently until Retson regained his composure.

"We'll do our best," Joe assured him. "But we'll need some clues. How long has Graham been missing?"

Retson folded his handkerchief and replaced it in his pocket. "Two months," he replied.

"You must have made some effort to find him in that time," Frank said.

"Of course. I went to the Granite City police when he didn't come home after a few days."

"Any results?" Joe asked.

"Nothing. Every lead petered out. Chief Carton calls it the most baffling case he's ever worked on. And he's cracked some big ones."

Frank stared out the window while he puzzled over the mysterious disappearance of Graham Retson. Then he remarked, "Sir, you obviously think we might succeed where the police failed. Why us?"

"I know your reputation as detectives," Retson replied. "According to the papers, you've helped your father on many of his cases."

Retson was referring to Fenton Hardy, the renowned detective, who had been a member of the New York City police force before becoming a private investigator. Frank, eighteen years old, and Joe, a year younger, were well experienced in tracking down criminals. Their first case was *The Mystery of the Aztec Warrior*, and their latest success, *The Bombay Boomerang*. But this seemed to be a different kind of mystery.

Retson continued. "That's not all. The point is, you're both about my son's age. There's a generation gap between Graham and me. But you fellows speak his lingo. You should be able to get through to him."

"We'll try," Frank said, "if we can find him."

Retson gave a deep sigh. "That's a relief. Stay right with the case. Money is no object. Spend whatever it takes. Go to the ends of the earth if you must, but find my son!"

"We'll give it all we've got," Joe vowed. "But we'll need some information from you."

"Such as?"

"Photos, letters, diary—anything that might give us a lead."

"I see what you mean," Retson said. "Well, I'll give you all the help I can. Come out to my place, Whisperwood, tomorrow. It's on a ridge of Granite Rock near the waterfall. Take the highway west till you see the wire fence round the property. You can examine Graham's personal belongings."

"We'll be there." Frank and Joe left the office, climbed into their convertible, and headed back to Bayport.

"What do you think of it?" Frank asked as he turned the car into the driveway of their home.

"Let's discuss it with Dad tonight," Joe suggested.

"He won't be home until late. But we'll see him in the morning."

At breakfast the next day Mr Hardy listened closely while his sons described their visit to Granite City.

"It's a real mystery," he admitted. "No wonder Retson's worried."

"Dad, can you give us a hand?" Joe asked.

Fenton Hardy smiled but shook his head. "I'd like to, but I'm tied up with a fake passport case. A ring of unsavoury characters is doctoring stolen United States passports. Strange coincidence, they were stolen in Granite City in a post office holdup two years ago. So I'm off to Washington this morning."

As the front door closed behind him the phone rang. Joe answered, heard a familiar voice, and turned to Frank with a grin. "It's Chet," he said.

Chet Morton was the Hardy boys' best friend. A plump, freckle-faced youth who jolted round town in an ancient jalopy, he was always involved in some new hobby.

Frank chuckled. "What's he up to?"

Chet was telling Joe excitedly, "I want to see you guys right away. Got a big deal on! If you sweet-talk me, maybe I'll give you a piece of the action. I'm coming over to your house pronto."

"No use, Chet," Joe said. "We're on our way to a meeting in Granite City."

Chet gave a low whistle. "You're on another case? . . . Say, is there anything I can do? Nothing too dangerous, of course."

He had helped the Hardys solve several mysteries. Though Chet was not fond of hair-raising assignments, Frank and Joe knew they could rely on him when the going got rough.

"We've just started," Joe answered. "We'll know more when we get back tonight. Come on over tomorrow and we'll talk."

"Okay," Chet replied. "And we'll discuss my big deal, too."

"Right." Joe laughed. He hung up and joined Frank for the drive to Granite City.

Beyond the outskirts of Bayport, Frank swung the convertible on to the highway leading west. After two hours the level terrain gave way to a section of hills and ravines. The car rolled through a pass cut in solid rock.

"There's the ridge Mr Retson mentioned," said Joe, glancing ahead at Granite Rock. "And that must be the fence round Whisperwood." He pointed to a tall barrier of heavy meshed wire.

"Right, Joe. It's a huge estate. I don't even see the gate yet. Oh, there it is." Frank guided the car past a stand of pine trees and stopped before a large iron portal guarding the entrance. A brass bell was mounted beside it.

Joe got out and tried to turn the massive handle. "Locked," he muttered. "And there's not a sign of a gatekeeper to let us inside this fortress."

Frank jangled the bell clapper, and the sound boomed through the grounds, but it brought no response. "Looks as if they don't want company," he muttered.

"Well, we've got an invitation," Joe said. "It's not polite for a couple of guests to keep their host waiting. So here goes."

Grasping the fence wire with his fingers, Joe got a toehold and climbed up the fence. He dropped down on the other side to the sound of tearing cloth.

"Ripped my jacket," he groaned. "Well, I made it, though. Come on."

Frank, who had followed Joe up the fence, jumped down. Together they walked towards the Whisperwood mansion, outlined against the sky at the summit of the ridge. A butler answered the bell.

"My name is Harris," he announced in solemn tones. "Mr Retson is expecting you. But you've torn your jacket, Mr Hardy. Here, let me have it and I'll see it's repaired before you leave. I'm so sorry I didn't hear the bell clapper."

Joe handed over the garment, then the butler ushered them into Retson's den.

Their client apologized when he heard about their experience at the gate. "I didn't expect you so early. You see, I do insist on complete privacy in Whisperwood."

"Think nothing of it, Mr Retson," Frank said. "Let's get down to the question of where your son might be. First of all, what does he look like?"

Retson lifted a photograph from the mantelpiece. "This was taken a few days before Graham disappeared."

Frank and Joe examined the picture. They saw a frail youth wearing long hair and glasses with round metal rims that made him appear owlish.

"Any distinguishing characteristics, Mr Retson?" Frank asked.

"Yes. Graham has a nervous habit of nodding his head while he's talking."

Joe looked hard at the photo. "He's not the rugged type, if I'm any judge."

"Hardly. Graham is very sensitive. In fact, he spends most of his time writing poetry."

"What started the feud between you two?" Joe wanted to know.

Retson snorted. "A cage of silly hamsters. Graham

brought the beasts home. I stood them as long as I could. Then one day when my son was out, I told the butler to get rid of them."

"Could we have a look at Graham's poetry?" Frank asked.

Retson opened a cabinet and pulled out a magazine. "Here, this is published by the private school he went to. You'll find his stuff on page 58. It's all Greek to me."

Frank spread the magazine on top of the cabinet. The boys began to read the verses.

"Say, this isn't bad," Frank said. "Your son has talent."

"But it doesn't tell us where he is," Joe mused. "We'd better have a look at his room."

Retson led the way up a broad staircase to a bedroom at the end of the hall. "I hope you'll find a clue here to Graham's whereabouts," he remarked, and left them.

The Hardys searched the closets, carefully looked through the bureau drawers, and examined the missing youth's collection of poetry books.

Joe was disappointed. "I haven't found anything here."

"Let's try the desk," Frank said.

They went through the drawers, beginning at the top centre, working down the left side and then turning to the right.

"Still nothing," Joe said. "No diary, no letters, no clues."

He started to slam the bottom drawer shut when Frank grabbed his arm.

"Wait a minute, Joe. What's this?" Frank reached to the back of the drawer and pulled out a crumpled piece of paper. Unfolding it, he read aloud four lines of verse:

> " 'My life is a walled city
>   From which I must flee;
>   This must my prison be
>   So long as I am me.' "

Frank turned the paper over. There were two more lines on the other side.

> " 'There is a way,
>   But what it is I cannot say.' "

Joe said, "This could be a clue! Judging by those first four lines, Graham wasn't too happy here."

"And the last two lines could mean he found a way to escape," Frank said.

Just then Mr Retson came into the room. Frank showed him the piece of paper. "Is this Graham's handwriting?" he asked.

"Yes."

"May we keep it? It might be a message in code."

"Certainly. Keep anything that will help you find Graham. Incidentally, you can stay at Whisperwood while you're on the case. There's an apartment over the old stable. The horses are gone, so we've had the rooms renovated and call it the guesthouse."

Frank and Joe decided they might accept the offer later on.

"We'd better get back to Bayport today," Joe said. "If we find it would be easier working from here, we'll be glad to park ourselves over the stable."

The butler showed the visitors out. "Here's your

jacket, Mr Hardy," he said to Joe. "I believe you will find the repairs satisfactory."

"Looks as good as new," Joe assured him. "Thanks a lot."

When the young detectives arrived home, Joe hung his jacket in the hall closet. Something crinkled in one pocket. He reached in and pulled out a folded page torn from a small notebook.

"What's that?" Frank queried.

"A bit of scribbling. Apparently somebody wrote it in a hurry."

"What does it say?"

Joe read, " 'Don't look for Graham. You'll ruin his life!' "

·2·

Bouncing Balls

"THIS is a warning!" Frank gasped. "Who could have written it, Joe?"

"Harris the butler could have slipped the paper into the pocket before returning my jacket."

"We'd better have a talk with Harris," Frank declared. "If he's trying to scare us off the case, I'd like to know the reason."

"You boys are jumping to conclusions," said a tart voice behind them. Fenton Hardy's sister was dusting the living room. Gertrude Hardy lived with her brother and his family. She loved her nephews dearly. But she never hesitated to give her opinion about the boys' detective work.

"I heard what you said about the butler," she went on, flicking her duster around a vase. "And I say you're jumping to conclusions. I've read enough murder mysteries to know that the butler is always accused."

"We're not accusing him, Aunty," Frank said. "He just seems to be the prime suspect at this point. Anyway, this isn't a murder mystery. At least we don't know that anybody's been murdered."

"We're involved in a missing-person case," Joe explained. "Graham Retson lived at Whisperwood near

18

Granite City with his parents. He's disappeared under mysterious circumstances."

"Granite City!" Miss Hardy sniffed. "That's a hundred miles from here. You'll burn a lot of fuel commuting back and forth!"

"Not necessarily," Joe replied. "Mr Retson offered to put us up at Whisperwood over his stable while we're hunting for clues. Besides, there might not be a criminal involved at all."

Gertrude Hardy clucked like a broody hen. "Stable indeed! Mr Retson should have offered you better lodgings. One of you might get kicked by a horse."

Frank and Joe soothed their aunt by assuring her there were no horses at Whisperwood to do any kicking.

"Well, I imagine you'll find some kind of danger there," Aunt Gertrude said. "So be careful." With this parting shot, she flounced out of the room.

Frank and Joe mulled over the strange disappearance of Graham Retson and the warning note. They decided to accept the industrialist's offer and go to Whisperwood the next day.

In the morning Frank and Joe were having breakfast with their mother and Aunt Gertrude when a series of rackety explosions erupted in the street.

"That's Chet's jalopy," Laura Hardy said.

The doorbell rang and Frank let their friend in. He was puffing with excitement as he entered the dining room.

"Morning, Mrs Hardy, Aunt Gertrude," he said. When he saw the food on the table, he halted in delight, rubbed his belt buckle, and glanced significantly at the women.

"Chester Morton, there's no mystery about what

you want," said Gertrude Hardy. "Can I tempt you with some pancakes?"

"Please do," replied Chet, who loved nothing better than eating.

Joe laughed. "After all, our buddy's only had one breakfast this morning. His inner man is telling him it's time for an encore."

Chet sat down and consumed a stack of pancakes at an alarming rate. He also drank two glasses of milk. Then he leaned back with a pleased expression. "That was just great," he said as the women cleared the table. "Thanks very much."

"Okay," Joe said. "What's the big deal you mentioned on the phone yesterday?"

Chet rolled his eyes. "You guys ever heard of golf ball scavenging?"

"Negative," Frank said. "What is it? A new hobby?"

"No, a get-rich-quick scheme. Duffers keep dunking golf balls in water hazards on most of the golf courses. Scavengers retrieve them and sell them. I'm a scavenger, and I'll cut you in if you're interested."

"We might be," Frank said, "when we have the time."

"We've got to go back to Granite City this afternoon," Joe told Chet.

"You can't do that!" Chet protested. "I'm counting on you. Hold everything. You've got this morning free, right?"

Frank and Joe nodded.

"Okay," Chet went on. "That's enough time to start operations. Let's go."

The three climbed into Chet's jalopy and drove to the farm outside of Bayport where he lived. On the way,

Chet explained how golf balls were retrieved.

"Many amateur divers and frogmen," he said, "descend into water hazards to scour the bottom. Professionals, however, don't go into the water. They use suction pumps and underwater vacuum cleaners.

"About sixty million balls are recovered every year," Chet stated, "and are resold for about fifteen million dollars."

Frank whistled. "That's a lot of money."

"Enough to buy several golf courses," Joe remarked.

"Sure," Chet said. "And I aim to get my share of the dough from the golf courses around Bayport."

At the Morton farm the three transferred to a small truck. In the back was a very large box with a petrol engine attached. Lines of small holes showed on one side, and a long hose dangled from one corner.

"Dad's letting me use his pick-up truck," Chet said. "I spent a week building the retriever. Come on. Let's go to the nearest course and see how my suction pump works."

When they arrived at the Bayport links, Chet explained his gadget to the club's golf pro. He was willing to let the boys have a try at the water hazard, providing they gave him half the golf balls they recovered.

The trio then drove to a pond at the third hole. Chet turned on the engine, pushed the nozzle of the hose down through the water, and began to vacuum the bottom.

A mixture of mud and water, sucked through the hose into the container, spewed out through the side holes and back into the pond. Loud rattling came from inside.

"Those are the golf balls!" Chet exulted. "They're

too big to go through the holes, so they're banging against the sides. We've struck it rich!"

"The pump works like a charm," Joe admitted. "Chet, for once you've come up with something practical."

About an hour later the pro rode up in a golf cart. He told them the recovery operation would have to wait until early evening because some golfers were impatient to play the third hole.

Chet wound up the hose and opened a door at the top of the container. Frank and Joe peered in. Several hundred golf balls—dirty and muddy from their stay in the pond, but otherwise in good condition—were piled up inside.

"We can sell these for a good profit," Chet said, "when we've cleaned them." After turning over half of the take to the golf pro, the boys tossed the rest into the back of the pick-up to dry off, and drove to Bayport.

As they went through the main intersection, a wild uproar broke out behind them. Horns blew. People shouted.

"What's wrong?" Chet muttered. "I didn't go through a stoplight!"

Joe, looking back, cried out, "We're paving the avenue with golf balls! The tailgate's open. We're losing them!"

Their cargo was streaming out of the pick-up into the crossing. Pedestrians went into frantic contortions as the golf balls rolled under their feet. Cars jolted to a halt. Traffic was snarled in four directions.

Chet pulled over to the kerb. "We're in for it now," he groaned.

"You can say that again," Frank muttered. "Here

comes the traffic cop. He looks pretty mad."

"And he's not too happy about running the obstacle course we just set up," Joe added.

"Everybody out!" the officer commanded the three youths. "Start picking them up!"

Frank, Joe, and Chet meekly climbed out of the truck and began gathering the golf balls. A group of youngsters pitched in for the fun of it. When the balls were back in the truck, Chet double-checked the tailgate before driving off.

"Lucky I didn't get a ticket," he sighed.

"And fortunately nobody got hurt," Frank said.

They arrived at the Hardy house to find their pals Phil Cohen and Tony Prito waiting for them. Phil was the sensitive, studious type, but could be counted on when Frank and Joe were on a dangerous mission.

Olive-skinned Tony, the son of a Bayport contractor, was another friend who frequently helped the Hardys solve mysteries.

The two were told about Chet's new business. They agreed to accompany him to the golf course that evening to complete the ball scavenging operation.

Frank and Joe drove to Whisperwood. They had dinner in a roadside restaurant. When they reached the estate, Retson showed them to his guesthouse. From a distance came a constant hissing sound.

"It's the waterfall," Retson explained. "It seems to be whispering all the time. That's why we called our home Whisperwood."

"Did your son ever come to the guesthouse?" Frank inquired.

"Yes, occasionally. You see, Harris used the place while a wing of the mansion was being renovated.

Graham liked him and visited him sometimes. Now the work on the house is done and Harris is back in his own quarters."

Joe described the incident of the note in his jacket pocket. "We'd like to talk to the butler about it," he said.

"Of course!" Retson replied. "Harris will have to answer to me if he's the one responsible."

Their host led the way back to the mansion, where they confronted the butler.

Joe handed the note to him. Harris became pale as he scrutinized the message. His eyes bulged. His breath came in gasps. He folded the note and handed it back. "Where did you find this?" he asked.

"In my jacket pocket, after you fixed it yesterday," Joe said.

Harris frowned. "If you think I wrote this, you are mistaken," he said.

"Can you prove that, Harris?" Retson asked harshly.

"Yes, indeed, sir. As you know, I make out the shopping list for the week. Here is the one I just wrote." Harris drew a sheet of paper from his pocket. "Compare my handwriting with the note Mr Hardy found in his coat."

Joe placed the two pieces of paper side by side. Frank looked on. The two scrawls obviously did not match!

"It seems someone else wrote the warning," Joe mused.

"But who?" Frank replied. "Who else lives in this house?"

"Jackson, the gardener," Retson said. "His wife is our cook. And of course there's Mrs Retson. My wife has had a nervous breakdown. She rarely leaves her room in the east wing. A nurse is on duty with her constantly. You can talk to Miss Hopkins if you want to. But don't bother Mrs Retson."

"We'll have to check out the whole staff," Frank said.

"Well, get on with the investigation first thing in the morning," Retson urged. "My son may have been kidnapped. Criminals may be holding him prisoner right now!"

Frank and Joe walked back to the guesthouse. "We're fresh out of clues," Joe commented.

"Maybe we'll come up with a theory after a little shut-eye," Frank said.

"That is, if we can get any shut-eye. Whisperwood gives me the willies. It's real spooky back here."

A high wind blew mournfully through the pines, and clouds scudded across the face of the moon. Granite Rock lay in deep shadows except for outcroppings of stone that resembled gigantic human figures trying to escape over the crest.

Despite the uncanny atmosphere, the boys fell into a deep sleep. They were awakened by a loud splintering sound in the middle of the night. A missile had crashed through the picture window into their room!

·3·

Careless Talk

"FRANK! What on earth was that?" Joe asked, fumbling for the light switch.

Frank had already jumped out of bed to the broken window. Bright moonlight gave him a clear view of the grounds. "No sign of the thrower," he reported. "Whoever it was ducked out of sight."

Joe turned on the small lamp next to his bed and the two searched around the room for the missile.

Joe reached under his bed. "Look," he said. "It's a golf ball!"

"I suppose it's a practical joke," Frank said. "But I don't think it's very funny."

"Whom do we know who might toss a golf ball in our direction?" Joe asked, raising an eyebrow.

"Chet Morton, that's who! Let's collar him if we can."

After dressing quickly, they hurried down the stairs and out the door. Joe circled the guest-house. Frank pushed through the bushes searching for a figure crouching behind them.

"When I spot an oversize shadow, that'll be our fun-loving pal," he said to himself.

Frank searched the bushes but found no one. Joe

reported failure too. Finally they returned to their room and slept soundly the rest of the night.

Early the next morning there was a knock on the door. Frank opened it. There stood Chet!

"Do come in," Frank invited. "We've been looking for you."

"Why?"

"What were you doing here last night?" Joe asked.

"What makes you think I was here?"

"This!" Joe showed him the golf ball. "It came through that window."

"Don't look at me," Chet protested. "I was home in Bayport!"

"You're here now," Frank put in.

"Sure. But I just arrived. I'm after golf ball scavenging contracts around Granite City. I just dropped by to see you two before making the rounds."

Frank shook his head. "You made a wonderful suspect. Now we're back where we started."

"Let me have a look at that ball," Chet said. He turned it over between his fingers. "Condor brand," he noted.

"Could find out where it came from?" Joe queried.

"Condors are popular," Chet said with an air of authority. "Even an expert such as myself might have trouble identifying a single ball. However, I'll ask around and see if any Granite City club sells Condors."

"How soon will you let us know?" Frank said.

"I'll stop by this evening and give you the info."

Chet drove off to the golf courses. Frank and Joe went to the Whisperwood mansion for breakfast, and told their host about the golf ball and the broken window at the guesthouse.

Retson also was puzzled, but finally he said, "I still suspect Harris."

"Why are you so down on your butler?" Frank inquired.

"Well, Graham spent a lot of time with Harris," Retson replied.

"More than with you?" Joe asked.

"Much more. I'd rather have seen the boy playing football. But no. He preferred writing verse. Harris said he liked the poetry, which could have been a come-on. He may well be part of a plot against my son."

The Hardys suggested checking the handwriting of the rest of the staff before accusing the butler. They set about gathering samples. Joe went to the kitchen, engaged the cook in conversation and persuaded her to write down a recipe for his mother.

Frank, buttonholing the gardener for a talk about the roses, managed to pocket a shopping list for seeds. Retson himself produced a memo written for Mrs Retson by Miss Hopkins, the nurse.

None of the samples of handwriting resembled that in the warning note found in Joe's jacket!

Frank looked disappointed. "We've learned what everybody's scrawl looks like, but that doesn't give us a lead."

"I still suspect Harris," Retson insisted.

"He could have had a confederate," Joe mused. "Maybe we should give him a lie detector test."

"I'll get him up here," Retson said. He pressed a button that rang a bell in the servants' quarters. The butler appeared.

Frank asked him, "Harris, you still claim to be innocent of that note, don't you?"

"Of course, Mr Hardy. I *am* innocent."

"Would you be willing to take a lie detector test to prove it?"

The butler blanched, but quickly regained control of himself. "Whenever you wish."

Joe offered to go to Granite City Police Headquarters and ask for a loan of a polygraph, the kind used in testing the veracity of suspects. He was back within the hour carrying a portable machine.

Harris sat patiently in a chair while the instruments for measuring pulse rate and blood pressure were attached to his body.

Frank set the graph which recorded physical reactions. Joe then directed a series of test questions at the butler. Then he said, "Harris, did you write that note I found in my jacket?"

"No."

"Do you know who wrote it?"

"No."

"Have you any idea where Graham is now?"

"No."

Watching the graph unroll, Frank saw that the pattern of the needle across the paper remained steady as the questioning continued. Finally he said, "Harris seems to be telling the truth."

Retson was clearly disappointed in the results of the test. He told the butler to leave the room and warned him to remain on the premises.

"I don't think he'll go anywhere," Frank said. "He seems like a loyal employee."

"Somebody here is disloyal!" Retson exclaimed. "How else do you explain away that note?"

Joe said, "You have to admit, Frank, it looks like an

inside job. Still, the handwriting provided no clue."

"Well, let's be thorough and give all of the staff a lie detector test," Frank said.

The Hardys told each employee about the surreptitious warning. No one seemed overly surprised to hear about it, although they all denied any knowledge of who sent it. Also, none of them objected to submitting to the polygraph test. In each case the results were negative.

Miss Hopkins, the nurse, said Mrs Retson was too ill to be questioned, and the boys did not pursue the matter. They repacked the equipment in thoughtful silence. They had drawn a blank. Besides being disappointed, they were slightly annoyed by the patronizing half-smile on Retson's face.

"Too bad," he said. "Now what kind of explanation can you come up with?"

"It'll take time to figure out," Frank said. "But there's an answer to everything. We'll solve this mystery sooner or later."

"I trust it will be sooner," Retson said as the Hardys left to return the polygraph. "I'm depending on your fine reputation as detectives to find my son!"

Frank and Joe were glum as they drove alongside a golf course on their way to Granite City Police Headquarters.

The green for the seventh hole lay close to the road, and a crawling sprinkler had come to rest near the edge of it, squirting water on to the pavement. Just as a car approached from the opposite direction, water splashed across the windshield of the Hardy's convertible, spraying them and momentarily blinding Frank's vision.

Cru-unch! They hit the oncoming car side on and came to a halt with screeching brakes.

Frank and Joe got out, as did two men from the other vehicle. One was a muscular individual wearing a slouch hat. His companion was young, slim, and had thick blond hair.

He managed a smile. "That was a pretty close shave," he said. "What happened? You seemed to swerve."

"Water from that sprinkler hit my windshield," Frank said.

The four circled the cars, examining the doors and bumpers. The convertible had a slight dent near the left door handle. The only damage to the other car was a scratch on the bumper.

The older man said, "If you're willing to overlook the dent, why don't you forget the small damage to my car? You know these insurance companies—miles of red tape."

"Fair enough," said Frank.

The man looked at the lie detector equipment in the back of the convertible and smiled. "Somebody's been put through a grilling, I see. You boys on the police force?"

"No, but we do detective work," Joe said.

"Are you on a case?"

"Yes, we're trying to pick up the trail of Graham Retson of Whisperwood."

"Ah, yes," the blond man said. "He disappeared some time ago. Think you can find him?"

"We hope to," Joe said.

"Come on," Frank urged. "We'd better be going. Thanks for your co-operation," he said, turning to the men. "Next time we'll be more careful about golf course sprinklers."

After the two cars had started off, Frank said, "Joe, you really yacked about our investigation. What's the idea?"

Joe looked embarrassed. "You're right, Frank. Sometimes I talk too much. I doubt, though, that those fellows had anything to do with the Retson mystery."

"Likely not, but there's no sense taking chances."

The boys returned the polygraph to the police. They thanked Chief Carton, who offered to co-operate with them in any way he could.

Then they drove back to Whisperwood. Frank parked the car near where the gardener was planting a small bush.

"This might be a good time to ask him a few questions," he said.

"Right," Joe agreed.

The boys walked up to the man. He was on his knees, firming the earth round the bush. When he saw the boys approaching, he looked up questioningly.

Frank came directly to the point. "Mr Jackson," he said, "how do you feel about young Graham's disappearance?"

The gardener trowelled some more earth on to the roots of the plant. "I just work here," he said calmly. "It's not my place to have any feelings about it."

"You must see a lot that goes on around here," Frank persisted. "Did Graham actually leave without you spotting him?"

"He did." Jackson was becoming surly. "I'm not his baby-sitter. And I don't keep a watch on the front door, either."

Just then the screen door of the kitchen opened. The gardener's wife stepped out. "I heard those questions about Graham Retson," she stated bluntly. "And let me tell you something. I'm glad that he's not cooped up here any more!"

"Can you help us find him, Mrs Jackson?" Joe asked.

"I wouldn't if I could," snapped the woman. "Why don't you mind your own business and leave the boy alone? He had good reason to run away!"

Mrs Jackson's tirade was interrupted by the sound of feet pounding along the brick walk. As Frank and Joe turned around, Chet Morton raced up to them.

His face was red from exertion. His breath came in big gulps. Wiping streams of perspiration from his forehead, he said, "Hey, fellows, I found out plenty!"

·4·

A Ghostly Figure

FRANK and Joe pulled Chet aside, and Frank asked, "What's up?"

"The Condor!" Chet puffed. "I've got the dope on it!"

"You mean the one that came through the window last night?"

"Not exactly," Chet answered. "But I've discovered who sells the Condor golf balls around here."

"Who's that?" Frank demanded.

"The golf pro at the Olympic Health Club. He's got a special concession. When you buy a Condor, you buy it from Gus McCormick."

"So Gus sold our ball to one of his customers?" Joe asked.

"That's my theory," Chet replied.

"That gives us something to go on," Joe said. "We'd better case the Olympic Health Club and see what gives over there."

Frank nodded. "That would be easy if Chet got a contract to retrieve golf balls from the Olympic water hazard."

Chet looked crestfallen. "Sorry, Frank. I've tried. I wangled two contracts from courses in town, but it was no dice at the Olympic. Say, I'd better get cracking with my suction pump. Business won't wait."

He left, and Frank and Joe resumed questioning the cook.

"Mrs Jackson," Frank said, "what did you mean when you said Graham had good reason to run away?"

"He wasn't happy here," she replied. "There were things he wanted to do that he wasn't allowed to."

"For instance?"

"Take those hamsters. They didn't do anyone any harm. And Graham got a lot of pleasure from them. Getting rid of them was a shame."

Her husband rose to his feet. "Be quiet, Martha!" he commanded. "You're talking too much."

"Mrs Jackson isn't revealing any secrets," Joe said.

"If Mr Retson wants to tell you about Graham, that's up to him," the gardener retorted. Turning to his wife, he asked crossly, "Do you want to get us fired?" He pulled her into the kitchen and the screen door slammed behind them.

Frank and Joe strolled over to the guesthouse.

"We've quizzed everybody except Mrs Retson," Frank pointed out. "She may have vital information about Graham. We'll have to talk to her."

"Retson might not go for the idea," Joe said. "Let's slip into the house when no one's looking."

As soon as darkness fell, the boys made their way through the grounds to the mansion. Circling round through the bushes, they reached the east wing of the building, prised open a window, and climbed over the sill into an unused room.

They went into the hallway and upstairs to the second floor where Mrs Retson had her apartment.

Joe knocked softly on the door. It opened. "What do you want?" asked Miss Hopkins.

"We'd like to speak to Mrs Retson," Frank said politely.

"Impossible! Mrs Retson doesn't receive visitors." The nurse started to shut the door, but Frank and Joe slipped past her before she realized what they were up to.

"Mrs Retson!" Frank called out, advancing towards the bedroom. "We must speak to you!"

"It's about Graham," Joe added. "And it's urgent."

The nurse followed, protesting all the while. No reply came from Mrs Retson. The three reached the bedroom doorway and peered in. They stood speechless.

The bed was empty!

Frank and Joe hastily searched the apartment. There was no sign of the woman anywhere. Joe pointed to an open window in the bedroom. A rope ladder was attached to the frame. "That's the explanation. She climbed out!"

"Your patient must be pretty agile," Frank said to the nurse as he looked out the window. Nobody was in sight.

"It's all your fault!" Miss Hopkins cried angrily. "When you barged in you must have frightened Mrs Retson. If anything happens to my patient I'll hold you responsible!" She pointed to the door. "Please leave immediately!"

"We're leaving," Frank assured her. "But we'll be back!"

As the boys went down the stairs, Frank said, "We'd better alert Retson that his wife is missing."

"Why don't we look for her first?" Joe suggested. "If

we tell him now, Hopkins might convince him it was our fault."

"Okay. Let's make a quick search round the premises," Frank agreed.

The boys left the house by the same route they had come in. They were about to split up when a loud cry echoed through the night air. A single word rang in their ears—a woman's voice screaming:

"Graham!"

Startled, Joe asked, "Where did that come from?"

"The waterfall. Come on!"

Frank pushed through the bushes and raced among the trees with Joe at his heels. The roar of the falls became louder with every step.

They turned up a narrow ravine. In the moonlight they saw the water spilling over the edge of a rocky cliff. It plunged into a churning whirlpool, from which a stream with a strong current coursed along the side of Granite Rock.

The Hardys moved towards the falls by stepping gingerly from rock to rock, struggling to keep their balance. "Once in that whirlpool," Frank warned, "and it could be the last swim we ever take. Watch your footing, Joe!"

The younger boy halted suddenly and pointed to the top of the waterfall. "Look!" he yelled.

High above them on a boulder near the edge of the drop stood the ghostly figure of a woman. Her head was held high. Her body was tense. She stared into the distance.

The boys wiped the spray from their eyes for a better look, but a rising wind whipped a scarf across the woman's face, concealing her features.

Frank was galvanized by the sight. "Joe, that woman may look like a wraith, but I'll bet she's Mrs Retson. I'm going to introduce myself."

The boys leaped over the rocky terrain. Suddenly Frank, who was behind Joe, lost his balance, clutched at the air, and fell into the water with a heavy splash.

The whirlpool took hold of Frank, bouncing him around like a cork. Desperately he struggled to escape from the swirling mass of water. A moment later he was thrown to one side. His head struck a rock with a thud and he blacked out.

Joe saw his brother go under, bob up, and float downstream. Frantically he dashed along the bank. Scrambling at breakneck speed across the boulders, he reached the spot where Frank was hurtling along helplessly towards certain death. Ahead was another drop full of razor-sharp rocks!

In the nick of time Joe reached down, grabbed Frank by the shirt collar, and dragged him to safety.

Frank lay quiet and Joe quickly applied mouth-to-mouth resuscitation until his brother regained consciousness. He gasped as he came round, "Thanks for fishing me out!"

Joe grinned. "As you said, this is no place for a swim."

Frank struggled to his feet. "The wraith—is she still up there?"

Both boys glanced towards the rock where the woman had been standing. A dense cloud covering the moon left the entire falls in darkness.

"She's probably gone by now," said Joe. "No use looking for her in this murk. We both might slip into the whirlpool next time."

"Joe, I didn't slip," Frank replied sombrely.

"What?"

"Somebody pushed me!"

"Did you see who it was?" Joe's voice was tense.

"No. But I think it was a man, judging by the force of the shove. He must have been lurking on the bank when I came along."

"Well, I didn't see anybody. I thought we were all alone at the bottom of the falls. Anyway, it proves something."

"Like what?" Frank asked.

"Somebody wants us off the Retson case. And he'll stop at nothing!"

"Which means we must be getting warm," Frank said. "Let's go back to the mansion. Perhaps Mrs Retson has returned by now."

They retraced their steps. As they approached the east wing, a figure way ahead of them ran across the lawn.

"A woman!" Frank exclaimed.

"Must be Mrs Retson!" Joe dashed off at top speed. Frank followed at a slower pace. But they were too late! The woman reached the building and began climbing up the side.

"She's going up the rope ladder!" Joe moaned.

"No doubt she's used to that contraption, the way she handles it," Frank said.

"Hey, what's this?" Joe said, picking up a piece of flimsy material torn from a scarf. He examined it for a moment, then put it in his pocket.

Since Frank was feeling exhausted from his ordeal in the whirlpool, they decided to call it a night. At the guesthouse Frank promptly fell into a deep sleep.

Joe lay in bed with his hands clasped behind his head, trying to make sense of the Retson riddle. "I wonder if Nurse Hopkins is in cahoots with Mrs Retson and knew where she went," he said to himself. Gradually he dozed off.

A hard pounding on the door snapped Joe wide awake. He looked at his watch. It was eight o'clock in the morning. Frank sat up, rubbing the sleep from his eyes. "What's all that noise about?" he asked groggily.

Joe got out of bed, opened the door, and confronted Harris the butler. He waved a cablegram wildly in Joe's face.

"It came this morning," he blurted out. "Now we know where Graham is!"

·5·

Away to Brazil

JOE seized the paper and read the message. *"Help,"* the cablegram said. *"Come Excelsior Grao Para. Do not reply. Just come. Graham."*

"You see," the butler remarked, "Graham must be in that hotel."

"Where is it?" asked Frank, who by now was wide awake.

"The cable was sent from Belem, Brazil. It's on the Amazon River, I believe."

"That's a strange place for him to be. Well, we'd better speak to Mr Retson right away."

"Yes, sir. He is waiting for you in his den," Harris said.

The Hardys found the tycoon looking very much relieved. "It's obvious what's happened," he chortled. "Graham has learned the error of his ways. He's got over all his nonsensical ideas and is ready to come home. The mystery is solved!"

"Looks as if there's nothing more for us to do," Joe observed.

"Wrong!" Retson retorted. "I hired you for an assignment, and it's still your case. Go to Brazil and escort my son home. Judging by his cablegram, he's in

41

some kind of trouble. Get him out of it, even if it's only an unpaid hotel bill."

Frank rubbed his chin thoughtfully. "That's okay by us, sir. But before we leave for Belem, we would like to talk with Mrs Retson."

The tycoon frowned. "Ordinarily I'd say no. But this new information about Graham is sure to cheer her up. Only make it short. I won't rest till I know you're on the plane to Brazil."

When Frank and Joe appeared at Mrs Retson's apartment, Miss Hopkins greeted them in stony silence. Had she told Retson about the incident the night before? Did she think the Hardys had? Her face showed nothing. She swung the door open and invited them in with a wave of her hand.

Mrs Retson was sitting in an armchair, a shawl over her shoulders and a blanket across her knees. Her head was tilted to one side and her eyes were half-closed. She seemed completely listless.

Frank suspected the woman was under sedation.

"Mrs Retson, we've come to ask you a few questions," Frank said.

The woman opened her eyes. "Questions? What kind of questions?"

"Well, we saw a woman at the waterfall last night. She resembled you!"

"It wasn't me!" Mrs Retson shuddered as she spoke and averted her eyes.

"This woman later climbed up a rope ladder to your room," Joe went on. "Who else could it have been?"

Mrs Retson's voice rose to a shrill pitch. "I don't know! I don't know! You must have made a mistake in the darkness."

"There was a full moon last night," Frank stated. "It lighted up the whole area of the waterfall."

"That explains what happened," she cried. "People often have delusions at the falls, especially under a full moon! You boys imagined you saw a woman."

Joe picked up a flimsy scarf from an easy chair. From his pocket he pulled the fragment of material he had found the previous night, and fitted it into a tear in the scarf. It matched perfectly.

Mrs Retson seemed terror-stricken at the sight. When Joe explained where the piece had come from, she slumped into unconsciousness.

"She's fainted!" Frank exclaimed. He began chafing her wrists while Joe massaged the back of her neck. Miss Hopkins came in quickly and held a glass of water to her lips.

Mrs Retson began to moan. She opened her eyes and gazed in bewilderment. After sipping a little water, she sat up. Joe adjusted the shawl, which had slipped down.

The nurse broke the silence. "That's enough. Mrs Retson isn't strong enough to be badgered like this. Do your investigating somewhere else!"

"We'll be leaving here soon," Joe promised. "We're going to Brazil to bring Graham home."

Upon hearing this, Mrs Retson raised a hand and cried out, "No! No! Graham is not in Brazil. He's right here!"

Startled, Frank begged her to explain herself. But she merely gave a knowing smile and refused to say another word.

Frank and Joe left the apartment, expecting the nurse to slam the door behind them. Instead, Miss

Hopkins joined the two of them in the hall.

"You must be mystified by Mrs Retson's remark," she said.

"That's putting it mildly," Joe replied.

Frank nodded in agreement. "What could she possibly have meant about Graham being right here?"

"She believes in extrasensory perception and psychic phenomena," Miss Hopkins explained. "She thinks a person can be in two places at once."

"So that's it," Frank said. "Thanks for telling us."

The boys went outside. Walking away from the mansion, they glanced back and looked up at Mrs Retson's apartment. They saw a face in the window. The woman herself was staring down at them with a pleading expression.

"I really feel sorry for her," Joe said. "She must be mentally ill. That explains her going down to the waterfall last night and calling Graham!"

The boys returned to the guesthouse. Chet Morton was there, and half an hour later Phil and Tony arrived. They had come to join Chet in the business of retrieving golf balls from the Granite City golf courses. The five discussed the latest events.

"So Joe and I will go to Brazil," Frank concluded. "Meanwhile, it would be a good idea if you guys could keep an eye on the Retson estate."

"How?" Chet asked. "You can't do it with a place this size from outside!"

"Maybe Retson will let you stay here. During part of the time you can scavenge golf balls, and when you're not busy, you can keep track of what's going on."

"Sounds good," Chet said with a grin. "It would save us money, too. Let's go see the big man."

The industrialist appeared gratified to know he could count on Chet, Phil, and Tony. "It'll be nice to have you fellows on the premises," he said. "Mrs Retson will feel much safer if we have muscular reinforcements as near as the guest-house. Not that I think anything will happen," he added.

Frank and Joe made plane reservations, then said goodbye to their pals and drove back to Bayport to get ready for the flight to Brazil. Their mother made lunch, then helped them pack their belongings. Laura Hardy always made sure the detectives in the family were properly equipped.

"I do hope you won't be gone long," she said.

"Not too long, Mom," Frank assured her. "It shouldn't take more than a few days."

"That's long enough to get caught by a boa constrictor or eaten by piranhas," came the voice of Aunt Gertrude, who had stepped into the boys' bedroom. "You'll probably get lost in the Amazon rain forest where the jaguars will take a bite out of you. Or the natives might nick you with their poison arrows."

"Aunt Gertrude, we're only going to Belem," Joe reminded her. "It's a modern city!"

"Anything can happen down there," Miss Hardy said sharply. "You boys had better look before you leap. Don't say I didn't warn you."

That evening Frank and Joe caught a connecting flight to New York. At Kennedy Airport they transferred to the jet to Brazil, and an hour later they were thundering through the air headed south.

The Hardys had the first two seats in their row. The window seat was occupied by a black-haired Brazilian in his early forties who spoke excellent English. He introduced himself in a friendly manner. "We will be on this plane for quite some time so we might as well get to know one another. My name is Joachim San Marten."

Frank introduced himself and his brother. "What kind of a city is Belem?" Joe asked their new acquaintance.

"Very romantic," San Marten replied. "It is at the mouth of the Amazon, and has buildings dating back to colonial times. Do not miss the Ver-O-Peso market. But remember that the Portuguese name means Watch-the-Weight. That's a wise rule to follow." He laughed.

Further conversation revealed that San Marten was a trader in wild animals.

"Zoos are always in the market for the snakes and big cats of the Amazon basin," he told the boys. "I buy them from the natives and ship them round the world. You have no doubt seen some of my animals in the United States. And why are you two gentlemen going to Belem?"

Frank said, "We're on our way to meet a friend in the city."

"Frank's afraid I'll spill the beans again," Joe thought and remained silent.

"Do you have good accommodations?"

"We are going to stay at the Excelsior Grao Para," Frank replied.

"Oh?" San Marten looked doubtful.

"What's the matter?"

"Nothing. It's just that this hotel has not the best reputation. It is said to be run by gangsters."

Frank grinned. "We'll watch out for the mob."

San Marten nodded. "Please remember, if I can be of any assistance, do not hesitate to call on me." He handed Frank his card.

"Thanks," Frank said. Then all three settled back in their seats for a snooze.

Hours later, in bright morning sunlight, the jetliner descended, and prepared for its landing at Belem. Through the window the boys could see the city. A riot of colour was reflected from red, green, and yellow tiled roofs. Small craft and freighters rocked gently in the harbour.

When they left the plane, the Hardys noticed San Marten waiting for a large crate that was being taken from the cargo compartment. It was covered by a tarpaulin.

"I wonder if one of our friend's dangerous animals is in there," said Joe.

"I suppose so," Frank replied. "Maybe he's brought back an American cougar for the Belem zoo."

After they were finished with the formalities at passport control and had claimed their baggage, they caught a taxi and soon arrived at the Excelsior Grao Para, which turned out to be a rather small hotel.

The desk clerk informed them that Mr Retson had checked out of his room.

"What? He's left?" Joe asked.

"Yes, sir. Mr Retson has departed."

"Where did he go?" Frank asked.

"He left no forwarding address."

"That's funny," Frank said, puzzled.

"Maybe he left a message for us in his room" Joe suggested. "Mind if we have a look?"

The clerk shrugged. "It's empty, so go ahead.

Number 225 he was in. I think it's open."

Frank and Joe left their bags at the desk, took the lift upstairs, and found the room. It was open and the key was in the lock. They walked inside.

"Let's give it a thorough once-over," Frank said.

They checked the dressers, the desk, and night table. Nothing. Frank searched the waste-paper basket but found no clues. Joe opened the closet. "Hey, here's something!" he said.

Joe brought out a leather jacket. It bore a label from a Granite City store. Methodically he searched the pockets. In one of them was a cigarette lighter.

"Look at his," Joe said. Out of curiosity he flipped the top open.

A sharp needle sprang out from a hidden trap.

It pierced Joe's thumb. He staggered back with a cry, went rigid for a split second, and then toppled over, unconscious!

·6·

Underground Voodoo

FRANK rushed over to where his brother lay on the floor. "Joe, what happened?"

Joe made no reply. His eyes were closed, and his face was pale. He breathed heavily as if gasping for air.

"I've got to get a doctor fast," Frank thought desperately. He went to the door, twisted the old-fashioned knob, and jerked hard. It did not budge! He tried shouting for help, but nobody heard him.

Frank ran to the telephone beside the bed. The desk failed to answer. Frantically, Frank poked his head out the window. There was a fire escape, but his heart sank when he saw that the bottom part of the ladder had been removed, leaving a thirty-foot drop to the pavement. He would need a rope!

Frank pulled the sheets from the bed, tore them into strips, and knotted the pieces together. Then he started to climb out the window.

Suddenly a click at the door caused him to turn round. "Hello?"

The door opened and San Marten stepped in. He looked in amazement at the torn sheets in Frank's hands and at Joe lying unconscious on the floor.

"What's going on here?" he asked.

"Quick, I need a doctor for Joe," Frank said. "He's been poisoned."

San Marten ran to the phone. The desk answered and he called for the hotel physician.

While they waited, Frank asked, "How did you get in here, and why did you come?"

"The key was on the other side and the door unlocked," San Marten replied. "I was in the neighbourhood and decided you might need some help in a strange city. The clerk told me you were up here. How was your brother poisoned?"

Just then the doctor hastened in. He set down his bag and kneeled beside Joe. After feeling the boy's pulse, he asked, "What caused it?"

Frank indicated the lighter. The doctor examined it closely. Then he pulled a syringe out of his bag and gave Joe an injection.

"The young man will be all right," he said. "But he could not have lasted much longer. He is suffering from a powerful poison. Fortunately he has a strong heart or he would be dead by now!"

"This seems to be a fiendish plot!" San Marten declared. "You will have to take precautions."

"Somebody in Belem doesn't like us," Frank agreed. "I'm glad you do, Mr San Marten. It's nice to have a friend in a strange city."

"I am happy to have been of assistance," San Marten replied. "If you take my advice, you will not remain at this hotel. Go somewhere else."

"We will," Frank assured him, "as soon as Joe's back on his feet."

While they were speaking, Joe came round. The doctor examined him and said he was out of danger.

When Joe stood up, he wobbled. "I'm a trifle queasy," he said. But gradually he felt stronger and the physician left.

"Incidentally," San Marten said, "where is the friend you were looking for?"

"We don't know. He checked out before we arrived," Frank replied.

"It is strange that the young man departed so suddenly," San Marten said. "Perhaps something happened to him."

"Graham must have been in a tizzy," Joe agreed. "After all, he left without his jacket."

"And his cigarette lighter," Frank added. "That is, if it was really his."

A bellboy opened the door and San Marten called him in.

"Perhaps you can give us some information about the former occupant of this room?"

"Yes, sir. A very rich American by the name of Graham Retson. About my age."

"What became of him?" Frank asked eagerly. "Did he say anything to you about where he was going?"

"All I can tell you is that he left the hotel in the company of two men. I do not know what their destination was."

"Did you know the men?" Joe asked.

"One of them," the bellboy stated. "I have seen him before many times at the Ver-O-Peso market. But I do not know his name or what he does."

Close questioning of the bellboy elicited no further information and he left.

"If you like, I will be glad to take you to the Ver-O-Peso market to look for your friend," San Marten said.

"We'd appreciate it," Frank said.

The boys took a room at the hotel, then sallied out into Belem with the Brazilian.

Crowds of people streamed past them on the streets. Rickety cars bumped over the cobblestones. A wisp of smoke drifting by carried the scent of roasting nuts.

San Marten smiled as he sniffed the aroma. "Nuts are one of the most important exports of our country. See this truck? Those big bags piled on top are full of Brazil nuts."

Joe noticed a monkey climb to the top of the sacks. He was about to call attention to him when suddenly one of the bags moved.

"Frank! Jump!" Joe yelled.

The massive bag smashed on the cobblestones where Frank had been. The truck stopped, the monkey disappeared, and the driver recovered his cargo.

"Thanks for the warning, Joe," Frank said. "I'd hate to be knocked off the case by a bag of nuts. But accidents will happen."

Joe was not convinced that it was an accident. The monkey had pushed the nuts. Could someone have put him up to it? Or was he just monkeying around?

The three stopped for lunch in a small restaurant, then continued on to the colourful market. They walked between stalls heaped with tropical fruits, sandals, and gewgaws.

Sellers offered their wares, buyers scoffed at prices, and haggling went on amid a din of Portuguese epithets.

Joe gestured towards one of the stalls. "How about a baby python, Frank? Or maybe you'd settle for some alligator teeth?"

"No thanks. I think I'll take a voodoo charm home to Aunt Gertrude," Frank replied.

Joe tried to find an opportunity to tell his brother about the monkey but San Marten did not leave their side.

Finally they stopped in front of a witchcraft stall, where a wizened, gnome-like old man offered to sell them weird idols, magical potions, and wax figures in which to stick pins.

San Marten spoke to the man in Portuguese, and turned to the boys. "We're invited to join a voodoo rite. Buru here claims he can conjure up a vision of where your friend is."

The witch doctor smiled and nodded, showing broken teeth.

"Tell him we don't believe in visions," Frank said.

San Marten smiled. "I'm sure you don't. But these dances are interesting to watch, and you do not get a chance like this often."

Frank shrugged. "Okay."

San Marten again spoke in Portuguese to the witch doctor, who bowed and gestured. Then he led the way through his stall, between piles of dried snake skins and jungle herbs, to a small door at the rear. He opened it, and a narrow spiral stone staircase lay before them.

Cackling softly to himself, Buru lifted a battered lantern off the wall, lighted it, and descended. The air became cool and the stone walls dripped moisture. The lantern threw flickering rays of light that only made the darkness behind seem more intense.

The old man stopped in front of a heavy wooden door and spoke in his native tongue. San Marten translated: "We are in an underground cellar far below the level of the street. The magical rites are held down here to prevent unwelcome intrusions by unbelievers, especially the police!"

The police! A shiver ran down Frank's spine. What kind of a place were they being taken to?

Buru pulled out a black key. The lock clicked and the door opened into a large musty room. Enormous dust-coated beams supported the high ceiling.

About twenty silent natives sat in a circle on the stone floor. All were dressed in flowing white robes. An earthenware jug passed from hand to hand around the circle, each man taking a swig as it reached him.

"My friends," San Marten whispered, "you have entered the world of macumba."

"Macumba?" Joe asked, puzzled. "What's that?"

"A form of voodoo. These people are convinced they can bring back departed spirits by means of a magical dance. The spirit possesses one of the dancers."

"They're not dancing now," Frank remarked.

"They are preparing for it by drinking the secret brew. A vile concoction, I assure you. I tasted it once."

The macumba mediums began swaying from side to side. They broke into a rhythmical chant and clapped their hands.

"This is the sacred song," San Marten explained. "By chanting these verses, they seek to placate the dead and open the path of communication."

The shadowy faces assumed ecstatic expressions as the Hardys watched. In the lamplight black eyes glowed like embers. The chant rose to a soaring crescendo.

Suddenly the nearest man got to his feet and began a jig. One by one the others imitated him, until they were all on their feet, stamping and waving their hands.

The circle began to move. Fascinated, Frank drew closer. The wild-eyed macumba dancers seemed to have hypnotized him. As if drawn by an invisible magnet, he moved into the middle of the ring, which revolved faster and faster.

Suddenly a piercing shriek brought Frank out of his trance. One of the natives fell to the floor, clutching at his throat. The others screamed and danced more wildly.

Frank looked around. The hair rose on the back of his neck.

"This is ridiculous," he thought. "I have to get out of here." He plunged between two of the dancers, looking for his brother and San Marten. A chill went down his spine when he realized that they were no longer with him.

Frank began a systematic search, making his way to the rear of the circle, and walking once around. No luck! Again he pressed himself between the ecstatically gyrating bodies to the centre. San Marten and Joe were nowhere in sight! Had they left?

Frank looked for the door. It had disappeared, too! His pulse beat like a jackhammer. He was trapped amid the zealots of voodoo!

·7·

Buru's Vision

WITH sinuous movements, hands reached out towards Frank. Was he about to become a victim of macumba rites?

"Not if I can help it," he thought. "I'll go down swinging before I let those lunatics get me!" He assumed a judo stance, ready to hit the first attacker with a karate chop.

"Cool it, Frank," came a low familiar voice. "It's me."

"Joe?" Frank was dumbfounded. In the dim light he could barely make out his brother's features.

"Right. Don't let the party costume fool you. I just put it on for this shindig. Same for my dancing partner here. He's not what he seems."

Frank recognized San Marten. "What's the big idea?" he demanded.

"San Marten suggested joining the dance," Joe said. "I figured you were coming, too."

"I thought we might learn something that would lead us to Graham Retson," San Marten said.

"Down here with these weirdos?" Frank shook his head. "Let's get out of here. We can resume our confer-ence when we get away from these shimmy-shakers."

56

The voodoo dancers were becoming more frenzied. Their chanting became stentorian, and their contortions more furious.

Frank saw Buru coming towards them as Joe and San Marten slipped back into their own clothes. The old man motioned to them, then led the way around the dancing circle, edging along so as not to attract attention, to a point where a big stone block stood against the wall.

Gesturing to the others to help, he began to push at the block. The rest pitched in, shifted the obstruction to one side, and gained access to an opening through which they had to crawl on their hands and knees.

They reached another stone staircase. Hastening upwards, they returned to the witch doctor's stall. With their hands they shielded their eyes from the daylight until they became reaccustomed to it.

The two Brazilians began an animated conversation. Frank tugged at Joe's sleeve and the boys moved off to one side, out of earshot.

"Wow! Am I glad to be back on earth!" Frank said.

Joe grinned. "Actually, it was fun!" Then he became serious. "A lot of strange things have happened since our arrival," he said. "That bag of nuts which fell off the truck, for instance. It was pushed by a monkey!"

"That figures," Frank said. "Somebody's after us. And I'd include San Marten among the suspects. I haven't yet discovered why he's so concerned about us."

"I think he's okay," Joe said.

"Maybe so. But I don't see why he brought us to this place. He can't take that voodoo stuff seriously."

"Of course not. He just thought it would be interesting for us to watch. I guess it was, too!"

"And what about his showing up at the hotel just at the right time? He claimed the door was open, but I'll bet somebody locked it after we went into the room. And how come part of the fire escape ladder was missing just when I needed it?"

"How's that again?"

Frank told his brother about his movements while Joe had been unconscious. "When I tried to call for a doctor, I got no answer. After San Marten had come in, the desk answered immediately."

"That doesn't prove anything. The clerk might have had another call."

"And how do you explain the locked door?"

"It could have been stuck."

"Then the bellboy walked in when nobody called for him."

"He might have been sent to take out the dishes. I saw a tray and a couple of glasses on one of the dressers."

Frank sighed. "Maybe you're right, but the whole thing is too pat, too—"

Just then San Marten beckoned to the Hardys. "Buru has a prediction about where to find Graham. He says he had a vision that your friend is going up the Amazon to Manaus."

"Where's that?"

"It's a port near the juncture of the Amazon and the Negro rivers nearly a thousand miles from here."

"Baloney!" Frank murmured to Joe.

The witch doctor sensed their scepticism. He smiled and spoke volubly.

San Marten said, "He warns that we had better

believe his vision. Otherwise serious harm might come to Graham. If you want to find him, go to Manaus."

"We'll think it over," Frank began, "and when we reach—"

He was interrupted by a rustling sound at the back of the stall. Furry fingers pulled the curtains apart. A simian face appeared in the opening. Frank and Joe saw a howler monkey about three feet tall, with silky black fur and a savage expression.

The Hardys got only a brief glimpse before the face pulled back behind the curtains.

"So you keep a monkey for a pet, Buru," Joe said.

When San Marten translated that remark, the witch doctor shook his head angrily and went into a torrent of negatives.

"He denies he has a monkey on the premises," San Marten reported.

"We saw it!" Frank insisted.

"Buru says that whatever you saw was caused by your imagination."

"Like his visions," Joe scoffed.

San Marten smiled. "Perhaps. Still I believe it would be better if I left your comparison untranslated. Witch doctors are not the best-tempered people in Belem."

Joe looked amused. "You mean Buru might place a curse on us?"

Sensing hostility, Frank said, "We'd better return to the Excelsior Grao Para."

"Not there, my friends," San Marten protested. "My home in the suburbs is at your disposal. Please use it freely as long as you stay in Belem."

Frank and Joe, however, would not be swayed. "You see," Frank stated, "we need to be in the city while looking for our friend. Thanks all the same."

"Some other time," Joe promised. "We'll take a rain-check just now."

They parted with friendly handshakes, and the boys went to the hotel. The desk clerk waved to them. "Mr Retson returned while you were out."

"Is he here now?" Joe asked excitedly.

"No. He came for his leather jacket and departed again."

"Did he give you any forwarding address this time?" Frank queried.

"All he said was that he was going to Manaus, and that he could not wait. He mentioned no address in that city."

The boys went to their room and Joe closed the door. "Good heavens, Frank! Buru was right. It's incredible!"

Frank suspected trickery. Joe, on the other hand, felt that the voodoo witch doctor might have some psychic power of insight. They discussed the case from every angle and tried to figure out how to proceed from here.

"Now we're faced with the monkey mystery, too!" Frank said. "Are you sure that sack of nuts was pushed by the monkey?"

"Listen, Frank. I told you!"

"Okay, okay. Don't let this give us the jitters. Was it the same one we saw at Buru's?"

"I don't know," Joe said. "Monkeys all look alike to me."

Frank sagged into a chair and let out a long breath. "San Marten bugs me."

"You worry too much," Joe said. "Tell you what. If it will make you feel better, why not have Dad inquire about him at the Brazilian Embassy in Washington?"

"Good thinking. We'll send Dad a cable."

"What about Manaus?"

"It's our only clue. I suggest we go, but proceed with extreme caution."

"I'm with you," Joe said. He took out a cablegram blank from the desk drawer and wrote: *"Need info Brazil Embassy Joachim San Marten. On way to Manaus re Graham."*

"I'll take it down to the telegraph office," he said when he was finished. "Better not trust the bellboy with it."

"I'll go with you," Frank said. "I'm starved."

The boys had dinner in a small restaurant near the hotel, then returned to their room. It was not air conditioned and seemed like an oven.

"We'd better get as much air as we can," Frank suggested, forcing the window wide open.

"Come to think of it," Joe said, "the fire escape would be a good place to sleep on a night like this. Natural air conditioning."

They showered and then turned in. Frank placed a flashlight on the table beside the bed for emergency use, which was an old habit with him.

Both boys slept fitfully, turning and tossing on sweat-dampened sheets. Suddenly both were wide awake. There was a strange noise in their room. Dimly they made out a figure bending over their clothes.

"A thief!" Joe thought.

Carefully Frank reached for his flashlight. Pointing it towards the intruder, he snapped it on. A cone of light stabbed through the darkness. It revealed a hideous-looking simian standing beside a chair, holding Frank's shirt in one of its paws. The monkey's nose was wrinkled, the eyes drawn into narrow glaring slits, and his fangs were bared in a ferocious scowl!

·8·

Fish Bait

FRANK and Joe jumped up and dived for the simian. Joe got a hand on a furry leg, but the animal scampered free. It dashed to the fire escape and swung down the metal framework from floor to floor, using its long prehensile tail as a fifth paw. The boys watched in dismay as the monkey finally leaped to the pavement and vanished around a corner of the hotel.

"That's the ugliest brute I've ever seen," Joe said in a shaky voice. "I'd consider it a nightmare if you hadn't seen it too, Frank."

"Oh, it was real enough," said Frank, who had been examining his clothes. "Real enough to make off with my wallet, key ring, passport and other identification papers."

Joe went through his pockets. "Good grief! I'm cleaned out, too!"

Frank sat down on the bed. "Joe, we're dealing with a monkey clever enough to be a professional burglar. A human being couldn't have pulled off the job more neatly."

"A human being put that monkey up to it!" Joe said.

An odd feeling swept over both boys. They felt as if they were in the grip of some evil power, as if a malevol-

63

ent force was bent on their destruction.

"Frank," Joe said, "we're stuck. No money, no passports, no nothing. What'll we do?"

"Go to the American Consulate," Frank said.
"Then I suggest we call San Marten and tell him our
sad story. If he's involved in it, we might as well stick
close to him. He doesn't know we suspect him, so
maybe we can pick up a clue."

At nine in the morning Frank asked the hotel clerk to
put him through to San Marten's home. After a brief
wait, the Brazilian's voice came over the wire. Frank
told him they had been robbed.

"I will help you," San Marten assured them. "Come
here for breakfast. Take a taxi at my expense. I will
instruct my servants to set two extra places."

Frank and Joe accepted his invitation, but first made
their way to the consulate. A United States official gave
them some cash, arranged for them to cable home for
money, and promised to have identification for them
shortly.

The boys thanked him, caught a taxi in front of the
consulate, and reached the suburbs of Belem in about
twenty minutes. It was an exclusive residential area of
large houses with broad lawns. Maids were sweeping
off front porches and washing windows. Gardeners
were spading the earth.

"Nice area," Joe commented. "The rich live well
here, too."

The Brazilian's home turned out to be a plush one. A
wrought-iron gate gave access to a walk flanked by
tropical flowers leading up to a big house. The door was
opened by a servant who ushered the boys through to a
patio in the rear of the property.

San Marten sat at a table beside a broad, deep swimming pool. Thick shrubbery grew a few yards from the pool on three sides; the fourth side facing the house was open.

San Marten rose. "I am very happy to see you here," he said, waving them to a couple of empty chairs.

Frank noticed the table was placed on the west side of the pool in the morning sun. They sat down with their backs to the glare.

A second servant brought in a platter of ham and eggs, which the boys ate with great relish. At the same time they discussed the theft by the monkey. San Marten seemed thoroughly mystified. He folded his napkin and placed it on the table.

"I will speak to the police immediately," he said.

"We'll go with you," Frank said.

"That won't be necessary. You stay here and relax. Enjoy a swim in the pool," San Marten said. "You'll find suits in the cabana."

Before they could object, he stepped into a light-blue sports car parked nearby and roared off in the direction of Belem.

Frank and Joe sat lazily in the sun for a while, then Joe said, "I think I'll take San Marten up on his swim invitation. How about you?"

"First we'll get rid of the breakfast dishes," Frank said with a grin. "Aunt Gertrude would never approve if we left the table like this."

He rang the bell for the servants, expecting someone to come and clean up the table. Receiving no response, he went into the house, found it empty, and returned to the patio.

"The help has vamoosed as well," he told Joe.

"Must be their day off," his brother guessed. "We'll have some peace and quiet for our dip."

"They were here when we arrived, so it's hardly their day off," Frank said, an uneasy feeling coming over him. "I think maybe San Marten is up to something."

Joe had already started for the cabana and quickly slipped into a pair of trunks which looked as if they would fit. Frank followed suit, still pondering the strange disappearance of the servants. As they emerged from the cabana, the sunlight reflected from the surface of the pool in blinding rays. Joe climbed on the diving board, where he poised for a back somersault.

Frank, shielding his eyes, spotted a slight movement down in the water. Suddenly Aunt Gertrude's warning rang in his ears: "Look before you leap!"

Leaning over the edge of the pool, he saw a small fish not more than eight inches long. It had a blunt face with an underslung jaw, a silvery bluish body, and a touch of red on its fins.

"Joe, don't dive!" Frank shouted.

The warning came almost too late and Joe had trouble regaining his balance. "Why, what's the matter?" he asked.

"You'll have company you may not care to meet. Come here!"

Joe descended from the diving board and peered down at the fish.

"Frank, there's more than one. In fact, a whole school. Wait a minute! I have a hunch!" Joe ran to the table where the breakfast dishes still lay. Seizing a piece of ham from the platter, he returned to the pool.

He tossed the ham through the air. It hit the water with a splash and had hardly started to sink when the school of small fish darted to it. They became a swirling horde of ferocious predators, tearing off mouthfuls and gulping them down. The ham was gone in seconds!

Frank and Joe shuddered.

Piranhas!

"No wonder San Marten and the servants vanished so suddenly," Frank muttered. "They set up operation bone yard for our benefit, but didn't want to witness the gory details. And the table was set up facing the sun to keep us from spotting the fish."

"Wow! I'm beginning to feel sick," Joe said.

"Come on," Frank said. "I've got an idea." He led the way into the kitchen and opened the refrigerator. They found a rib roast, two large hams, a big loin of pork and a leg of lamb.

"Our host must have been planning a party," Frank said. "Joe, help me carry these!"

The boys lugged the meat outside. "In they go!" Frank said as they tossed the provisions into the water.

The piranhas were on them in a flash. The water boiled with the assault. In a few minutes only cleaned bones lay at the bottom of the pool.

Suddenly the front door slammed. Frank and Joe dodged into the shrubbery, crouched down, and parted the leaves. The two servants walked warily across the patio to the pool.

One laughed, elbowed his companion, and pointed to the bones. The other guffawed as if he had just heard a good joke.

"They think they're looking at our remains," Joe whispered.

Frank nodded. "We'd better get off the premises before they find out the truth. Come on!"

As they slipped through the shrubbery Joe tripped and fell. Frank paused to help him up. Then came the sound of pursuers.

The boys careered past large bushes and small trees towards the fence at the back of the property. Frank scrambled to the top. Joe followed, barely escaping the clutching fingers of one of the servants.

"They'll come after us!" Joe panted.

They ran down the street and turned a corner.

"In there!" Frank replied, pointing to the nearest building. It was a low neat structure with the sign BIBLIOTECA beside the front door.

"It's a library," Frank said. "And look how we're dressed."

The dark-haired, pretty girl at the reception desk was startled by the sudden appearance of two boys in swimming trunks. Readers looked up from their books and newspapers to see what all the commotion was about.

The boys asked for help and the girl, in halting English, said, "I will get police. You wait."

Frank and Joe squatted behind some bookshelves. A few minutes later a squad car transported the Hardys to headquarters. The chief, Captain Vasquez, spoke English quite well.

Frank asked for San Marten, but was told he had not come to headquarters. Then the boys went over the morning's events repeatedly, only to be met with grins of disbelief.

"Americanos good with joke!" said a lieutenant, bursting into loud laughter.

"Joachim San Marten would never do anything like this," the captain insisted. "He is a respectable man."

"Send your men to investigate his swimming pool," Frank urged.

Vasquez hummed and hawed, but finally agreed. The squad car went out. It returned ten minutes later and the two policemen reported nothing unusual about San Marten's pool.

Frank was crushed. "The servants must have removed the piranhas and the bones," he said weakly.

"We will forget your fish story," Vasquez said, shaking his head, "and let you go this time. Get out of these swimming trunks. We will find your size among clothing left by former prisoners."

"Thanks," Joe said glumly, disappointed that nobody believed them.

The boys changed, then left. As they walked into the lobby of the Excelsior Grao Para, Frank grabbed his brother's elbow. "Sh! Look over there at the desk!"

"San Marten!" Joe gasped.

The Brazilian was in a towering fury. His face was flushed, his body trembling. He pounded the desk with his fist.

"Where are the Hardys?" San Marten demanded in English.

"Sir, I have no idea."

San Marten seized the man by the lapels and shook him. "Where did they go? Where can I find them?"

"Sir, if I knew, believe me I would tell you," the clerk gasped.

Thrusting him aside with a contemptuous gesture, San Marten wheeled round. The Hardys hastily ducked behind a large pillar. Had they been fast enough? Had their murderous enemy seen them?

·9·

A Curious Number Seven

SAN MARTEN motioned savagely in the Hardys' direction. He started walking towards the pillar behind which they were hiding.

"He's spotted us!" Joe warned.

"Get ready," Frank muttered. "We'll have to fight our way out of this one!"

San Marten's vigorous strides brought him quickly abreast of the pillar. The boys could see the angry tightening of his jaw. Tensely they prepared for a counter-attack.

The Brazilian, however, did not circle the pillar. He walked straight past towards a man in the doorway at whom he had been gesturing. The pair disappeared out of the hotel.

Frank mopped the perspiration from his forehead. "Wow! That was close."

"Let's scram while we're still in one piece," Joe urged.

"Right. But we'll need our suitcases."

"How do we get to the room—by asking the clerk for the key?"

Frank grinned. "I'd rather not. Let's take the fire escape. Since we paid one night in advance when we registered, I suggest we forget about checking out, too."

The boys managed to climb up to their window unseen. They jumped into the room, took their bags, and went out the same way.

"Where to now?" Joe asked.

"There's a park a few blocks down the street," Frank said. "San Marten won't think of looking for us there. We'll have to hang around for a while until money from home arrives."

They found the park practically deserted. Seated on a bench under some spreading tropical foliage, they were able to talk freely with no fear of eavesdroppers.

"San Marten can't be operating against us all on his lonesome," Joe remarked. "He must be the leader of a gang."

Frank agreed. "Try this for size, Joe. The gang kidnapped Graham Retson, took the money he withdrew from the bank, and are now holding him for ransom. They're out to get us before we rescue Graham."

"You're on my wavelength, Frank, coming through loud and clear."

Frank paused to think over the problem. "I can't figure out where Manaus fits in. That clue might be a plant to lure us up the Amazon so San Marten and company can ambush us."

"On the other hand," Joe countered. "Graham could really be in Manaus. Our job is to find him, so we can't ignore the whole thing."

"Besides," Frank said, "if it's a trap, we may be able to turn the tables on the gang. Forewarned is forearmed, as Aunt Gertrude would say."

"I'll buy that," Joe said. "But how do we get to

Manaus? If we take a boat upriver, it'll take weeks before we arrive."

"We'll have to fly."

"San Marten will have the commercial lines watched," Joe predicted. "And I doubt if we can rent a plane without identification papers. That second-storey monkey grounded us."

"Maybe the man at the consulate can give us some advice," Frank said. "We'll have to check in there anyhow for our money. I hope it has arrived."

Carrying their bags, Frank and Joe returned to the American Consulate, which was near the park. The man they had spoken to that morning greeted them with a smile. "Your money is here," he said. "I'm having your passports cancelled and you will have new ones soon."

Frank explained that they wanted to fly to Manaus and the man made a quick phone call. He spoke in Portuguese, smiled, and hung up.

"This should do the trick," he said to the Hardys. "Go to the airport on the edge of town. A pilot by the name of Rico Armand is waiting there. He has a small private plane and will fly you to Manaus."

"Thank you very much," Frank said, and the Hardys walked out of the office.

They hailed a taxi and an hour later were at the airport. They found the pilot, a handsome youth in his early twenties, who spoke English.

Armand shook hands, mentioned his fee, and the boys paid in advance. Then the three took off.

They circled over the vast delta of the Amazon, heading upriver. The east coast disappeared behind them, and the rain forest extended on both sides like a huge green carpet. It looked never-ending.

Smaller tributary streams could be seen snaking through towering trees before emptying into the broad river.

The plane flew on and on, and it seemed nothing else existed in the world exept those countless miles of jungle beneath their wings.

Two refuelling stops were made at intermediate air-strips. Armand followed the Rio Negro from its confluence with the Amazon, and finally Manaus came into sight.

Frank and Joe looked down on hundreds of canoes in the river, paddled by natives headed for the waterfront market with cargoes of fruit and vegetables. The build-ings of the city were a conglomeration of styles, running from primitive huts to old colonial and modern high-rise buildings.

One building in particular stood out—an ornate structure of pink and white marble. Frank and Joe stared in disbelief.

"How did that ever get into the jungle?" Joe asked.

"That's the old opera house," Armand replied. "Manaus used to be the rubber capital of Brazil. The wealthy planters had the best of everything, including opera."

"The city must have gone downhill since then," Frank remarked.

"Brazil's rubber doesn't sell too well these days," said the pilot. "Can't compete with the East Indies. So Manaus is pretty much what you Americans would call a ghost town of the Amazon."

"How do people make a living now?" Joe asked.

"Partly from tourism. Manaus is a free port and you

can buy things duty free. That's one reason I see more visitors in Manaus every time I come."

A message from the airport tower came over the radio: "Wait for permission to land." Armand began to circle. His fuel gauge showed the plane could not keep flying much longer.

"I don't understand the delay," he said nervously. "I'll have to land without permission if this keeps up."

"Frank," Joe muttered, "this may be San Marten's doing."

The fuel gauge pointed to *empty* and the three aboard were braced for a crash landing when the control tower finally gave the okay.

"Down to the last drop of fuel," Armand commented as they taxied to a halt. In the terminal they found out that a maintenance truck had been stalled on the runway.

After a quick sandwich at the airport the boys said goodbye to the pilot, then took a taxi to a hotel in the middle of town. After checking in they began to scout Manaus for Graham Retson. None of the hotels had any record of him, so they turned their attention to the rooming houses. It was not until the next day, however, that they struck a lead.

"Yes," said the owner of a small rooming house, a German named Bauer, "Graham Retson was here, but left yesterday. I found this paper in his room. Maybe it will help you."

Frank took the piece of paper. It was dirty and wrinkled as if it had been crumpled into a ball and tossed aside. He examined the crudely scrawled message. It was dated May seventh and said: "I am being taken to a small boat next to the Argentine freighter in

Manaus harbour. My captors intend to take me farther up the Amazon. Help! Graham Retson."

Joe whistled and pulled his brother aside. "Frank, this is a real clue!"

"You're wrong, Joe."

"Why?"

"Look at the date. The seven has a bar through it. That's the European way of writing the number. No American would do it like that. Another thing. Today is May seventh. The landlord said Graham left yesterday. He's in cahoots with San Marten, Joe! Bauer wrote the note himself. They're trying to trick us!"

"We'll trick them in return!" Joe declared. "They want to get us aboard their boat for a one-way voyage to the bottom of the Amazon. Instead, we'll stay off the boat and listen to what's going on."

"With our bug, you mean?" Frank asked. "Great idea."

The boys went back to their hotel. Frank opened his suitcase and drew out a length of coiled wire from a hidden pocket under a false bottom. One end of the wire had a set of earphones attached. From the other dangled a sensitive metal sphere. The Hardys had often used this detection device to listen in on conversations at long range.

They walked to the harbour at nightfall. Frank pointed to the lights of a hulking vessel anchored there. "That's the Argentine freighter, Joe. And that small boat beside it has to be the one we're looking for."

"Okay, I'll go to work."

Frank, holding the earphones, sat down behind some crates on the dock. Joe stripped quickly to his shorts, then slipped into the river carrying the wire, which payed out from the bank as he swam. Reaching the boat, he carefully planted the bug on one of the port-holes.

"The insect is ready to strike," Joe announced when he came back to Frank, shaking the droplets of water off his body. Then he began to put on his slacks and shirt.

"Hurry," Frank said suddenly. "We're having company."

Two men walked down to the water's edge and stopped a few yards from where the Hardys were concealed. Obviously convinced that they were alone in the darkness, they spoke clearly in English. The Hardys recognized the voices.

"San Marten!" Joe whispered.

Frank nodded. "The other guy sounds like Bauer—that guy at the rooming house."

San Marten spoke in more informal English than they had ever heard him use before. "Are you positive every angle's covered? I don't want any slips, mind you."

"Don't get upset," his companion replied. "Diabo is standing guard. No one can sneak past him. He's fool-proof."

"Okay," San Marten said with satisfaction. "Soon the river will have the Hardys."

"Joachim, that was a good idea to lure them to Brazil. With Graham on our hands back north at—"

A sudden noise caused Frank and Joe to whirl round.

They saw the monkey with the evil face charging at them! He was so close that they did not have a chance to move. Snapping and snarling ferociously the animal catapulted into the Hardys. The force of the assault toppled them over into the river!

·10·

Adrift on the Amazon

FRANK and Joe plummeted down through the water until they steadied themselves. Kicking convulsively, they shot back to the surface.

At once the howler monkey was on them, clawing their backs with his hind paws, nipping and scratching at their heads.

Frank twisted around and pulled the creature off Joe. Their combined strength was too much even for their savage assailant. Suddenly the monkey wrenched himself from their grasp. Streaking through the water, he made for the shore.

"Don't let him get away!" Frank spluttered.

But a fusillade of shots changed the Hardys' minds. Bullets skipped off the surface of the river and whined into the darkness.

Joe halted abruptly, treading water. He turned back towards Frank. "We can't get to the shore," he warned.

"Let's swim downstream," Frank suggested.

"And quick," Joe said. "They're coming after us!"

The *put-put* of a motorboat echoed across the water, growing louder as the craft cut the distance between it and the boys. Frantically Frank and Joe swam out into the river. The motorboat gained on them rapidly.

Just then a pleasure launch came gliding in their direction. The lights of the cabin threw a sheen over the Rio Negro. Three or four couples were dancing to the rhythm of a small band.

"Follow me!" Frank gasped. "To the other side!"

Waiting until the launch was slightly upstream from him, he took a deep breath and submerged. Kicking hard, and using his arms in a powerful breaststroke, he arched down under the launch. The keel scraped his back as he passed. His lungs were bursting for want of air when he came up on the opposite side of the craft. Reaching out, he grasped a railing just above the water line.

A split second later Joe bobbed up beside him. They clung to the railing side by side, gasping for breath. The launch carried them swiftly down the river.

"Now what?" Joe asked. "Shall we call the skipper?"

"Better not," Frank said. "There's no telling who's on board. San Marten's confederates would be only too happy to arrange a reception committee for us."

They clung to the launch until it passed the confluence of the Rio Negro and the Amazon, a few miles below Manaus. Feeling safe, they dropped off and swam to the shore.

"I've had it," Frank said, flopping down in a patch of tall jungle grass.

"Rest a while," Joe said. "I'll get us a snack."

He walked off into the jungle and returned ten minutes later with a big bunch of bananas. Voraciously they ate the fruit, tossing the skins over their shoulders as they worked through the bunch.

"At least we won't starve here," Frank observed.

"We're okay," Joe said, "as long as we don't get

eaten. I'd hate to wake up and find a hungry jaguar staring me in the eye."

"There's probably a lot of them in this area," Frank said. "Hear those monkeys chattering in the trees? Jaguars feast on monkeys."

Joe pondered Frank's remark. "That reminds me. We've learned the name of the beast that's been annoying us—Diabo."

"Which means devil in Portuguese," Frank said. "You couldn't think of a better name for that horrible creature."

Joe yawned. "We've left him far behind. Now it's me for dreamland."

They both were soon sound asleep on the banks of the Amazon. The sun had risen by the time they woke. After breakfasting on bananas and berries, they walked along the shore, waving and shouting at boats passing by in the middle of the river.

"No go," Joe said after a while. "They're too far out to notice us."

"We'll have to build a raft," Frank stated. "There are plenty of fallen trees in the jungle. They'll do for logs."

The boys began hauling tree trunks out of the nearest patch of jungle. When they had gathered about a dozen, Frank lined them up in a row. Joe pulled down some thick, sinuous creepers from the trees to use as rope. Skilfully they braided the creepers over and round the logs. The result was a seaworthy raft. Flat driftwood provided a pair of paddles.

The boys gave their craft a stiff push into deep water. Then they scrambled on to it and began paddling towards the middle of the Amazon.

The strong current caught the raft, propelling it along at a rapid rate. "No use fighting this," Joe panted. "The best we can do is travel on a diagonal line downstream."

Dipping their makeshift paddles rhythmically into the water, the boys managed to guide their raft towards the lanes followed by river traffic.

Frank ceased paddling and looked around at the bare expanse of water, sky, and jungle. "We seem to have the Amazon all to ourselves."

Joe also shipped his paddle. "Well, we're far enough out, Frank. There'll be boats coming by and we'll be able to hitch a ride back to Manaus."

He rose to his feet, shaded his eyes with his hands, and squinted up the river. A dot on the horizon grew larger. The outline of a substantial vessel took shape.

"Tour ship coming," Joe announced jubilantly. "I'll flag it down." Taking off his shirt, he fastened it to his paddle by the cuffs. Then he began to wave his improvised flag at the ship, which slowed down and eased alongside.

A rope ladder swung down over the railing. The boys quickly mounted to the deck. In the captain's cabin, they told him that they had become lost in the jungle on the previous night.

"Where do you wish to go?" the captain asked.

"To Manaus," Frank answered.

"We will be glad to take you."

"Thank you very much, sir."

Frank and Joe freshened up and had a second breakfast. "Good thing we've still got our money," Frank said with a grin. "It got soaked, but it'll still buy us what we need."

"How about a plane trip back to Belem?" Joe asked.

"Good idea. The only thing is, who's going to take us?"

Joe shrugged. "We'll just have to make it to the airport and play it by ear."

It was about noontime when the Hardys arrived in Manaus. After getting their bags, they took a taxi to the airfield and Frank inquired if Rico Armand happened to be there.

The airport manager, a rotund Brazilian with a bald head, shrugged. "If you know his plane, go out and look around. There are many small planes coming in here and I do not know all the pilots by name."

The boys made a methodical search of the field.

"Hey, Frank," Joe said, "doesn't that crate look like the one we came on?"

"Sure does. I recognize the number. Wow, are we in luck!"

"Tell you what," Joe said. "I'll stay here by the plane while you try to locate Armand."

"Okay." Frank left. He returned a half hour later without the pilot. "Somebody told me he'd be flying out about three o'clock," he said. "But no one knows where he is now."

"We'll wait right here," Joe said. "It's our best bet."

The boys squatted down beside a hangar from where they could keep the plane under surveillance. Rico Armand appeared about a half hour later. He was surprised to see the boys, who quickly asked for a ride back to Belem.

"Sure, get in," the pilot said. "I'll be glad to take you."

They arrived in Belem in the evening and found a

small hotel to spend the night. After dinner they discussed the situation.

"What next?" Joe asked, stifling a yawn.

"Obviously the Brazilian angle was nothing but a wild-goose chase," Frank said. "We were lured here by San Marten and his gang to be eliminated."

"Suppose Retson had come instead of sending us?"

"Then no doubt he would have run into the same difficulties."

"Too bad we didn't learn where Graham really is," Joe said with a sigh.

"Back north most likely meant the United States. I vote we return to Granite City and work on the case from there," Frank said.

"I'm with you. Maybe we can get our papers tomorrow."

At the American Consulate the next day the Hardys were greeted by the same man they had spoken to before. "Your passport problem is solved," he told them. "The lost ones have been cancelled. Here are a couple of identification cards that will enable you to return home."

"Thank you, sir," Frank replied.

The young detectives made plane reservations and sent a cable to their family, saying they would be on a late-afternoon flight from Belem to New York. Then they taxied to the airport, bought tickets, and boarded a jet.

Before they left the ground, Joe, who was at the window, nudged his brother. "Frank, look at that!"

They saw a crate with a howler monkey being lifted into the hold of a plane operated by another airline The animal stood on its hind legs, grasping the bars, and peered through with sharp black eyes.

"Would you say that's Diabo?" Joe asked.

"Hardly. This one has a pleasant face, not at all like the leering monster we tangled with."

They landed at Kennedy Airport the following morning. After they made their way through customs, they found Chet Morton waiting for them with a big grin.

Joe clapped their freckle-faced friend on the shoulder. "Chet, how did you know we were coming?"

"I had something to do for my dad in New York. Before I left, your mother called me. She got your cable and asked me to let you know your father's coming in on the shuttle from Washington just about now. He'll join us for the connecting flight to Bayport."

The three youths went to the shuttle terminal coffee shop to kill time while waiting for Fenton Hardy. They took a booth near a window where they could see the planes coming down for a landing.

After the waitress had served them, Frank sipped his coke. "How's business, Chet? Last we knew Phil and Tony were joining forces with you in the golf ball project."

"Anyone drown in a water hazard yet?" Joe needled their rotund pal.

Chet downed a bite of doughnut. "You guys don't take scavenging seriously enough," he said. "Business is booming. We've recovered about a thousand balls. At least a hundred bucks apiece for each of us."

Frank brought the conversation round to the mystery. "Chet, what's going on in Whisperwood? Everything quiet out there?"

"Quiet!" Chet exclaimed. "Are you kidding? Mrs

Retson had completely disappeared!"

Frank drew a sharp breath. "Disappeared!" he repeated incredulously.

"Gone! Scrammed! Vamoosed!" Chet replied.

"Give us the facts," Joe said grimly.

"First I learned about it was when I went up to the house the day after you left. Mr Retson blew his top. Told me his wife had vanished from her room."

"What about Hopkins the nurse?" Frank put in. "She must have been on duty."

"Says she heard nothing. She was eating her lunch in another room. When she returned, she found the bed empty. She's been having hysterics. Claims you two upset Mrs Retson so much she just up and ran away."

"So we have two mysteries," Frank said. "First it was Graham, now it's his mother."

"There must be some connection," Joe observed. "I'll bet San Marten is behind this too."

"Maybe Mrs Retson received a secret message from Graham," Chet ventured. "He might have let her know somehow where she could find him."

"It's possible," Frank replied. "Joe and I failed to locate Graham in Brazil." He told Chet about their trip.

Suddenly Chet said, "Do you know a guy who wears a Panama hat?"

Frank shook his head. "I can't think of anyone."

"Me either," Joe chimed in. "Why?"

"There's a man standing in the doorway who seems awfully interested in you!"

·11·

Dangerous Stranger

JOE casually turned round for a look. The doorway was empty!

"Whoever it was, he's gone," Joe said.

"Well, he sure gave you fellows the once-over," Chet stated. "Kept staring at you as if you were his long-lost cousins."

A sudden thought caused Joe to sit bolt upright. "What if this character followed us from Belem, Frank! Maybe it was San Marten!"

"What did the man in the Panama hat look like?" Frank asked.

"Small, scrawny. Has blond sideburns. Wears steel-rimmed spectacles."

Joe breathed a sigh of relief. "It wasn't San Marten, thank goodness."

"Could be one of his gang," Frank stated. "On the other hand, maybe the man thought we were somebody else and realized his mistake."

"Well, I watched him for a while to make sure," Chet said. "He never took his eyes off this booth till Joe turned round."

"Listen, they're announcing Dad's plane," Frank said.

Joe nodded. "Let's go outside and meet him."

The boys quickly paid their check and went to the gate. The detective came through shortly and shook hands with all of them.

"How much time do we have before our flight leaves for Bayport?" he asked.

"An hour, Dad," Joe replied.

"Then let's park ourselves somewhere and compare notes about our investigations."

"Okay, Dad," Frank said.

They went to the airline waiting room, where they settled themselves in easy chairs round a low table. Mr Hardy kept a firm grip on his black briefcase.

"This is loaded with vital documents," he said in an undertone. "I'd be in big trouble if a thief grabbed it and got away."

"Have you had any breaks in your investigation of the passport gang?" Joe asked.

"Yes. A man carrying one of the stolen and doctored passports was apprehended at Kennedy Airport."

Chet looked glum. "Then there's nothing for us to do, Mr Hardy. You solved the case without us."

The Bayport detective smiled. "Not quite, Chet. Our suspect clammed up. I'll have to run down more clues before I collar the ringleader. You fellows and your pals may come in handy before we round up the gang. By the way," he continued, "how's your own case progressing? Have you found Graham Retson?"

Frank described their fruitless quest for Graham in Brazil and Joe told about San Marten's attempts to eliminate them, including an account of the hideous Diabo.

Mr Hardy frowned. "I didn't think the Retson case

was going to be that dangerous," he said, sounding
worried.

"That isn't all, Dad," Joe went on. "We haven't
found Graham, and now Mrs Retson is missing."

"Come again?"

"Chet can explain. He was there."

Chet repeated the story of how Mrs Retson had
vanished from her room.

"As I understand it, Chet, you, Phil and Tony were
supposed to keep Whisperwood under surveillance,"
Mr Hardy said mildly.

"Correct, sir," Chet said. "But we were out golf ball
scavenging when Mrs Retson got away."

A voice over the loudspeaker announced that the
plane for Bayport was ready to board. Gripping his
briefcase firmly under his left arm, Mr Hardy led the
way to the ramp. Once on board, he retired to the back
of the lightly loaded plane to examine some papers.
Frank and Chet took two seats together, while Joe sat in
the same row across the aisle. There was nobody
behind them. Only a few passengers were scattered
around the rest of the cabin, and several went to sleep
as soon as the plane became airborne.

Chet unbuckled his seat belt and returned to the
subject of golf balls. "You want to know the system I've
worked out so we don't miss any?" he asked.

"Sure," Frank said.

"Well, Phil and Tony work as my divers."

"What do you need them for? I thought the suction
pump did the trick," Joe said.

"It does, in most cases. But some of the water-holes
and lakes are too deep and my hose doesn't reach down.
So I hold a large basket on a long rope and let Phil and

Tony fill it up. We've brought back quite a haul every time."

"And that way *you* don't get wet," Frank noted.

Chet assumed a hurt look. "You guys know me better than that. I'm the brains of the operation. I've got to direct traffic topside."

Frank and Joe kept needling their pal. Suddenly he jarred them by saying, "Something mysterious is going on at the Olympic Health Club!"

"I thought you couldn't get a contract there," Joe said. "How did you get in?"

"Oh, I didn't," Chet admitted. "But I have an agreement with the golf course next door. During the night I saw strange things over at the Olympic. So did Phil and Tony. They'll back me up."

"What kind of strange things, Chet?" Frank asked.

"Flickering lights on the roof. They flashed on and off, then went out for good. We never saw that happen before. Couldn't figure out what it meant."

"Was that all?" Joe inquired.

"No. There were peculiar noises, too. Like someone shouting. At first I thought I was hearing things. But when Phil and Tony came up from their dive, they heard it too."

"Did you investigate?"

"We climbed over the fence and sneaked into the golf course. But whoever was there had gone by the time we made it."

As the boys talked, Fenton Hardy looked up from his papers. He noticed a man rise and walk slowly down the aisle. The passenger then eased himself into a seat behind Frank and Chet, who never noticed him.

Sensing something sinister about the man, Mr

Hardy strode down the aisle and paused to observe the stranger a few steps to the rear.

Covertly the man drew something from his pocket. Shielding his hands with his body, he fiddled with the object until a metallic clicking sound occurred. He hunched over, feeling for the space between the seats in front of him, where Frank and Chet sat. With the other hand he guided a long slender tube into the space.

"Just a minute!" Fenton Hardy said sternly. He grabbed the man by the collar and hauled him out into the aisle. As he did, the plane hit some turbulence, jostling the passengers. Fenton Hardy was thrown to one side. The other man fell to the floor heavily, with the tube under his hand. He lost consciousness!

A stewardess ran up to inquire what was wrong. "This!" said the detective. He picked up the tube, which had a sharp needle projecting from one end. "It punctured his wrist," Mr Hardy went on. "It might be poison. He needs a doctor."

The pilot radioed ahead, then made an emergency landing at an airport near a small town. An ambulance rushed the stricken man to a hospital while Fenton Hardy and the three boys followed behind in a police car.

In the emergency room an intern examined the stricken passenger and the tube, then administered an injection.

"Was it poison?" Fenton Hardy asked.

"Yes. Definitely. The antidote seems to be working, although he nearly died. Who is this man?"

The officer went through the victim's pockets. When he pulled out a United States passport, Mr Hardy asked to see it. It was issued to Harold Solomon.

"It's not genuine," the detective said.

"How do you know?" the officer asked.

"It's my business to know," Mr Hardy replied, and showed his credentials to the policeman.

"Then we'll hold Solomon on several charges," the officer said. "Attempted murder and carrying a false passport."

Frank, Joe and Chet, meanwhile, discussed the bizarre case. "A poisoned needle!" Frank shuddered. "And it was meant for us!"

Chet walked over and looked at the ashen face of the stranger, who was still unconscious. "You want to know something!" he said suddenly. "That's the guy who was watching you in New York!"

·12·

The Monkey Mask

THE boys peered down at Solomon, whose eyelids began to flutter.

"He must belong to San Marten's gang," Joe said. "Probably a professional killer."

"That's a good theory," Fenton Hardy agreed. "I've checked his clothing. No identification marks. But his suit, shoes, and hat are all South American style. I'd say he's from Brazil. But here's the clincher."

The detective held a ticket between his fingers.

"What's that?" Joe asked.

"A baggage claim check for a crate back at Kennedy Airport. Guess what's in the crate!"

Joe gasped as the truth suddenly dawned on him. "A monkey!"

"Right. The claim check is clipped to a health certificate declaring the animal has had all its shots and can be brought into the United States."

Two more policemen, one a captain, entered the hospital as he was speaking. Introductions were made. "Good to meet you, Mr Hardy," the captain said. "We can always use an assist from America's number one private eye."

"Thanks for the compliment," the detective replied.

"But the praise actually belongs to these young men. They can tell you what happened."

Frank described the trip to Brazil. Then Chet reported how the man in the Panama hat had kept them under surveillance at Kennedy Airport. Joe explained his theory that the man belonged to San Marten's gang.

"That seems to make sense," the captain said. "We're here to take Solomon into custody—if that's really who he is. He's conscious now. All of you can come along and hear what he has to say for himself. We've examined the plane, by the way. It's clean."

The doctor said the patient was well enough to leave the hospital. Two squad cars took the group to headquarters.

After the prisoner was seated and given a drink of water, he was advised of his rights to consult a lawyer before answering questions. He nodded and even refused to divulge his name.

"It really isn't Solomon, is it?" the captain asked. "And what's your nationality?"

"None of your business."

"Where did you get the metal tube with the poisoned needle?"

"It isn't mine. I happened to fall on it in the aisle. And I won't have any more to say until I see a lawyer."

"That's your privilege," the officer replied.

The prisoner was taken to a cell. Fenton Hardy summoned the three youths aside for a conference on their next move.

"I'll stay here to press charges against Solomon," he said. "What plans do you have?"

Frank made a quick decision. "I think we should go

back to New York with that baggage claim check. The crate calls for a look-see."

"That's what I had in mind, too," Joe agreed.

The police provided photographs of the ticket claim check and the health certificate and kept the originals for evidence.

"I'll continue on to Bayport," Chet remarked. "I'll brief the folks back home on the latest news from the Hardys, and then hit the road for Granite City."

The group broke up. Frank and Joe returned to the airfield with Chet, and soon everyone was airborne.

Frank and Joe had lunch aboard the plane. Upon landing at Kennedy they hastened to the warehouse where the animals in transit were kept. They told the attendant that a friend had supplied them with the photographs and asked them to take a look at the monkey. He would pick the animal up later. The man told the boys to follow him and led the way through the building.

It was an enormous structure lined with cages of many sizes.

"This must be how Noah's Ark looked," Joe said as they walked along. "I've already counted a baby hippo, a pair of lions, a sackful of snakes, and a wild assortment of zebras, tapirs, and antelopes."

"Not to mention plain old cats and dogs," Frank said with a grin. "Who owns these animals?" he asked the attendant.

"Well," the man replied, "the domestic animals are mostly pets belonging to passengers. The rest are bound for zoos, menageries, and circuses."

"San Marten's line," Joe muttered to Frank. "He told us he was a wild animal trader. Remember?"

"Yes. But that obviously was a cover-up."

Suddenly another attendant came dashing through the warehouse. "A snake has gotten loose!" he yelled. "A king cobra!"

The Hardys knew that cobra venom was among the deadliest of all. And the king cobra was the biggest of the poisonous serpents, reaching a length of twelve feet or more!

"Where is it now?" asked the first attendant.

"I don't know. I found the lid to its box ajar. It slipped out unnoticed. Goodness knows where it is!"

"Okay, everybody be careful," the other man warned. "Don't step into a dark patch on the floor without looking to see if it moves. And don't feel around the tops of the cages with your hand. This cobra could be lurking anywhere. And it strikes like greased lightning."

"We'd like to help capture the cobra," Frank offered. "We've had experience with them."

"Fine. Let's spread out and go over this warehouse yard by yard. First one to spot it, sing out loud and clear."

Joe moved to the area housing the birds. In one cage an Andes condor flapped its wings. A dozen brilliantly hued parrots lent a splash of colour to the dim interior of the place. Some jungle fowl began to cluck and scold.

Joe edged towards them. A slithering movement behind him caused him to turn. Around the corner of the cage whipped a king cobra at least twelve feet long!

It reared three feet off the floor. The hood spread wide open, and the reptile began to sway slowly from side to side. Its eyes locked on to Joe's with a malevolent stare.

Sweat poured down the boy's face. His hands felt clammy. "It's too close to miss me," he thought.

For what seemed like an eternity, Joe stood as immobile as a statue. If he turned to run, the cobra would strike. The fangs would pierce his leg, pumping venom into his blood stream that would cause him to die in agony. Joe's nerves started to give way. He would have to move!

Suddenly a cord dropped over the serpent's head, pulling it to one side. Frank stood there holding the creature securely in the loop of a snake hunter's rod. The cobra writhed and twisted, hissing ferociously, but it could not break the hold of the loop. Skilfully Frank manoeuvred the snake over to its box, dropped it in, and slammed the lid.

Trembling from head to foot, Joe sat down on the next cage. He was too shaken to speak.

"Take it easy," Frank advised. "When I heard the jungle fowl clucking, I figured they were scared of something. So I hustled over for a look. But I didn't expect to see you cornered by the runaway snake."

Frank gave Joe a minute to rest. Then they went to the cage corresponding to the number on the baggage claim check. Inside sat a howler monkey. He looked like the one they had seen at the Belem airport!

He chattered and gazed at them with a gentle demeanour, holding out one paw appealingly as if to shake hands.

Frank rubbed his chin. "We thought this critter was too nice to be Diabo. We were right, weren't we?"

"Absolutely. I'll never forget the way Diabo snapped at us. This is an amiable monkey. Must be from a better jungle family."

The boys turned to leave. As they neared the door on their way out, two men walked in. One was dressed in a whipcord jacket and corduroy pants. The other had on a trench coat and a snap-brim hat. Their faces were hard. They beckoned to the attendant, who was walking a few steps ahead of the Hardys.

"We came to get a monkey you have here," Corduroy Pants said.

"May I see your claim check?"

"Forget it, buddy," Snap-brim growled. "We lost it. But we know the number. That's good enough for us. It's good enough for you."

As the attendant eyed the intruders nervously, Frank pulled Joe behind a cage with baby hippos.

"What's the number?" the warehouse man asked.

"Forty-two-o-seven-six."

The attendant led the way back to the cage he had shown the Hardys.

"I'll have to call the supervisor," he told the men. "I'm not allowed to give you the monkey without a claim check."

"That's all right," Snap-brim said. "Meanwhile we'll go see our little pet."

"Did you send your friends to look at the monkey?" the attendant asked timidly.

"What?" Snap-brim looked puzzled.

"Never mind," Corduroy Pants said impatiently. "Call the supervisor. We're in a hurry."

As soon as the attendant had left, the two men grasped the cage by the corners. Grunting and swearing, they manoeuvred it out of the warehouse as fast as they could to a station wagon parked nearby.

Frank and Joe, ducking behind crates, had trailed

the two men to the spot where the monkey cage had stood, then followed them to the door. They saw Snap-brim and Corduroy Pants lifting the cage into the rear of the vehicle.

As they did, the cage tilted and a package wrapped in brown paper fell out on to the road. The men did not see it. They hopped into the car and drove off.

"We've got to follow them!" Frank said. The boys ran out of the warehouse. Joe pounced on the package, which was small enough for him to slip into his jacket pocket. Frank took down the licence number of the men's car, at the same time flagging a taxi. The boys jumped in, and Frank ordered the driver to follow the station wagon.

It moved fast in the heavy traffic at the airport. The driver kept right on its tail, zooming round and past slower cars. It was a close race until the station wagon whizzed through a red light.

The taxi had to stop. Disappointed, the boys watched their quarry vanish into the myriad of cars headed for New York City.

"No use trying to catch up with them now," Frank said, and told the driver to return to the airport. They got out and paid the fare.

Joe suddenly remembered the package he had picked up. "Let's see what is in it," he said. "Maybe it'll give us an idea of what to do next."

He unwrapped the brown paper and took out a rubber mask of a hideous countenance. The snout was misshapen. The eyes were mere slits of hatred. The fangs were bared in a savage scowl!

"A monkey mask! It's the face of Diabo!" Joe exclaimed.

·13·
One More Chance

"THE face of Diabo!" Frank repeated. "Now I get it. This hideous mask is a form of pyschological warfare. It sure can scare the wits out of a victim."

Joe turned the mask over, noting how the rubber would stretch under a simian's jaw and over the back of its head. The earpieces were broad and thick, almost like earmuffs.

"Do you suppose," Frank said, "that the monkey in the cage really was Diabo?"

"That howler was friendly," Joe replied. "I can't imagine him spitting and snarling like Diabo."

Frank snapped his fingers. "Joe, something else just occurred to me. If San Marten knows this fellow Solomon, then the Brazilian may be involved in Dad's passport case, too! Remember, Solomon had a doctored passport."

"Wow!" Joe shook his head. "This San Marten is really a master criminal. Playing two rackets at the same time."

"Except that we don't know for sure that the monkey is Diabo."

"I can't believe he is," Joe said. "But it would be a strange coincidence if he wasn't."

Frank and Joe took a plane back to Bayport. At home they held a long session with their father after dinner.

"I go along with your suspicion of San Marten as far as the passport racket is concerned," Mr Hardy said. "The man's an enigma. The Brazilian Embassy hasn't been able to come up with any information on him. All they know is that he lives in Belem, has no police record down there, and doesn't court publicity."

"Anyhow, maybe we can help each other in our investigations," Frank said.

"Right. If I smash the passport gang, it may lead me to Graham Retson. Or, if you fellows find Graham, you may find the gang's ringleader at the same time."

Early the next morning Frank and Joe drove back to Whisperwood to join their buddies. Chet was in high spirits. "I hope you guys are doing as well as we are," he greeted them.

"Just how well is that?" Joe asked.

"We retrieved a couple of hundred more golf balls last night," Phil said.

"Most of them in pretty good condition, too," Tony added. "They'll bring in a lot of clams after we put them in the washing machine."

"Tonight," Chet said, "we'll be working the big water-hole at the Olympic Health Club."

"I thought they wouldn't give you a contract," Frank put in.

Phil winked. "They wouldn't let Chet in the place. But Tony and I wangled the contract."

"It was easy," Tony said. "We just walked in and said how about it and they said okay."

"Wait a minute," Chet interrupted. "You guys were my bird dogs. I let you go ahead, that was all. I could have made the deal if I had wanted to."

When the boys' laughter at his bragging had sub-sided, Frank and Joe asked Chet about Mrs Retson. They were told she was still missing. The Hardys went to the mansion to report to their client. Harris opened the door.

"Mr Retson is in the den," he said and escorted them in.

Retson was seated at his desk, looking over some papers. He glanced up in surprise.

"Hello, Mr Retson," said Frank. "We're sorry to hear about your wife."

"What? Oh yes. More trouble. All I seem to have is trouble. Well, where's Graham?"

"I'm afraid we haven't found him," Frank said. He explained about San Marten and the wild-goose chase up the Amazon.

"So you failed!" Retson exploded. "I should have known this case was too big for a couple of amateurs!"

"Sir, we haven't failed completely," Frank said cool-ly. "We have reason to believe that your son was kid-napped. Chances are he is somewhere in the United States."

"And is being held captive by San Marten and his gang," Joe added.

"Nonsense!" Retson said. "I don't believe there's any such person as this San Marten you keep talking about."

Retson composed himself and in a lower voice added, "I'll give you one more chance. But if you don't find my son pronto, you're fired."

"Mr Retson, have the police investigated the disap-pearance of your wife?" Frank asked.

"Yes, yes. They're working on it. You don't have to concern yourself with that."

"She and Graham might have been kidnapped by the gang!" Joe put in.

"I doubt it," Retson said sharply. "A rope ladder was found hanging down from her window. I believe she completely lost her mind and ran away. You leave that up to the police. Just find Graham!"

The Hardys returned to the guesthouse. On the way Joe said, "Retson brushed off his wife's disappearance quite casually."

"He sure did," Frank agreed. "And he doesn't seem to take us very seriously, either."

"We'll have to do something to convince him that he can rely on us," Joe said. "But what? We haven't got a single clue to go on."

"Let's try the Olympic Health Club," Frank said. "Those flickering lights and the noises Chet reported might mean something. Also, remember the Condor golf ball which was thrown into our window the first night? That points to the Olympic too, according to Chet."

Joe nodded. "Let's join the scavenging operation tonight and check out the premises. Another thing. What should we do about Mrs Retson?"

"Nothing. I'm sure once we find Graham, we'll find his mother."

Chet was enthusiastic when he heard that the Hardys would join him that night. "We can use all the help we can get. We'll even cut you in on the profits!" he said with a grin.

During the rest of the day, Frank and Joe kept the mansion and the staff under surveillance, but nothing unusual happened. At nightfall the five boys drove to the club in Chet's pick-up with the suction pump in the back. The Olympic golf pro, Gus McCormick, let them in, waited while they transferred the pump to a golf cart, and watched them vanish into the darkness over the golf links. Frank wheeled the cart up to the edge of the water-hole, which was a distance from the clubhouse.

"This is a combined operations strategy," Chet said pompously. "We'll have four units acting under central control."

"Where's central control?" Joe asked.

Chet slapped his chest. "Here!"

"Shall we synchronize our watches?" Phil asked jokingly. "Oh, I forgot. I don't have any."

"Neither do I," Tony said. "I won't be able to tell the time when I'm in the pond."

"I'll keep time for all of us," Chet told them.

"Where do Frank and I come in, General?" Joe asked.

"Frank, you handle the hose to the suction pump. Sweep up all the balls along the edge. Joe, you take the basket and gather the booty that Phil and Tony bring back from the water-hole. Let's go, team!"

By midnight the boys had a basketful of golf balls, and the suction pump container was loaded.

"All right, time to go," Chet said. "We've gathered all the wealth in this place. Those balls in Joe's basket look pretty good to me. Let's take a gander at the container. It'll probably have to be cleaned out."

He lifted the lid, took a peek, gave a low whistle and called, "Hey, fellows, look at what we dredged up tonight!"

Reaching in, he brought out a woman's shoe.

Tony chuckled. "Some lady player must have gone back to the clubhouse barefoot."

"That's not all," Chet said, reaching into the container again. This time he came up with a badly rusted pistol. The other boys looked in amazement.

But before anyone could comment, a loud cry echoed over the golf course. Lights flickered on the clubhouse roof!

·14·

Big Deal for Chet

"THOSE lights must be a signal to somebody!" Joe said excitedly. "Let's get over to the clubhouse and see what's going on!"

Frank grabbed his arm. "Take it easy. Somebody's coming."

The Hardys slipped away into the darkness just as several men ran up to the water-hole. "What are you doing here?" one of them shouted.

Chet explained.

"Who gave you permission?"

"Gus McCormick."

"We have a contract with Gus," Phil said. "We get half the golf balls we retrieve, and he gets half. It's a fifty-fifty deal."

The man grunted angrily. "Well, the deal's off. Gus had no business making it. Now, you three, get out of here. And don't come back or I'll make it hot for you!"

He and his companions strode off towards the clubhouse and the Hardys moved back to the water-hole.

"Those roughnecks are really mad about something," Frank said. "I wonder what's bugging them."

"Beats me," Chet replied. "All the other pros gave us

104

the go-ahead without any beefing by the management. What's so special about this place?"

"Gus acted as if he were in charge," Phil commented. "He was glad to let us do all the work while he was getting half the profits."

"Something fishy's going on," Frank declared. "Remember the shout we heard? And the flickering lights? And the pistol we dredged up?"

"What'll we do now?" Chet asked.

"We'll have to get off the premises," Joe replied. "Let's go back to Whisperwood."

"And we'll contact the authorities tomorrow," Frank added. "Chief Carton might want to take a look at that gun we found."

The Hardys drove into Granite City early in the morning, taking the pistol and the shoe with them. They found the chief at his desk and explained their reason for calling on him.

Carton toyed with a pencil. "I haven't been out to the Olympic Health Club often," he said. "It's a private outfit and no member has turned up on the police blotter yet. However, this pistol calls for an investigation. I'll have it put through tests in our crime lab. Want to come along and watch?"

"Sure would," Joe said, and told the chief about their own private lab at home.

The fingerprint expert could find no prints on the pistol, but the serial number became visible after the weapon had been carefully scraped. Also, it was still in good enough condition to be fired by the ballistics expert, who returned a while later to the lab with his report.

Carton left the office and returned with a file folder.

Then he placed the ballistics report and the open file side by side. He rubbed his chin and commented, "This is very interesting."

"What, sir?" Frank asked.

"A man held up a post office in Granite City two years ago. His name was Roscoe Matthews. This is our file on him." He tapped the folder. Then he hefted the weapon in the palm of his hand. "And this is the holdup gun!"

"Are you sure?"

"The serial number proves it belongs to Matthews. And a bullet found at the crime scene matches the one just fired in our lab."

"Is Matthews a dangerous criminal?" Joe wanted to know.

"Highly so. During the robbery he shot a guard in the shoulder. He would have killed him except the guard's badge deflected the bullet. We put out an all-points bulletin on Matthews, but he dropped out of sight."

A sudden thought struck Joe. "What kind of loot did Matthews get away with?"

"That's the strange thing," Carton answered. "He ignored the money. All he took was a batch of pass-ports."

"Passports!" Frank exclaimed. "That's what our dad is working on right now!" He gave Carton a quick explanation of both their father's case and their own.

"Do you have a picture of Matthews?" Joe asked.

Carton pulled a photograph out of the file. It showed a broad-faced blond man with a long nose and a slight squint. It was not San Marten, as Joe had secretly hoped, and Carton had no further information to give.

"Was Matthews a member of the Olympic Health Club?" Frank asked.

Carton shook his head. "No. How the gun ever got into their water-hole is a mystery to me!"

"Talking about the water-hole," Joe said, "we also found a shoe. It probably doesn't mean anything, but we brought it along anyhow." He pulled the shoe from the paper bag in which he had carried the two items.

Carton looked at it. "All I can say is it hasn't been under water very long."

An idea flashed into Frank's mind. "Maybe it belongs to Mrs Retson!"

"She might have lost it running away," Joe added. "Or—or do you suppose she was murdered?" he said, his face registering shock.

Carton stared at the shoe. "I'll find out if it belongs to her. If it does, we'll have to dredge the water hazard at the Olympic golf course."

On the way back to Whisperwood the boys discussed the latest turn of events. "I sure hope it's not Mrs Retson's shoe," Joe said.

"Chances are it's not," Frank told him. "Any number of women play golf there. And why should she have run across the course? She would have been seen, recognized, and brought back. Don't forget, she left in bright daylight."

"The question is, did she go on her own or was she kidnapped," Joe mused.

"We've got to zero in on the Olympic Health Club fast, Frank. All these mysteries may be part of one big package."

Back at the guesthouse, the Hardys found Phil and Tony preparing to leave for Bayport.

"What's up?" Joe asked.

"We've picked the golf courses clean around here," Phil answered. "Now we'll give the duffers a chance to dunk some more, then we'll come back for another scavenging operation."

"You're taking off when mysteries are busting out all over," Frank protested.

"We'll be here in a jiffy if you need us," Tony assured him. "Just give the word."

"How about you, Chet?" Joe asked.

Before Chet could reply, the phone rang. He answered, then beckoned Frank and Joe to listen in.

A strange voice asked, "Are you the guy who cleaned out the water-hole at the Olympic Health Club last night?"

"Correct," Chet said.

"Then you're in possession of everything that was dredged up?"

"Correct."

"How would you like to make a fantastic deal for the entire haul?"

"What kind of deal?"

"A cool thousand bucks!"

Chet let out a low whistle. Frank gestured to him to keep the stranger talking.

"That sounds great," Chet went on. "How come—?"

"You wonder why I'm offering so much?" the man interrupted. "Well, I want the golf balls plus everything else your suction pump brought up."

"Like a gun and a shoe?" Chet asked casually.

There was a moment of silence. Then the man said, "I mean everything. Understand?"

"Sure. Will you come over here? Or shall I bring the stuff to your place?"

"Neither. Put it in a golf bag and leave it tonight under the tall elm in the woods south of the Olympic Health Club. Come back tomorrow night, and you'll find your money in a paper bag under the same tree."

The phone clicked off and Chet gulped. "Wow! I'm in the middle of a dangerous mission!" He looked pleadingly at his friends. "I'll need some protection!"

"Don't worry," Frank said.

"I wonder how this guy knew where to find you, Chet," Joe mused.

"That makes the whole business even stickier," Frank replied. "We're on to something big here. Whoever phoned knew the gun was down there, and must be connected with Matthews."

"It could have been Matthews himself," Joe said.

"Who's Matthews?" Chet asked.

Joe told about the ballistics test on the pistol.

"Hey, I'm getting out of here!" Chet quavered. "I don't want to get mixed up with any gunman."

"You'll have to pretend you're going through with the deal," Joe replied. "Besides, there's a thousand bucks in it for you."

"That's what you think! He won't pay!"

Joe grinned. "True. But he won't know if you gave him the gun until he opens the bag. Meanwhile, we can get a look at him."

Swiftly Joe outlined his plan. He took a golf bag from the closet, poured a stream of balls into it, then crumpled up some newspapers and forced them down on top of the balls. Then he lifted the bag in his two hands, testing the weight.

"That's not bad," he said with satisfaction. "Let's hope our plan works."

After lunch Tony and Phil left for Bayport, wishing their friends luck with their case.

"We'll need it," Chet said, apprehensive about their impending mission.

At night the trio drove to the woods near the Olympic Health Club. Frank and Joe circled through the trees, and crouched behind a clump from which they could observe the tall elm. Chet walked openly to the tree. He placed the golf bag upright against the trunk, then went back to the car, got in and waited.

The minutes ticked away. When the moon rose, leaves and branches cast weird shadows on the ground under the elm. In the distance a dog howled.

"My foot's going to sleep," Frank complained in a whisper.

"And I'm getting a backache," Joe replied. "Chet always comes out on the right end of our stakeouts. I imagine he's snoozing comfortably in the car—"

Joe stopped at the sight of a moving shadow. Someone was in the tree.

"Get ready to charge!" Frank advised. "We can't let him escape!"

The figure moved from limb to limb in an agile descent. Bounding to the ground, it turned in the direction of the Hardys, who looked directly into the leering face of Diabo!

Before either of them could move, the simian seized the golf bag and scampered off into the darkness. Pursuit was futile.

"Outwitted by that monkey again!" Joe exploded.

"But he provided a good clue," Frank said. "Old

Diabo is the pet of San Marten, so San Marten is definitely in league with Matthews or his pals. Everything points to the Olympic Health Club as their headquarters!"

"As you always tell me," Joe said wryly, "don't jump to conclusions."

Just then Chet ran up. As Joe had guessed, sleep had overtaken their hefty pal and he had missed the monkey episode.

They drove back to Whisperwood in silence, pondering the odd twist in the case.

At breakfast the next morning the phone rang. The same man was calling Chet.

"Buddy, you pulled a fast one on me last night. But you'd better not try that stunt any more," the man threatened. "You'll hear from me again, and this time make it real or you'll never hunt for another golf ball!"

The phone went dead. Chet looked pale under his freckles. He stretched uncomfortably. "You know," he said, "I'm really not anxious at all to go out of business!"

"You won't," Frank said. "Don't worry. Just sit tight here while we go and check out the Olympic Health Club."

"Okay," Chet said as Frank and Joe left.

At the reception desk of the health club they met Gus McCormick, and told him that they would like to play golf.

"Impossible!" the pro snapped. "It's only for members—the names in here." He slapped the register on the desk.

"Suppose we're the guests of a member?"

"Then it's okay."

"Mind if I have a look at this book?" Frank inquired. "Maybe we know somebody who belongs here."

"Help yourself."

Frank ran his eye down the list of names, while Joe looked over his shoulder. Finally he came to J. G. Retson.

"Can we go in as Mr Retson's guests?" Frank inquired. "We know him quite well."

"He'll have to tell me so himself," said Gus. "Sorry, those are the rules."

"I'll call him." Frank phoned their client, but he was not at home.

"Too bad," said Gus.

"Was Graham Retson a golfer?" Frank asked.

"No. He stuck to table tennis. Usually played with one of our caddies, Harry Grimsel."

"Grimsel? Is he here now?"

"Yeah. In the locker room. Go right through that door if you want to talk to him."

"Thanks."

Frank and Joe went in and found a slim young man putting some golf clubs into a locker. When he turned round, they recognized him. One of the pair in the car they had hit!

·15·
Midnight Pursuit

"HI, Harry!" Joe greeted him. "Long time no see!"

"Remember us?" Frank added. "We met you on the highway."

Grimsel pushed his long hair out of his eyes. "Oh, now I remember," he said. "What can I do for you? Want a game of golf?"

"Maybe later," Joe said. "First we want some information."

"Like what?"

"Does Mr Retson play the Olympic golf course?"

"Yes. I've caddied for him lots of times. He's not much of a player, though. Too hot-tempered. Has a habit of throwing his clubs in the water hazard after a bad shot."

"How well did you know Graham Retson?" Frank inquired.

"Pretty well. We played table tennis together. He talked a lot about himself. Said he couldn't get along with his father and wanted to run away."

"Did he ever tell you where he was planning to go?" Joe asked.

"Well, he mentioned a number of places," the caddy said, knitting his brows as if trying to remember. "The

113

South Sea Islands, India, Ceylon, Hong Kong, and—"

"Brazil?" Joe interrupted casually.

"No—yes, he did say something about Brazil, but I forget what."

Frank realized that they would not get anything useful out of Grimsel and shrugged. "Maybe he went to the moon. How about some golf now?"

"Okay," the caddy replied. He went off, saying he had to make a phone call first. He returned a few minutes later and supplied the Hardys with clubs and golf balls, then led the way out a side door to the first tee. They each hit a solid drive. Soon there was a putting duel on the green. Frank sank a long putt and took a one-stroke lead.

"Say, you guys play better than most of the club members," Grimsel remarked.

The course wound round the back of the clubhouse. After sinking their shots, Frank and Joe would step aside from a hole and take a good look at it.

"This place is a lot bigger than it looks from the front," Joe muttered to Frank while Grimsel was making his last shot on the ninth hole.

"It seems they've added an entire new wing to the old building," Frank said. "And see that ventilator on top? Must be the biggest unit in Granite City."

On the next hole, Joe stood a few yards to one side as Grimsel started to swing back.

"Do you know anything about howler monkeys, Harry?" Joe asked.

The question broke the flow of the caddy's movement. The ball sliced, struck Joe on the side of the head, and bounded down the fairway.

Joe slumped to the ground as if he had been clubbed

with a bludgeon! Frank rushed to examine him.

"Gosh, I didn't mean to hit him!" Grimsel exclaimed, worried.

Frank looked at the bruise over Joe's left ear.

"I don't think he's badly hurt," he said. "But he's out for the count. We'd better get him back to the clubhouse. You stay here. I'll go for a golf cart."

Frank started off at a run. He was hardly out of sight when Joe stirred. As his eyes focused, he saw Grimsel standing in front of him.

"Sorry I bashed you like that," the caddy said.

"So am I. That's what I get for talking while you concentrated."

"Think you can make it to the clubhouse? Your brother went for a cart, but they all might be in use."

Joe rose to his feet and took a couple of steps. "I'm okay. But what a headache I've got!"

As the two neared the clubhouse they heard loud angry voices. Rounding the corner they found Frank being escorted to the front steps by Gus McCormick. Behind him was a large stout man with a flushed face.

"That's Charles Portner, the general manager," Grimsel whispered.

Portner was furious. "Throw this trespasser off the premises!" he ordered, pointing to Frank. Then he noticed Joe. "Bounce that one, too! He's not a member either. They've got a nerve using our private golf course!"

Portner caught the guilty expression on Grimsel's face. "You didn't give them permission, did you?"

The caddy was silent.

"Answer me!"

"Mr Portner," Harry whined, "I thought it was okay

as long as a member of the staff was with them."

"It wasn't okay. And it won't happen again because you're fired!"

At that moment a police car drove up to the clubhouse. Two officers got out and climbed the steps. "I'm Lieutenant Cain," one of them said. "What's going on here?"

Portner calmed down. "Nothing to bother you with, Lieutenant. Just a couple of trespassers."

"That's your affair," said the other policeman. "We've come on a different matter. Concerns the wife of one of your members."

Portner tucked his chin in and cocked his head. "Who, may I ask?"

"Mrs J. G. Retson. She's disappeared from her home in Whisperwood. We're checking the neighbourhood."

Frank and Joe listened intently as the conversation went on. They quickly realized that the police were being purposely mum about the pistol and the woman's shoe.

"Has Mrs Retson been here at the club recently?" Lieutenant Cain asked.

Portner tapped his forehead. "No. She hasn't been around for at least three months. Of course, I can't swear to it. I might not have seen her."

Portner hesitated, then went on, "A woman has been seen around here several times after nightfall. She ran across the golf course."

"Did anyone recognize her?"

"No."

"Could it have been Mrs Retson?"

Portner frowned. "I have no way of telling. She appeared in the dark, and disappeared in the dark."

"Okay, Mr Portner," said Lieutenant Cain. "We'll continue our search. And let us know if you catch the mysterious lady of the golf links."

As the squad car rolled off down the driveway, the Hardys strolled back to their convertible.

Joe said, "A woman's been running across the golf course. And we've found a woman's shoe at the bottom of the water hazard. How do you figure it?"

"Even if it turns out to be Mrs Retson's shoe, it still doesn't mean she's been murdered," Frank said, trying to cheer both of them up. "Let's give Dad a call when we get to the guesthouse. I think I'd feel better if we could talk it over with him."

Back at Whisperwood, Frank put a call through to Bayport. His mother answered.

"Dad's out of town," she reported. "He's checking some new clues in that passport case. How are you boys?"

Frank decided not to worry her by talking about their latest suspicion. He merely said that they were collecting evidence at the Olympic Health Club.

"A health club sounds safe enough," Laura Hardy said with a soft chuckle. "Stay close to it. And I'll tell Dad you called when I hear from him."

Frank hung up. "We'll take Mother's advice and stick close to the Olympic Health Club. But it may not be as healthy as she thinks!"

That night the boys left Chet in the guesthouse and drove to a road bordering the club. They turned off the lights, parked the car in a stand of trees, and set off for the golf course. At the rear of the clubhouse thick shrubbery provided good cover. They settled down there to keep the place under surveillance.

An hour dragged by. Two. Three. The drone of cicadas lulled Joe to sleep and Frank had trouble keeping his eyes open. Finally they took turns dozing off. Just before dawn headlights flashed into view and two cars turned into the long driveway leading to the clubhouse.

Tensely alert, Frank and Joe crept forward as five men got out. They entered the building and reappeared in a few minutes. One car started off with three passengers. Two men lingered beside the second car and talked in low voices.

"Let's tail this one!" Frank whispered.

They raced across the golf course and climbed into their convertible just as the vehicle came out of the driveway. In total darkness Frank shadowed it, keeping the tail-lights in sight.

The driver ahead sped to the Granite City airport, where he parked near the airstrip. Frank stopped at a distance. Nobody left the waiting car.

"Let's sneak up and spy on them," Joe said.

"Okay." Frank pulled the key from the ignition. Hunched over, they made their way close to the other car. They noticed that only the driver was in it. Obviously the other man had stayed behind at the club.

Suddenly a plane sounded overhead. A small craft came down through the darkness for a landing. It taxied to the edge of the lighted runway and a man stepped out. He hastened to the waiting car and climbed in beside the driver. Who was he?

The boys moved closer and crouched behind a bush near the car. A match flared in the front seat. The newcomer bent forward to touch the flame to his cigarette.

The flickering light played over the man's face. *San Marten!*

·16·

The Ambush

THE match went out, leaving only the burning tip of the cigarette visible in the darkness. San Marten and his friend conversed in low tones.

Frank whispered in Joe's ear, "Let's jump them!"

Joe bolted forward, seized the handle, and flung the door open. He grabbed San Marten by the lapels and started to pull him out when suddenly a powerful spotlight snapped on behind the Hardys, catching them sharply in the white glare.

"We're ambushed!" Frank cried. "Run for it, Joe!"

They turned and ran. San Marten and his companion leaped from the car, and were joined by the man with the light. The three raced after the boys.

In his haste, Joe's foot caught in a vine. He tumbled head over heels, landing on his back. Before he could regain his feet, their pursuers pounced upon him.

Running like mad, Frank was unaware of what had happened until he reached the convertible. Only then did he realize he was alone. He jumped behind the wheel, started the engine, and swung the car around, roaring back to the scene. San Marten and his accomplice had disappeared, and so had Joe. The sound of a motor could be heard in the distance, diminishing gradually in the direction of the highway.

Frank set out in desperate pursuit of Joe and his captors. By the time he reached the highway, the gang's car was out of sight.

Frank made a quick judgment. The Olympic Health Club! "That's where this caper began," he thought. "That's where it will probably end."

He drove to the top of a hill that overlooked the clubhouse. Peering down at the valley, in the first light of day, his eyes followed every turn and twist in the highway for miles ahead. Not a thing moved on the road!

"They must have gone the other way," Frank reasoned. He decided to drive to Granite City and report Joe's capture to the police.

The sergeant at the desk took down the particulars. Frank was turning away, wondering what to do next, when a familiar figure emerged from the office of Police Chief Carton.

"Sam Radley!" Frank exclaimed in amazement. "What are you doing here?"

Fenton Hardy's assistant, a pleasant sandy-haired man, was dressed in a tweed jacket and slacks. He wore heavy shoes and a battered felt hat.

"Hello, Frank," Radley said. "I'm here on a case of my own."

"What's the scoop?"

"Tell you later. First clue me in to what you and Joe are doing."

Frank rapidly described the Retson case, beginning with Graham's disappearance and ending with Joe's kidnapping.

"I'm convinced that we'll find the key to the mystery

in the Olympic Health Club," Frank concluded. "A lot of fishy things have been going on there."

Radley raised his eyebrows and Frank continued, "The general manager seems awfully anxious to keep us away from the place. And now—what about your case?"

Radley rubbed his chin thoughtfully. "When I was in New York a few days ago," he said, "I met an old partner of mine. We used to specialize in missing-person cases. He asked me if I'd undertake an investigation for a good friend of his."

"Who's the good friend, Sam?"

"Mrs Retson of Whisperwood!"

"Mrs Retson!" Frank exclaimed. "And we thought she might be dead. We've been wondering if her body was at the bottom of the Olympic water hazard where we pulled up a woman's shoe and a pistol."

Radley shook his head. "She's in New York in a state of near collapse. Her doctor's keeping her under sedation."

"How did she get there?"

"She climbed out of her bedroom window, caught the bus to New York, and asked her friend to look for Graham. He passed the assignment on to me."

"That's strange," Frank said. "Mrs Retson knew Joe and I were on the case. Why didn't she co-operate with us?"

"Because you're representing her husband."

"What's the difference? They're both looking for their son!"

"That's true. But you're to bring him home. I'm supposed to prevent him from coming home. 'Prevent him at all costs,' was how Mrs Retson put it."

Frank grimaced. "Sam, we're working at cross purposes here."

Radley shook his head again. "Not really, Frank. Mrs Retson thinks her son is in danger. So do you and Joe. Let's rescue Graham and then worry about bringing him home."

Frank started. "What about Joe? We've got to rescue him before we do anything else!"

The sergeant left the desk and approached them. "We've got a tip on that getaway car with your brother," he told Frank. "It was spotted speeding up the road to the abondoned Milten Dairy Farm."

"How do we get there?" Frank asked.

"Take the highway south from Granite City for ten miles. Look for the big Milten sign on the right-hand side. I'll dispatch a car as soon as I can."

Frank and Radley, who carried a small suitcase, hurried out, slid into the convertible, and zoomed down the highway. At the Milten Dairy sign Frank turned off, and the convertible bounced along a rutted dirt road. It led to a complex of barns and sheds.

"Slow down, Frank," Radley said. "There's a car in that big thicket over there."

"It's San Marten's!" Frank replied. He parked behind the thicket, and they got out.

"Look—footprints!" Radley said in a low voice.

The trail led to a run-down house. Carefully the two sleuths edged up to it and peered over a window-sill into a dingy room.

Through the dim light Frank and Sam saw Joe sitting in a chair with his hands tied behind him. San Marten and two other men were taunting the captive with threats.

"You'd be wise to answer my questions," San Marten was saying. "Or I'll let Belkin and Moreno go to work on you. They have ways of making people talk!" He turned to one of the men. "Right, Belkin?"

"You'd better believe it," said Belkin. He pulled out a switchblade knife and tested the edge with his finger. At the same time Moreno turned his face and Frank recognized him. He was the driver of the car the boys had hit alongside the golf course when the sprinkler had obscured their view! Harry Grimsel had been with him.

Joe tugged frantically at the ropes and San Marten clouted him across the face.

As Joe moaned, the door splintered open. Frank and Sam Radley burst in. San Marten and his men spun round, mouths agape.

Frank floored Belkin with a swinging right and fell on top of him. Radley bowled over San Marten and tripped Moreno at the same time!

·17·
Golf Ball Artillery

THE criminals bounded to their feet and a wild mêlée ensued. Punches, karate chops, grunts, and curses filled the room as Joe sat helplessly looking on.

Frank decked San Marten and Radley staggered Moreno with a forearm smash. As Frank and Sam turned to face Belkin, the third member of the gang lifted a chair and knocked both of them to the ground. San Marten pulled himself up shakily.

"Let's go!" he yelled and raced out, followed by his two confederates.

Frank and Sam rose slowly, shaking their heads to clear the cobwebs.

"Thanks," Joe said. "You did a great job."

Frank quickly untied his brother and they dashed towards the big thicket. Radley was the first to spot San Marten's car moving out. It gained speed and disappeared.

The Hardys and Sam jumped into the convertible, eager to take up the pursuit. To Frank's horror the car keys were gone.

"Oh, no! I shouldn't have left them here!" Frank chided himself.

"Don't fret," Sam said. He pulled a pad from his

pocket and wrote something. "I got the licence number. We can phone it to the police."

"Hey, what's that?" Joe said. A glint in the sun had caught his attention. He walked over to it. Nearby in the grass lay the car keys, wet with dew and reflecting the sun's rays.

Frank started the engine and they sped away. At the first public phone booth they stopped and Joe reported to Chief Carton. After a short conversation he told the others that the getaway car had been stolen the day before. "The chief checked the licence number right away. They're on the lookout for it. And another thing—the shoe we found in the water-hole was not Mrs Retson's. Wrong size!"

Frank grinned. "I'm glad about that. Otherwise they might have started dredging the water-hole." As he started the car again, Radley asked Joe:

"What kind of information was San Marten trying to get out of you?"

"He wanted to know about Dad's investigation of the bogus passport ring."

"So he knows Dad's on the case," Frank remarked.

"He sure does. He kept asking where Dad is right now."

"This proves what we suspected," Frank said. "He's in on the passport racket."

"What else did he want to find out?" Radley went on.

"All about Graham Retson. Where is he now? What's he doing? When is he coming home? Things like that."

Frank whistled. "Those were trick questions. We know that he knows where Graham is. He was on a fishing expedition to see how much we've learned."

"That reminds me," Radley said. "How about a bit to eat? There's a restaurant ahead."

"Great idea," Frank agreed. "I'm starved."

Over ham and eggs, they continued to analyse the Retson case.

"We forgot to tell Sam about this," Joe said suddenly and pulled a piece of folded rubber from his pocket.

"The monkey mask!" Frank exclaimed. "How could that have slipped our minds!"

Radley was amazed at Joe's account of Diabo. "This could be very important," he said. "I'd like to take this mask with me. Something tells me it might come in handy before the mystery is solved."

"Where are you going, Sam?"

"To the Olympic Health Club. I called and told them I had arthritis and signed up for the two weeks' treatment they advertise."

"How come you're zooming in on Olympic, too?" Joe wanted to know.

"Mrs Retson is convinced Graham's being held there," Radley revealed. "As a patient, I can do some snooping. See if I can find any trace of him."

"Olympic seems to be San Marten's headquarters," Frank pointed out. "Won't he recognize you?"

"Unlikely," Radley said. "It was pretty dim in that building and he didn't get a chance to see my face. Anyway, it's worth a try."

They got up. "I'd better call a taxi," Sam said. "It would look suspicious if you dropped me off."

When the taxi arrived, Radley got in and waved goodbye.

"Good luck," Frank said, then the Hardys drove on to Whisperwood. Chet was waiting in the guesthouse.

He looked worried and rushed to meet them.

"The guy who played that monkey trick on us called again," he said.

"What did he want this time?" Joe asked.

"His offer of a thousand bucks still stands," Chet replied. "He only wants the pistol."

"What did you say to that?" Frank asked.

"I told him I didn't have it," Chet replied. "But he wouldn't believe me. Said I'll end up in the water-hole myself if I don't deliver the gun."

Frank and Joe agreed it would be safer for Chet if he returned to Bayport right away. They hid behind the suction pump in the back of his pick-up, so they would be on hand if the anonymous caller tried to ambush the truck. They intended to see Chet safely beyond Granite City, planning to return to Whisperwood by bus while their pal continued on home.

Chet was freewheeling the pick-up down a side road towards the highway when a car with two men came racing up behind. He steered to the right, but the other car refused to pass. Instead, the driver cut diagonally into Chet's lane, forcing him off the road into a ditch.

The pick-up truck bucked over a couple of boulders, tilted precariously, and jarred to a halt.

Chet leaped from the cab and ran to the rear of the truck. The two men came after him.

Frank and Joe peered out from their hiding place. *San Marten and Grimsel!*

"Let's see how good my pitching arm is," Frank muttered. Plucking a golf ball from the suction pump container, he took aim and bounced it off San Marten's head.

Joe promptly grabbed a couple of balls and fired

away. Chet quickly leaped on the truck and joined the artillery.

San Marten and Grimsel tried to ward off the barrage with their hands, but the boys kept pitching too fast. Their targets bent over, shielding their heads with their arms.

"Cease fire!" Chet yelled finally. Jumping from the truck, he ploughed into Grimsel with both feet. His weight knocked the caddy into a quivering heap.

Frank and Joe raced after San Marten and subdued him. Quickly they bound his hands with rope from the truck, then tied up Grimsel.

"You'll pay for this!" San Marten snarled.

"Save it for the judge," Frank advised him.

"What'll we do with them now?" Chet asked.

"Take them down to headquarters. Chief Carton will be delighted to see them, no doubt."

The men were lifted into the truck. Frank and Joe stood guard over them, while Chet drove to headquarters. When they arrived, the Hardys announced a citizen's arrest and turned the pair over to be booked.

San Marten and Grimsel were told that it was their constitutional right to consult with a lawyer before making any statements. Then Chief Carton ordered both to be fingerprinted.

At this point San Marten panicked. He resisted the procedure so furiously that it took two officers to hold him while a third cleaned his fingertips preparatory to rolling them in the ink.

The Hardys watched intently. Why would San Marten lose his nerve like this?

"I'll bet he has a record," Frank said to Joe.

San Marten scowled savagely at the Hardys, but he

saw that further resistance was futile. He stood stolidly
as his fingers were rolled in the ink and recorded on the
FBI standard fingerprint card.

"Send the prints to the FBI," Chief Carton said.
"But first check our files to see if we have anything on
him."

"Give me a few minutes, Chief," said the officer who
had taken the impressions. He left the room.

Carton was discussing the Retson case with the Hardys in his office when the man returned and placed a
report on the chief's desk. Carton picked it up, read it,
and dropped it with a puzzled frown.

"This is unbelievable!" he said.

·18·

Bad News

FRANK and Joe looked curiously at the police chief. "What's the matter?" Frank asked.

"It doesn't add up," Chief Carton replied. "Here, take a look. Who would you say this is?" He pushed a photograph across the desk. Frank, Joe, and Chet studied it.

"It's Matthews," Joe said. "We saw his picture before."

"That's right," Carton replied.

"What are you getting at?" Frank asked.

"San Marten's fingerprints match those of Roscoe Matthews!"

The boys looked dumbfounded.

"It can't be!" Joe exclaimed. "No two people have exactly the same fingerprints."

"It follows that Matthews and San Marten are the same person!" Frank declared.

He re-examined the photograph of Matthews. "San Marten seems to have a narrower face," he commented.

"And his nose is much shorter," Joe observed.

"Also, no squint," Chet said.

Carton nodded. "San Marten's hair is black, not

blond. Of course that's easy to do with dye. But the other features are so different!"

"Plastic surgery," Frank surmised.

"That's possible," Carton agreed. "It's an old dodge among the criminal elements. Sometimes a crook's mother wouldn't recognize him after the operation." The police chief stared off into space.

"The thing that doesn't fit into this theory is the difference between the behaviour of Matthews and San Marten. Your Brazilian buddy appears to be quite sophisticated and tricky. Matthews wasn't like that at all, according to our records."

"Matthews' personality must have changed along with his face!" Joe said. "It's been done by other criminals."

An idea struck Frank. "Remember Graham Retson's poem, Joe?"

"I sure do."

"What poem?" Carton asked.

"We found it in Graham's room and weren't sure what it meant," Frank said. "It goes like this:

'My life is a walled city
From which I must flee,
This must my prison be
So long as I am me.
There is a way,
But what it is I cannot say.' "

Carton was thoughtful. "Are you implying Graham Retson wanted to change his identity?"

Frank got up and paced around excitedly. "It sounds far-fetched, but we know San Marten changed his, and Graham is mixed up with San Marten. Isn't it possible that both did the same thing?"

"I don't know," Carton said. "If Graham decided to do this voluntarily, why would San Marten have kidnapped him?"

"I doubt that San Marten would tell us," Joe said. "But maybe Grimsel will volunteer some information."

"Good idea," Carton said, and had the caddy brought in.

He looked frightened. Carton advised him of his constitutional rights, then began to ask him questions. Grimsel answered most of them. Gradually his confidence returned. He even became boastful.

"I know something that could blow the Olympic Health Club wide open," he bragged.

"All right, give us the facts," the chief said.

The caddy smirked. "I'm not that dumb. I know what happens to informers. They end up in the water. Very dead.."

"You mean the water hazard on the golf course?" Frank asked in a nonchalant manner.

"Never mind what I mean," Grimsel said surlily. "I'm not talking any more."

Grimsel was taken back to his cell.

"Here's what we do next," Carton said. "We'll get a search warrant for the Olympic Health Club and investigate the place, based on the discovery of the gun."

"We'd like to go along," Frank said.

"Why not? You boys collected most of the evidence so far."

After the warrant was obtained, Chief Carton and two detectives drove to the health club. Frank, Joe, and Chet followed in the pick-up truck. The manager met them as they entered.

"Search warrant, Mr Portner," Chief Carton said

and presented the document for inspection.

Portner turned pale. He examined the warrant briefly, then said, "Go right ahead. We have nothing to hide."

The officers went to inspect the manager's office. Meanwhile, Frank, Joe, and Chet made a tour of the facilities. First they visited the swimming pool, where about twenty members were splashing around. Next they paused in the doorway of the exercise room. Several men were lifting dumbbells and pedalling stationary bikes.

"Nothing suspicious here," Joe said.

Then they went to the gym. Two teams were playing basketball. Another group of four was tossing a medicine ball.

Suddenly Frank felt a thump between his shoulders and pitched forward on his face. The medicine ball had flattened him!

Joe helped him up. Frank was gasping for air.

"Sorry, fellow," a balding man apologized. "My aim isn't usually that bad. I hope you're not hurt."

"Just shaken up," Frank said, and moved on to the steam room with his pals.

Three men were sitting around in thick bath towels, soaking up the heat.

The boys immediately recognized the figure nearest them—Radley! But neither they nor Sam gave a sign that they knew one another.

"Whew!" Radley said to no one in particular. "I could use some ventilation in here!"

Was he trying to give them a hint?

"It's rather hot," Frank agreed. "I don't think I'd like to stay very long."

Sam did not continue the conversation, however, so the boys left. Outside, Frank said in a low voice, "Sam meant to tell us something with that remark. There was no other reason for him to speak."

Joe nodded. "But what did he mean?"

Frank shrugged. "I wish I knew. Just keep it in mind, maybe it'll make sense later."

"Okay. Let's get back and see if the police discovered anything."

They found Portner talking to Carton about Grimsel. "I fired the caddy," said the general manager. "His record here was bad. He broke the rules many times. That's why he's no longer with us."

"Know anything about a man named San Marten?" Carton inquired.

"No."

"A fellow named Matthews?"

"Never heard of him. Really I'm quite unfamiliar with the people you mention. We have so many members and patients who come here for treatment just for short periods that it's impossible to know everyone's name."

The two policemen came back from their search. Carton asked, "Any results?"

"No," one of them replied. "The place appears clean."

Portner looked from one to the other. "At least you could tell me what you were expecting to find?"

"Oh, nothing in particular," the chief replied. "It just so happened that a gun was found in your water hazard which belonged to a fugitive from justice."

"Well, I do hope you're satisfied. I don't want our members disturbed by all this!" The general manager seemed genuinely distressed by the police visit.

"All right, Mr Portner," Carton said. "We'll clear out and let you—"

The phone rang on the desk. Portner answered, then said to Carton, "It's for you."

The officer took the phone. After a brief conversation, he hung up. "Back to headquarters on the double!" he said, his face tense.

As they hurried out to the cars, Frank asked, "What's up?"

"San Marten staged a jailbreak!"

"How did he get away?" Joe asked.

"He had a confederate spring him," the chief replied grimly. He climbed into the squad car.

"You mean another member of his gang?" Frank asked.

"Not on your life!" Carton said. "It wasn't a person at all. San Marten was helped by a monkey!"

·19·

A Telltale Bug

THE news of San Marten's accomplice stunned the Hardys and Chet.

"How did he escape?" Joe asked.

Carton shrugged. "We'll have to wait till we get to headquarters."

The police car drove off, and the boys followed in Chet's pick-up truck. When they arrived, Officer Jensen, who had phoned the chief, supplied the details. "Near as I can figure, the monkey climbed down from the roof, got hold of the bars to San Marten's cell, and wedged himself through. He brought San Marten a plastic explosive and a gun."

"And San Marten did the rest," Joe commented, feelingly.

Jensen nodded. "He planted the explosive under the lock and blew it off. The men on duty came running back to find out what happened. They saw a lot of smoke, dust, and falling plaster."

"Where was San Marten?" Frank asked.

"Under the bed. He scrambled out with the gun in his hand, got the drop on them, and made them throw their gun belts into his cell. Then he locked them in another cell and beat it with the monkey."

"Did the guards get a good look at the animal?" Joe inquired.

Jensen nodded again. "That's one of the strangest things. They said it was the most repulsive creature they've ever seen. A leering, snarling little monster. About three feet high with a long tail and blackish fur."

"Diabo!" Joe gasped.

"What did you say?" Officer Jensen asked with a baffled frown.

"A Brazilian howler monkey we happen to know," Frank said. "Your description fits him perfectly."

Joe explained their experience with Diabo. "We think that horrible face your men saw was a rubber mask."

"A masked monkey! That's a new one on me!" Jensen snorted. "But that was not the only confederate San Marten had when he broke jail. A car was waiting for him outside. San Marten and Diabo jumped in and were gone before we could do anything about it."

"Did Grimsel get away at the same time?" Frank wanted to know.

"No. San Marten left him behind. I've put a special guard on the caddy's cell."

Frank, Joe, and Chet went back to Whisperwood. In the guesthouse Chet slumped into an easy chair. "I'm bushed," he announced. "How about you guys going to the kitchen and rustling up something for the inner man? Make mine milk and ham sandwiches."

Frank chuckled. "Those threatening phone calls don't seem to have affected your appetite, Chet."

"Please, Frank. Don't remind me. Just bring on the eats."

"Okay, okay."

While they were munching on their sandwiches, Joe remarked. "As long as San Marten's still at large, none of us is safe."

"And don't forget the guy who's been phoning me about the pistol found in the water hazard," Chet said. "He's after us, too!"

Joe took a sip of milk. "When we saw Sam in the Olympic steam room, he mentioned the word ventilation. What could he have meant?"

"You know," Frank said, "the ventilation apparatus at the club is huge. Maybe for a reason. I vote we go back tonight and check it out. And it might be a good idea to take some detecting equipment."

"Lucky we've got a spare bugging device," Joe commented. "The other one must have sunk to the bottom of the river when the monkey pushed us into the Amazon."

When it was dark the boys put a scaling ladder and a mountaineer's rope aboard the truck. Then Chet drove to an inconspicuous dirt road and parked in a concealed spot. The three got out, took their gear, and stealthily approached the Olympic Health Club.

The new wing of the club loomed high above. They could barely make out the oblong shape of the ventilator on top.

"We'll have to go all the way up," Frank said in a low tone.

"Not me!" Chet muttered. "I'm volunteering for low-altitude duty."

Joe snickered. "Your weight would probably break the rope. We'll all be better off if you stay below and hold the ladder steady."

They anchored the scaling ladder near some large

bushes. Chet placed his feet against it, and the Hardys climbed the rungs. Frank was first. Joe followed with the rope.

The ladder fell far short of the top. Frank surveyed the gutters and the ventilator, trying to figure out how to get the rest of the way up to the roof. He spotted a two-inch pipe sticking up at one corner of the ventilator.

"That's the hold we need," he thought. Gripping the top rung with one hand, he reached for the rope with the other.

Frank made three tosses before the noose dropped over the pipe. He tested the rope for security, then hoisted himself hand over hand, gaining added leverage by walking up the wall with his feet. Clambering over the gutter, he gestured to Joe to follow.

Joe gripped the rope tightly, then swung himself upward. His feet hit the wall at an angle that caused him to veer wildly away from the building. As he swung back, he felt for the top rung with his right foot, intending to steady himself before making a second attempt to climb up.

His foot probed into empty space! The ladder was gone! Joe dangled at the end of the rope with nothing beneath him except a two-storey drop to the ground!

Desperately he strained every muscle to keep his grip on the rope. Finally he managed to wedge both feet against the wall. Hand over hand, foot by foot, he climbed up until he was high enough for Frank to lean over and haul him on to the roof.

Joe lay there for a moment, gasping for breath.

"What happened to the ladder?" Frank asked.

"We'll have to ask brother Morton about that."

"Come on. Let's take a good look at the ventilator," Frank urged.

Cautiously they crept along the roof until they reached the equipment, which hummed softly. Through an opening they peered far down into a dimly lighted room, far below.

"Let's see if someone's down there," Frank whispered. He removed the listening device from his jacket pocket and lowered the cord into the ventilator shaft. The bug descended and dropped through one of the chinks in a metal grate at the bottom.

Frank held up a hand to indicate that was far enough. He and Joe crouched over the earphones. Sounds came through clearly. A group of men were talking loudly!

"We got the dope on Radley," said one. "He's a fuzz. Works for Fenton Hardy. We'll have to do him in before he sets the Feds on us."

A second voice startled the eavesdroppers. It was San Marten's! "I told you to screen Radley before accepting him for treatment!" he hissed. "Arthritis! What a dodge! And you fell for it!"

"You weren't so quick on the uptake yourself," accused a third voice. "Whose bright idea was it to lure the Hardys to Brazil? Who promised us they'd never come back? We should have knocked them off here in Granite City like I wanted."

The first man spoke again. "Now they have the evidence they need. If they spill what they know, we'll all do time in the pen."

"Stop caterwauling," San Marten commanded. "We can get out of this mess if we keep our heads. I'll devise a new plan."

"I hope it works better than the old one," came a surly reply.

"This one will be foolproof," San Marten promised. "We'll finish off the Hardys and Radley, and get away with the loot. Break it up for now."

Chairs scraped over the floor. The scuffling of feet indicated that the men were rising. Frank motioned Joe to draw the bug up.

"We've heard enough," he whispered. "Let's get away from here and alert Chief Carton!"

"Right," Joe said. "I sure hope Chet's got the ladder up again!" He grasped the cord and pulled on their listening device. It was stuck! He gave the cord a jerk. The bug banged against the metal grating.

"What's that?" San Marten exclaimed.

"Somebody must be spying in the ventilator shaft!"

"Alert Portner and his guards!" San Marten screamed. "And turn the signal lights on. Hurry!"

Lights began to flash on and off at the corners of the roof. Frank and Joe rushed to the parapet, leaving the bug in the shaft. Frank beamed his pocket flashlight. No ladder!

"We'll have to find another way!" Frank ran to the other side of the roof. But there was no alternate escape route in sight!

Suddenly a trap door flew open. Three armed guards sprang out and seized the Hardys at gun-point. They were hustled through the trap door and into a lift for a rapid descent to the room below.

There the lift stopped and the men hurled Frank and Joe out. The boys picked themselves off the floor and were confronted by five men with brutal, cruel, animal-like features.

The men were wearing monkey masks!

"Five oversized Diabos!" Frank said in amazement.

"So you know all about Diabo." The speaker was San Marten. "You're about to meet him again!"

With those words he opened the door of a cage in the corner of the room. Diabo emerged, wearing his hideous mask. The beast looked more sinister than ever because in one paw he held a thin, razor-sharp dagger.

San Marten boomed, "Play your game, Diabo!"

·20·

Unmasking the Gang

THE howler monkey obeyed the command and began a weird caper. He jigged madly round Frank and Joe, waving his arms and throwing his body into contortions. At the same time he rasped out a stream of eerie snarls and whines.

"That's the voodoo dance of the macumba witch doctors!" Frank gasped. "The same as we saw in Belem!"

Diabo circled closer, flailing the stiletto. Another step, and the ferocious simian would be near enough to stab the boys.

Over the monkey's shoulder, Frank and Joe saw a door open. A sixth man slipped into the room. He, too, was wearing a monkey mask. Just as Diabo poised for a thrust at the boys, the sixth man pulled a gun from his pocket.

"Stop!" he shouted.

Startled by the sound, the monkey turned his head. Frank jumped forward and seized the paw that held the dagger. Joe gripped Diabo by the other arm. While the newcomer held the men in check with his gun, Frank and Joe hustled the animal over to the cage, forced him in, and slammed the door.

144

"Thanks," Frank said to their rescuer. "You got here just in time."

"It's a pleasure," came a familiar voice behind the mask. *Sam Radley!*

Sam pulled off his mask. As he did, one of the gang members picked up a small chair and hurled it at him, knocking the gun from his hand. Two men jumped the detective, while the other three went after Frank and Joe.

Frank met the first attacker with a stiff right-hand punch that put him down for the count. Joe felled second with a karate chop. They wrestled the third to the floor, and subdued him after a violent struggle.

Radley took care of his two opponents by grabbing their shirt collars and cracking their heads together. He picked up his gun, and as the gangsters recovered, ordered them to line up along the wall. Sullenly they obeyed.

Then the door opened again. Fenton Hardy rushed in, followed by Chief Carton and a contingent of police. Chet Morton was at their heels.

"Dad!" Frank and Joe cried out in surprise. "How did you get here?"

"I had a late appointment with Chief Carton. A man was caught with a falsified passport in New York, and he spilled the beans regarding the Olympic Health Club. While I was talking to the chief, Chet rushed in and gave us the word."

"Right after you went up on the roof, I heard someone coming so I took the ladder and ducked," Chet said. "Then, before I could set it up again, those lights went on. I was worried plenty, but I see you have the situation here well in hand."

"Sam gets the credit for that," Joe said, and quickly explained to his father what had happened.

"So that's it," Mr Hardy said. "I was wondering how he got in on this caper. You did a great job, Sam."

"You mean your sons did, Fenton," Radley replied. He walked over to the prisoners and began to remove their monkey masks.

"Belkin!" Joe exclaimed as the first face became visible. "The guy who wanted to carve me up with his switchblade knife!"

Radley jerked off the second mask.

"Moreno, our Brazilian buddy's other strong-arm man," Frank told his father.

The third man to be unmasked was San Marten. "No surprise," Joe commented. "We recognized his voice."

When Radley ripped off the fourth mask, the Hardy boys were startled. "Buru!" Frank exclaimed. "What's a Belem witch doctor doing in Granite City? But you're really an American criminal posing as a witch doctor."

Buru's guilty look confirmed Frank's deduction.

Radley reached the end of the line. Putting his fingers under the chin part of the last mask, he wrenched it off. Everyone gasped in amazement. *J. G. Retson!*

"Caught red-handed!" Fenton Hardy declared. "You've got a lot of explaining to do, Mr Retson."

"Wait a minute," said Sam. "There's somebody waiting outside who should be in on this." He went to the door and beckoned. A young man entered. He wore long hair and spectacles that gave him an owlish look. His face was pale.

"Meet Graham Retson," Sam Radley introduced the youth. "He's ready to provide some answers to the questions that have puzzled us in this case."

"Wow!" Joe said, shaking hands with the youth. "We tramped all over Brazil looking for you!"

"Believe me, I wish you had found me sooner," Graham said. "As it was, Sam was just in time to rescue me from the sauna room before I passed out. They locked me in there and turned up the temperature!"

Frank looked at Sam Radley and his father. "How about letting us in on all the details?"

"To begin with," Mr Hardy explained, "San Marten and his gang have been running a Change-Your-Identity operation here at the Olympic Health Club. Criminals were outfitted with new faces, personalities, and passports, which were in ample supply from the post office heist. Of course, the documents were doctored to fit their new owners."

"How did they ever get away with it?" Joe asked. "This health club is a big place, and to keep an operation like this secret—"

"They had everything set up in this room," Radley put in. "It is cleverly concealed from the rest of the building. No one who worked here knew about it, except Portner, Grimsel, and the three musclemen who acted as the ground patrol. Every time those signal lights on the roof flashed on, they checked the premises for unwanted intruders."

With a sidelong glance at San Marten, who stood in silent rage, Carton said, "We've arrested those four already. Grimsel, incidentally, was never really fired. That was just an act Portner put on to underline his 'no trespassers allowed' policy."

"Sam, how did you ever find out about this room?" Frank asked. "We've been here with the police searching the whole place and came up with nothing!"

"It took me a while. It is only accessible by a hidden lift. See that cubicle over there? It's the operating room where the gang's doctor—Buru, incidentally—performed plastic surgery."

"Wow! And we thought he was a witch doctor," Frank said.

"What about personality changes?" Joe asked.

"They brainwashed people," Sam said. "Mostly criminals. For an exorbitant fee they gave them psychiatric treatment, including hypnosis. Moreno here, who poses as a strong-arm man, is really a licensed psychiatrist. Exhibit A—San Marten himself."

Now Graham Retson spoke up. "I learned about their operation by accident. They made me a prisoner in the club."

"You mean you never ran away from home?" Joe asked.

Graham shook his head. "I was going to leave after I found out my father was involved with that gang. I went to the bank and withdrew money, but the bank president notified my father immediately and he intercepted me on my way from the bank to the airport."

Graham paced back and forth as he related the past events. "I tried to escape a few times, but I could never get far enough before they found out. Those lights flashing on and off were signals for the guards to look for me. Once I got as far as Whisperwood—"

"Were you the one who threw a golf ball through the guesthouse window?" Joe interrupted.

"Yes. I thought Harris was there. I didn't know he had moved back into the main house. He was my friend, and I was trying to signal him. My father caught me that time. Another time I almost made it to the waterfall. I heard my mother call me. Then Grimsel and Moreno seemed to appear out of nowhere and Moreno clubbed me. I heard them talking later about Grimsel spotting you at the falls that night."

"So he was the one who pushed me into the water," Frank said.

"Graham," Joe said, "how did your mother know that you were at the Olympic Health Club?"

"I don't think she actually knew for certain. It must have been terrible for her. It caused her breakdown, no doubt. Sam Radley told me about that."

Graham looked at his father accusingly. J. G. Retson flushed.

"I owed money to their loan sharks and couldn't pay it back. So they forced me to work with them. I have many important contacts in industry and was able to launch many of their clients in various businesses. For that the gang charged an extra fee. You discovered the scheme, Graham, so we had to hold you prisoner in the club. I worked out arrangements to send you abroad, however. You would have had your freedom and enough money to live on. Look, Graham—"

"Forget it," Graham said disgustedly.

Frank spoke up. "Why did you insist that we investigate Graham's disappearance, Mr Retson?"

"To make it look good. My wife was suspicious, and I had to convince her that I was eager to find the boy. I didn't want to hurt her, believe me—"

"So you put that note in my jacket to throw suspicion on the butler," Joe cut him short.

"Also," Frank said, "you sent us on that wild-goose

chase to Brazil. You had your nerve, complaining when we returned without Graham!"

Joe turned to Sam Radley. "How did you ever hit on that ventilator clue, Sam"?

"Well," Radley replied, "I had found out about this underground room. But as a patient, I couldn't possibly get down here without being suspect. I figured the only way to investigate was through the ventilator shaft from the outside. I tried it once but almost got caught."

"Not almost," Frank said. "We heard them say that Radley was the fuzz. They knew, and were probably waiting for a good opportunity to get rid of you."

"I guess that just about winds up the case," Fenton Hardy remarked to Chief Carton.

"There's one thing that hasn't been explained yet," Frank spoke up. He went over to the monkey cage. Diabo glared at him through the bars.

"Joe, give me a hand here," Frank said. "I want to see what makes this monkey tick." He opened the door to the cage. Immediately the monkey growled menacingly, and Joe had to use all his might to keep him down while Frank removed the mask.

As soon as the boy had pulled the rubber mask off, the monkey calmed down. A pleasant, gentle simian face emerged, and bright eyes glanced around the gathering in a friendly way. Diabo seemed to be wondering which of these human beings would be good for a handful of nuts or a banana.

Fenton Hardy shook his head in disbelief. "That's the most astonishing transformation I've ever seen," he said. "Diabo must have been trained to be vicious only when he had the mask on. I wonder how."

"Here's a possible answer," Frank said. He turned

the rubber mask inside out, revealing a couple of tiny earphones hidden in the thick earpieces. "Somebody's been radioing instructions to Diabo."

Joe observed San Marten move his head uncomfortably, as if his collar were too tight. The boy went over to examine the prisoner closer.

"Just as I expected!" Joe exclaimed. He removed a collar mike and followed the cord to a sending unit concealed under San Marten's shirt.

The Hardys studied the apparatus. Finally Fenton Hardy said, "I see it now. High-frequency signals sent out between oral instruction could drive the poor animal crazy." He turned to San Marten. "You're a sadist!"

"Dad," Frank said, "I think Diabo's first piece of monkey business was tossing a bag of nuts at me from a truck in Belem."

"Wait a minute, Frank," Joe said. "He wasn't wearing a mask then."

Frank laughed. "You're right. He was strictly monkeying around on his own that time."

"But he had the mask on when he burglarized our room at the hotel," Joe went on.

"And when he pitched us into the Amazon," Frank added.

"Diabo's a very versatile monkey," Chet put in.

"So is the whole gang, in a sinister way," Frank muttered. He was thinking of his first day in Belem. "I wonder if that hotel clerk at the Excelsior Grao Para was in with the gang."

Retson answered. "No. San Marten had someone pose as Graham at the hotel."

"What about Bauer in Manaus?"

"He's a confederate," Retson confirmed.

Frank addressed San Marten. "He was with you that night at the dock when you had us thrown in the Amazon, wasn't he?"

The man shrugged.

"We'll inform the Brazilian police about Bauer," Chief Carton said.

"One more thing," Chet said. "Who phoned me about the pistol?"

"I did," Moreno grumbled.

Chief Carton motioned to his men. "Take the prisoners to headquarters."

Joe Hardy grinned at his brother. "Well, I'm glad that's over. I don't want to do anything more serious than scavenge golf balls with Chet from now on!"

"Count me in, too," said Frank as everyone filed out.

But neither Frank nor Joe were aware that they would have little time to participate in Chet's project. A new case, *The Shattered Helmet,* would soon involve them in a chain of exciting events.

Upstairs in the lobby Frank turned to Graham Retson. "You know," he said, "our first clue in this investigation was a poem we found in your room. It goes like this:

>   " 'My life is a walled city
>   From which I must flee;
>   This must my prison be
>   So long as—' "

"I remember that," Graham interrupted.

"We figured you were thinking about escaping from home, or even changing your personality when you wrote it. Were we correct in thinking that?"

Graham chuckled. "Sorry, Frank. You were on another wild-goose chase."

"Then what does the poem mean?"

"You'll have to ask the author, not me. I copied it out of a magazine!"

*With a banshee yell Joe jumped upon the figure of
Kitten Cole.*

The Hardy Boys® Mysteries

THE SHATTERED
HELMET

The Shattered Helmet was first published in the UK
in 1979 by William Collins Sons & Co. Ltd.

·1·

A Weird Welcome

"CAN you tell a Greek by looking at him?" asked Joe Hardy.

"Stop kidding," his brother Frank replied, "and keep an eye peeled. This is quite a crowd. We may miss him."

The boys scanned the faces of incoming passengers hurrying to the baggage claim area of Bayport Airport. They were waiting to meet Evangelos Pandropolos, a Greek student who would attend Hunt College with them for a few weeks while taking a course in film-making.

"There he is!" Joe exclaimed.

The youth at the claim centre looked exactly like the photo he had sent the Hardys. He was shorter than Frank and Joe, had wavy black hair, keen dark eyes, and a handsome face. At the moment he looked perplexed.

"He's in trouble!" Frank said. "That big blond guy is trying to take his suitcase!"

Frank and Joe hurried over to Evangelos. He and a tall, good-looking young man were grasping the handle of the same suitcase. The man, who was slightly overweight around the middle, carried an expensive movie camera in his other hand.

"Evangelos!" Frank said. "What's the matter?"

The Greek youth turned and smiled. "The Hardys? What an embarrassing way to meet you. This person wants my suitcase." He spoke excellent English with a pleasant accent.

The tall man broke in, "Listen here! I'm Leon Saffel, and this is my bag, bud. Come on, let go!"

"I beg your pardon," Evangelos replied. "Perhaps if we both let go, I can prove to you that it belongs to me!"

His adversary sneered. "You foreigners are all alike. Always want to prove something." With this he gave a furious tug. Evangelos let go at the same moment.

Saffel stumbled backwards over another suitcase and landed flat on his back, desperately clutching his camera with one hand and the bag with the other. He lay stunned for a moment. Meanwhile, a crowd had gathered to see what all the excitement was about.

Frank and Joe tried to hide a look of amusement, then each grasped one of Saffel's arms and helped him to his feet.

"Leave me alone!" Saffel fumed. "If this camera is damaged I'll have you all arrested! I'll sue you!"

"Calm down," Evangelos said. "It was your fault."

"You asked him to let go," Frank added. "Now, let's get this straightened out."

As he spoke, a uniformed baggage claim agent pushed through the crowd and asked if he could be of help.

"Yes, sir," Evangelos said. He opened his ticket folder, took out a claim check, and handed it over. "This man has my bag."

8

The agent compared the numbers. "That's right. This suitcase is yours." He took it from Saffel and gave it to the Greek.

"B-but—" Saffel stammered in disbelief.

"Here comes another one like it," the agent said, pointing to the conveyor belt. He stepped forward, grasped it, and asked Saffel for his claim check. Then he verified the suitcase as his.

Saffel looked embarrassed as the three boys walked out of the terminal building to the parking lot, where the Hardys' car waited.

"Evangelos," Frank said, "you entered Bayport with a bang!"

"How's that?"

"With plenty of excitement," Joe said, smiling.

"Quite unfortunate," Evangelos said. "I hope it isn't a bad omen." Then he added, "Please call me Evan. Now which is Frank and which Joe?" He reached into his pocket and pulled out two photographs. "I get confused." He studied the boys' faces as they stood beside their car, then referred to the pictures. "Ah, yes. You're Frank, the older one."

"Right, I'm eighteen."

"And, Joe, your hair is light—almost the same colour as the unfortunate Mr Saffel's."

Joe laughed. "I'm just about a year younger than you and Frank."

"Good. Now I have you straight, I think," Evan said and shook hands with his new friends.

Joe swung the bag into the boot, then slid into the rear seat. Frank beckoned Evan to sit beside him. "We'll give you the fifty-cent tour of Bayport on the way home," he said and drove out of the parking area.

9

The adjacent highway led through open country to the outskirts of town. Bayport was a city of fifty thousand inhabitants located on Barmet Bay, a sweeping indentation on the Atlantic coast. Evan watched the unfolding panorama with rapt attention. He smiled when Frank drove along the waterfront, where two freighters were berthed at wharves and smaller boats lay at anchor in the bay.

"Just like in Greece," he said. "We like the sea and ships." He added, "I'm really excited about our studies at Hunt College."

Evan had heard about the summer course from Frank and Joe. The three boys were pen pals, members of an international camera club.

"Our friend, Chet Morton, has enrolled, also," Frank told the visitor. "He's a movie-making buff, too."

"It'll be great fun," Joe said. "The campus is out in the country about fifty miles from Bayport."

"What kind of camera do you have?" Frank inquired.

"A new Cyclops," Evan replied. "It's in my suitcase."

"Great. Say, that was a beauty Saffel had. Joe and I own good ones, but not that fancy."

Finally Frank drove to the Hardy home on Elm Street, a shady avenue of one-family houses, and pulled into the driveway. The boys got out. Joe took care of the suitcase, and Frank escorted Evan inside.

Waiting to greet him were the Hardy boys' parents and their Aunt Gertrude. Evan seemed shy as introductions were made.

"We're so glad you could come," Mrs Hardy said,

taking Evan's hand in both of hers. "Please make yourself at home."

Evan smiled, shook hands with Mr Hardy, and bowed to his sister Gertrude, an angular woman with pessimistic views of her nephews' detective activities.

"It is very kind of you to ask me to stay overnight in your home," said Evan, then added warmly, "I think Americans—like Greeks—are very hospitable people."

Aunt Gertrude's face brightened. "Evangelos," she said, "you seem like a very nice young man. The proper kind of companion for Frank and Joe."

"Now wait a minute, Aunty," Joe said. "You make it sound as if our friends were a bunch of freaks."

"Yes," Frank added. "What about Chet and Biff and all the rest? What's wrong with them?"

Gertrude Hardy raised her eyebrows. "I'm not referring to *them*. What I mean are those terrible criminals you and your father often get mixed up with."

Mr Hardy smiled. "Frank and Joe often help me on my investigations, Evan," he explained.

Evangelos Pandropolos knew from their correspondence about Mr Hardy's profession, but since he was not an American, he did not realize how famous the detective was. Fenton Hardy, formerly with the New York City Police Department, had left the force to set up his own agency in Bayport when his sons were quite young. They had grown up steeped in police lore and had gained a reputation in their own right.

Starting with a case known as *The Mystery of the Aztec Warrior*, Frank and Joe had proved their keen sleuthing ability. Their latest adventure, *The Masked Monkey*, had taken them to Brazil in the hair-raising quest for a missing youth.

Laura Hardy smiled. "Their cases often are dangerous, but I have confidence in my boys. Come now, supper is nearly ready. Frank and Joe, why don't you show Evan to his room?"

The three went upstairs to the guest room, which was small but comfortably furnished.

"Our room is next door," Frank said. "You can share our bath."

As Evan unpacked, he remained silent, as if thinking about something. After putting his shirts in the dresser drawer, he turned to the Hardys. "This could be a very lucky day for me," he said.

"How so?" Frank asked.

"Meeting a detective family like yours."

"Don't tell me you have a mystery to solve," Joe quipped as they trooped downstairs.

"It's almost an impossible one," Evan said. "I'll tell you about it later."

The delicate aroma of Aunt Gertrude's apple pie mingled with the smell of sizzling roast beef. It sharpened the appetites of the three boys.

During the meal, conversation switched from one subject to another—the film school at Hunt, cameras and lenses, American television.

"Speaking of television," Joe said, "Dad's on a very interesting assignment right now."

"It's the first of its kind for me," Mr Hardy explained. "I'm a consultant for a TV documentary exposing a crime syndicate."

"Dad knows how criminals operate," Frank put in. "He's really digging out a good story about Twister Gerrold's operation."

The Hardys told Evan that Twister Gerrold was a

crime overlord who kept in the background and let his assistants do the dirty work.

"His real name is Filbert Francisco Gerrold," Frank said, helping himself to another slice of beef. "The mention of it infuriates him."

"Is it an odd name?" Evan asked.

"Guess he thinks it's too fancy a name for a gangster," Joe replied. "Ol' Filbert Francisco's getting pretty nervous about the documentary. Dad has unearthed some juicy new evidence against him and his gang."

Aunt Gertrude sniffed. "Nothing good will come of it, I tell you, Fenton. You should stay away from such evil men before something terrible happens to all of us." She paused and held up a finger. "What was that noise?"

Everyone was silent for a moment. "I don't hear anything," Joe said.

"I certainly did," Aunt Gertrude insisted.

"You're jittery," Frank said. "Would it make you feel any better if I turned on the outside alarm system?"

"Yes, please do."

Frank rose from the table to activate an electric surveillance system protecting the Hardy property.

"Okay," he said after he returned. "Now we can eat our dessert in peace. By the way, Evan, what's that mystery you were talking about?"

Fenton Hardy leaned forward in his chair. "You're involved in a mystery? You've come to the right place."

"Let's hear it," Joe said eagerly. "We're ready for an exciting new case!"

Miss Hardy clucked disapprovingly, but listened intently as Evan began to spin his tale. "You are probably aware that Nicholas Pandropolos, the Greek shipping magnate, is my uncle."

"We were wondering whether you were related," Joe said. "How does it feel to be the nephew of a millionaire?"

Evan grinned. "It's not my money. Anyway, he wasn't always rich. When he was young, Uncle Nick was very poor. At fifteen he signed on a ship as a sailor. About that time, some boys in my hometown near Mycenae discovered an ancient helmet which probably belonged to a Greek warrior."

Evan went on to say that a curator from an American museum who was touring Greece had seen the helmet. It was split in the back, as if by a sword, and had several undecipherable letters inscribed on the front above the nosepiece. They were copied down, but no picture had been taken of the helmet.

"The curator told about a museum in Los Angeles that might be interested in buying it," he said. "Since Uncle Nick's ship was going to California, he was entrusted by the townspeople to take the helmet with him."

Aunt Gertrude drew in her breath. "Don't tell me he lost it!"

"Someone else did. When he arrived in California, Uncle Nick made friends with a movie cameraman who was working at the time on a film called *The Persian Glory*. They needed an authentic Greek helmet so Uncle Nick loaned it in exchange for a bit part in the movie. The prop department somehow lost the old treasure."

"What a shame!" Laura Hardy said.

"It was quite a blow to Uncle Nick," Evan continued. "He returned to Greece very sad. The

14

townspeople forgave him, but he never forgave himself. He really wants to find the ancient helmet."

"That's like looking for a needle in a haystack," Frank said.

"Too difficult an assignment for you?" Mr Hardy teased.

"Are you kidding? We'll give it a try."

"You will?" Evan could hardly believe his good luck. He swallowed the last bite of pie, thanked his hosts, and asked to be excused.

"I'll go upstairs and write Uncle Nick immediately," he said.

"Use the desk in our room," Frank suggested. "You'll find paper in the top left drawer."

Evan was gone only a few seconds when the Hardys heard him cry out in alarm. Frank and Joe dashed up the stairs three steps at a time.

"What happened?" Frank asked as they burst into their room.

Evan pointed to Joe's bed. On the spread lay a hairy tarantula. As the boys stared at the creature, the alarm system suddenly shrieked a warning!

·2·

Start Worrying!

FRANK grabbed the empty waste-paper basket beside the desk, turned it upside down, and trapped the spider on the bedspread. Then the three boys dashed downstairs and outside, where Mr Hardy was beaming a powerful torch around the grounds.

"See anybody, Dad?" Joe asked.

"No. The intruder was scared off."

Frank quickly explained about the tarantula on Joe's bed. "Obviously whoever put it there sneaked in before the alarm system was turned on, and it went off when the intruder was making his getaway."

Mrs Hardy and Aunt Gertrude, who had stepped out into the back yard, heard Frank telling his father about the spider.

"A tarantula in our house!" Aunt Gertrude cried out. "Oh, Laura, I understand they multiply fast. We'll have tarantula eggs all over the place!"

"Don't worry, Gertrude," Mr Hardy said. "We'll destroy it before it can lay any."

"Let's see how the prowler got up to the first floor," Frank suggested.

"I'd say he climbed the drainpipe," Joe said, pointing to the metal tubing located behind a rhododendron bush. It extended past the boys' window to the gutter at the end of the sloping roof.

Frank took his father's torch and carefully parted the bush. "Footprints!" he announced. "But, Dad, they're so small—like a child's!"

At that moment a blast shook the Hardy house. Glass from the window above rained down on the rhododendron. Frank jumped back to avoid being hit.

"What in the world was that?" Joe exclaimed.

"Something exploded in our room!" Frank said.

Evan stood by open-mouthed at all the excitement. Then he followed the others upstairs.

Joe's bedspread was torn, so were the sheets. A piece of wood from the frame had hit the mirror and shattered it. The waste-paper basket had been blown to the ceiling, where the circular bottom had made a mark.

"The spider!" Evan cried out. "What happened to the tarantula?"

"It was a fake," Frank said grimly. "Someone made a clever imitation, concealing an explosive device."

"But why?"

"Obviously this was a warning," Mr Hardy said. "I'm probably putting too much heat on Twister Gerrold. One of his favourite methods of retaliation is to threaten members of someone's family."

"What a welcome to Evan," Joe said.

The Greek youth grinned. "I must say life has been exciting since I arrived in Bayport."

After scanning the bedroom for clues, Frank found that the window screen had been forced open.

"Who could it have been?" he wondered aloud.

"Kitten Cole is my guess," Mr Hardy replied.

"Who?"

17

"Kitten Cole," the detective repeated. He told his sons that Cole was a famous cat burglar and lock expert. "He's been part of Gerrold's gang for years," Mr Hardy said. "And he has very small feet."

"You mean Gerrold gave him the job of leaving the tarantula to warn you to give up the investigation," Evan asked Mr Hardy.

"Probably. Come on, I'll show you what Cole looks like." Mr Hardy led the way to his study, opened a file cabinet, and removed a dossier. Cole's mug shots showed that he was an odd-looking man. He had a small, narrow face, a receding chin, and an upturned nose. His height was five feet, and he weighed only ninety pounds.

Cole's record showed that he had served several terms in prison. But he had been out for the last three years.

"Well, I'd better call the police," Mr Hardy said and dialled Chief Collig's number. The Chief, who was a good friend of the family, said he would have his men check on the Hardy residence and also be on the look-out for Cole.

Aunt Gertrude, who had been quiet up to this time, finally regained her composure. "I told you I heard a noise," she said. "But no one believed me!"

"You're right," Mr Hardy said. "We should have investigated. You see, you're a better detective than all of us."

Mrs Hardy threw up her hands in despair. "It'll take us a week to straighten out this mess!"

"Don't worry, Mother," Frank said. "We'll give you a hand after the police investigation."

Before long, two young officers arrived. When they

had finished dusting for fingerprints and made casts of the footprints under the rhododendron bush, they gathered tiny parts of the explosive device. Then they questioned the family and left.

Everyone helped to clean up. Under Aunt Gertrude's able direction, the job was completed sooner than had been expected.

Finally Evan sat down to write his letter. He had just finished and come downstairs to join the others when loud backfiring could be heard in front of the Hardys' home. Heavy feet clomped on to the porch and Chet Morton called through the front screen door to announce his arrival.

Chet was as tall as the Hardys, with a broad back and a waistline which was far from trim. He was known all over Bayport for his enormous appetite.

"Hi, come on in, Chet," Joe said. "We'd like you to meet our guest."

The two boys shook hands. "How's everything in Greece?" asked Chet.

"Quiet in comparison to America," Evan said with a grin.

"If you want excitement, you came to the right place."

"Yes, I found that out already."

"No kidding. What happened?"

Frank and Joe told about the intruder and the explosive tarantula.

"Well, it might be dangerous around here," Chet said, "but Aunt Gertrude's baking makes up for everything. How about it, Aunty? Any of that apple pie left?"

"I'll get you a piece," Miss Hardy replied.

"You know she always saves some for you," Frank

said. "You've got influence!"

As Chet ate his pie, Joe said to Evan, "Chet's big on film-making. He's going to drive to Hunt College with us."

"Right," Chet said. "Lots of people here are interested in the subject."

"It's popular world-wide," Evan said. "Young people in Greece are very keen on it."

"Living on campus ought to be fun," Chet said. "I wonder what kind of chef they have up there."

"There you go again," Frank said. "Always thinking about food."

"An army travels on its stomach," Chet remarked solemnly. "And movie people have to live too."

"What kind of films have you made?" Evan asked. "I'd like to see them some time."

"You said the wrong thing," Frank said with a laugh.

"Would you really like to see some of my work?" Chet inquired. "I just happen to have a couple of reels in the car."

He hastened outside to his jalopy and returned with the films. Joe set up the screen while Frank readied the projector.

"I'm warning you, Evan," said Joe, "that Chet is his own greatest subject."

"Oh, cut it out," Chet replied. "In the country, where I live, there aren't too many people around."

"You got a cow and some chickens!" Frank teased. "But of course they're not as gorgeous as you."

"Sorry to disappoint you, but this film happens to be about Iola," Chet said haughtily as the projector began to whir.

A lovely girl in a swimsuit emerged from a pond, stretched, threw back her long dark hair and ran towards the camera in slow motion.

Evan was spellbound. "Who is that beautiful girl?"

"My sister," Chet said proudly.

"Really?"

"I know it's hard to believe," Frank commented.

"I certainly would like to meet her," Evan said.

"Forget it, pal," Joe quipped. "I never introduce her to a prospective rival."

"Is she your girl friend?"

"I've been dating her."

Evan sighed. "Too bad for me. Well, Chet, I must admit the photography is excellent."

"I like to use outside natural light," Chet said. He explained details as the film went on for about ten minutes. When he rewound it, Frank said, "Now that you've seen Otto Preminger at his best, we'd better get our things ready so we can leave after breakfast tomorrow."

The next day was sunny and warm. The boys stowed their cameras and suitcases in the boot. Mr and Mrs Hardy cheerfully wished them a good time at the film school, but Aunt Gertrude was less than enthusiastic about the trip.

"Be careful of criminals!" she warned. "That thug who climbed up the drainpipe last night might follow you. Lock the doors and windows of your room."

"But, Aunty, it's summer," Joe said as he slammed the boot shut. "We'd suffocate."

"Better than being murdered in your sleep," she said dolefully.

"All right." Frank grinned. "We'll be extra careful."

The trio left in high spirits, but Frank, who was driving, checked his rear-view mirror occasionally. Nobody seemed to be tailing them, although a red car passed them once before dropping behind in the slow lane.

"That's a cool foreign job," Joe remarked idly. "I go for that neat white trim."

At noon they stopped at a café for a sandwich. Frank locked the car doors before going in. When they returned after the meal, he exclaimed, "Hey, look, What are these beads on the front seat?"

"*Komboloi*," Evan said.

"What's that?" Chet asked.

"Worry beads." Evan explained that many men in Greece play with strings of beads. "It keeps their hands busy and is said to be relaxing. Personally I don't use them."

"But what are they doing in the car?" Chet asked. "Didn't you lock it, Frank?"

"Sure did."

"Do you suppose that Kitten Cole, the lock expert, was following us?" Joe conjectured.

"Probably," Frank said. "He wants us to start worrying."

"As if that explosive tarantula wasn't enough," Joe said.

Frank nodded. "We'd better keep our eyes open from now on," he said. "Well, let's get going."

A few miles from the town of Hunt they passed a spectacular waterfall cascading down the side of a wooded hill. A sign read *Silver Mine Falls State Park*. Shortly afterwards, they reached their destination.

Hunt College proved to be an attractive, small school

with modern buildings set against a green, sloping hillside. A quiet river ran through the glade.

The boys registered at the office and were directed to a dormitory. Their room, A-14, was large and airy, with double-decker bunk beds on either side. The window was some ten feet above the grassy lawn and commanded a pleasant view of a tree-lined path which led to the other buildings.

The rest of the afternoon was spent exploring the campus. One part of the river widened into a small basin where a flock of ducks paddled about.

It was early evening when the boys went to the cafeteria for dinner. They sat at a large table with other young men and women. After the meal a dozen students gathered around a piano. Seated at the keyboard was a smiling man in his thirties playing popular tunes.

While Chet was working on his second dessert, Frank, Joe, and Evan joined the group. Just then a tall, blond, young man entered the room. He wore a green-and-yellow checkered jacket and a red scarf tucked around his neck.

"Good night!" Joe said. "Look who's here—Leon Saffel!"

Evan's eyes widened. "Is he an instructor?"

"If he is," Frank said, "we might be in for a rough time!"

·3·

Firecracker Plan

LEON SAFFEL'S gaze swept across the room, but he showed no recognition of the boys as he walked towards the piano. He squared his shoulders, tugged at the lapels of his jacket, and fussed with his scarf.

"Oh, boy!" Joe said. "Isn't he cute?"

"Don't be jealous," Frank quipped.

By now Chet had joined his companions and the Hardys clued him in. Chet watched as Saffel squeezed on to the bench beside the pianist and smiled into the faces of those gathered around.

"Yep. He probably is a prof," Chet said. "If he has it in for you guys, I suggest you get a refund and split."

"And you?" Joe asked.

Chet studied his fingernails. "I'll stay, of course. Ol' Chet can make friends with a polecat."

"Then he's your man," Frank said. He got four bottles of Coke from a nearby machine and handed them out. Sipping their drinks, the boys edged closer to the piano. The player ran his fingers up the keyboard and broke into a familiar camping song.

Everyone joined in and the formality of a new situation melted into carefree camaraderie. A slim girl with long jet-black hair hopped on to the piano and gave a solo performance of one of the verses. The students clapped. Leon Saffel, however, cleared his throat and said:

"My dear, that was quite good, but you tend to go flat in the higher register. You should really take vocal lessons."

"I say she's very good!"

All eyes turned to the speaker. He was in his twenties, wore a green sweater, had reddish hair and a full beard.

"Thank you," replied the girl and blew him a kiss. Then she looked hard at Leon. "I do take lessons."

A high-pitched laugh of embarrassment filled the room. The girl continued to stare at Leon and added, "Perhaps you could give me some pointers. I presume you're a teacher."

"Oh, no. I don't teach. I'm a student here."

Chet, who was taking a long swig of Coke, tried to swallow, but choked. The Coke sprayed from his mouth as if from an atomizer. It hit Leon in the back of his neck, dripping all over his collar and the silk scarf.

Several girls held their hands to their faces to suppress giggles, but a few boys openly guffawed.

Saffel wheeled round and glared at Chet while daubing at the wetness with a breast pocket handkerchief.

"I'm sorry, Leon," Chet said. "It was one of those things. I get the hiccups sometimes."

"Well, get them somewhere else!" Saffel fumed. Then he did a double-take. "How come you know my name?"

"Why—er—I've heard about you."

"How's that?"

"Some of my friends saw you lying down in Bayport Airport."

Saffel's eyes scanned the other faces. "So! You're here!" he said, having discovered the Hardys and Evan.

Frank stepped forward. "Look, Saffel. Why don't you let bygones be bygones? We're all here to learn something about film-making, and we should be friends." He held out his hand.

Leon tossed his head. "I'm particular about my friends!"

The red-haired young man said, "You fellows better kiss and make up now, because you might be working together later on."

"Says who?"

"Says Jeff Riker, one of your instructors." He winked at the pianist and left.

"You'd better believe him," said the player. He started another lively tune and the tension was broken.

Half an hour later the pianist stopped playing. He walked over to the Hardys and their friends. "I'm Johnny Almquist," he said, and shook hands. "I teach English at Hunt and drop in for a looksee during the film course." He continued in a low voice, "Don't be too hard on Saffel. I understand he's a rich kid. Sort of spoiled, you know. He ate in town tonight because he didn't like the carrots on our menu."

"He sounds like a doll," Frank said, then added, "Thanks for the tip. We'll try to be nice to him."

"Okay. See you around. Don't forget, the first meeting is at nine tomorrow morning."

Before going to bed, the boys told Chet about their latest mystery—the search for the ancient helmet.

26

"Sorry," Chet said, "but I think this is one case you're not going to solve."

Evan looked disappointed and Chet added, "You've got absolutely nothing to go on."

"Well," Frank reasoned, "if we could dig up a copy of *The Persian Glory*, we could find out what the helmet looks like and take it from there. And Hunt might just be the place to start. Some of these film people might give us a lead."

The first lecture next morning was given by Jeff Riker in a small theatre packed with young people.

"Motion pictures used to be strictly entertainment, but are now beginning to gain recognition as an art form," Riker said. "As we discuss techniques, we will study old films at the same time."

The theatre darkened and two reels of a classic comedy were shown. Discussion followed about the overdrawn acting and the fine lighting for the period in which the movie was made.

"With the arrival of sound movies," Jeff went on, "not much attention was paid to the oldies. Many were mislaid in studios. Some were destroyed by fires. Others were stolen. But films have a way of turning up in some forgotten vault or dusty attic, or in the hands of private collectors."

Frank whispered to Joe, "Jeff Riker would be the one to ask about *The Persian Glory*."

After class the instructor was besieged by enthusiastic questioners. The Hardys had to wait until lunch to talk with Riker. They found him sitting alone at the far end of the cafeteria.

"Hi, fellows," he said as they approached. "What can I do for you?"

27

"We're looking for an old film," Frank replied.

The boys told about the lost helmet, the recovery of which hinged on locating the movie in which it was used.

"There are no photos of this helmet?" Jeff asked.

"Not one."

"What's the name of the film?"

The Persian Glory."

Riker let out a low whistle. "That's one of those lost movies. Collectors have been trying to find a copy for years."

Frank sighed. "What rotten luck! Well, don't tell anyone about this, please. The fewer who know about our search the better."

Riker agreed.

After lunch there was another class. A woman instructor stressed the mood in film-making.

She said, "I want you to go out this afternoon and shoot some footage indicating mood."

Several hands were raised in question. What kind of mood? Where could it be found? Would it be illustrated by people or locale?

'That's up to you. Film whatever you like," she said. "Tranquillity, excitement, or whatever."

As they left the class to get their cameras, Joe said, "I vote for excitement."

"Like what?" Chet asked.

"Like photographing a waterfall, for instance," Joe replied. "Remember Silver Mine Falls we passed on the way?"

"Not a bad idea," Frank agreed.

The boys got their cameras, loaded them with 16-millimetre film, jumped into their car and headed

28

towards Silver Mine Falls. On the way Chet suddenly cried out, "Hey, Joe! Stop a minute."

Joe had hardly braked the car on the side of the road when Chet opened the door and jumped out. He made a beeline for a small roadside stand covered with red, white, and blue bunting. A big sign beside it announced *Fireworks*.

"Chet, come back here," Frank called out. "We haven't got time for that!"

But Chet had already made a purchase, which he slipped into this pocket. He hastened back to the car and slammed the door.

"What did you buy?" Evan asked.

A wide grin spread over Chet's freckled face. "Fire-crackers."

"You've got to be kidding! We're up here for some serious work, and you want to go round shooting off firecrackers!" Joe shook his head.

"Not shooting off," Chet said. "They're for a special purpose."

"Like what?" asked Frank.

"I intend to set them off tonight to scare our fancy friend, Leon Saffel."

"Oh no you don't!" Frank said. "You'll have us thrown out of Hunt before we get started."

"That's right," Joe agreed. "Hand them over, Chet."

"B-but—"

"Come on," Joe urged. "All we need now is a big ruckus to blast our chance for finding a clue to *The Persian Glory*."

"Okay," Chet replied and gave the package to Joe, who slipped it in the pocket of his windbreaker.

29

Then he drove off again. Shortly afterwards, he turned into a parking area several hundred yards from the falls.

Carrying their cameras and tripods, the group set off along a narrow path which led to the bottom of the falls. From high up on the hillside the water leaped down in three cascades until it frothed into a whirlpool basin.

A rushing stream carried it off under a bridge and finally to the river which flowed past Hunt College.

"This is mood all right," Joe said. He set up his tripod and filmed the swirling waters.

Evan said, "I think we could get better shots from high above. Look, there's a trail going to the top."

Chet had already started up, and the others followed. The way was steep and rocky, running parallel to the falls which cut a swath through the heavily wooded hillside.

At the foot of the top cascade was a large shallow basin which sloped slightly downwards and was dotted with big boulders. Evan jumped nimbly from one to the other until he reached the far side. There he set up his camera.

Chet climbed to one of the boulders in the middle of the rushing water. Perched up high, he had a dizzying view of the two cascades plunging below him to the valley.

Meanwhile, Frank and Joe ventured a little higher on the trail. From Frank's vantage point, he had a clear shot of almost the entire falls. As his camera began to whir, Joe suddenly cried out, "Look out, Frank!"

A rock, hurled from somewhere above, missed Frank's head by inches. It continued down the gorge and scored a solid hit on Chet's camera!

30

·4·

Trailed by an Amazon

THE camera fell from Chet's hands into the swift-running water. He jumped in and began groping for it. But his fingers clutched only slippery stones. Suddenly his feet shot from under him. He fell and was swept towards the edge of the basin! Wildly he grasped at a rock and slid off. A foot from the drop-off he gave a desperate lurch, wedging himself between two boulders.

In a moment Evan had leaped to his assistance. Both boys worked their way to the side of the falls where Frank and Joe helped them on to the bank.

"That was pretty close," Frank said soberly.

Chet managed to catch his breath. "Who threw the rock?" he asked. "Did you see it?"

"No. It came from over our heads. Somebody farther up the trail must have heaved it."

Chet removed his shirt and wrung it out. He looked at Frank from the corner of his eye. "Do you suspect that Saffel did it?"

"It's possible," Frank said. "We'll check him out."

"I think it was somebody from Twister Gerrold's mob," Joe said.

They hastened back to Hunt, where some of the

31

students had already arrived with their mood films.

"Let's have your work," Jeff said, "and we'll send it out for rushes."

"I don't have any," Chet said, and told Riker what had happened.

"That's too bad. There's a camera shop in town. Perhaps you could rent some equipment."

At dinner that evening the Hardys made discreet inquiries regarding Saffel. A girl told Joe that Leon had been photographing ducks in the river. But she did not know whether he had spent all afternoon there. Neither did anyone else.

Next morning Jeff continued his lecture on the first motion pictures. "Film was dangerous in the old days," he said, "because it was made of volatile nitrate. One film, in a vault in Argentina, exploded and blew the whole place apart. In fact, just moving a can of nitrate film could cause it to explode."

He continued, "But now we have a triple acetate, or safety film. The manufacturers say it has a life span of four hundred years."

Riker explained that nitrate stock could be copied on acetate, but that it was costly and time consuming. "The old Charlie Chaplin films have been copied that way, and they're still very popular."

The boys returned to their room after the lecture. Joe unlocked the door with his key, then stopped short and exclaimed, "Look at this! The place is a mess!"

The others crowded in to see the torn-up condition of their quarters. Desks and chairs had been knocked over. Clothes that had been pulled from dresser drawers were strewn about the floor. Two study lamps lay broken.

"Here's how the prowler got in," Frank said, pointing to the open window.

"The cameras!" Evan said. "What happened to our cameras?"

The boys found their equipment where they had left it, safely tucked away in a closet.

"If the intruder was here to steal something, he certainly missed the only thing that was worth a lot," Frank said.

The Hardys scoured the room for clues. When nothing turned up, Joe stepped out the window on to a brick ledge and dropped down to the ground. There he found footprints. Most were indistinct, but one set of toe prints told him that the intruder had sprung up to grasp the ledge before hoisting himself into the room.

Joe searched to the right and left. Suddenly an object lying under a low bush caught his eye. He pulled out a white work glove. On it was a smudge of black paint. He climbed back into the room and showed it to the others.

"Maybe the guy wore gloves," Chet said, "so as not to leave fingerprints."

"But why the black smudge?" Evan asked.

"He might have used them for a paint job," Frank conjectured.

The boys checked and found nothing missing. "Maybe the fellow wasn't a thief," Joe said. "This could be malicious mischief."

The Hardys reported the vandalism to the school authorities, who notified the campus police.

The boys straightened their room and after lunch drove into town to find the camera shop.

Frank pulled into a parking lot and they walked

along the quaint business section, looking into display windows.

Chet glanced over his shoulder and whispered, "Frank, I think somebody is trailing us."

The quartet lingered in front of a sports shop and looked back to see a tall girl wearing a sweat shirt, dungarees, and sneakers. She had a winsome face, short auburn hair, and large hips. In her right hand she carried a shopping bag.

The girl stopped and looked the other way until the boys moved on. Then she followed again.

Chet said jokingly, "I think she's got a thing for you, Joe. Maybe she's just too bashful to speak up!"

"Well, there's one way to find out," Joe said. He turned and walked towards the girl. "Is there something we can do for you?" he asked.

She nodded with downcast eyes. "I—I guess I'm a little nervous. I don't usually talk to strangers."

"Don't worry about us," Joe said. "We're perfectly harmless. I'm Joe Hardy. Come on, I'll introduce you to the others."

Joe walked ahead of her and said, "Fellows, this is—?"

"Thelma Sanger," she said. "I live here. My father has a farm outside of town."

Chet brightened. "My family has a farm too! What do you grow?"

"Corn, potatoes, tomatoes, and some tobacco."

Frank said, "Thelma, we're taking the film-making course at the college."

"I know," she said. "That's what I want to talk to you about."

Joe noticed a park across the street and he suggested

they all go there and sit on the grass.

When they were settled under a shady elm tree, Frank began, "Now tell us, Thelma, how do you know we're taking the film course?"

"I was watching you at the falls."

"Really?"

"Yes. I followed you up the trail, because I wanted to find out what you were doing."

"We didn't see you," Evan said.

"I was sort of hiding," the girl said shyly and looked at Chet. "I saw what happened."

"To my camera?"

"Yes. I think I heard a man sneaking off into the woods. But—well, it might have been a deer."

"I'm glad you told us about it," Frank said. "Why didn't you talk to us right then and there?"

"I don't know. I guess I didn't have the nerve." She looked at Chet again. "I know all about the falls. I've explored them since I was a little girl." She put a hand in her shopping bag and pulled out a camera.

Chet look dumbfounded. "Hey, that's mine! Where did you get it?"

"When you left, I climbed into the basin where you dropped it. I found it between the rocks."

"Thanks! That's great! I guess the film's ruined, but otherwise it doesn't look too bad."

"Let's take it into the camera shop," Frank suggested. "They can check it out."

They all trooped across the street and entered the shop. The proprietor examined the camera carefully. He noticed a dent in the housing, but the lens, spring-wind motor, and shutter were undamaged.

"Thanks again, Thelma," Chet said. "Can I get you

35

a reward? Something like a chocolate soda?"

"Yes, I'd like that."

As they started up the street Frank said, "Chet, you go on with Thelma. We'll see you back at school."

"Okay." Chet waved gaily and the two entered a soda shop.

Frank, Joe, and Evan got into the car, drove round a monument in the centre of town, and headed over the bridge towards Hunt College.

At the entrance to the campus they passed Jeff Riker driving in the opposite direction. There was a screeching of brakes, then he backed up.

"Hi, fellows," he called out. "I've been looking for you."

"What's up?" Joe asked.

"Oh, just an idea I had that might help you. I'll tell you later. Suppose I come to your room after dinner tonight?"

"Fine," Frank said and drove on.

Chet arrived just before dinner. He had thumbed a ride back to school and met Frank and Joe who were strolling across the campus. They had left Evan reading in the lounge.

Chet was smiling, and patted his stomach with satisfaction.

"Did you enjoy your soda?" Frank said.

"You bet. All three of them. And brother, can Thelma pack 'em away! She kept up with me!"

"Yes, I would say she looks well-fed," Joe said. "Does she play tackle or guard on the high school team?"

"Cut it out," said Chet. "She may be big, but she sure has personality. Besides, she likes me!"

Banter about Chet's new girl friend continued through the dinner hour. When they finally left the cafeteria, Jeff Riker joined them. They went to their dorm and closed the door. The four boys sprawled on the two lower bunks, while Riker straddled a straight-back chair.

"I think I can help you locate a clue to *The Persian Glory*," he began.

"How?" Joe asked.

"There's an old film actress living in New York named Betty Love. Her hobby is collecting movie posters from way back. If she has one about *The Persian Glory*, it might list the names of the actors, producers, and writers. If any of those old-timers are still living, they might give you some kind of clue."

"Great!" Frank said. "By contacting them we could perhaps learn who has a copy of the film."

"Precisely."

"Do you know Betty Love's address?"

Jeff nodded. "When you met me on the road I was going to the telephone company office. I found her name and address in a Manhattan directory."

"Suppose we go to see her tomorrow!" Evan said enthusiastically. "It's Sunday, and we won't miss any classes."

"Why not?" Frank said. "The sooner the better."

Footsteps sounded in the hall and disappeared as the boys discussed their plans. Suddenly Evan put a finger to his lips. "Listen!"

There was a rustling noise outside the door.

Frank got up, quietly turned the knob, then suddenly flung the door open.

Leon Saffel fell into the room!

·5·

Tricky Leon

SAFFEL fell to the floor, then scrambled to his feet, red-faced.

"Welcome to our room," Joe said. "Why didn't you knock?"

"I know why," Chet said. "He had his ear to the keyhole."

"That's not true!" Saffel protested. "I was just about to knock when the door opened."

"All right, cut the baloney," Frank said. "What do you want?"

"I want to talk to Jeff." Saffel admitted that he had seen the Hardys and the instructor leaving the cafeteria together.

Riker seemed more amused than annoyed. "Okay, Saffel, what is it?"

"You know I've got connections," Leon replied. "I know where we can get those rushes done very cheaply indeed."

"We already have a good film lab," Jeff said. "Even if I could get a lower price, I wouldn't want to change at this point."

Saffel shrugged. "I'm only trying to help."

"Thanks just the same," Jeff said as Saffel left.

38

"Why is he spying on you?" Riker asked the Hardys. "Do you have any idea?"

Evan told of the unpleasant scene at the airport. "I don't think he likes us because of that," he said.

"But that wouldn't explain the eavesdropping," Jeff said with a frown.

"He's trying to harass us for some unknown reason, perhaps," Joe said, and told about their room being ransacked.

"I don't like to see things of this sort going on at Hunt," Jeff said. "If there's any more trouble, please let me know."

"Roger!" said Frank. "Thanks for the information about Betty Love. We'll fly to New York and talk with her."

"I'll come with you," Evan offered.

"Me too," said Chet. "I'd rather stay here and shoot some film, but I don't want to be the only one."

"But you'll have Thelma," Joe needled.

Evan rubbed his chin. "Okay, Chet, we'll both stay. But, Frank, can't we help in some way?"

"Sure," Frank said. "See what Saffel's up to. And remember, lock the room and the window when you leave."

"Just as Aunt Gertrude told us," Joe added with a wry grin.

The next morning the Hardys rose first. "We're off to see Lady Love," Frank said. "Dress neatly, Joe."

Chet rolled over in his bunk, rubbed his eyes, and sat up on one elbow. "Quit kidding me about my lady love," he said.

The Hardys laughed and Frank threw a pillow at Chet. "Down, boy. We're not talking about Thelma."

Evan was awake by now and wished the Hardys good luck.

The boys said goodbye, drove to the nearby airport, and parked the car. Their flight would leave in half an hour and return from La Guardia Airport early in the afternoon.

They picked up their tickets, had a quick breakfast, and boarded the plane. Soon they were winging over the green countryside.

The pilot set his course along the Hudson River, which glistened like a silver ribbon. But near New York City, the atmosphere became cloudy.

When the buildings of Manhattan loomed out of the haze, Frank checked the address which Jeff had given him.

"Let's take a taxi direct from the airport," he suggested.

On the way to the city, the driver was talkative.

"That address is in a good neighbourhood," he said. "Nice old brownstone houses. You gonna visit your grandmother?"

"How did you know?" Joe asked.

"A lot of nice elderly ladies live in them buildings," the driver replied. "Most of 'em have dogs. They gotta be careful. Lots of burglaries around here."

The taxi stopped in front of a quaint building. The boys paid the driver, mounted the front steps, and Frank pushed the button under the name B. Love.

Soon a buzzer sounded and the Hardys entered. Halfway down the hall a door opened a crack, and a high, trilling voice said, "Who's there?"

It was accompanied by the sharp barking of a dog.

Frank announced who they were and that they

would like to talk about old movie posters. The dog yapped some more and Miss Love commanded silence. "Are you from Hunt College?" she asked.

The boys were taken aback. "Yes," Joe said. "But how—?"

"Come on in," she interrupted. "Greta won't hurt you."

The door opened wide to reveal a fragile woman. Betty Love's face still retained traces of the beauty of her youth. She was short, prim, with fading blonde hair and a small straight nose.

Greta proved to be a saucy Pekingese. She sniffed the boys' trouser legs, then curled up on a velvet hassock and eyed them suspiciously.

"Have a seat," Miss Love said cordially. "This is just the strangest coincidence. An hour ago I sold a number of my posters to a very nice young man. He was also from Hunt College. Why do you look so startled?"

Frank tried to gain his composure. "We were looking for *The Persian Glory*. Did you—?"

"Yes. That was among them. Are you the young man's friends?"

"Was he tall, blond, and a little bit on the heavy side?"

"Oh, yes. And he had such delightful manners. He was so fond of Greta—even guessed she was named for Garbo." The actress petted the dog. "His name was Segal—Oh no, Sapphire—"

"You mean Saffel? Leon Saffel?" Joe spoke up.

"Yes, that's it. He's already a film director and intends to produce a spectacular."

"That sounds like him," Frank muttered. "Well, we were trying to find an authentic Greek helmet used in

41

that old movie. We don't know what it looks like. And now—"

"*Persian Glory* was one of the finest," Betty Love said. "In fact, it was my very favourite. I played the princess."

"Then you remember the director?" Joe said.

"Certainly," the actress said. She knew not only the director, but the entire cast and the production people.

As Frank made notes, Miss Love rattled off name after name, then gave a big sigh and let her hand fall limply into her lap. "That was yester-year, I'm afraid. Only one person from all of those is still alive."

"Who's that?" Joe asked eagerly.

"Buster Buckles."

"Oh, we know about him," Joe said. "His movies are being revived right now. Can you tell us where he lives? Maybe he has a copy of the film."

Betty Love laughed and her hands fluttered. "Oh, that's impossible," she said. "There are no more copies of *The Persian Glory*. But Buster—I think you might find out something about him from Actors Equity, even though he's retired."

She jotted down the name, address, and phone number. "They keep tabs on those old-timers," she said.

"Miss Love, you've been very helpful," Frank said as the boys rose to leave.

"Goodbye, Greta," Joe said and received a growl in reply.

On the street, Frank remarked, "Leon Saffel is one up on us, Joe."

"That's because he was so nice to Greta. But we've got the information we wanted!"

Frank chuckled. "The great director probably heard our plans when he was listening at the door last night."

"No doubt about it," said Joe. "We're kind of early for the plane. What say we walk over to Times Square?"

The boys strolled to the busy intersection. Then they went down to the piers to look at the ships. They ate a snack of hot dogs and sauerkraut at a street vendor's cart before getting a taxi back to the airport and boarding the plane.

When the Hardys arrived at Hunt, the first thing they saw was a group of young people gathered around Leon Saffel's display of old posters which were spread on the grass.

"What'd I tell you?" Joe said. "He's gloating already."

They walked closer and Saffel flipped over one of the posters so the Hardys could not see it. He gave them a sarcastic look.

"Something tells me you've been to the big city," he said. "That's my turf. Country hicks should stay away."

There was no reply, and Leon went on, "I hear you like to visit old ladies. Did Betty Love give you my regards?"

"Yes. By the way, what's that spectacular movie you're going to make?" Joe needled.

This time there was silence on Saffel's part. The Hardys coolly walked round the display and Frank said, "You know, Joe, I can see right through the back of this poster here. Behind it is the one about *The Persian Glory*."

"Yep," said Joe. "I can see it, too."

The onlookers became interested, and Frank continued. "Oh yes. There's the name of the director—Bart Lund, and the producers, Soderbeg and Lister."

"And don't forget the cast of characters," Joe said, and proceeded to rattle off the list of names.

The students started laughing as Frank clapped his brother on the shoulder. "You'll get an A in clairvoyance, Joe."

Then one of the girls said, "Say, Leon, I thought you weren't going to show that poster to the Hardys. They seem to know all about it!"

Saffel picked up his posters and walked away with a scowl on his red face.

"I guess that evens the score," Joe said.

Frank grinned. "Right. Now let's go find Chet and Evan."

They were not in their room, so the Hardys had dinner alone. Shortly after dark Chet wandered into the dormitory, starry-eyed.

"Don't tell us," Frank said. "You had a date with Thelma."

Chet rolled into his bunk and heaved a sigh. "She's wonderful!"

"So she's the greatest," Joe said. "Where's Evan?"

"There's nobody like her in Bayport, or anywhere else for that matter. You know, she beat me at Indian wrestling three times out of five! You know, the hand-type."

"I'm sure she can also lift you off the ground with one hand," Frank said. "Now listen to me, Chet. Where's Evan?"

"What biceps!" Chet hugged his pillow. "She'd be great working on a farm!"

Joe grabbed Chet's legs and pulled him on to the floor. He hit with a soft thud.

"What's the idea?" Chet complained.

"You're not listening to us!" Frank said. "Would you mind coming back to reality for just a moment?"

"Okay, now I'm listening," Chet said, finally roused from his daydream.

"Have you seen Evan?"

Chet jumped to his feet. "Gosh, no. Not since this afternoon. Do you think he's in trouble?"

·6·

A Clue on Film

"Don't panic," Joe said. "I doubt if he's in trouble."

Frank looked serious as he thought about it. "With Gerrold's gang after us," he reasoned, "I wouldn't be too sure about that."

Chet told them that he and Evan had spent nearly all day together making films. "Then I had this date," he concluded, "and Evan went into town."

"Alone?"

"Yes."

"Let's hunt for him," Joe suggested. "Chet, why don't you stay here just in case he comes back while we're gone."

"Okay."

As the Hardys left the room, Chet picked up a film manual and began to study.

The Hardys had not quite reached the parking lot when they heard whistling in the darkness ahead. The figure coming towards them was in a happy mood.

"It's Evan!" Joe exclaimed, running towards their friend.

"We were worried about you," Frank called out. "Where've you been?"

"I met some Greeks!" Evan said. He had a white bag in his hands and held it up.

"What's in it?" Joe asked.

"Baklava, Greek pastry. It's delicious. But you'll have to eat it with a fork. It's sticky."

On the way back to their room, Joe said, "Say, who were the Greeks you met?"

Evan told them that he had gone to town for a long walk and had become hungry. "I found a Greek restaurant," he explained. "Their special today was dolma, grape leaves stuffed with rice and meat."

"Sounds delicious," Joe said.

"It is. The proprietor's name is George Kolouris. He has a wife and son, and all three were very cordial. They're from Sparta. That's on the Peloponnesus near my hometown."

When the three arrived in their room, Chet was very much relieved.

"I'm sorry you worried, Chet," Evan said. "Here, this will make you feel better." He offered Chet and the Hardys the sweet and sticky baklava.

"Hm!" Chet said, savouring the thin pastry with nuts and honey. "This is just as sweet as—"

"Thelma!" Joe put in.

Chet raised his eyebrows. "How do you know?"

"Just guessed."

The next morning as the boys were finishing breakfast a messenger from the administrative office entered the cafeteria. He paged Evan.

"Over here," Evan said and stood up.

"Cablegram for you."

Evan read it and clutched the message in his fist. "Let's go back to the dorm," he whispered. "It's important—and secret."

Frank surmised that it in some way was connected

with their case. His hunch proved correct.

Behind the locked door of their room, Evan read the cablegram from his Uncle Nick.

The shipping magnate said that the cryptic writing copied from the helmet had just been deciphered by an eminent Greek scholar. It indicated that the headgear might have belonged to King Agamemnon.

"Agamemnon! He was very important!" Frank exclaimed.

"That means the helmet is of great value," Joe added.

"Priceless," Evan said. He refreshed the boys' memory about the Greek king. "Agamemnon had been away fighting the Trojan War for ten years, and shortly after he returned to his castle he was slain."

"Maybe he was wearing the helmet on the day he was killed," Chet conjectured.

"There are conflicting stories as to his death," Evan stated. "For all we know, Chet's theory might be correct. Anyway, if Uncle Nick gets this helmet, he wants to give it to the Greek government. But anyone else could sell it for a fortune!"

Frank and Joe were eager to get on with the search for the shattered helmet. However, it was too early to call Actors Equity in New York, so they went to the morning lecture first.

The subject concerned light when shooting with colour. The instructor, a middle-aged man connected with a New York studio, explained that lighting could be a very complex process.

"When it is flooded all over the scene, the results figuratively resemble a picture postcard, devoid of any style," he said. "The Victorian era in film-making is over, however, and the matter of prime importance is to express the dramatic element of the film."

The boys were busy writing notes. The light that comes from the sky, they learned, has a bluish tint, whereas light reflected from the ground has a brownish cast. In like manner, light reflected from leaves and foliage has a greenish quality.

In a question-and-answer period Evan remarked that reproduction of colours in some movies was not exactly accurate.

"That's true," said the instructor. "The only things that must be faithfully reproduced are colours of recognizable objects, such as the American flag and flesh tones, for instance." He added that great care must be taken to shield certain objects and the skin surface of the human body from unwanted colour reflections.

"And now," he said, "your project for this afternoon will be to combine good colour rendition and an action scene. At three o'clock we will review the rushes which were taken on Saturday."

The boys phoned Actors Equity after class, but the line was busy. "We'll try again later," Frank said. "Meanwhile let's have lunch."

During the meal they decided to use Chet for the action shots in the colour rendition. The stout boy was agreeable and did a series of comic tumbles which made everyone laugh. Then he disappeared for a while to get some footage of his own.

When they had finished their project, they tried Actors Equity again, but could not get through. There was no more time left and they hurried to the theatre to watch the rushes.

Jeff was in charge. He said, "Now you'll see what you

did for the art as film producers."

The efforts were short and amusing. One was a mood picture of children at play. Saffel's gliding ducks were well filmed and drew praise from Riker. The Hardys' shots proved interesting, Joe's in particular. It panned along the edge of the woods before centring on the waterfall.

"Wait a minute!" Frank said suddenly. "Can you run that scene backwards, Jeff?"

"Sure. Is there something you wanted to see?"

"I think I noticed a face in the woods."

The projectionist reversed the film slowly.

"There it is!" Frank cried out. "Can you hold that frame?"

Although a bit fuzzy, the picture showed a man peering out from behind a bush. He had a heavy black moustache and wore what looked like a chauffeur's cap.

"Okay," Frank said. "You can roll it again."

When the session was over, the boys hastened outside to discuss Frank's discovery. Evan said, "You know, fellows, that could have been a Greek by the waterfall."

"How so?" Frank asked.

"His features were Greek, and his hat was just like the ones that the Greek sailors wear."

"You think he threw the rock?" Chet asked.

"He couldn't have," Joe remarked. "It came from over our heads. The man in the picture was below us and on the other side of the falls."

"He might have seen who did it, though," Joe said. "I vote we go back to the falls and look around for clues."

The boys stowed their cameras in the closet and

hastened to the car. Soon they were at the foot of the falls, and climbed towards the spot where the mysterious man had been hiding.

They crisscrossed the area, their eyes glued to the ground. The grass was trampled down in spots and they found some broken twigs, but that was all.

Suddenly Chet let out a low whistle. "Hey, what's this?" He bent down to pick up a small, blue bead lying on a fallen green leaf.

The boys examined it carefully.

"It's a worry bead," Evan said. "I told you the man could have been a Greek!"

"I wish we knew where to find him!" Joe said.

"I have an idea where he could be," Chet quipped. "In a Greek restaurant!"

"Wait a minute, Chet," Frank said. "You might be right. Let's go see Mr Kolouris!"

They drove to town, parked in front of the restaurant, and went in to question the proprietor. He was a short man with a pleasant face and dark, curly hair.

After Evan introduced his friends, he said, "Would you like some more dolma? I just made it a little while ago."

"Not this time," Evan said. "We'd like to find out if a certain person has come here to eat."

Frank described the man in the film, stressing the Greek-type hat.

Mr Kolouris thought for a moment, then smiled broadly. "Yes. He was here for lunch a couple of days ago!"

51

·7·

The Mysterious Red Car

CHET'S hunch had proved correct, and he beamed with pride as Frank asked, "Was this fellow a Greek?"

Mr Kolouris looked at Evan and smiled. "Yes. He was busy with worry beads. The string had broken and he was putting them together again while his soup cooled." He added after a moment's pause, "Besides, he had a Greek passport sticking out of his shirt pocket."

Evan reached in his jacket and pulled out his own blue passport. "Like this one?"

"Yes, the same."

"Did you notice anything else about him, Mr Kolouris?" Joe asked.

The Greek's plump wife, who had been listening, spoke up. "I saw his car. Would that be of help to you?"

"Yes, of course!" Evan said excitedly. "What was it?"

"A small foreign car. Red with white trim."

"*Efharisto,*" Evan said.

"*Parakalo.*"

"What was that?" Chet asked.

Evan laughed. "Nothing more than 'thank you' and 'you're welcome'. I can see you fellows will have to learn Greek."

He asked the woman if she remembered the licence number of the car, but she did not. As the boys left the restaurant, Chet whispered to Evan, "How do you say thank you?"

"*Efharisto*. It sounds like F. Harry Stowe."

"I think I can say that," Chet declared. At the door he turned round and waved gaily to the Greek couple. "Harry F. Stowe!"

When the Kolourises looked perplexed, the Hardys laughed and Chet realized the mistake. "F. Harry Stowe," he corrected himself.

"*Parakalo*," Mr Kolouris said with a grin. "You sure can speak Greek well!"

As the boys drove towards the campus, Frank reminded the others of the red car which had passed them on the first day of their trip.

"I'll bet it was the same one this Greek fellow was driving," he said.

"You think he planted the worry beads on our front seat?" Chet asked.

"Yes. But Kitten Cole must have been with him, because whoever did that pulled a nifty lock job."

"A dangerous pair," remarked Joe. "We'll have to watch out for them."

The following morning Frank went to a phone booth and called Actors Equity again. This time he reached them without delay. Buster Buckles, he learned, lived in a suburb of Los Angeles. His telephone number was 748–2948.

Frank opened the door a crack and quickly clued in the others. Then he called California, using the family's credit card number.

The voice at the other end was obviously a recording.

It told Frank that Buckles' phone had been temporarily disconnected.

"Oh nuts!" Frank said, stepping out of the booth. He told the boys the result of his call.

"Do you suppose the old boy has died?" Joe asked.

"I don't think so. Actors Equity would have known about that."

"I've got it," Joe said, snapping his fingers. "Let's get in touch with Rena Bartlett."

"The Hollywood columnist?" asked Chet.

"Sure. She knows all about the actors."

"It's worth a try," Frank agreed and went into the booth again. It took him a while before he reached the columnist's office in Hollywood, where he spoke to a secretary. She was cordial, but insisted that he put his request in writing to Miss Bartlett, who was very busy.

"But this is urgent!" Frank pleaded. He told of the call to Actors Equity and of Buckles' disconnected telephone.

"All right," she finally said. "I'll see what I can do. Hold on."

A few seconds later a voice said, "Rena Bartlett."

Frank introduced himself to the columnist and explained their problem in finding a copy of *The Persian Glory*, and their search for the shattered helmet.

"What an interesting story," she said. "Just the thing to use in my television show."

"But, Miss Bartlett," Frank said, "this is a secret mission. We don't want the whole world to know about the helmet!"

There was silence on the other end for a few moments. Finally Rena Bartlett said, "Will you promise to let me know the solution—first?"

"Certainly," Frank said. "You'll get an exclusive report if we find the thing."

"That's a deal. Now, as to Buster Buckles. He and his dog are touring the Southwest in a half-ton pick-up camper. Last time I heard he was in the Sangre de Cristo mountains near Santa Fé, New Mexico. So far as I know, he's still there. I'd love to have him and his dog on my show. And you, too. What's your name again?"

"Frank Hardy. But please, no publicity until we solve the case!"

"Don't worry. You can rely on me."

Frank thanked her and hung up. When the others heard the latest news, Joe said, "We're getting somewhere, Frank! Let's fly down to New Mexico."

"But what about our film-making course?" Chet asked.

"We'll have to see what kind of arrangement we can make," Frank said. "Right now we'd better get to class. It starts in five minutes."

They went to the theatre to watch the action colour rushes. Even with the few lectures they had attended, the students had improved noticeably. Evan's film had been selected as a good example, and everyone chuckled at Chet's antics.

After the work of other classmates had been flashed on the screen, Jeff announced, "That's all for today."

"What about Frank's and mine?" Joe asked.

"You drew blanks."

"What?"

"There was nothing on your film. Sorry."

The announcement was greeted with mixed derision and needling. Saffel's boos were exceptionally loud.

Frank and Joe were dumbfounded. If it had happened to only one, it would have been understandable. But both?"

"Maybe the film was faulty," Frank said as they hurried back to the dorm.

"But I used the same kind!" Chet said.

The boys made a beeline for the closet where the cameras were kept. They opened them and examined the inside mechanisms.

"Good grief!" Evan cried out. "It looks as if someone sprayed paint on your lenses! They're all blacked out!"

"Ruined! Our cameras are ruined!" Joe fumed. "And I'll bet it was Saffel who did it! Under the guise of ransacking our room!"

"But what about Chet's equipment and mine?" Evan asked. "Wouldn't he have damaged that too?"

"Not necessarily," Frank said. "It's Joe and me he can't stomach. Come on. Let's go find him!"

Saffel was not in his dorm. One of his room-mates, Ron Kennedy, said that he had driven off in his car a few minutes before.

"Where did he go?" Joe asked.

Ron tilted back in his chair with a humorous grin. "How come you want to know? It seems you and Leon aren't exactly buddies."

"We're not. And if it's a big secret, Ron, don't tell us where he went. We just wanted to give him something."

"In that case," Ron said, "I'll tell you. He mentioned something about the falls."

"Thanks," Frank said and turned to go.

"What is it you're going to give him?" Ron inquired.

"A punch on the nose!" Joe said.

The boys hurried to their car. They drove off through

town and took the road to Silver Mine Falls. Joe was at the wheel. He braked the car just before their destination and rolled slowly into the parking area.

Evan said, "There's his car." It stood at the far end of the lot. Near it was a foreign red car with white trim! Two people were in the front seats.

As Frank drove closer, one of them suddenly jumped out. Leon Saffel!

The red car drove off, kicking up a cloud of dust that concealed the licence plate.

Leon hurried towards his own car, but the Hardys and their friends intercepted him.

"Not so fast, Leon," Frank said.

"What do you want?" Saffel's face showed fright and anger.

"Did you paint our cameras?"

"I don't know what you're talking about."

"You broke into our room and sprayed paint on the lenses!" Frank insisted.

Leon denied this vehemently.

"You climbed into our window!" Joe said. "We found your footprints below the ledge."

"Tell it to the campus cops," Leon replied with a smirk.

"We did that already. But we haven't reported that we found your fingerprints on the cameras."

"You couldn't have!"

"Because you wore gloves?"

Saffel did not reply. He slid into the front seat of his car and fumbled with the keys.

Chet, meanwhile, glanced into the back seat. "Wow! Look at this, Frank!" He pointed to a white glove and a can of spray paint.

Saffel reached over the backrest, grabbed the paint can, and jumped out of the car. He started running across the parking lot, with Joe in hot pursuit.

Suddenly he whirled round, aimed the nozzle at the boy, and pushed the release button.

Black spray shot towards Joe's face!

·8·

Motorcycle Monsters

THE can of spray paint hissed at Joe as he swung around to avoid it. He felt the wetness on the back of his head.

Saffel moved in to get a closer shot. At the same time Frank shouted a warning. Joe delivered an elbow thrust, which caught Leon in the mid-section. With a grunt he dropped the can to the ground.

Joe whirled about, and with an open hand dealt Saffel a resounding blow on the side of the face.

Leon staggered backwards, all the fight gone out of him. By this time Frank and Chet had raced over, with Evan on their heels. They surrounded the stunned adversary. Joe wiped the black paint from his blond hair with a pocket handkerchief.

"What's the big idea?" he fumed. "Saffel, you must be crazy! If that paint had gone into my eyes, it could have blinded me!"

"Can't you guys take a little joke?" Leon asked shakily.

"I'd say it's a pretty rotten joke," Frank said. He picked up the can and examined it. "This is what you sprayed on our cameras."

"I don't know anything about any cameras."

59

"Don't be stupid," Chet said. He showed him the white glove. "This matches the one we found under our window. How can you deny the evidence?"

Leon's mouth twitched. He looked from one boy to the other. "All right, I did it," he said finally. "But don't beat me up!"

"Nobody wants to beat you up," Frank said. "We prefer not to get physical, but you don't give us much choice."

"Why did you do it?" Joe demanded.

"I was trying to get even," Leon admitted.

"Then let's stop this feud right here and now," Frank said. "It's getting ridiculous."

"But you'd better pay for the repair of the cameras," Chet said.

"All right."

Joe shot a question, hoping to catch Leon off guard. "Do you know Twister Gerrold?"

"Who?" Leon's face showed no emotion.

"Forget it."

"Can I go now?"

"Not yet," Frank said. "Who was the joker in the red car?"

"I don't know."

"You were talking to him."

"Yes, but I didn't ask his name. He was Greek," Leon added. He said that the man had approached him on campus and suggested that they meet in some quiet place.

"We'd only been here a minute when you came along."

"Well, what did he want from you?"

"Said he wanted a job done."

60

"What kind of job?" asked Evan.

Leon shrugged his shoulders. "He was about to tell me when you interrupted."

Frank said, "I'll advise you not to get into any more trouble."

"Okay. Let me go now." Leon jumped into his car and drove off.

The boys discussed the latest events. Why would the Greek stranger want to talk to Leon? What kind of job did he have in mind? Did it have anything to do with the Hardys?

"I've got a strong hunch it has," remarked Frank.

"And that means trouble for us," added Joe.

The boys drove back to the campus and had lunch. Then they went to their dorm, locked the door, and mapped out their sleuthing strategy.

Both Frank and Joe were eager to track down Buster Buckles in their quest for *The Persian Glory.*

"Our film-making course here is important," Frank said, "but we have a job to do. And I don't think it can wait any longer."

"That's right," Joe agreed. "I have a strange feeling about this case. That man in the red car gives me the creeps. He's up to no good."

"If Leon was the one who threw the rock at Chet's camera, and Red Car saw him," Frank conjectured, "Red Car might have figured that Leon has something against us. So he gets in touch with our joking buddy and asks him to do a job—"

His voice trailed off. The others nodded silent agreement to Frank's theory. But what was the job Saffel was to do?

"If you two plan to split," Chet finally said, "where

does that leave Evan and me?"

"Stay and continue," Frank advised.

"Not me," Evan spoke up. "Remember, I got you into this mystery and I want to help you solve it."

"That takes care of that, then," Chet said. "I'm coming, too. We can always take the course some other time."

Frank hesitated. "I'd rather you stay here, Chet."

"Why?"

"Someone has to keep an eye on Saffel and Red Car. They're up to no good."

"Besides," Evan put in shyly, "Thelma's here."

"That's right," Joe said. "She'd be heartbroken if you left."

Chet broke into a smile. "Maybe you guys are right. I'll stay."

"Okay," Frank said. "Would you take our cameras to the shop in town and have them fixed? We'll leave as soon as we can."

He and Joe hastened off to see Jeff Riker and reported their plan to him.

"Too bad you won't be able to finish the course," Jeff said. "But I know how you feel about your case. Maybe you can take the course later."

"I hope so," Frank said. "We sure enjoyed it."

Since they planned to purchase knapsacks and sleeping bags in New Mexico, the boys took a minimum of clothing in a duffel bag and mailed the rest home. They called their father, who promised to make ticket arrangements for them right away and to wire some money to Santa Fé.

At eleven o'clock the next morning the Hardys and Evan boarded a plane for Chicago, where they would transfer to the Santa Fé flight.

At the window-seat, Evan's eyes were fixed on the landscape. The vast green forests and lakes, interspersed with towns and cities, had him spellbound.

"I didn't know there was so much undeveloped land here in the United States," he said.

"You haven't seen anything yet," Joe said. "Wait till we get out west!"

The flight from Chicago was at extremely high altitude, and only when the plane was on its descent did the Greek boy marvel once again at the countryside.

The forested mountains of the Sangre de Cristo gave way to rolling hills dotted with juniper bushes and rabbit brush. Evan said the semi-arid land was much like the hills around Athens.

After they had landed at Santa Fé, the travellers checked at the airline counter. Their money had already arrived.

They took a taxi to the La Fonda Hotel, where they checked in, then went directly to the office of the *New Mexican,* the town's leading newspaper.

Frank spoke to the city editor, Felix Montoya, asking what he knew about the presence of Buster Buckles in the nearby mountains.

"Oh, he's quite a character," Montoya said. "Last time I heard about Buster, he was camping at Chimayo."

He walked over to a wall map and pointed out the location of the Spanish settlement north of the city, known for its rug-weaving.

The boys thanked the editor for the information and left. Next they bought knapsacks and sleeping bags at a sporting goods store called The Trading Post, and visited a motorcycle rental agency. The Hardys had had experience with trail bikes in an adventure called *Danger on Vampire Trail*. They knew what they were looking for and soon selected three sturdy Hondas. Evan remarked that this machine was also well known in Greece. The rental agreement was signed, along with adequate insurance coverage.

In the evening they strolled round the central plaza, which was swarming with Pueblo Indians. The men wore jeans and cowboy hats, the women voluminous skirts and colourful shawls. The Greek boy was surprised to hear so much Spanish spoken on the streets.

The following morning they started out, their gear strapped to the back of the cycles.

Evan's face glowed with irrepressible delight. The new country, the keen crisp air, and the promise of high adventure made his blood tingle with excitement.

The turn-off to Chimayo opened on to a rough road that snaked through dun-coloured hills. Finally they came to a small settlement of low adobe houses and a few shops.

The riders parked their cycles in front of a store bearing a sign *Indian Rugs and Blankets*. They entered and asked the proprietor if he had seen Buster Buckles. Did he know where the old actor was encamped?

The man, leathery-faced and friendly, said that Buckles had been camping near the town. "But he left two days ago," he added.

"Do you know where he went?" Frank asked.

The man waved his hand. "Towards Taos. I hear Buster wants to stay there a week or so."

"Well, we've nearly got him," Joe said as they left the store and had a quick sandwich. Then they mounted their bikes again and started towards the main high-way.

"Hey, look what's coming!" Frank shouted.

From round a bend halfway down the hill appeared seven motorcycles. The Hardys and Evan pulled far to the right side, allowing plenty of room for the oncomers to pass single file.

But instead they approached en masse, blocking the way completely. The lettering on their jackets could be seen plainly: *Monsters*.

The pack stopped, as did the Hardys and Evan. The leader pushed up his goggles, revealing a tough-looking face with squinty eyes. On his helmet was the name Jock. Standing astride his bike, he said, "Where you guys going?"

"To Taos," Frank replied.

The leader turned to his companions and laughed. "They *think* they're going to Taos!"

"What do you mean?" Joe asked. "Why don't you just move aside and let us pass!"

"Anybody who rides a cycle should be ready for a challenge," Jock said with a grin.

"Like what?"

"How about a hill-climbing race, dudes?"

"We're not out for any hill-climbing," Joe replied.

"That's what you say! I say you're just in the mood for a race."

The three boys exchanged glances. The Monster pack laughed in derision.

"All right," Frank said. "We'll race you up a hill. Then we'll be on our way again."

Jock ordered his pals to turn round. They retreated along the road a hundred yards, then turned sharply right on to a small trail which led to the top of a lava flow.

The black hill was strewn with boulders, and from the many tyre tracks on the trail, the Hardys deduced that this must be the Monsters' practice place.

The bikes assembled on a plateau just below the steep incline. Jock pulled the goggles over his eyes.

"All right, you foreigners," he said sarcastically. "I'll give the signal. The guy who reaches the top first is champ."

"Are there any rules?" Evan asked.

"Oh, now, isn't he polite," one of the Monsters said with a sneer.

Another shouted, "No rules. Every man for himself!"

Frank turned to Joe and said, "Fifty-four, twenty-one, thirty."

His brother recognized their football signal. The play was on an off-tackle run, in which Frank led his brother through the line.

Joe acknowledged with a slight nod. Frank would go first and he would follow slightly behind.

Now the racket became a din as the riders gunned their machines and waited for Jock's signal. A mad scramble started. Dirt and pebbles were spewed into the air from spinning tyres. The pack jumped into motion.

Soon it became evident what no rules meant. One of the Monsters cut off Evan. His cycle slewed to one side. The Greek regained control, only to be cut off by another gang member.

This time his front wheels hit a boulder. Evan flew from the seat and landed in a patch of rabbit brush as his cycle skidded on its side.

Frank and Joe gamely fought their way uphill, dodging Monsters while trying to retain equilibrium. Jock and a buddy were in the lead, with Frank following and Joe close behind.

The Hardys had ridden cycles in Bayport and had had some hair-raising experiences, but none like this!

The Monster ahead of Frank swerved to cut him off. Frank braked momentarily, then, with a burst of speed, nudged the rear wheel of the rider. With a look of surprise the Monster veered out of control on a sandy spot.

Watching from below, Evan saw the pack thinning out. Two of Jock's men had bumped each other, and were out of the running. The others kept on like a pack of hounds after Frank and Joe.

Now the top of the hill was in sight. Jock turned his head to see the Hardys in pursuit. He let Frank come even with him on the left, and both riders, their heads bent low, tried to gain the advantage.

Suddenly Jock's foot kicked out. The blow caught Frank on the thigh and he swerved momentarily. Jock followed the advantage by pulling ahead. His rear wheel brushed against the front of Frank's machine, which skidded over to one side, and out of the race.

Jock glanced back to hurl an epithet, unaware that Joe had gained on his right.

Now the Monster leader had another Hardy challenging him! He tried the same trick, kicking out his foot viciously. But Joe, who had seen what had happened to Frank, was ready. He gave Jock a karate blow against the shin.

More surprised than pained, the Monster let up for a split second. Joe burst into the lead and reached the small circular plateau on the summit. There he stopped his machine and waited.

Jock arrived first and threw off his helmet angrily. "What was the idea of whopping me like that! You threw me off balance!"

"So what?" Joe retorted. "No rules, remember?"

The motorcycle leader fumed. Soon the others had gathered round. Frank said, "Nice going, Joe." He turned to Jock. "Now we'll be on our way."

Jock clenched his fists and stepped forward menacingly.

Evan said, "We made a deal, didn't we? We had the race and Joe won. What are you getting uptight about?"

Jock turned to his pals, searching their faces for an answer. One of them, a short boy who looked like an Indian, said, "I guess a deal's a deal. Let them go, Jock."

Frank, Joe, and Evan drove down the hill, on to the bumpy road and finally reached the highway.

They sped towards Taos, looking back over their shoulders occasionally. But the Monsters were nowhere to be seen. Finally they slowed down and took a short break.

"I'm sure glad our buddies aren't playing tag," Joe said, stretching out in the tall grass to the side of the road.

"They slightly outnumber us," Frank agreed. "A real fight with that gang would be all we need."

Evan said, "I have heard of motorcycle gangs in your country, but I never expected to encounter one!"

Frank laughed. "Just stick with us and you'll get into all kinds of tight spots."

Ten minutes later they mounted their cycles again and continued towards their destination.

On the outskirts of town, the boys made inquiries at several filling stations, but nobody had heard of Buster Buckles.

"I guess only the old-timers know about him," Joe said. "Before we go any farther, how about some chow? There's a café over there and I'm starved."

Frank and Evan were, too, and they pulled into the café parking lot. Several trucks were standing in front.

"Maybe we can find out some information about Buster here," Joe suggested as they went inside.

Over steaming plates of stew and crusty bread, the young adventurers relaxed. They asked the waitress about Buckles, but she knew nothing. However, a rancher in a sombrero who had overheard the question said that he had seen Buckles camping near his spread.

"Where is that, sir?" Joe asked.

The man smiled and shook his head. "It wouldn't do you any good if I told you. Buster's not there now. He just up and disappeared. I was hoping he'd stay a little longer. He's quite a character."

The boys thanked the rancher and started on their apple pie à la mode when suddenly a patron sitting next to the window pointed and cried out, "Stop! You'll run right over them!"

·9·

The Disappearing Act

PATRONS craned at the window to see what was happening. A husky man in a red plaid shirt exclaimed, "That's my truck! What's going on?" He made a dash for the door.

By this time the boys had caught a glimpse of what was happening. A huge trailer truck was backing up to where their cycles were parked.

"Oh, no!" Joe cried out. "Stop it!"

The three motorcycles were knocked down and the wheels of the huge truck passed over them with a metallic crunch!

Customers jumped up and rushed to the door, all trying to get out at the same time for a look at the destruction.

"Get that guy!" someone called.

"Where'd he go?"

When the Hardys reached the truck, nobody was in it. The man in the red shirt looked at the damage to the motorcycles and shook his head. "Now who'd do a thing like that?"

"I'd like to know, too," Frank muttered. "These are our bikes!"

Introductions were made. The trucker's name was

Tim. "It was done on purpose!" he said. "But I still have the keys." He hefted them in his big hand. "The guy must have been a clever lock-picker."

"Oh, oh," Evan said. "That sounds like Mr Cole."

The boys questioned witnesses, but none of them had had a good look at the culprit, although all agreed that he was a small man.

Joe pressed through the crowd to a phone booth and called the police. Shortly afterwards, a patrol car pulled up with an officer wearing a wide-brimmed hat. He asked questions and took notes.

"Do you have any enemies?" he said to the Hardys.

"A few," Frank replied.

"Who are they?"

The boys looked at each other. Enemies indeed. They seemed to have more than a few.

Frank continued as spokesman. "We had trouble with a motorcycle gang, the Monsters, after we beat them in a hill-climbing race."

"I know them," the patrolman replied. "They haven't been around here today. Who else?"

Frank briefly told about their harassment by Kitten Cole. "My guess is he flew out here after us."

"And there seems to be a mysterious Greek who's in the act, too," added Joe.

After Frank gave descriptions of the men, the patrolman said he would be on the lookout for them. But he doubted whether he could press charges.

"It's only your guess that they did it," he said. "We don't have any witnesses to the act. All we know is that a man jumped out of the truck and disappeared before anyone got a good look at him."

"We realize that," Joe said, adding, "Is there a place

in town where we can get these bikes repaired?"

The officer recommended a cycle shop operated by two young proprietors. "Their place is open late," he said.

Tim offered his sympathy. "I feel real bad about this," he said, "since it was my truck that caused the damage."

"It wasn't any fault of yours," Frank said.

"Well, anyway, I'll help you pick up the pieces and haul 'em to the repair shop. Here, give me a hand with this bike."

Together they lifted the wrecked motorcycles on to the truck. Then Tim climbed up behind the wheel. Evan joined him in the cab, while Frank and Joe rode in the back.

Tim said, "Some guys want to stop you from going wherever you're going."

"Well, they won't!" Evan said emphatically and the Hardys smiled at his determination.

The mechanics at the repair shop assessed the damage. The front wheels of the three cycles had been badly crushed. Fortunately, the shop had spare parts on hand. It would take two days, however, to finish the job. Luckily the rental agency's insurance would cover the damage.

"We'll just have to stay in Taos until the bikes are ready," Frank said.

Tim dropped them off at a motel, and they thanked him for his help. "It's my pleasure," he said. "I'll be delivering around town and picking up more cargo. Hope to see you again."

"Under better circumstances," Joe said, laughing, and they shook hands.

The next morning was spent sightseeing around Taos. The historic old town, once a frontier settlement, was now the centre of a burgeoning art colony, with shops displaying the works of young artists. Evan browsed around while Frank and Joe went to police headquarters in the afternoon.

There was still no clue as to who had sabotaged their cycles. When the Hardys asked about Buster Buckles, however, the police knew all about him. A local newspaper reporter had written a story several days ago.

"I think we still have a copy," said the sergeant, who was in charge. The boys eagerly read the article, which said that the comedian would be heading back to California by way of Arizona.

Joe asked the sergeant if he would contact the State Police in Arizona to find out if they had information about Buster's whereabouts. At first the officer was hesitant. "He's not a missing person, is he?"

"Not exactly," Frank replied, "but we'd sure like to find him." He told of their search for the shattered helmet.

Finally the sergeant agreed and put a query on the teletype machine. Almost immediately an answer came back from Flagstaff.

Buster Buckles' mobile caravan had broken down on the highway, and the State Police had given him assistance. He was camped not far from the Grand Canyon. Directions for reaching the site were supplied.

The Hardys thanked the sergeant and hastened off to find Evan. He was in an art gallery, buying a small painting to send back to Greece.

"You're going to see more of our beautiful West," Frank told him. "Lots of rocks, and very few people.

73

We're going away out West to Arizona."

The next day the repairs on their bikes were finished and they started out around lunchtime towards Arizona. They had not gone far before they passed Tim and his truck. He gave several blasts on his big horn and motioned them to stop.

They pulled off to the side of the road and Tim called out, "I get a little lonesome driving this big hack. How about taking a ride with me?"

"Okay," Frank said, and Tim let down a ramp so they could stow their bikes inside. Evan sat in the rear. Frank and Joe sat up front.

They drove along, talking about everything from baseball to surfing. About a hundred yards farther on, near the Arizona border, a car passed them on the right.

Joe glanced out the window and looked down at the driver as he flashed by. The man had a pinched face. A passenger was sitting beside him but Joe could not see his face. A third man with blond hair sat in the back.

"Frank, look!" Joe exclaimed.

But before his brother could lean over to see any of the occupants, the car had sped on ahead. It was a maroon Buick sedan with New Mexico licence plates. The Hardys memorized the number.

"I'm sure that the driver was Cole," Joe said.

"Luckily we're in this truck," Frank said. "If that car had overtaken us when we were on our bikes—wow!"

"Where do you suppose they're going?" Tim asked.

"That's another mystery," Joe said.

They approached the next truck stop and the Hardys scanned the area for any sign of the maroon car.

"There it is!" Frank said suddenly as he recognized

the licence number. "They must be in the restaurant!"

"Are you going in to see?" Tim asked.

"Yes, but not through the front door. Joe and I'll go around the back way. Evan and you had better stay here. This could be dangerous."

"You know," Frank said as he stepped down from the cab, "that guy in the back seat might have been Saffel."

"That's a wild guess," Joe said. "But we'll see."

They entered a screen door in the back of the place, which led to the kitchen. As the chef and a waiter stared at them, they mumbled apologies and entered a hallway leading to the dining room. At the end of the hall was a beaded curtain. From behind it came the murmur of voices.

"Careful," Frank whispered. They reached the curtain and peeked through the beads.

Cole and the mysterious Greek were seated five feet away! But there was no sign of the blond man.

Frank and Joe eavesdropped as Cole spoke. "So far so good. The boss'll pat us on the back for bugging the Hardys and the Greek kid."

"Don't get cocky," the Greek answered in fluent but heavily accented English. "We have to find Buckles before they do or he'll shoot us in the back!"

The Hardys were thunderstuck!

How did these men learn of their plans? Were they after the helmet, too, or did they just want to prevent the Hardys from finding it?

The Greek, who was fingering a string of worry beads, spoke again. "The kid's gone for the big stuff. If the Hardys show up again—*teliose!*"

"You mean it's curtains for them?"

"Right."

Suddenly Frank and Joe heard footsteps behind them. Turning, they saw the waiter approaching with a large tray of food held high in his right hand. The boys pressed flat against the wall to give him room to pass, but it was not enough.

The man stubbed his toe against Joe's foot. He lost his balance and tumbled towards the boy.

Joe and the waiter fell headlong into the dining room!

·10·

Flash Flood

THE food flew into the air, some of it spattering on to Cole and the Greek. Both men jumped to their feet, cursing.

As Joe arose from the slippery floor, they recognized him and bellowed abusive remarks.

Joe raced back along the hallway. Frank was ahead of him. The Greek and Cole ran after them, slipped on some mashed potatoes and gravy, and fell to the floor. By the time they reached the back entrance, the Hardys were not in sight.

Frank and Joe had made a dash for the truck, flung open the door and dived to the floor of the cab.

"What's going on?" Tim asked in surprise.

"Those guys are after us," Frank said. "I think they were the ones who ran over our bikes. Tim, see what they're up to."

The truck driver reported every movement of the dishevelled pair as they searched the parking lot. "They're looking for your bikes," Tim said with a chuckle. "And are they mad!"

Finally Cole and the Greek gave up the search and returned to the restaurant.

Tim set off down the highway. After several miles he

had to turn off in another direction so he stopped to let the Hardys out. The boys unloaded their bikes and thanked him for the ride.

Tim waved and drove off. Before mounting their cycles, Frank said, "You know, the blond character was not with the two men. Maybe he's 'the kid who's gone for the big stuff'. I'd like to call Chet and see if Saffel is still at Hunt."

"Let's stop at the next phone booth," Joe agreed.

A mile farther on they found a highway telephone. Frank went inside and made a person-to-person call.

In a few seconds Chet was on the line. He was delighted to hear from the Hardys and began asking questions about their case.

Frank said, "Listen, Chet, I don't have much time. What I want to ask you is this: has Saffel left school?"

"Matter of fact, yes."

"When?"

"Right after you left."

"Have you seen the red car?"

"No! Not since the day we saw it at the falls."

"Thanks, Chet. How's Thelma?"

"Great, just great! I've gained five pounds eating goodies at her house."

"How's the film course?"

"Super. I'm taking lots of footage of Thelma."

Frank chuckled and hung up. "Joe, Saffel's gone."

"He might have followed us," Joe said. "Well, let's go and keep our eyes open."

Just before sundown the boys arrived in the area where Buckles had been reported to be camping.

They made several inquiries about a man with his dog and were directed to a mobile caravan which had parked in a shady glen. Driving close to it they stopped and approached the mobile caravan. Joe knocked on the door. A woman answered.

"Sorry," the boy said. "I think we made a mistake."

"Who are you looking for?" she asked.

"Buster Buckles, the old actor," Joe said. "We were told that he's camping in this area."

"You mean the movie funnyman with his little dog?"

"Yes, that's the one."

A man appeared behind the woman and joined in the conversation. "He wasn't very sociable," he said.

The couple told the boys that other neighbours had reported Buster was on his way to Bald Eagle Mountain.

"Hardly anybody goes there," the man said. "No facilities."

Frank looked at a road map. Bald Eagle Mountain was not far away. The elevation showed 6,100 feet.

"Do you think we can make it before dark?" Evan asked.

"If we push hard," Frank said.

They hopped on their bikes again and set off. In the distance a great mass of black clouds began to settle into a valley.

"That storm's a long way off," Joe thought. But minutes later lightning forked through the sky. The valley became dark with rain, and the setting sun produced a full rainbow.

Frank, in the lead, held up his hand in a signal to stop at a crossroads. They checked their maps again and found that the road leading to Bald Eagle Mountain turned left, into the same valley where they had seen the storm.

They continued on, riding parallel to an arroyo with only a thread of water trickling through it. But the riders noticed that the stream grew larger by the minute. Now the road dipped down over a bridge to the other side of the broad gulch.

Frank and Joe crossed the bridge first. Evan was third in line. He stopped, fascinated, and reached for his camera. The Hardys did not notice his absence until they had gone several hundred yards.

Suddenly Joe shouted and Frank turned to look. To their horror they saw a wall of water swirling down the arroyo.

"A flash flood!" Frank cried out as he wheeled his cycle around. "Evan, come on, hurry!"

The Greek boy, however, seemed mesmerized by the oncoming flood. He took some more footage. Frank and Joe raced towards him at full speed. They braked to a screaming halt at the edge of the bridge and waved their arms wildly.

All at once Evan realized the danger. He stowed his camera and hopped aboard his cycle. As he did, the first wave of water swept several inches above the bridge. Evan gunned his machine and the wheels set up a spray as he flew across the span.

Seconds later three feet of muddy, boiling, sandy water flooded over the bridge, carrying pebbles and debris, just as the three cyclists reached higher ground.

They stopped to look back at the phenomenon. Evan's hands were shaking a little. The roof of a cabin swirled against the bridge, tearing apart like matchwood. Three uprooted pine trees followed. The span shuddered as they banged against the superstructure and stuck there.

"I just got out in time." Evan said. He promised to be more careful in the future.

"You'd better," Frank said with a grin. "We don't want to send you back to Greece in a coffin!"

The cyclists followed the uphill road, which gradually became nothing more than an indistinct trail. Off to one side, in a grassy gully, they spied cattle being urged along by a lone cowboy. They waved to him and drove over to ask if he had seen Buckles.

"The old man with the dog?" the man said.

"Yes," Frank replied.

"Are you looking for him, too?"

"What do you mean, too?"

The horse grew restless and the cowboy leaned over to pat the animal's neck. "A young fellow like you asked the same question about an hour ago."

"Was he blond?" Evan inquired.

The cowboy nodded. A smile crossed his wrinkled face. "You'll find the old guy up there on the mountain," he said. "But I'm warning you. He's about as friendly as a wounded grizzly bear."

"Thanks," Frank said. "You've been a big help."

The trio drove quietly around the cattle, found the dim outline of the trail again, and continued on as evening settled.

Frank said, "Do you suppose it was Saffel who asked the cowboy about Buster?"

"We'll find out," Joe replied.

But soon it became too dark to follow the trail. Finding the elusive Buster Buckles would have to wait until morning. They made camp at the base of three towering pine trees, ate some canned food, and crawled into their sleeping bags.

The sighing of the wind blowing through the treetops lulled the weary travellers to sleep. Frank was awakened at dawn. He had been dreaming that he was swimming in choppy water. Suddenly he realized that something was lapping against his forehead.

The boy opened his eyes slowly and saw the face of a friendly fox terrier. He reached up, patted the dog, and called to the others. "Look, fellows. We've got a mascot."

Joe and Evan crawled out of their sleeping bags, put on their dungarees and shirts, and combed their hair. The terrier continually jumped up and down, and Joe said, "Hold still while I look at your collar."

Attached was a small tag. Joe studied it and whistled. "Hot dog! If this isn't luck. Little Bozo belongs to Buster Buckles!"

"Which means," Frank said with a whoop, "that he's close by."

"Come on, pooch," Joe said. "Take us to your master!"

The dog yapped several times, then headed up the hill through a stand of trees.

"If we ride our bikes, we might scare the daylights out of the old boy," Frank said. "I don't think he'd appreciate that. Let's go on foot."

The dog cavorted around, yapping at his new-found friends, and led them over a small hill. Down the other side, not more than three hundred yards, was a mobile caravan. Several shirts had been hung on the roof to dry.

The boys followed the dog to the door and Frank called out, "Hello, Mr Buckles!"

Someone stirred inside. Then the door opened and a

wrinkled face poked out. The grey hair was dishevelled, and the eyes were full of sleep.

The face showed annoyance at being rudely awakened. The man retreated for a minute, then reappeared, wearing glasses.

"What in thunder!" he growled. "Where did you find my dog?"

"In our camp," said Joe and introduced himself, Frank and Evan.

"Hello and goodbye," Buster Buckles said churlishly. "Look, I came out in the wilds here to be alone. If you want my autograph, I'll give it to you, and then you can buzz off."

"Please wait a minute, Mr Buckles," Frank said, trying to soothe the old fellow. "We're very sorry to bust in on you this way. But it's very important."

"What's more important than a good night's sleep? I don't usually wake up till nine."

Frank laughed. "Well, your dog woke us up at daylight."

"Teddy, you shouldn't have done that!" Buster scolded the dog. "His name's Teddy—after Teddy Roosevelt."

A smile appeared on the comic's thin lips. "All right, boys, I'm over my morning grouch. Now you may call me Buster. Let's have coffee. I've got to fix myself some breakfast. Will you join me?"

"Sure thing," said Joe. "We're hungry, too!"

Buster brought out a portable cooking stove, lighted it, and put several slices of bacon in a large frying pan. It started sizzling, and a mouth-watering aroma scented the brisk, morning air.

The actor did not talk much, and the Hardys decided

not to ask any questions until they had finished eating. They sat down on the ground after Buckles declined their offer to help. He removed the bacon, cracked eight eggs into the pan, and brought a loaf of bread from his larder. Then he passed around paper plates.

"Dig in," he said simply.

After they had eaten, Buster said, "Now, tell me, what brings you here?"

Frank explained about their quest for the helmet and *The Persian Glory*.

"So you're old movie bugs, eh?" Buster said. "Let me tell you, there was more guts in those pictures than there is today. Why, these young upstarts—"

"But do you know where we can find a copy of *The Persian Glory?*" Frank asked impatiently.

"I thought you might be coming to that," the actor said, leaning forward on his camp stool. "I think—"

Just then a thunderous explosion rent the air and shook the ground!

·11·

Cheese Bait

"IT'S an earthquake!" Buster Buckles cried out, and dived headlong into his mobile caravan. Tail between legs, Teddy slunk in after him.

At first the boys looked at each other in stunned silence. Then Frank exclaimed, "Something's happened over the hill!"

They raced up the slope towards their campsite. When they reached the brow of the hill, they looked down on a scene of utter devastation!

At the place where the bikes had stood there were now three shallow holes in the ground. The machines had been blown to bits! Parts dangled from the pine trees. A wheel had smashed into a rock, and a handlebar stuck out of the ground. Only the sleeping bags were still intact and lay crumpled on the ground about thirty feet away.

In stunned disbelief, the boys walked down the hill to the site of the demolition.

"This is terrible!" Evan whispered. "We've been dynamited!"

"Our enemies are really desperate to get us out of the way," Joe said.

"Somebody must have been spying on us," Evan

conjectured, "and when we disappeared over the hill, set up the explosives."

Frank nodded. "Good thing they didn't go off while we were sleeping!"

The three boys poked around the debris for clues. After searching in vain, Frank said, "Remember what Cole said in the restaurant? 'The kid's gone for the big stuff.' That kid could have been Leon Saffel going for the dynamite!"

The boys made one more round of the area. This time they picked up their sleeping bags and the motor-cycle licence plates, one of which had become embedded in the trunk of a pine tree.

"I think the police and insurance company will need these for evidence," Frank remarked as they trudged back over the hill.

Waiting on the other side was Buster Buckles, a rifle on his shoulder.

"Hey, Buster!" Joe called out. "Put the shooting iron away. The varmints are gone!"

"Oh, it ain't real," Buster replied, explaining that the gun was an old comedy prop he carried along to scare off snoopers.

The actor bombarded them with questions about the explosion. Upon hearing the details, he blanched.

"Listen, I'm getting out of here!" he declared.

"But the bad guys are gone!" Frank insisted.

"How do you know they won't come back? Maybe they'll blow up my caravan next! The whole world's gone cuckoo. You can't even find peace in the wilds of Arizony."

Frank agreed they should leave and report the bombing to the police.

"Could you give us a ride to the next town?" he inquired.

Buster nodded. Then he said, "Hey, what was that you were asking about *The Persian Glory*?"

"We are looking for a copy of the film," Joe said. "That's why we're here. Do you have one?"

Buster shook his head. As the boys moaned their disappointment, he added brightly, "I think I have an out-take, though."

"What's that?" Evan asked.

Buster explained that an out-take was film footage that had been clipped out for one reason or another.

"It might have been a poor shot," he said, "or cut to tighten the action. Or, perhaps, the film was just too long."

He went on to say that one old Hollywood movie had been eight hours long. "They edited out six hours of it. Boy, was the director ever mad!"

"But how come you have out-takes of films?" Frank asked.

Buster explained that his hobby had been to collect them. "I used to splice them all together," he said. "It made a very funny movie. You could hardly follow the plot." He slapped his knee with delight. Suddenly his face turned serious again.

"We're getting out of here, boys," he said, and carried the little stove back into the camper.

Frank pressed for more information. "Do you really have some footage on *The Persian Glory*?"

"I think I do. I'm not sure."

"Where is it?"

"At my place."

"You mean your home in California?"

"That's right. I have cans of film in the back of the garage. They're under a pile of junk, but I'm sure I could find them."

"Then let's go!" Joe cried.

Buster looked reproachful. "What's the hurry? I came here to fish!"

"But—but Mr Buckles, this is important," Joe said. "It can't wait!"

Frank signalled his brother to be quiet. Then he said, "All right, Buster. It's your vacation and up to you how long you want to stay. But after that, may we go to California with you?"

"Sure." When Buster was certain that every scrap had been picked up from the campsite, he spoke again of the fishing trip.

"I tell you," he said, "those trout are that long!" He indicated the size with his hands.

"Please," Frank pleaded, "can you drop us off at the police office so we can make the report while you go fishing?"

Arms akimbo, Buster gave them a look of annoyance. "The fish are in a little lake at the top of this mountain. It's nowhere near town. We'll fish first, then find the cops!"

The boys stepped to one side and discussed the plan. Travelling on foot in these wilds, they reasoned, was almost impossible. They would have to go along with the old man's wishes.

Buster climbed behind the wheel. Frank sat beside him, while Joe and Evan rode in the back.

It was a bumpy ride over the trackless ground to the summit of the nearby ridge.

"Only a few Apaches and cowboys know about this

lake," Buster said. "And those little rascals are waiting for their cheese!"

"Who? The Apaches or the cowboys?" Frank asked.

"The trout, of course. They love cheese. That's what I use for bait."

"Fish also like bread. Maybe we can give them a whole cheese sandwich," Frank quipped.

"Okay, wise guy. You'll see!"

Soon a small blue lake came into view. It lay in a crater, reflecting the cloudless sky overhead.

Buster parked the caravan beside a boulder and they got out. "I've only got three rods," he said. "You can use two of 'em."

"Go ahead, fellows," Evan said. "I'll walk around the lake." He wandered off along the rocky shoreline.

Buster sliced off a piece of American cheese and cut it into small cubes. "Put these on your hooks," he said to Frank and Joe, "and watch the fun."

The Hardys did. They flicked out their lines and the cheese dropped into the lake. Joe's bait had sunk no more than six inches when he felt a swift strike.

"Wow! I've got one!" he yelled.

Buckles was already reeling in a fat, flopping trout. "What did I tell you?" he asked with a happy grin.

In a short time the three fishermen had caught all they could possibly eat in one meal. Frank had just unhooked a shimmering beauty when the mountain silence was broken by a sharp cry.

"That's Evan!" Frank said, alarmed.

The cry came again.

"He must be in trouble! Come on, Joe. Let's go!"

The Hardys dropped their rods and set off among the boulders until they caught sight of Evan. He stood with his back against a slab of brown rock, tense and motionless, staring at something.

"Good grief!" Joe whispered. "Look at that rattler!"

The sidewinder slithered towards the Greek boy, its tongue flicking. Quietly Frank and Joe picked up stones. Joe hurled his. It missed.

Frank dashed in close and the snake turned its head, weaving from side to side.

"Watch it!" Joe cried.

Crash! Frank's rock hit the reptile directly on the head. As the creature writhed, Joe finished it off with another blow.

"Thanks," Evan said weakly. He pulled out a handkerchief and mopped his forehead. "It really *is* dangerous in America. Say, how's the fishing?"

"Tremendous," Joe said. "We'll have some for lunch."

The three walked back to the mobile caravan cautiously, watching for sidewinders. But they had no more trouble.

Buster had already set up his stove. The boys cleaned the fish, and soon a delicious aroma filled the air. After the meal, Buster caught some more trout which he stored in the small freezer of his mobile caravan. Finally he pulled in his gear.

"Have you had enough fishing now?" Frank asked.

The man tilted his straw hat and grinned. "Yep. Let's go find the sheriff."

He turned the mobile caravan round and started back. Suddenly another car appeared, bouncing over the rough terrain.

"It's the State Police," Frank exclaimed.

The vehicle stopped nose to nose against the mobile

caravan and two officers stepped out. Buster and the boys did the same.

The policemen identified themselves as troopers Jones and Olivio and studied the four travellers.

Frank said, "We were just going to look—"

Olivio interrupted and pointed a finger at Joe. "We want you to come with us for questioning!"

·12·

Suspect Joe

"ME? For questioning?" Joe stepped forward. "What seems to be the trouble?"

Olivio advised Joe of his legal rights. "You don't have to tell us anything," he said. "And we can get you a lawyer in town."

"We don't need any lawyer," Frank said hotly. "We've done nothing wrong. Now will you please tell us what this is all about?"

Trooper Jones searched the mobile caravan, while Olivio explained why Joe Hardy was under suspicion.

"There was a theft of dynamite at a construction job near here," he said. "A blond boy was seen slipping away with three sticks. The watchman got a good look at him."

"But what makes you think it was me?" Joe asked.

The officer said the police had been on the lookout for a blond youth, and a rancher had reported seeing such a person in the area.

As his partner spoke, Jones stepped out of the mobile caravan holding something in the palm of his hand.

"Where did you get this blasting cap?" he asked sternly. "What was it doing in one of your sleeping bags?"

92

"Listen," Frank said, "if you'll give us a chance to explain, we can clear the whole thing up."

"Go ahead."

Frank told about the bombing episode, which had destroyed their motorcycles. "Come with us," he concluded, "and we'll show you the place."

"All right," Olivio said. The police car followed the mobile caravan to the site of the explosion.

After the lawmen had looked around, Jones said, "Dynamite all right. But how do we know that you didn't steal it and the stuff went off by accident?"

"We wouldn't be here if it had," Evan said. "We'd have been blown up."

"Well, you'll have to come to headquarters," Olivio said. "Stay right behind us and don't try to get away."

The town, twenty-eight miles distant, was the county seat. It comprised a courthouse, a movie theatre, garage and a dozen shops, surrounded by a scattering of frame houses.

The troopers entered their office, where a bronzed man in his thirties was seated behind a desk. He had jet-black hair and eyes to match. A plaque on his desk read *Captain Popovi*.

Jones said, "Captain, we found a blond boy who answers the description Callahan gave us."

The captain, whom the Hardys figured to be an Indian, rose from his desk, sat on the edge of it, and looked keenly at the impatient quartet.

"Have a seat." He pointed to a long bench, and turned to Olivio and Jones. "Go get Callahan."

Then he listened quietly while the boys related what had happened on the mountain.

Captain Popovi said that he had read about Buster

Buckles touring the area. He was glad to meet him, and also a visitor from Greece.

"But what brought you three boys out here?" he asked.

Frank smiled. "It's a long story, Captain."

"Go ahead, tell it. It'll be some time before Callahan gets here."

"Who's he?" Buster asked.

"A witness. Now go on with your story."

Frank told about their search for *The Persian Glory* and how they had come to find Buster Buckles.

"We've been harassed all along," Frank said. "But this bombing is the worst yet."

The captain said he was well-acquainted with the machinations of the Gerrold gang. He also knew of Mr Hardy's reputation and concluded, "If you're innocent, we'll know soon enough."

After nearly half an hour Olivio appeared with a man even older than Buster Buckles. The fellow had a flowing white moustache, gnarled brown hands, and walked with a decided stoop.

"We have a suspect, Callahan," the captain said.

"Where?" The old man looked into the faces of the four seated on the bench.

"Stand up, Joe Hardy," the captain said.

Callahan took a long look at Joe. "He's young, and he has blond hair. But he's not the kid that ran off with the dynamite."

"Are you sure?" Popovi asked.

"Positive. The thief was sort of fat in the middle, even though he was about the same height."

"All right, that does it," the captain said. He stepped forward and shook hands with each of the four. "Sorry to detain you like this. But you understand."

While Callahan was driven back to his job, the Hardys chatted briefly with Captain Popovi. He promised to be on the lookout for Cole and the Greek suspect, as well as the dynamite thief.

"Goodbye and take care!"

Outside headquarters, the Hardys urged Buster to head for California immediately.

"The way you boys eat," he protested, "we have to get more supplies."

They chipped in some money and bought groceries to stock the larder. "That ought to hold us for a while," Buster said.

After an overnight stop, they continued on the straight highway, with Frank and Joe spelling Buster at the wheel.

The miles could not fly fast enough to suit the Hardys as they neared their destination. Finally they crossed the border and drove through the jagged mountains at the western edge of the state.

It was evening when the little mobile caravan pulled up in front of the home of Buster Buckles. It was an old-fashioned bungalow located in a run-down area. A small one-car garage stood in the rear of the weed-covered lot.

Joe was all for plunging directly into a search for the film. But Buster said, "What's your hurry? It's late. We'll look for it in the morning."

He parked in front of the house and led the way inside. The interior of the bungalow had a musty smell and the boys helped Buster open all the windows.

Evan said, "Mr Buckles, what does a can of old film look like?"

The old man said the tin was about fifteen inches in diameter and an inch and a half deep. "It holds a thousand feet of thirty-five millimetre film," he explained. "Now look, I have only one bed. So bring your sleeping bags in. I'll make a snack, then we'll all hit the sack."

"Okay," Frank said. "But I'd like to call home and let my folks know where we are. Is there a phone nearby?"

"I've got one," Buster said.

"Yours is disconnected."

Buster grinned. "I had that done before I left, but it's on again since the first of the month. That was yesterday."

Frank called his father and told him of their adventures so far. When he came to the dynamite episode, Mr Hardy interrupted. "I know about that."

"What?"

"The mob's harassing you to get me off the investigation. I received a note after they dynamited your bikes, saying that the next time it wouldn't just be the bikes but you too."

Frank whistled. "I wish I'd called sooner."

"So do I. I wanted to warn you but couldn't get in touch. From now on, be extra careful."

"Okay, Dad. Don't worry."

In the morning, after Buster had made pancakes for everyone, he took a key from a shelf and beckoned to the boys.

"Now we'll go look for the film." He led them to the garage and unlocked the door.

Inside sat a dusty compact car. Around it on three sides was an assortment of junk—old tyres, empty oil cans, a ladder, garden tools, and an ancient bicycle.

"I'd better take the car out first," Buster said, "or we'll never get to the stuff." He drove the automobile into the street and parked it there. Then he walked to the front of the garage.

"I think the film is in this corner somewhere," he said, pointing to a dirty tarpaulin. Under it was a piece of black oilcloth, sticky with age.

Frank and Joe lifted it to reveal a dozen film cans covered with cobwebs. Frank brushed away a layer of dust with the back of his hand. Then he, Joe, and Evan each picked up a can.

"Be careful," Buster warned. "Those things can explode!"

· 13 ·

Los Angeles Rendezvous

HEEDING Buster's warning, Frank, Joe, and Evan gingerly carried the tins into the house and placed them gently on the dining-room table.

"Let's examine these reels right away," Joe said.

Frank agreed. If *The Persian Glory* was in one of the cans, they might not have to bother with the others still in the garage.

Lids were removed with great caution. Inside lay the old nitrate celluloid, its pungent smell rising from the tins.

Buster unreeled and examined them one at a time as the boys peered over his shoulder.

"Look at that," Frank said. "Part of an old Tom Mix movie."

Evan read a caption and asked, "Who was Eddy Polo?"

Buster explained that he was the hero of an adventure series in the days of the silent films.

The first two cans contained several dozen out-takes. But none of them was from *The Persian Glory*.

Buster had just started to examine the third reel when the house was shaken by a muffled roar. He put down the film and they all raced outside.

Black smoke billowed from the garage. An instant later the frame structure was engulfed in red flames.

"Good heavens, the film's blown up!" Buckles cried out. "Run for your lives!"

His warning was hardly necessary, because the heat forced all of them back to a respectful distance.

Buster rushed into the house and phoned the fire department. Five minutes later three fire engines screamed to the scene.

While the young detectives looked on, crestfallen and silent, the firemen quickly attached their hoses. Two streams of water gushed into the inferno, whipping up sparks and blackened ash.

Joe was glum as he watched the garage fall with a shower of sparks. "Frank, now we may never solve this mystery!" he muttered.

Buster seemed to be in a trance. His eyes were fixed on the flaming boards which gradually disintegrated.

"Are you insured?" Frank asked him.

He nodded, coming back to reality. "But I'm glad the car wasn't parked inside," he said.

A policeman, who had joined the scene, approached the actor. With him was a man carrying a camera in his hands.

"What happened? How did it start?" the officer inquired.

"I guess something shifted and fell and the old film just blew up," Buster replied.

"Old film? You mean nitrate? That stuff's dangerous. You shouldn't have it around."

"Well, it ain't around any more," Buster said.

"It must have started by spontaneous combustion," the policeman deduced.

Joe thought it could have been set off deliberately and said so.

"Set off by whom?" the policeman asked.

"The people who have been tailing us," Joe replied. "Either someone else wanted to get that film, or wanted to prevent us from having it."

"What film? And who are these people you're talking about?"

The boys told their story briefly, and Frank noticed that the man with the camera took notes.

"What are you doing that for?" the boy asked.

"I'm a reporter for the *Afternoon Gazette*," the man replied.

When Frank heard this, he got a sinking feeling in the pit of his stomach. Publicity was the last thing Evan and the Hardys wanted.

"Does all this have to go in your newspaper?" he asked.

The man smiled pleasantly. "You bet it does. Can't you see the headline? *'Old-time actor involved in modern drama. What secret lies in* The Persian Glory?' Wow!"

He turned and hurried off, stepped into a car, and disappeared.

The usually smiling Evan was a picture of dejection. His mouth dropped at the corners. "Now everyone will know about the helmet!" he said gloomily.

The firemen, meanwhile, continued to douse the smouldering remains of the garage long after the flames had subsided. Finally they left the blackened mess.

Buster led the boys back into his house. "Let's look at the last few out-takes," he said, picking up the film and unreeling it slowly.

"No—no. That's not it." He rolled off a couple of

more feet and his eyes focused sharply. "Wait a minute!" he said, and held the film up against the light. His hands began to shake.

"Boys, if I'm not mistaken, this is it! Yes, here's Cornelius Doornheim, who played the lead, and he's wearing the helmet."

The surge of excitement was electrifying. Frank, Joe, and Evan pressed closer for a better look.

"Be careful!" the actor cried. "You'll knock me over and we'll all explode!"

He rolled up the film again and placed it back in the can. "I don't want to put this in my projector," he said. "It would be better to have it copied on safety film first."

"Do you know a lab who would do it?" Frank asked.

"Yep!"

"Great! Can we go right now?"

"Why not? Follow me in the car. I'll take the mobile caravan and return it to the rental agency."

On the way Joe remarked, "We might as well get two copies. Jeff Riker would love to have one, I'm sure."

The technician at the laboratory promised to make two copies by late afternoon.

Buoyed by enthusiasm, they drove back to Buster's bungalow. A few blocks away they stopped for petrol at a service station. While they were waiting, Frank's eyes lighted upon a maroon Buick up on the rack.

"Joe! See that car with the New Mexico licence number?"

"The one Cole and Greek were using!" Joe exclaimed.

"Right. They must have followed us here and are spying on us."

101

"Now we know for sure they set the fire," Joe said. "Let's talk to the mechanic." He and Frank approached the man who was working on the car, while Buster and Evan stayed behind.

"We've been trying to get in touch with a Greek friend of ours," Frank said. "But he's moved. I believe this is his car. Do you have his address?"

"The car belongs to a Greek, all right," the mechanic replied. "George Dimitri."

"That's our friend," said Frank.

"I don't have his address. He said he'd pick up the car tomorrow or the day after."

"What's he driving in the meantime?" asked Joe.

"A blue Chevy. He rented it from the place down the street. You want me to give him a message?"

"No. We're leaving town tonight. Thanks all the same."

At Buster's house, the young detectives went into a huddle to map out their strategy.

"We'll have to stake out that garage, then follow Dimitri when he picks up the Buick," Frank said.

"Do you think Buster will give us his car for the whole day?" Joe asked.

"I wouldn't even ask him. We can't impose on him like that. Let's rent one. But first I want to call Dad. It just occurred to me that he might know something about George Dimitri."

Mr Hardy did indeed. "He's a shady character who came from Greece not long ago and joined the Gerrold mob. What his racket is I don't know yet. I'll try to find out."

Frank then told his father about their planned stake-out.

"No need to rent a car," Mr Hardy said. "Sam Radley is in Los Angeles right now. Call him at the Ambassador Hotel. He might be able to do the surveillance job for you."

Frank called his father's operative, who had assisted them on many cases, and reported what had happened. Sam promised to watch the garage the following two days.

Later Buster went out to get the afternoon paper. At the bottom of the front page was a three-column picture of his burning garage. He handed the paper to the boys. "Take a look at that story!" he said.

They read the report and groaned in dismay. All details of their quest for the old movie had been given to millions of readers in the Los Angeles area!

Frank shrugged. "Well, our enemies knew all about it, anyway. What difference does it make at this point whether the whole world knows?"

At five o'clock Buster received a call from the film lab. The copies were ready and could be shown in the lab's viewing room.

"Fine," Buster said. "We'll be over after dinner."

"All right," came the reply. "Mr Simmons is going to stay late today anyhow. He'll wait for you."

When Buster and the boys left an hour later, they looked cautiously about to see if anyone was spying on them. Only a motorcycle sped past. Nothing else. Still, Frank had the uncomfortable feeling that they were being watched. He kept looking out the car's rear window all the way to their destination, but saw nothing suspicious.

When they arrived at the lab, it was closed, but Mr Simmons let them in. He locked the door after them and ushered them to a room on the first floor that looked like a miniature movie theatre.

On a small table in the back of the room were the two copies of *The Persian Glory* out-take. Mr Simmons put one of them in a projector.

"Make yourselves at home," he said while adjusting the film.

They sat in the front row on comfortable cushioned seats, and in a few minutes the old silent movie flashed on the screen. The Hardys realized that *The Persian Glory* must have been a high-budget enterprise. A scene showed hundreds of people attacking an ancient castle, then came a close-up of a young man.

"Evan, that's you!" Joe exclaimed.

Evan laughed. "It's Uncle Nick. We sure look alike!"

Nick Pandropolos walked to the lead man who wore the ancient Greek helmet.

"Can you return that shot?" Joe asked Mr Simmons. "We're interested in the helmet."

"Sure." Simmons ran the film backward.

"There! Hold it."

The boys studied the headgear. The top was rounded and a long piece of metal extended down to cover the nose.

"Could you make us a couple of enlargements of that frame?" Frank asked Mr Simmons.

"Be glad to." Simmons turned the light on, rewound the reel, and said, "Did you take the other copy of the film I left on the table over there?"

"No," Frank said. They stared at the table. The reel was gone.

"It's been stolen!" Joe exclaimed.

·14·

Surprise Phone Call

NONE of them had seen anyone enter the screening room. The theft must have been accomplished when the lights were out!

The boys ran downstairs to the main floor. The door stood open, but by the time they reached the street there was no sign of anyone who looked suspicious.

Joe and Evan went in one direction, Frank and Mr Simmons in the other. They questioned passers-by. No one had seen a man running away from the lab building. Half a dozen queries produced no results, but finally Joe talked to a man who was standing on the opposite side of the street waiting for a taxi.

"Yes, some guy came out of that building—a short, wiry fellow. He took off fast and kept looking back over his shoulder," the man said.

Joe and Evan thanked him and hastened back to the others.

"Obviously it was Kitten Cole," Joe said. "He must have followed us somehow, picked the lock, and come in while we were viewing the out-take."

"May I use your phone?" Frank asked Mr Simmons. "I'd like to report this to the police."

"Go ahead."

Frank made the call, then asked when they could pick up the enlargements.

"Tomorrow. Do you want me to make you another copy of the out-take?"

"Yes, please, And thanks very much for your trouble."

Back at Buster's house, over cups of tea, they pondered the new events.

"I don't think Dimitri and Cole set the fire," Frank said. "They not only wanted to prevent us from having the film, but they wanted it themselves."

Joe nodded. "Let's give Chet a call and see if there's anything new at his end," he suggested.

It took a few minutes to get in touch with Chet. When he finally came to the phone he was out of breath.

"Hi, fellows. I ran all the way. What's up?"

Frank told him what had happened.

"Wow! You sure had a lot of adverse action out there," Chet said.

"True. How about you?"

"Nothing happened here. Red Car never showed up again."

"That figures. By the way, how's the romance?"

"Great, just great. And boy! I'm learning a lot about film-making. I'm going to be a director some day."

"Okay, Chet, keep your eyes open." Frank hung up.

The boys retired for the night after watching a show on Buster's television. Next morning they were awakened by the persistent ringing of the telephone.

Buster Buckles reached it first. "Who? . . . Who do you want? . . . Yes, they're here. Hold on, please."

Joe Hardy had wriggled out of his sleeping bag and Buster handed him the phone. "It's for you. A woman."

106

"Hello, this is Joe Hardy."

"Joe, this is Betty Love. I'm here in California."

"Oh—Miss Love, how did you find us?"

The woman chuckled. "I read the papers." She added, "I'd like you to come and see me. I have some information for you."

"What kind of information?"

"I don't want to discuss it over the phone. Do you have a pencil? Then write down this address in Hollywood and come over right away."

Joe fumbled for a piece of paper in his jacket pocket and wrote down the address. When he finished he thanked Betty Love and hung up.

"What was that all about?" Buster asked.

"Betty Love wants to see us."

"Betty Love, the actress? I remember her. She played in *The Persian Glory*."

"She was the one who told us about you. Now she says she has some more information. Obviously about *The Persian Glory*."

Buster scratched his head. "You've got an awful lot of enemies. Suppose that wasn't Betty, but a trap?"

Frank nodded. "I was just thinking that myself. On the other hand, we have to pursue all possibilities. Buster, would you go with us? You and Evan can wait outside, and if we don't come out in ten or fifteen minutes, call the police."

"You bet!" Buster said. "But let's eat first, eh? Who wants to get trapped on an empty stomach?"

After breakfast they left. Again, there was no sign of any tail, but to be on the safe side, Buster drove in and out of side streets and made a quick U-turn at a filling station to throw off any possible pursuer.

The address which Betty had given them proved to be a lovely home on a tree-lined street. Buster and Evan stayed in the car, while Frank and Joe walked up the front steps and rang the doorbell.

A strange woman opened the door, smiled, and beckoned them inside. Their footsteps were muted by a thick Oriental rug which led to a gracious living room. Seated in a high-backed chair beside the marble fireplace was Betty Love.

She smiled. "Frank and Joe, I'd like you to meet my friend Marian Stewart. She's another old actress like me."

After the boys were seated, Betty Love went on, "I was going through some things Marian kept in storage for me over the years. I found an old diary which might be of interest to you."

"Does it have to do with *The Persian Glory?*" Joe asked.

The elderly woman nodded, reached for a leather-bound book lying on the table beside her, and opened it.

She leafed through the yellowed pages until she found what she wanted. The entry was dated a few years after Nicholas Pandropolos had returned to Greece. It said that the old, authentic Greek helmet had been found at the studio.

"I remember now," Miss Love said, "the director was going to send it back to Greece, but with one thing and another he didn't and it wound up in the storage building."

"Maybe it's still there!" Joe said, hardly able to contain his excitement.

"No, I'm afraid not," Miss Love said, shaking her

head sadly. "All of the things were sold at an auction when the company dissolved three years ago."

"Who bought the stuff?" Frank asked.

The woman did not know, but told them that a story about this had been printed in the newspapers. "It was in the spring," she said.

Frank and Joe thanked Miss Love for her information. "You really put us on the trail of the helmet," Frank said. "I'm sure we can track down who bought the things."

The boys hastened out to tell Evan and Buster the good news. "Next stop the newspaper office," Frank said.

A clipping from the newspaper's library provided the next clue. While viewing microfilm of the feature story, the Hardys learned that a dealer named Mervin Hecht had bought the entire contents of the movie company warehouse, including stage settings and props of all kinds.

The boys thanked the librarian for his help and hastened back to Buster, who was temporarily double-parked in front of the office.

"Come on, or you'll get me a ticket!" he said. "Where to next?"

Joe consulted the notes they had taken in the newspaper office. Hecht's shop was in Hollywood and turned out to be a small place next to an interior decorator. The three boys entered and were greeted by a slender man wearing a wide tie and a carnation in the lapel of his blue jacket.

When Frank asked about his purchase from the movie company, he replied, "That was a few years ago. I didn't keep the stuff long. The sets I sold to amateur groups and the junk—saddles, bridles, Civil War uniforms—went to a New York outfit." He paused and looked at them quizzically. "Just what are you looking for?"

Frank avoided a direct answer. "We're trying to find some old props used in a certain movie. We're studying film-making."

"Well, maybe the New York shop still has some of the stuff," Mr Hecht said. He pulled a business card from his pocket, turned it over, and wrote on the back.

"The place is called the Antique Salon," he said. "I can't remember the address, but you can look it up in the telephone directory."

The boys thanked him and left. Frank slid in beside Buster, and Joe and Evan hopped in the back.

"Something funny's going on," Buster said tensely. "A blue Chevy pulled up behind me and a guy got out. He peered through the window of Hecht's shop while you were in there!"

"What did he look like?" Frank asked.

"Stocky, dark hair."

"Did he have a moustache?"

"I couldn't see."

"Where did he go?"

"Back in the car and drove off. Do you suppose he was following you?"

"Sounds like it might be Dimitri," Frank said.

They returned to the bungalow and had a late lunch while they continued to discuss the man in the blue car. "If he goes to see Hecht," Frank said, "he'll learn the same thing we found out."

"In that case, we'd better get to New York as soon as possible," Joe declared.

110

Just then the phone rang. Frank picked it up. The caller was Sam Radley.

"I've been trying to get through to you fellows," he said. "Listen! This is urgent!"

·15·

Cat and Mouse

FRANK pressed the receiver to his ear and motioned for silence. "What's the scoop, Sam?"

As he listened, Frank's eyes reflected intense excitement. "All right, we'll find the place. Meet you in your room."

Frank hung up. "How about that! Dimitri left with the maroon car. He had a passenger. From Sam's description it was Kitten Cole."

Radley had followed the car to a motel ten miles north of the city. "They're on the ground floor," Frank said. "Sam took the adjacent room and set up an electronic surveillance. He wants us to take over while he guards the exit."

"Why doesn't he have them arrested right away?" Evan asked.

"Not enough proof, but the eavesdropping might reveal further clues to the whole operation."

Buster was told about the phone call from Radley, but he had a headache and decided to stay home. However, he offered them his car.

When they left the house, the boys noticed a motorcycle across the street. The rider tried to start it, but the machine did not respond.

Frank said, "You know, I think that fellow passed here when we drove to the film lab last night. Maybe he's spying for Cole!"

Joe shrugged. "If he is, he's out of luck right now."

The cyclist seemed to pay no attention as the trio started off in Buster's car. A superhighway carried them north at a rapid clip and soon they reached the motel. A pine woods stretched out to the right of it, providing an isolated setting.

Frank drove into a clearing in the woods and parked the car out of sight. "Sam's in Room 29B," he said as the boys walked to the motel.

The boys found the door and knocked. Sam Radley, sandy-haired and grinning, let them in. After he and Evan were introduced, Sam said, "Right now these guys seem to be sleeping. It might be a long wait. Keep tuned in at all times. I'll stay outside and watch the driveway."

"Good idea," Frank said. He took the headset of the listening device and Sam quietly left the room.

Not a word was spoken in the adjoining room until nightfall. Then the phone rang.

"Yes?" one of the men answered. He listened for a while, then said, "Rotten luck. Well, I hope they didn't go far."

He hung up. "That was Mitch. The Hardys and their friend took off and he couldn't follow because his bike kept stalling."

"Too bad," said a man with a Greek accent, obviously Dimitri. "Did they leave in the old man's car?"

"Yeah."

"Then they'll be back." There was silence until Dimitri resumed the conversation. "I'm glad you got the film, Kitten. Twister's going ga-ga to lay his hands on the prize. Then he wants to get out of sight for a while. I can't blame him. Pressure's too much. After the next shipment to Greece we're going to lie low."

"Yeah," Cole said. "No use to risk your necks. By the way, what happened to the kid?"

"He high-tailed it back to New York. Got cold feet. But Twister found him."

"Look," Cole's voice came again. "We'd better call him. He'll want to know about Hecht."

A number was dialled, and Dimitri asked for Gerrold.

Frank felt utterly frustrated. The gang knew about the studio props, and if Gerrold were told, he would get to the Antique Salon before they could!

But luck was with them. Gerrold could not be found, and Dimitri hung up. "We'll have to wait until we get back to New York," he said.

Frank turned and whispered, "Cole's got the film. We can have him arrested for the theft!"

Joe nodded. In a low voice he called the police, after which Frank told him and Evan the rest of the men's conversation.

He had hardly finished when the phone next door rang again.

"Hello?" Cole said. After a few seconds' pause, he uttered a string of oaths, followed by, "Impossible!"

There were a few minutes of silence, then a door slammed, and footsteps sounded outside.

"They've split!" Frank cried out. "The guy on the switchboard must have tipped them off!"

By the time the boys raced from their room, the criminals were nearly out of sight. Dimitri rushed past the office and right into Sam Radley. He bowled the detective over and sprinted down the driveway to the road.

Cole had run off towards the woods. Joe and Evan dashed after him, while Frank helped Sam to his feet. They started after Dimitri just as two police cars zoomed into the driveway.

An officer jumped out of the first one and ordered Frank and Radley to halt. By the time the two had identified themselves, the Greek was gone.

Joe and Evan, meanwhile, raced through the woods, looking for Cole. Suddenly they came upon a wire fence barrier. On the other side, the land dropped steeply down to a superhighway, where cars whizzed by at seventy miles an hour.

"If Cole climbed the fence," Evan reasoned, "he might have hitched a ride. What do you think?"

Joe was sceptical. Stopping on the freeway could cause a mammoth pile-up. "I doubt if someone would pick him up."

Radley, Frank, and a policeman arrived at the fence. "Well," the officer said, "I guess the other one got away too." He obtained the description of Cole and left. Radley and Frank followed, but Joe and Evan lingered behind.

Soon all was still again in the dark pines. Joe whispered, "Don't make any noise. I have a hunch Cole is still in these woods. Let's wait a while."

The two moved quietly beneath the domed canopy of inky blackness, tensely alert for the slightest sound. Minutes ticked by, a quarter of an hour passed. Joe was about to give up when he heard a slight rustle. It seemed to come from directly overhead.

Suddenly something brushed against Joe's face, startling him. He reached out in the dark to grasp the end of a thin rope. A thud followed as someone dropped down, landing lightly on the spongy ground, inches from the boys.

With a banshee yell Joe jumped upon the figure of Kitten Cole. Evan joined in. The three rolled and thrashed about, shouting at the same time and calling for help.

Finally they pinned each of Cole's arms to the ground as a light appeared among the trees. "Joe, Evan!" Frank called out. "Where are you?"

"Over here!"

Soon the flooding light revealed a dishevelled Kitten Cole, tightly in the grasp of his captors. Frank was accompanied by the policemen, who had stayed to question the switchboard operator and examine the men's luggage.

Cole was frisked and the stolen film found in his pocket. Then handcuffs were snapped on his wrists. Cole was advised of his constitutional rights as an arrested person, then led away.

Half an hour later everyone met at headquarters. Sam Radley, who was going to stay in Los Angeles for a while, pressed charges against Cole for the theft of the film. He promised to send the reel to Jeff Riker when the police released it. Cole remained silent.

Finally the boys returned to Buster Buckles' house, where Frank phoned home. Mrs Hardy answered. She said that their father was in New York and gave the number of his hotel. Joe made the second call and reached the detective.

Mr Hardy congratulated the three young sleuths on

their work. "I'm still gathering information on the Gerrold mob," he said. "I just hope I'll have enough solid evidence to have him arrested before he disappears."

"So do I," Joe said. "We're coming to New York. Dad. Will you make our flight arrangements with your credit card?"

"Sure. I'll call you back and let you know what plane I booked you on."

The detective managed to get mid-morning reservations for the following day, and after breakfast the boys called a taxi and said goodbye to Buster Buckles.

He was sorry to see them go. "You made me feel young again with that mystery of yours," Buster said as he shook hands with each of them. "Be sure to visit me when you come west again."

On the way to the aiport they picked up the enlargements from the film lab, as well as the out-take. Frank and Joe each pocketed one of the pictures and stowed the reel in their duffel bag. They reached the plane with only minutes to spare.

After landing at Kennedy International Airport they went directly to Mr Hardy's hotel. It was a happy reunion, and stories were exchanged over an early dinner. After the meal the boys looked up the Antique Salon in the telephone book. The company had two shops, one in the Bronx, the other in Manhattan on Third Avenue near Sixtieth Street.

The following morning, while Mr Hardy pursued his investigation, Frank and Evan went to the Bronx, and Joe visited the shop on Third Avenue.

It was full of old statuettes, vases, sundry pieces of art, and oriental antiques. Joe told the manager that he was looking for spears and helmets.

"Putting on a school play?" the white-haired man asked.

"Could be," Joe replied.

"Well, follow me," the man led Joe into a back room piled high with articles of all kinds. "Take a look," he said. "If you see anything you like, bring it out."

Joe's eyes roved around. There were wooden spears, along with other theatrical accoutrements—but no helmets. Then he noticed a huge Swiss cowbell, the kind used to decorate cattle when they came down from the high Alps in October. He remembered reading about the festival held at that time.

Joe was curious. He lifted the bell to ring it. *Under it lay an ancient helmet!*

Joe set the bell aside and picked up the helmet. The back had a cleft as if it had been struck by a heavy sword, and above the nosepiece was a cryptic inscription.

Hands trembling, Joe pulled out the photograph of the shattered helmet and compared it with the antique. There was no doubt. This was the prize they were looking for!

Trying to hide his excitement, he cradled the helmet in his left arm and walked to the front of the shop.

"Find something?" the manager asked.

"I guess this will do," Joe said.

"I'm glad," the man said with a smile. "I'll give you a real bargain since you're a student. Twenty-five dollars."

Joe took the money from his wallet. The man wrote a receipt, wrapped the helmet, and gave it to him.

Success at last! Joe felt as if there were wings on his

heels. He stepped out into the sunlight on Third Avenue, thinking about the cheers that would greet him when he delivered the shattered helmet.

But as Joe looked for a taxi he felt a sharp blow on the back of his skull. He slumped to the sidewalk, and at the same time the helmet was snatched from his hands!

·16·

Flight to Greece

By the time Joe woke up, a crowd of people had gathered. The antique dealer and two other men helped him to his feet.

The boy rubbed the back of his neck and winced. "Who hit me?"

The shopkeeper said that three men had jumped him. One delivered the blow, another had snatched the helmet. All three had turned the corner and dashed towards Lexington Avenue so quickly that nobody could give a good description of them.

With a hasty thank-you, Joe turned the corner. To find his assailants, he realized, would be almost impossible, but he would try. He reached Lexington Avenue and glanced both ways, but saw no one who was carrying his package.

As he trotted towards Park Avenue, questions raced through his mind with computer speed. Had his attackers followed him to the Antique Salon? Had Dimitri ridden in the same plane from Los Angeles to New York? Had these men already attacked Frank and Evan?

Joe crossed Park Avenue and was hurrying towards Madison when he spotted three men half a block ahead

120

of him hailing a taxi. One of them carried a bulky package. *The helmet!*

Joe bolted foward, but the car was off in the traffic before he could reach it. Then another cab pulled up and a passenger got out.

Joe hopped in and pointed to the taxi with the three men, which had stopped for a red light. "Follow them!" he said.

"Playing cops and robbers?" asked the driver.

"Please! Don't lose them in traffic!" Joe begged. "They're thieves!"

"I'll stick to 'em like glue. Relax."

When the signal changed to green, their quarry went north on Madison. The boy craned forward to get a look at the passengers, but all he could see was the backs of their heads.

The pursuit led across Sixty-third Street, then north on Eighth Avenue. The lead taxi stopped near Seventy-second Street and the men got out. Joe handed his driver a five-dollar bill and ran after them. One of the fugitives, who looked like Dimitri, turned and spied Joe. Abruptly the men ducked into a place called the Peloponnesian Restaurant.

As Joe reached the door his way was blocked momentarily by a couple who were leaving. Then he rushed inside, glancing about wildly. Where had the thieves gone?

The manager, a handsome man in a black jacket, approached him. "Are you looking for someone?"

"Three men! They came in a minute ago!"

"Not only that, but they ran out the back way!" the manager said disapprovingly.

Joe did the same, dashing through the kitchen and

into an alley that led to a parking lot on Seventy-third Street. The men were nowhere in sight. Joe hurried to the street and looked in all directions. His quarry was gone.

Dejectedly he returned to his father's hotel. Frank and Evan had already arrived. Joe told what had happened. "I wonder how they knew which Antique Salon had the helmet!" he said glumly.

"I can answer that one," Frank replied. "The salesman in the Bronx told Evan and me that a Greek fellow had been there before looking for a helmet. Since he had none, he sent him to the Third Avenue branch."

"That must have been Dimitri. He was one of the guys who bopped me. I recognized him when he turned around. The second man could have been Saffel. But who was the third?"

Frank had an idea. "Dad, do you have a picture of Gerrold with you?"

"Sure." Mr Hardy went to his briefcase and produced a photograph of the racketeer. He had an intelligent face and curly brown hair.

"Let's show this to the manager of the Peloponnesian Restaurant," Frank suggested.

The boys returned to the restaurant, where the manager confimed that Gerrold was one of the fugitives who had run through his establishment.

Back at the hotel, they mulled over the case. Why was Gerrold so eager to get the helmet? Could he have learned of its real value? Did it have any bearing on Mr Hardy's investigation of the underworld?

"My head is spinning," Joe said, "from the bump *and* the questions. Now what?"

"I think the gang will go to Greece," Mr Hardy said.

122

"That's it, Dad!" Frank said. "Dimitri told Cole that Gerrold wanted to get out of here for a while."

"Let's fly to Greece!" Joe urged.

"Good. I'll be your guide," Evan said.

Mr Hardy nodded. "Make reservations right away. I'll wire Evan's parents and tell them you're coming."

All planes to Athens were filled for the day, but there were seats available for the following day on three flights.

The young detectives decided to travel separately so they could cover all three. They inquired whether Dimitri or Gerrold were booked on any of the planes, but the reply was negative.

"But that doesn't mean anything," Mr Hardy said. "They could have used aliases. Watch carefully for them."

The boys made their preparations. Evan's flight took off first, with Joe's following. Frank's plane left in the evening. When it was airborne, Frank got up and moved around slowly, studying faces.

None of the passengers seemed to resemble Gerrold or Dimitri. But then Frank noticed a man fingering worry beads. He had no moustache, but he did have dark hair, and his stocky build looked like the Greek's!

Frank spoke to a stewardess. "Isn't that man over there named Dimitri? I think I know him. But I don't want to make a mistake."

"I'll find out for you," the girl said and went over to the man. When she returned she said, "Yes, his name is Dimitri."

Frank decided to confront him at once and walked over to his seat. "You might as well give up now, Dimitri," the boy said. "I'm going to tell the captain that there's a fugitive on board!"

The man rose and looked at Frank quizzically. "What on earth are you talking about?"

"You know what I'm talking about. You're tied up with Gerrold and Kitten Cole!"

The passenger laughed loudly. "Listen, you've gone off your rocker. You're talking Greek to me."

Suddenly it dawned on Frank that the man spoke English without the slightest accent. Could he be wrong?

"Your name is Dimitri, isn't it?" Frank asked.

"That's right," the man replied. "Dimitri Jones from Keokuk, Iowa."

Frank was tongue-tied. "B-but I thought you were Greek!"

"Half Greek," the man said. "My mother came from Thessaly. That's how I got the name Dimitri."

Frank felt his face grow hot from embarrassment. "I'm sorry," he said. "I guess I took you for somebody else. Please excuse me."

"I think you read too many detective stories," Mr Jones said, shaking his head.

Frank slumped back into his seat. "Boy, what a boo-boo," he thought. "I'm glad Joe and Evan weren't here!"

Suddenly two strong arms grasped him from behind. They locked around his head so tightly that Frank could not utter a sound!

124

·17·

Masquerade

FRANK struggled but the grip grew tighter. Suddenly the vice-like hold relaxed and he heard a familiar chuckle.

Wheeling round, Frank looked up into the jolly moonface of Chet Morton!

Chet moved forward and lowered his hefty frame into the seat next to Frank's.

He grinned broadly. "Frank Hardy supersleuth. I knew you'd be in trouble without me!"

"All right!" Frank groaned. "And how did you get here just at the right time?"

"Your guiding angel sent me. Actually it was Aunt Gertrude. I phoned your house and she told me you were coming to New York. The school had planned an optional field trip for this week and I begged off. Came into town and spoke to your father. He told me about your trip. It sounded exciting so I rushed to the airport and almost missed the plane. Well, anyway, here I am."

"I don't believe it! You spent all that dough for the fare just to join us?"

"Besides having the important mission to look out for you. Also, I'm making a documentary film."

"No kidding. On what?"

"Dumb detectives. Oh, no. Grecian beauties," Chet corrected himself as Frank gave him a playful punch.

"For the Greek beauties you broke away from Thelma?"

Chet winced. "Frank, to tell you the truth, I was glad to get out of there."

"How come?"

"She wanted to get engaged!"

Frank doubled over with laughter.

"Anyway, she fed me too much," Chet went on. "Look at this!" He patted his well-rounded midsection. In the next breath he said, "When's dinner?"

Frank sighed in mock despair. "There you go again. Now listen to me. This whole thing is rather serious." He brought his pal up to date on the latest events. "Chet, we'll have to scrutinize everybody on this plane."

"I've got an idea," Chet said. "I'll start my documentary right here with the passengers. That way I can look at everybody real close."

Chet took his camera and went up and down the left aisle, filming short footage of passengers he thought looked interesting. Meanwhile, Frank strolled down the right aisle and carefully scrutinized each person.

Chet deviated from his task for a moment to smile at a pretty girl. Then his eye caught the middle-aged man beside here. He had grey sideburns and light hair.

Seeing Chet's camera, he quickly held a magazine before his face. Chet was alerted immediately. He made his way to Frank and told him about the bashful passenger.

"This guy really acted suspicious, Frank!"

126

"Some people are camera shy," Frank said. "Did you say he was middle-aged?"

"Yes."

Frank pulled out Gerrold's picture. "Is that him?"

"No. He's quite pale and has light hair."

"Then it's not Gerrold. And it doesn't sound like Dimitri either. But I'll take a look on my way back."

Chet returned to the man. The girl beside him had left her seat and Chet slipped into it. He tried to start a conversation.

"Great flight we're having," he said.

The man mumbled something unintelligible.

"I'm from Bayport," Chet went on. "Where do you live?"

The man coughed, put a handkerchief to his face, rose from his seat and made his way to one of the rest rooms.

Chet joined Frank. "That guy is definitely suspicious," he declared, and told of his attempt to make a conversation.

"We'll watch him," Frank decided.

Twenty minutes passed before the man finally appeared. Frank and Chet stood in the aisle and observed him take his seat.

"He's built just like Saffel," Frank said. "And his hair colour is the same. But Leon's not that old!"

"He could be in disguise."

"Let's sit down. They're just beginning to serve dinner."

Frank took the seat next to the suspect, while Chet established himself on the other side of the aisle. Not a word was said.

Frank observed the man from the corner of his eye.

127

He sniffed and seemed nervous. A stewardess slid trays of hot food before the passengers. Fillet steak, mashed potatoes, and carrots. Frank picked up his fork and began to eat.

The suspect sat stiffly. He ate a small piece of meat and a dab of mashed potatoes. The carrots he pushed off on to his bread plate.

Something flashed through Frank's mind. *Leon Saffel couldn't stand carrots!*

"Well," Frank thought to himself, "here we go again." He took a deep breath, then said to the man in a low voice, "Quit playing games, Leon!"

A fork clattered on to the tray. Saffel's hands shook from fear and fatigue.

"All right, I give up!"

Chet's eyes bulged. "Holy crow! It's really Leon!"

"In disguise," Frank said. "You had us fooled for a while. Now tell me, why did you get mixed up with that Gerrold gang?"

Saffel sighed. "You really embarrassed me at Bayport Airport the first time we met. I wanted to get even. Dimitri saw me smash one of your cameras at the falls. He approached me later and asked me to help him harass you guys."

"Did he tell you why he was after us?"

"No. I didn't realize how serious the whole thing was until they made me steal the dynamite and blow up your bikes. I took off after that and went back to New York, but they found me and threatened to kill me. I knew they weren't fooling, so here I am."

Frank remembered Dimitri saying to Cole in the motel room the kid had high-tailed it back to New York and that Gerrold had found him. "It seems Saffel's telling the truth," the boy said to himself.

Chet addressed Leon. "Did you follow the Hardys and Evan to Santa Fé from Hunt?"

Leon nodded. "I wore this disguise. Cole and Dimitri took another flight and we met out there."

"Who ran over our cycles in Taos?" Frank asked.

"Kitten Cole did. He started the truck."

"I thought so. Now, what are you doing here?"

"I don't really know. All Gerrold and Dimitri told me was to go to Greece and meet them there."

"Where are they now?"

"They took a private plane out of Teterboro, New Jersey, and flew to Bermuda. From there they planned to go to London, and from London to Athens."

"Were you with them when they stole the helmet from Joe?" Frank asked.

Leon nodded. "Sorry Dimitri clouted your brother." He shrugged wearily. "Look, I'll do anything if you can get me out of this!"

"We'll try," Frank promised. "Where are you supposed to meet them?"

"Outside the arrivals building at Athens Airport. There's a line of taxis and I'm to walk towards the end of the line. That's all they told me."

Frank had an idea. "Listen, Chet, how about you taking Leon's place? You can put on his disguise and get away with it, at least for a little while. You two have about the same build. We'll follow you, and when you need help, give us a signal. Okay?"

"Sure. I'll try anything," Chet agreed.

It was early next afternoon when the huge jet descended towards Athens International Aiport. Chet had donned Leon's disguise and fixed up his face with

129

make-up Saffel had in his bag.

"Now you know what you're going to look like in a few years," Frank needled his chum.

The plane landed, and the next twenty minutes were taken up by passport control and customs. Finally they walked out of the arrivals building. A long row of taxis stood ready.

Chet, his movie camera over one shoulder, strode to the end of the line. Frank followed, with Leon behind him at a safe distance.

Suddenly the door of the taxi next to the last swung open, an arm reached out, grabbed Chet and dragged him inside. As Frank and Leon raced towards the vehicle, it took off with a burst of speed!

·18·

Sympathetic Vanides

MOMENTARILY stunned by the turn of events, Frank stood helpless as the taxi sped away with Chet. Then he beckoned to Leon, and the two got into another waiting cab. Frank told the driver to follow the getaway car.

The man turned round and asked Frank to repeat his instructions.

"Get that guy! Hurry! Follow him!" Frank said.

But the driver only shrugged. "Which hotel, sir?"

"No, no. I want you to—"

The other taxi was out of sight by now. Frank tried to hide his frustration. Resigned, he reached in his pocket, pulled out the address that Evan had given him, and showed it to the driver. He nodded, smiled, and started the car.

Evan's family had an apartment near the centre of the city. When Frank and Leon arrived there, Joe and Evan were the only ones home. They gasped in amazement when they saw Leon. "Where did you get him?" Joe blurted out.

Frank told about the capture on the plane, and Leon apologized again for what had happened in the past.

"All right, forget it," Joe said. "I'm glad you're on our side now."

131

"That's the good news," Frank said. "Are you ready for the bad?"

"Oh, oh," Joe said. "Let's have it!"

"It's about Chet."

"Was he hurt at school?" Evan asked with a worried look.

"No. He was kidnapped at Athens Airport."

"What?"

When Frank had given the details, Evan quickly telephoned the police and gave a description of Chet. He also mentioned the fact that he carried a movie camera. The police promised they would contact all taxis in the city and be on the lookout for the kidnappers.

Evan also mentioned that Gerrold was a known gangster in the United States and the officer thanked him for the information. He promised to get in touch with them immediately if he had any leads.

It was five o'clock when Evan's parents arrived, surprised to find visitors. They had been away for the weekend and had not received Mr Hardy's cablegram.

Mr and Mrs Pandropolos were gracious people and welcomed their guests warmly. They were immediately apprised of all that had happened.

"Oh, how terrible!" Mrs Pandropolos said when she heard about Chet. "Have you called Uncle Nick yet?"

"No," Evan replied. "We were keeping the line free in case the police should call."

Just then the phone rang. Evan snatched it from its cradle. He listened, then spoke briefly in Greek. Finally he hung up.

"The police think they have a clue!" he said excitedly. "A cab driver found a movie camera on the floor of his taxi and turned it in. We are supposed to go over right away and see if we can identify it."

Leon remained behind while Frank, Joe and Evan took a taxi to headquarters. With Evan as their spokesman, they introduced themselves and a lieutenant showed them the camera.

"It's Chet's, all right," Joe said. "See, here's the dent where the rock hit it."

Frank said to Evan, "Ask the officer to have the film developed. Chet might have left a clue."

The officer agreed. While the boys waited, the film was removed from the camera and quickly processed in the police laboratory. Then the lieutenant put it in a projector and showed it on a small screen.

First appeared the faces of the aeroplane passengers, including Leon Saffel holding up the magazine. Next came a series of disconnected shots. Several frames showed blurred buildings. This was followed by clear footage, revealing two close-up profiles.

"Dimitri and Gerrold!" Frank cried out. "Now we know for sure they kidnapped Chet!"

The last shot focused on the ruin of an ancient arch.

"That's Hadrian's Gate," Evan said. "One of the famous landmarks of Athens."

"What do you make of that?" Joe asked Frank.

"It's probably where they got out of the taxi. And Chet, the fox, left his camera on the floor. The question is, where did they go from there?"

The lieutenant promised to continue the search. "We will alert police all over the country in case the kidnappers try to flee," he declared.

The boys thanked him and left. They decided to go to Hadrian's Gate first thing in the morning to see if they could pick up the trail of the kidnappers.

After breakfast the next day Evan's parents left for work in the government offices. Leon, who had come down with a bad cold, stayed in the apartment, while Frank, Joe, and Evan set out to Hadrian's Gate.

It stood on one side of a very busy street not far from Evan's house. The Greek boy explained that it had been built in ancient times to separate the Greek and Roman settlements in the city.

The boys looked around. Across the street Frank spied a car rental agency. "Hey!" he said. "Maybe they rented a car and took off into the mountains."

They waited for the light to change, then raced across the street and into the agency. A pretty girl greeted them cordially.

"Ah, Americans," she said. "You would like to hire a car?"

"No," Frank said, and explained what they were looking for. He pulled out Gerrold's photo. "Did this man come in here yesterday and rent a car from you?"

She scrutinized the picture. "He came in the afternoon and took a tan Fiat."

"Was anyone with him?" Joe asked.

"Two men waited outside in a taxi."

"We have to catch up with these men," Evan said. "Could you give us the licence number of their car?"

The girl looked it up on a voucher. "But I don't know where they went," she said.

"Did the man ask for a map?" Frank inquired.

"Yes, he did."

"Try to remember," Frank urged, "if he mentioned anything about his plans."

The girl frowned in deep thought. "He spread the

map out over here. Ah, yes, I do remember. He followed the national highway with his finger. And I believe he indicated Delphi."

"Thank you very much!" Evan said. "You've been a great help."

The boys were elated when they left the rental agency. They took a taxi back to Evan's house and from there relayed the information to the police.

Minutes later the doorbell rang. The caller was Nicholas Pandropolos, Evan's famous uncle. He was a tall, portly man with a high forehead, rugged face, and a handshake to match. He was very much upset over Chet's disappearance.

Evan told him about the Delphi clue and asked, "Could we use your car, Uncle Nick? We want to follow Gerrold."

"Of course," Uncle Nick said and looked at Leon. "I think you should stay here until the criminals are caught. You might be their next target."

Leon nodded gratefully.

"What do you suppose the mob will do with Chet?" Evan asked his uncle.

"They can't let him go; he knows too much. On the other hand, he would be a nuisance to take wherever they went."

"That leaves only one alternative," Joe said, "and I don't want to think about it!"

"If we could find out more about George Dimitri," Frank mused, "it might lead to a clue. His friends, connections, a former job—"

Uncle Nick's eyebrows shot up. "You know, I remember that a man named George Dimitri worked once for my competitor, Spiro Vanides. He got into some trouble and was dismissed. Perhaps this is the same Dimitri."

"Do you think we could talk with Mr Vanides?" Frank asked.

"Well, Vanides and I have never seen eye to eye in business matters, but I don't think he'd refuse you any information. Let me drive you to his office. You can take my car from there. And, Evan, I'll tell your parents."

"Thanks, Uncle Nick," Evan said.

Half an hour later they met Spiro Vanides in a plush new office building. He was younger than Evan's uncle, with straight black hair combed back, a thin face, prominent jaw, and slender frame. He appeared very agitated over the kidnapping, and when he heard that Dimitri was a suspect, he shook his head.

"If it is the same man, he is no good. He worked for my company some time ago. But we dismissed him because of cargo thefts. Our security men suspected Dimitri but lacked enough proof to have him arrested."

"Do you know any of his friends?" Frank asked.

Vanides shrugged. "Unfortunately, no. But I will try to find out more information for you. Perhaps some of my employees will know. I will call you later."

They thanked the shipper, then set off immediately for Delphi in Uncle Nick's Mercedes Benz. With Evan at the wheel, they raced north over the national highway, making a turn-off at the exit marked Levadia. Near the outskirts of the town, Evan pulled into a roadside haven called The Friendly Stop.

"How come this place has an English name?" Joe asked.

Evan said that tour buses and foreign travellers

stopped here for refreshments. "Let's go inside and find out if Gerrold and company were here."

"Good idea," Frank agreed. "I'm starved, anyway."

In his native tongue Evan asked the manager if he had seen Gerrold and Dimitri, and showed him Gerrold's photograph.

The man gesticulated and pointed to the parking lot.

"What'd he say, Evan?" Frank asked eagerly.

"They stopped here yesterday. Gerrold came inside and bought some pastry. Meanwhile, there was quite a commotion. A boy was struggling in the back seat and a man was holding him down. Gerrold said he was suffering from a fit, and that they were taking him to Delphi."

"Poor Chet," Joe said as they started off again after a quick snack. "No one realized what trouble he's in."

The road snaked through rolling hills and along the slope of a steep mountain. It was late afternoon when they arrived in Delphi. The Hardys marvelled at the seat of the ancient Greek civilization, where ruins of temples stretched up the hillside to a magnificent marble amphitheatre.

"The stadium is even higher up. You can't see it from here," Evan said. "But we'd better not take time for sightseeing."

They drove into town and questioned many people. But no one had seen their quarry. Finally they struck gold at a filling station at the western end of Delphi. The attendant told them that a tan Fiat had stopped the day before and that one of the passengers had had a fit. The two men with him had mentioned that they were taking their sick companion to a doctor in Mesolongion.

Now the way led downhill, curving like a roller coaster through a grey forest of olive trees. After an hour Frank spelled Evan at the wheel. The road led upwards in hairpin turns over a bare mountain, then down again into a long, narrow valley cut by a placid stream.

All at once the valley was filled with grey clouds.

"A storm's coming our way," Evan said. "I've seen them before. Something like in Arizona, only more suddenly."

Rain came down in a torrent. Frank turned on the wipers, but they could not keep up with the flood of water. Straining to get a glimpse of the road, he bent over the wheel, driving slowly.

From the steep hillside on the left several rocks rolled across the road, then without warning—*crash!* The back end of the car slewed around as a boulder bounced off it.

The boys got out to look at the damage and were drenched in seconds. They found that the rear wheel was crushed.

"It's hopeless!" Frank groaned. "We'll have to move the car off the road."

The three pushed and hauled until finally the vehicle was on the shoulder.

The boys jumped back inside, soggy and shivering. They took some dry clothes from their bags and changed. Half an hour later the clouds disappeared and the setting sun broke through the dripping landscape.

"We're in a great fix," Joe said. "Your uncle's car is wrecked, Chet's lost, and we're stranded!"

"Not a bright outlook," Evan agreed. "And this is a pretty deserted area. We might have to wait hours for a car to come by."

"Maybe we can go for help," Frank suggested.

"Somebody must be living out here."

"Let's look then," Evan agreed.

They trudged down the road for half a mile, then Evan pointed uphill.

"There's a shepherd's place," he said.

"Where?" Joe asked.

"The long, low stone structure. See it now?"

"Yes. Blends right into the hill."

They climbed the slope until they reached the cottage. Evan knocked on the rough-hewn door and a peasant woman answered. He explained their predicament.

A short conversation followed during which the shepherd arrived, prodding his flock into the small stone enclosure next to the hut. The Greek couple suggested that the boys have supper and stay overnight.

"The valley is full of boulders. They drop down for some time after the storms are over," the shepherd said.

Frank, Joe, and Evan thanked their hosts, ate with them, then settled down on piles of straw at one end of the long room. Near dawn all three awakened at the same time.

"What's that?" Joe asked.

"Sounds like a helicopter," Frank replied. "And it seems to be getting closer!"

The boys dashed out and looked up into the grey sky. A small chopper was landing far up on the hillside.

"What luck!" Joe said. "Maybe that guy can give us a lift!"

They raced up the hill, slipping and sliding in the soft mud. Soon they saw a small hut nestled against the dun-coloured mountain. The boys began to shout.

The helicopter was now at rest, its rotor whirring slowly. Suddenly a familiar cry shrilled through the air.

"Help! Help!"

"It's Chet!" Evan exclaimed.

"You're right!" Frank gasped. "And look, they're dragging him to the chopper!"

·19·

The Caves of Corfu

CHET, whose hands were tied, put up a fierce resistance. When he heard his friends' shouts, he threw himself to the ground and kicked violently.

His captors realized there would not be enough time to get Chet into the helicopter. They ran to the chopper and it rose into the air amid a maelstrom of wind and noise.

Evan, first to reach Chet, unbound his hands. The boy winced as the circulation in his wrists resumed, but quickly recovered from his ordeal. His friends surrounded him and rapidly fired questions at him.

Chet said he had been brought to the hut by Dimitri and Gerrold the previous day, and was left there, tied to a post.

"Where did they go?" Frank pressed.

"I don't know. They mentioned the word Kerkira a lot, whatever that means."

"That's the Greek name for Corfu!" Evan said. "An island off the north-west coast near Albania. Maybe that's where they went!"

"Who were the guys with the chopper?" Frank asked.

"I have no idea. They just appeared a little while

ago. Didn't say where they were going to take me. Now tell me, how did you get here just in the nick of time?"

Frank and Joe took turns explaining the latest events. Suddenly Chet clasped his stomach. "I feel weak! I haven't eaten since yesterday!"

"We know a place where you can get breakfast five minutes from here," Evan said.

"Let's go!"

The boys worked their way back to the shepherd's hut, where they had goat's milk and bread. Then they thanked their hosts and returned to the Mercedes.

They found a national police car parked alongside. One of two officers was taking down their licence number. They looked surprised at the four boys.

Evan explained their predicament in Greek and the police radioed to Navpaktos for a service car. Then Evan told the officers about Chet's rescue and the helicopter take-off. They promised to notify Athens, call the Pandropolos family, and keep a lookout for the chopper. Then they left.

Two hours later a mechanic arrived. He had brought a spare wheel and replaced the smashed one. After paying him, the boys set off westward towards Corfu.

The narrow highway twisted and turned before it made a sweeping loop in the descent towards Navpaktos, a small town on the Gulf of Corinth. There they stopped for petrol and oil.

"Let's keep on going," Evan said. "If we're lucky, we'll catch the last ferry from Igoumenitsa to the town of Corfu." He showed the Americans a map. The road led west to Mesolongion, then northward to Ioannina and west again to the coastal town of Igoumenitsa.

The boys spelled one another at the wheel. Frank

drove for the last few miles. He skilfully negotiated the tortuous mountain road, which finally dropped down to the seacoast.

Evan pointed. "There's the ferry! It's loading. Hurry, Frank, and let me out when you come to the toll-house."

Frank slowed enough for the Greek boy to hop out, then sped to the last position in a line of cars boarding the ferry.

Evan came back with their tickets in time, gave them to the ferryman, and joined his friends aboard the boat. The whistle blew a mournful note and the craft eased out of the harbour for the crossing to Corfu.

The two hours' sailing time seemed like an eternity to the Hardys. The sun lowered into the waves and not long afterwards darkness spilled over the Ionian Sea. By the time the steel ramp clanked down on the wharf at the town of Corfu, the sky was inky black. Headlights creeping off the ferry illuminated a broad plaza, bordered by shops and hotels.

"How about some chow and beddy-by?" Chet asked. "I'm beat."

The others agreed. "We can't do any investigating this time of night, anyway," Frank said.

They registered at the Hermes Hotel and had dinner.

"Wake me up after you catch those crooks," Chet said when they were back in their room. "I think I will sleep for a whole week."

The next morning, however, he rose with the others, eager to pursue the suspects. They had breakfast in the hotel's coffee shop and the waiter gave Evan directions to the local police station.

Half an hour later the four boys entered headquarters, where Evan conversed in Greek with the sergeant on duty. He told of their mission to capture Dimitri and Gerrold and their search for the ancient helmet.

"So! You, too!" The policeman smiled as he replied in English. Seeing their puzzled looks, he went on, "Yes. We are hunting for them. We know all about Gerrold and Dimitri through a teletype from Athens."

"Any luck yet?" Frank asked.

"We found the tan Fiat—abandoned. And a small boat is missing."

Evan looked amazed. "You mean they took off for Albania?"

"It is possible."

"They'll be caught and tossed in jail over there," Frank reasoned.

"Not likely. Dimitri is an Albanian. He will ask asylum for his friend, the American gangster," the policeman said.

Frank let out a whistle. "Dimitri—an Albanian?"

"Yes. He crossed the strait illegally some years ago, obtained a fake Greek passport, and eventually slipped into the United States."

Joe said, "So he knows this area well."

"Yes. But our men are patrolling the strait and have not seen them. There is a good chance the fugitives are still on Kerkira."

Evan thanked the officer. "If you learn anything, will you leave a message for us at the Hermes?"

"Certainly."

Evan looked discouraged. Outside, he pointed north-east across the narrow belt of water to whitish hills rising starkly not more than ten miles distant.

"There's Albania. Not a very friendly country. If

those criminals got away, goodbye to the helmet!"

"There's still hope," Joe said. "Those hoods could be holing up somewhere, waiting for a good chance to make a break for it."

"The question is, *where* could they be hiding?" Chet said.

Evan was thoughtful for a few moments. "If they stole a boat, they have to hide that, too. There are many caves along the shore. Perhaps they're using one of them!"

"Let's get a boat and look," Joe said.

The boys hastened to the waterfront and rented a sturdy eighteen-foot craft with an inboard engine. Evan purchased a detailed map of the island and they set out with the Greek at the wheel.

The coast swung north in a curve until nearly touching Albania at a place called Kouloura.

"It's only a mile and a half across at that point," Evan said.

Unlike the area around Athens, Corfu was clothed in green hills that sloped down to the water's edge. Part of the shore was rocky, with caves cut deeply into the limestone. In other places, lagoons provided harbours for small boats and beaches for bathing.

Evan held his course a quarter mile offshore. "There's Dassia," he said. "English people vacation here a lot. Not many Americans." He pointed out the settlement and continued north.

The coast became more rocky, caves more abundant. Whenever a large one came into view, Evan sailed closer and they examined it carefully.

Now Albania hardly seemed more than a stone's throw away. It looked chalky white in the midday sun.

"Let's put in at Kassiopi for lunch," Evan suggested. Kassiopi was a small harbour edged with a low concrete bulkhead. Behind it were several restaurants.

"That's my kind of detective work," Chet said. "Water sports and food." While the others made fast the boat, he headed straight for the nearest restaurant. When his friends caught up, he was trying to make the waiter understand what he wanted.

While lunch was being prepared, the young detectives asked several people if two men resembling the fugitives had been seen in the area. They showed Gerrold's picture round, but got no result.

Finally the waiter beckoned them to an outdoor table. Evan shot one more query at him. The waiter cocked his head, examined the photograph, and lifted an eyebrow.

"Yes, I saw this man. I made up a dozen sandwiches this morning for him to take out, together with two Thermos flasks of hot coffee."

"Where did he go?" Frank asked.

The waiter shrugged.

Nevertheless, the boys were elated. "Those crooks must be hiding somewhere nearby," Joe said, "biding their time. It's unlikely they'd leave in broad daylight. Let's hurry and continue our search."

When they had finished, Evan took the helm again and skilfully guided the boat as close to the shore as he could without scraping the bottom.

Every navigable cave was entered and the work grew tedious and tiring.

"We'll never make it by nightfall," Chet said, shielding his eyes from the low sun.

"I'm not giving up yet," Evan stated grimly.

They continued their search until dusk, but then the light became so dim that the boat was in danger of being ripped by underwater crags.

"We'll have to call it a day," Joe said.

"Okay," Evan agreed. "I guess—hey, what's that?"

An aircraft engine broke the stillness.

"It's a chopper!" Chet cried out. "Look, the same kind that nearly got me!"

·20·

Bang-up Roundup

THE helicopter landed on a rocky promontory not far from where their boat lay hidden by a jutting boulder. A man appeared, seemingly out of the ground, got into the chopper and the craft took off.

"He must have come from the rear entrance to a cave," Frank said excitedly.

"Yes, I see the opening," Joe said. "Right behind that rock."

Evan cut the engine and began manoeuvring the boat with an oar. "Should we go in?"

"We don't really know if the cave is empty," Frank said. "Someone else might still be there."

Evan paddled the boat softly through the water and finally stopped at the entrance to the cave. The boys sat silently for a few minutes, straining to pick up a sound. There was none.

Finally Frank said, "Let's go in. Joe, you stay here as a lookout." He took a torch from a locker and the boys climbed over the rocks inside the cave, using their light as sparingly as possible. They passed several cracks and crevices in the crumbling limestone walls, then came upon a flat area floored with hard-packed sand. Footprints were all over the place.

Suddenly the light fell upon a small boat with an outboard engine.

"No doubt the stolen one," Evan said. "Hey, look at this!"

On the floor of the boat lay a neatly-tied, brown carton. Evan reached for it.

"Wait!" Frank commanded. "It might be a booby trap." He cut the string carefully, then gingerly opened the top of the carton. *Inside lay the shattered helmet!*

"Wow!" exclaimed Chet. "Look at that!"

"Quiet!" hissed Frank. "They might hear us!"

"Of course we hear you!" Dimitri's voice boomed out. They whirled round to see the Albanian and Gerrold step out of the shadowy crevice. Dimitri held a brilliant torch.

"I wouldn't touch that helmet!" he said.

"Says you," Frank declared. He picked up the box. "Come on, Chet. Show Evan how to . . . "

Suddenly a voice behind the boys spoke with chilling effect. "Put that helmet down!"

Frank turned slowly to look into the nose of a nickel-plated pistol.

"Spiro Vanides!" Frank gasped.

Evan said, "You—you—I can't believe it!"

"Neither will anybody else," Vanides said coldly. "I wanted this helmet and I have it, thanks to my friends—and of course your good detective work."

The three boys were stunned by Vanides' admission.

"You risked an awful lot for the helmet," Frank said. "Why?"

"Why?" The shipper waggled the gun towards Evan. "Because of his Uncle Nick, that's why!"

"My uncle never harmed you!" Evan protested.

"Oh no? He gets the fat shipping contracts. He's praised for his charity. He wants Agamemnon's helmet to present to the state! More praise, more glory!"

Vanides' face flushed with hatred. "Now I have the helmet and Nick's favourite nephew and assorted trash from the United States!"

Frank stepped forward impulsively.

"Don't move or I will shoot you!" Vanides snarled.

Dimitri said, "We have the fat kid again. Can't seem to get rid of him! And that's your fault, Vanides. Your chopper pilot should have dropped him off in the Gulf of Corinth! Same as we planned to do with that stupid Saffel before he got away!"

"Quiet!" Vanides ordered. "Where is the other Hardy boy?"

"He's not with us," Frank stated.

"Brilliant observation!" Vanides said sarcastically.

"You're not so smart yourself," Frank said, "or you wouldn't have pulled this caper. All you have is us, a broken helmet, and a lot of trouble."

"Trouble?" Vanides laughed. "You are in trouble. I have won!" His grinning confederates joined in his pleasure. "As for the helmet," he said, "it goes to the Moscow Museum of Antiquity—benefactor Spiro Vanides."

Gerrold interrupted at this point. "And as for you kids, what a great ransom!"

"No!" Vanides' voice rose. "They will go to the bottom of the Ionian Sea!"

"But we could get a million dollars for them!"

"Listen! You might be boss in the States, but I am boss in Greece. You will do as I say!"

Frank saw Twister flinch and quickly pressed the

150

advantage. "What do you know! Filbert Francisco isn't the big shot any more!"

The taunt threw the gangster into a rage. His face grew livid and he lunged towards Frank.

At that instant the whole cave reverberated with the deafening sound of explosions.

"Joe's back with the cops!" Chet shouted.

Vanides stood dumbfounded for a second. The gun slumped momentarily. Frank knocked it from Vanides' hand with a karate chop. At the same time Chet and Evan set upon their tormentors with strength born of desperation.

The cave was filled with groans and grunts as the battle raged evenly. The sudden appearance of Joe gave the boys the advantage. He kayoed Gerrold with a smash to the point of his chin. Chet took care of Dimitri while Frank and Evan tied up the hapless Vanides.

Then Frank picked up the gun with his handkerchief and pocketed it as evidence. As the other two were being tied, he asked, "Where are the police with the guns, Joe?"

His brother grinned wryly. "Guns? What guns?"

"The explosions!"

"Oh, those were firecrackers. Thank Chet. I still had them in my windbreaker."

Chet chuckled. "I had a hunch we'd need them!"

The boys stowed the helmet in their boat, then carried the three men outside.

Frank scanned the sky for the helicopter, but it had disappeared. Evan guided the boat into open water and it chugged towards the town of Corfu.

Meanwhile, accusations flew from gunwale to gunwale. One prisoner set himself against another in rage over being outsmarted by a handful of boys.

Frank and Joe asked questions that helped to supply some missing facts in the case. Dimitri spoke freely, revealing the motive for the caper.

It all started, he said, when Cole was assigned by Twister Gerrold to harass the Hardys because of their father's investigation. When these tactics failed, Dimitri joined Cole at Hunt College to kidnap Frank and Joe.

"Why didn't you?" Joe asked.

"Before we had a chance to, Vanides learned through Nick Pandropolos' secretary that the shattered helmet might have been Agamemnon's and was worth a fortune. That changed things. Now we followed you to find the helmet."

"But you kept harassing us. Why?"

"Gerrold hoped it might eventually have an effect on your father and he would drop the investigation."

"But how does Vanides tie in with Gerrold?" Frank asked.

"Shut up!" Vanides shouted and glared at the Albanian, but Dimitri continued.

"Vanides is a smuggler. Twister is his partner in the States. What Vanides asks, Twister does."

The town of Corfu came into sight now. When Evan docked, Joe went to get the police. The officers were amazed to see Vanides tied up, and for a while were inclined to believe his story that the boys had kidnapped him.

Back at headquarters, however, they radioed Athens and soon had the truth. The Athens police, meanwhile, seized Vanides' helicopter when it landed there and arrested the pilot and his companion.

Two days later, after Evan's Uncle Nick presented the shattered helmet to the museum at an impressive public ceremony, a reception was held for all the participants. Both Mr and Mrs Hardy had arrived by plane in time for the event, which was covered by radio, television, and the press.

While Frank, Joe, Chet, and Evan received official accolades, a movie camera whirred to record the event. The boys glanced up to see Leon Saffel, one eye pressed against the viewer. He waved and the young heroes returned the greeting. If Leon's camera had been a crystal ball, they might have foreseen their next adventure, to be known as *The Clue of the Hissing Serpent*.

"Hey, Joe!" Frank said suddenly. "We forgot to do something!"

"What's that?"

"Cable the news to Rena Bartlett in Hollywood!"

The sickles gleamed in the midday sunshine.

The Hardy Boys® Mysteries

THE CLUE OF THE HISSING SERPENT

·1·

A Runaway Balloon

"YOUR father sounded desperate," Aunt Gertrude said, looking worried. "He wants you to meet him at four o'clock in the lobby of the Treat Hotel at Oak Knolls. Better hurry!"

Frank and Joe Hardy had just arrived home from a swim at the Bayport pool when their agitated aunt met them at the kitchen door. The telephone message seemed innocent enough, but Aunt Gertrude always feared the worst for her famous detective brother Fenton.

"Oh, yes," she continued, "he mentioned the word *Falcon*. What does that mean?"

"*Falcon!* Holy crow, Frank, let's go!" Joe urged excitedly.

The boys bolted out of the door and into their car. Joe took the wheel and they sped off.

Falcon was a secret word used by the two young detectives and their father. It meant *danger ahead*. But what was the danger Fenton Hardy had foreseen in their meeting?

They mulled it over as they hit the speed limit and arrowed along the highway due west from Bayport. Mr Hardy had not mentioned any new case. Hence, if there

7

was danger, it had sprung up suddenly. Frank and Joe were worried.

Dark-haired Frank, who was eighteen, glanced at his watch. "Three o'clock. We should make it in time."

Joe, a blond seventeen-year-old, nodded. "I just hope it doesn't rain. Might slow traffic."

The sky, which had been bright and sunny during the morning, had turned ominously grey in the west and a chilly wind began to dissipate the late June heat.

"Looks like a storm is heading our way," Frank said. "And traffic's slowing already. But it can't be because of the weather. I wonder what happened."

"I guess there's been an accident." Joe craned his neck out of the window for a better look. But all he could see was a line of cars moving at a snail's pace. Horns were honking impatiently. Then traffic stopped completely.

People began stepping out of their cars, and Joe did the same. Suddenly his eyes grew wide in amazement.

"Frank! I see the trouble!"

"What is it?"

"A balloon! Flying pretty low and coming closer to the road. Everybody's stopped to look at it."

Frank reached into the glove compartment and grabbed binoculars which the boys kept handy. He jumped out to scan the green-and-white striped balloon. Like a giant pendulum, it whipped dangerously back and forth.

"It must be caught in some kind of crazy wind current," Frank said. "Here, take a look, Joe."

Now the balloon was no more than a hundred yards away. Joe focused on the two passengers hanging desperately to the sides of the basket.

8

"What are they going to do?" he cried out. "Land on the highway?"

Suddenly the balloon veered to the right, coming to rest in a field beside the road not far from the Hardys.

Frank pulled the car over to the side. "Come on, Joe. Maybe we can be of some help."

A lot of other motorists had the same idea, and soon a huge crowd raced across the pasture to where the balloon was gradually deflating.

The boys were in the forefront and reached it first. The two balloonists were just climbing out. Frank's jaw dropped open in amazement as the younger one turned around to face them. It was none other than their staunch friend Chet Morton!

"Hello, Frank. Hi, Joe," Chet said.

"What in the world are you doing here?" Joe demanded.

The chunky, freckle-faced youth squinted up at the collapsing balloon and remarked casually, "I'm taking lessons. Didn't want to tell you until I became a full-fledged balloonist."

His companion walked up to the group. "Oh, fellows," Chet said, "this is Mr Albert Krassner. And these are my friends, Frank and Joe Hardy."

The man seemed to be about forty, with thinning black hair and a paunch. He had a broad, fleshy face, full lips, a wide nose and slightly droopy eyelids, which made him look half asleep. Yet there was a brisk alertness in his voice as he spoke.

"Glad to meet you." He extended a pudgy hand to the young detectives. "We really got into trouble. A sudden wind came up and we tried to land, but a faulty vent prevented us from getting down fast enough. We

9

almost drifted on to the highway!"

"A faulty vent?" Joe asked.

Chet nodded. "You pull a cord to vent when you want to descend more rapidly than simply letting the balloon's air cool. The vent lets the air out—the longer you hold it open, the quicker. Ten feet above the ground you rip the top if the wind is high. It pulls off the circular panel and lets the hot air out in a rush."

"I see," Joe said. "But you have to be just above the spot where you want to land to do that."

"Right," Chet said.

Krassner went back and continued to deflate the balloon, answering questions of other onlookers. The Hardys took Chet aside and asked him about his new friend.

"He's a rich guy," Chet said. "An investment banker. Belongs to the Lone Tree Balloon Club near Oak Knolls."

"How'd you meet him?" Frank inquired.

"I used to hang around the club," Chet said. "Krassner took a liking to me and offered these lessons free."

"This could have been your last lesson, Chet!" Frank said. "You almost got killed!"

"And if you're such a buddy of ours, how come you didn't let us in on your new hobby!"

"Now don't get sore," said Chet. "I told you, I wanted to make it a surprise."

"It sure was," Frank said. Then he glanced at his watch. They had twenty minutes to reach their destination. "We've got to meet our dad at the Treat Hotel in Oak Knolls," he said. "See you later."

Traffic had started to unsnarl with the aid of two

State Police officers. As the boys hastened to their car, they saw a small truck drive across the field to retrieve the balloon. A small black sports car followed it.

"Probably Krassner's," Joe commented. "Looks like an Italian job."

The Hardys crept along for a while until they could pick up speed. Joe passed dozens of cars, but eased off when the needle exceeded the speed limit. "If we get a ticket, we'll never get there on time," he said.

Finally they reached the exit for the small town of Oak Knolls. By now it was ten minutes past four. When they drove into the parking lot, the clock on the tower in the town square stood at four-twenty.

The boys rushed into the hotel. "Any message for Frank and Joe Hardy?" Frank asked the desk clerk.

"No, nothing. Were you expecting to meet someone?"

"Yes." Frank looked worriedly about the lobby.

"Would you like accommodations?"

"No, thank you," Joe replied. He noticed a meeting room off to one side with the door open. The boys walked in. The place smelled smoky and cigarette butts lay in numerous ashtrays. Printed agendas were scattered on folding chairs and long tables.

On a dais at the far end of the room stood a blackboard. Chalked on it were numbers indicating that a business meeting had taken place.

"Maybe Dad attended," Frank mused. "It couldn't have ended long ago." He took a closer look at the blackboard. In one corner something was printed in small letters. "Joe," he exclaimed, "it says *Mayday Room 211 Falcon!*"

"Dad's in trouble!" Joe said. "In Room 211!"

11

Suddenly both were startled by a voice behind them. "The world's full of trouble!"

Frank and Joe whirled to confront Albert Krassner.

"W-what are you doing here?" Joe asked.

Krasser smiled blandly. "Chet told me where I could find you. He also told me you're the famous Hardy detectives."

"We're not famous," Frank said. "But our father is."

Actually, Frank and Joe had become as famous as Fenton Hardy, who had retired from the New York Police Department to set up his own private practice. Starting with an adventure called *The Mystery of the Aztec Warrior*, the Hardy boys had solved many baffling cases themselves. Their previous one was known as *The Shattered Helmet*.

Joe said, "Mr Krassner, if you want us to join your balloon club, we can't talk about it now."

"No, no. It's not that, I want you to help me!"

"How?" Frank asked.

Suddenly Krassner's face contorted with pain. He grabbed Joe by the shoulders. Before the boy could move, both landed on the floor with a thud.

·2·

A Custom-made Rocket

JOE pushed the man away and sprang to his feet, but Krassner did not move.

"He's out cold," Frank said. "Must have had some kind of attack!"

The Hardys knew that ill people sometimes carry instructions on them in cases of emergency. Joe went through the man's pockets. "Here's a bottle," he said. "And a note wrapped around it!"

They read it quickly. If Krassner suffered a heart seizure he was to be given one tablet under his tongue.

Frank administered the medicine. Seconds later Krassner opened his eyes. The Hardys helped him up and to a comfortable position on a sofa.

Joe ran out to get a glass of water. When he returned, some colour had come back into Krassner's pale, puffy face.

He spoke in a shaky voice. "Sorry to be such a nuisance, boys. Guess I had too much excitement for one day. And I'm sure glad you found my pills."

"Think nothing of it," Frank said. "Why don't you just rest here a while? We'll be right back."

Krassner nodded and the two walked out of the conference room. "This is all very strange," Frank whispered. "We'd better find Dad fast." They hurried through the lobby and up to the second floor.

In front of Room 211 they stopped and listened quietly. At first they heard nothing. Then there was a thump and a low moan.

"Let's break down the door," Joe said.

"Wait," Frank replied.

He tried the knob. It turned and he pushed the door wide open. Inside, midway between a bed and a dressing-table, lay Fenton Hardy. He was bound hand and foot and gagged. The boys rushed over and freed their father. Stiffly the detective sat up and rubbed the back of his head.

"I thought you'd never get here," he murmured.

"Sorry," Frank said. "We were delayed by a balloon."

"What?"

"We'll tell you later, Dad. Get up now. Easy."

As they helped Mr Hardy to a nearby chair, Joe noticed a piece of paper stuffed into his shirt pocket.

"What's this?" he asked.

"I don't know," Mr Hardy replied.

Joe took it and read the message. "Dad, it says, 'Keep your mouth shut.' "

"Fat chance!" Frank exclaimed. "Dad's a pretty hard man to intimidate."

The detective smiled wryly and told his sons what had happened.

"It all started with a telephone call to Sam Radley," he began, referring to an operative who had often helped him in his investigations. "The caller wanted Sam to bug the home of Conrad Greene in Ocean Bluffs."

"The United States chess champion?" Frank asked.

"That's the one."

"But why?" Joe queried.

"The world championship is coming up soon," Mr Hardy said. "It might have something to do with that. Anyway, when Sam told me about it, I went in his place to see his so-called client."

"And met with him downstairs," Frank concluded.

"Correct. When I arrived, there were two men in the room. Obviously there must have been a group of people who had just left. I don't know whether the two men had any connection with them or not. They told me their names were Smith and Jones."

"Sounds as phony as a three-dollar bill," Joe said. "What did they look like?"

"Smith was short, slender, with long pointed fingers. He had a slightly Mongolian look. The other fellow, Jones, was strictly Anglo-Saxon. Long face, typically English, I'd say. Narrow thrusting chin. Both were in their late thirties.

"What I wanted you boys for," Mr Hardy went on, "was to tail these men."

"Don't worry. We'll find them if they're anywhere in this area," Frank assured him.

"Anyhow," Joe said, "you told them it was no go on the bugging deal."

"Right. Then they invited me to Room 211 to talk it over some more. I excused myself on the way out because I forgot my briefcase. That's when I put the message on the blackboard."

"Good thing you did," Frank said.

Mr Hardy nodded. "When I entered Room 211, a third person conked me from behind."

"Do they still think you're Radley?" Joe asked.

"I don't know. In any case, this illegal wire-tapping must be stopped. If Smith and Jones find some dishonest detective to put a tap on Greene's phone, it could lead to real trouble."

Mr Hardy felt better now and they went downstairs. Krassner was not in the meeting room, so they questioned the clerk at the desk.

He said that 211 had been rented as a hospitality room for a sales meeting of Eco Incorporated. "I've never heard of that company," he told them. "But one of the salesmen mentioned Associated Jewellers. They're a house-to-house operation with headquarters in Bayport."

"Did you see the gentleman who came in after us?" Frank asked.

"Oh yes. He left a little while ago."

The Hardys thanked the man and went outside. Frank and Joe explained about the delay on the highway and how Krassner had suffered a heart seizure.

"He sounds like an odd character," Mr Hardy said. "Wanted help and didn't tell you why."

"Maybe he changed his mind," Frank said. "What now, Dad?"

It was decided that Frank and Joe would investigate the assault, because Mr Hardy was occupied with a case involving Hong Kong custom tailors.

"The Association of Menswear Retailers wants me to track down this fraud operation," the detective said. "About half a dozen men are involved. They take orders for custom-made suits from Hong Kong, request a fat down payment, and disappear. It shouldn't take too long to crack it. Crooks like this aren't too bright."

Mr Hardy drove out of the parking lot and the boys followed in their car. At home, Mrs Hardy met her three men, as she called them, and asked, "What's this big mystery Gertrude was telling me about?"

Frank gave her the gist of what had happened and added, "Don't worry, Mother. Things are under control."

Mr Hardy made a few phone calls, then said to his sons, "Eco Incorporated and Associated Jewellers are not listed in any trade register I can get hold of, but Associated Jewellers are in the phone book. I think Eco was just a phony cover for that company. I suggest you check it out."

"Will do," Frank said.

"I also called Conrad Greene's home to warn him about the wiretap, but no one answered."

"We'll have to try again," Frank said. "Let me see if I can get in touch with Chet to quiz him about Krassner."

Chet was home and took Frank's call. "Boy, Krassner was full of praise for you," he reported. "I just saw him a little while ago. Said you helped him when he had an attack."

"Do you have any idea what he wanted to talk to us about?" Frank asked.

"No. But why don't you drop by the balloon club tomorrow and ask him? He usually comes over early. Besides, I want to show you the place."

"We'll be there."

Right after breakfast the next morning the Hardys started out for the club. Near Oak Knolls they turned off the highway at a sign announcing Lone Tree Balloon Club. A narrow lane led through the woods and to an

17

open meadow. Off to one side was a frame structure no larger than a two-car garage. A single, large oak tree stood next to it.

Out in the field Chet Morton and another youth were busy unfolding the envelope of a red-striped balloon. Joe parked beside the clubhouse and the Hardys walked up to their friend.

"Hi, guys," Chet greeted. "I'd like you to meet Ken Flippen. Just call him Fearless. That's his nickname."

Frank and Joe shook hands with a slightly built boy of sixteen. A shock of black hair hung over his eyes and he tossed his head occasionally.

"Sure glad to meet you," Fearless said with a friendly grin. "Chet's clued me in on your detective work. Says you're on another important case. That must be exciting!"

Frank gave Chet a slit-eyed look. "What have you been telling people?"

"Can't I brag about my friends—a little?"

"Very little," Joe said, and turned to Fearless. "Don't believe everything this big panda tells you. By the way, what are you fearless about?"

"Aw, nothing."

"I know," Chet said. "When he was a kid, he hung on to a rope and got pulled into the air by a balloon. Hung on for ten minutes until it came down."

Fearless looked embarrassed, and Frank said, "There you go again, bragging about your friends!"

They all laughed and Chet said, "Fearless knows a lot about balloons. His father and two other men own this one. We're practising inflation."

Fearless was pleased to tell the Hardys about his balloon. It had a two-man aluminium gondola or bas-

18

ket, and was lifted by hot air. Two propane gas tanks lay on the floor of the basket, and from each a stainless-steel tube led to a multiple pilot-light structure mounted on a metal framework above the gondola.

"When the pilot pulls this cord," Fearless said, "the blast valve releases propane which is ignited by the pilot light." He demonstrated, and a roaring blast of flame shot upward.

"This goes into the open mouth of the balloon," the boy went on, "keeping the air inside hot, or heating it more if it's cooled."

"Hey, that's amazing!" Joe said. "You can carry your own hot-air furnace with you."

"Right. This balloon is made of flame-resistant nylon. If by accident the flame melts a hole in the fabric, it will not burn the balloon up."

Chet and Fearless proceeded to shoot hot air into the bag, and Chet said, "If you want to descend gradually, you don't shoot any more air in and the balloon will come down."

"There sure is a lot to know about ballooning," Frank said. "Chet, when will you get your pilot's licence?"

"Maybe in a month," Chet said proudly.

Joe changed the subject. "Where's Krassner?"

"He didn't show up." Chet said. "That's unusual. I expected him early this morning, but maybe he doesn't feel too well. Why don't you wait a while?"

Frank shook his head. "No, we have some work to do. We'll catch up with him later."

"So long, Fearless," Joe said.

"Come back for a ride someday!"

"We will."

The Hardys went to their car, looking back once towards the balloon which was now partially inflated.

"Chet sure does latch on to some good hobbies," Frank said as they drove back to Bayport to investigate Associated Jewellers.

Their office was near the waterfront, and turned out to be a relatively new one-storey building. Across the street stood an ancient three-floor wreck of a house bearing a sign: *Danger. Building Condemned.*

The boys parked and entered the jewellery company. In a waiting-room were three chairs and a writing table. The door at the far end opened and a woman appeared.

"Are you answering our ad?" she asked.

Frank hesitated, "Why—er—"

"Then come right in. Mr Jervis will talk to you."

The inner office contained four filing cabinets, a number of chairs, and a cluttered desk. Behind it sat a pale, thin man wearing thick-lensed glasses. A name-plate on the desk read: *Reginald Jervis.*

"Have a seat," he said with an ingratiating smile. "You're rather young, but we could use two men right now. What is your experience in door-to-door sales?"

Before either had a chance to reply, Jervis went on, "We have a fine line of jewellery, and if you succeed in selling it, we have another most attractive offer."

Finally Frank interrupted. "We don't want a job, Mr Jervis."

"What? Then why are you here?"

"To ask some questions."

"About what?"

"About Smith and Jones. Who are they?"

"Never heard of them!" Jervis snapped.

"And you've never heard of Eco Incorporated, either, I suppose," Joe put in.

Jervis rose from his chair and pointed a finger at the door. "Get out!" he said.

"So you don't know Smith and Jones?" Frank said coolly. "Well, there are other ways to find out about them."

The boy's calm demeanour infuriated Jervis. "I said get out!" he yelled. "Or I'll throw you out myself!"

21

·3·

Tricky Surveillance

THE man pushed back his chair and took a step towards Frank and Joe.

"You don't have to get physical," Frank said. "We'll go."

Back in their car, Joe said, "We sure touched a sensitive nerve. Something fishy's going on at Associated Jewellers."

Frank nodded. "Jervis was really on edge. Now I'm sure Smith and Jones are connected with that outfit."

Joe suggested they visit the Bayport Better Business Bureau. "Maybe they can shed some light on Jervis's company."

The Hardys drove along the waterfront, past a number of Chinese-operated shops known as Little Chinatown. They stopped at a hamburger place for a quick snack, then proceeded to Main Street, where the Better Business Bureau was located.

They were cordially received by the woman in charge of consumer protection. In answer to Frank's question, she replied that she had heard of Associated Jewellers. The Bureau had received numerous complaints of high-pressure salesmanship and shoddy merchandise.

"The company is on our list," the woman said. "So far, we haven't enough solid evidence against them to warrant a lawsuit."

"Has the public been warned?" Frank asked.

"There was a report in the newspaper," the woman replied. "But I'm sure that many people did not see it."

When the boys returned home they found that Mr Hardy, in response to a tip from Police Chief Collig, had gone off to question several persons who had been cheated by the jewellery peddlers.

"He'll be home later," Mrs Hardy said.

"I wish we could watch one of their salesmen in action," Frank said.

"Perhaps you can," Aunt Gertrude spoke up. "But for goodness' sake, be careful. If they cheat people, there's no telling what else they're capable of."

Her nephews looked perplexed. "What are you talking about?" Joe asked.

"Mrs Snyder," Aunt Gertrude said.

"Well, what about her?"

"Mrs Snyder—you know, the one who lives on Lincoln Street—has arranged for an Associated Jewellers representative to come to her house. I just spoke to her a few minutes ago. Your father had already left. She told me a very nice man phoned her and offered free earrings for letting him show their products."

"When will he call?" Joe asked.

"I don't know exactly when. You'll have to ask her."

"Gee, thanks, Aunty," Frank said. "This may be a big help in our case."

Just then the telephone rang. Frank answered. It was Krassner, inviting the boys to his home in a suburb of Bayport that evening.

"We'll be there," Frank said. "How about eight-thirty?"

"Roger. See you then."

"This sure is a big day for us," Joe said. "Come on, Frank. We've got a lot to do."

The boys had just stepped out of the house for the short walk to Mrs Snyder's home when Biff Hooper came along with his hound dog, Sherlock. Biff was a tall, athletic high school pal of the boys.

"Hi, Biff," Frank said. "Is Sherlock taking you for a stroll?"

"Something like that," Biff replied with a friendly grin. "Matter of fact, I dropped by to ask you how about some tennis after supper tonight? I've got Tony Prito lined up for doubles."

"Sorry," Joe said. "We're busy."

"Official business?"

"Yes. We're interviewing one of Chet's friends. He may have a case for us."

"You mean Krassner, the balloon guy?"

"How'd you know that?" Frank asked in surprise.

"Chet was in town at noon. He keeps me posted on your doings."

Frank laughed. "Good old Chet. He's a balloon buff now."

"It's a good sport," Joe said. "I'm getting interested myself."

"Where are you guys going?" Biff asked.

Frank told him.

"I'll walk you over," Biff offered as Sherlock strained at the leash.

The trio turned a corner and proceeded along the block to the fifth house on the right. On the front steps

24

sat a huge, tawny cat. Sherlock lunged, nearly pulling the leash from Biff's hand.

"Hold it, Sherlock!"

The hound let out a mournful bay and the cat raced up a mimosa tree on the front lawn. The commotion brought an elderly couple to the porch. The man looked over the top of his eye-glasses.

"Get that hound out of here!" he ordered. "He's scaring Princess!"

"All right. No harm meant," Biff said politely. "So long, fellows. See you later."

As he left, Frank addressed the couple. "You're the Snyders, aren't you?"

The woman nodded with a prim smile.

"We're Gertrude Hardy's nephews Frank and Joe. May we talk to you a minute?"

"Of course."

Mrs Snyder preceded the boys into the house while her husband went to retrieve Princess from the mimosa tree.

"You see, we love cats," the woman said. "Not that we don't like dogs, too, mind you."

It was then that the boys realized that there were cats all over the house. They seemed to blend into the furniture. Frank counted six in the living room.

"Please be seated," Mrs Snyder said. "But be careful of our pets."

One of them jumped off the sofa where Frank and Joe were sitting. At the same time Mr Snyder entered, carrying Princess. He dropped down in an overstuffed chair and stroked the animal in his lap.

"We're sorry about the dog," Frank said, knowing that it was the wrong time to ask for a favour.

25

"Don't worry about it. Tell us what we can do for you," Mrs Snyder said.

"We understand you're expecting a visit from an Associated Jewellers salesman," Frank began.

"Yes, he's coming tomorrow."

"Well, there have been complaints about this company. High-pressure salesmanship and shoddy merchandise. It might have something to do with a case we're investigating, and we'd like to listen to what this man has to say to you."

At that moment he felt a terrible tickle in his nose and let out a resounding sneeze. "Excuse me, please."

Mr Snyder nodded. "How are you planning to listen in?"

"We could conceal ourselves somewhere."

"Goodness! Wouldn't that be dangerous?" Mrs Snyder asked.

"I doubt it," Frank said. "Anyway, we'd be here to protect you."

"I don't like it," Mr Snyder said.

"Don't be grumpy," his wife intervened. "What would Gertrude think if we turned her nephews down?"

"Then may we come?" Frank asked hopefully.

"Certainly. The salesman is due at two. Why don't you stop by at one-thirty?"

Mr Snyder looked none too pleased but did not object. The boys expressed their thanks and left.

At home, Frank and Joe praised Aunt Gertrude for her aid. "Did you know the Snyders have a houseful of cats?" Joe asked as the family sat down to dinner.

"Oh yes. One named Princess Golden Girl of Bayport is a champion."

When the meal was over, the boys set out for Krassner's home. It was located in a wooded area about twenty miles out of town.

The sun was setting as they neared the property. Suddenly they heard a strange hissing noise.

Frank slowed down. It was not from the car, but seemed to come from overhead. Both looked up in amazement to see a weird balloon. Hot air was gently shooting into the envelope with a sound like auto tyres on a wet pavement.

"Look at those crazy colours!" Joe exclaimed as the craft drifted over the woodland. It was mottled in shades of green, blue, and yellow, and its central decoration was an evil-looking, twisting serpent of the same hues.

"Someone has an artistic touch," Frank said admiringly. "Let's follow it to see where it lands. It was flying pretty low."

"Okay. We have half an hour to spare, anyway."

They turned around and a hundred yards farther on found a narrow lane leading into the deep woods.

Overhanging branches brushed past the car as it probed deeper into the forest along the rutted trail. The slow going was maddening. But finally they reached a clearing.

Off to one side was a tumble-down barn, and beside it a stark blackened chimney—all that remained of a burned-out farmhouse.

"Look," Frank said. "There's the balloon. And their truck got here ahead of us."

They could see why. A good blacktop road was no more than a hundred yards away on the opposite side of the clearing.

27

Frank and Joe parked the car and trotted towards the barn. Perhaps the serpent balloonists were from the Lone Tree Club.

Behind the old building the deflated envelope was being packed up. Three men worked with great rapidity, and the balloon and gondola were loaded on to the truck. The men jumped in.

"Hey, wait a second!" Frank called out as he and Joe ran forward.

The truck started up and the Hardys hailed it again. But instead of slowing down, the driver accelerated. Frank and Joe moved to the side of a gully, because it was coming right at them!

"Holy crow!" Joe exclaimed. "They're trying to run us down!"

"Jump!" Frank cried out.

·4·

A Hissing Blast

DIVING headlong, Frank and Joe cleared the side of the road and landed in a bramble patch as the truck sped by.

Joe rose painfully from the thorny foliage and Frank followed him, pulling bramble thorns from his hair and clothing.

"Did you get the licence number by any chance, Joe?"

"Oh, sure, I jotted it down while flying through the air!" he quipped. "Frank, do you think those guys have something to hide or are they just nasty?"

"I'd say both."

They brushed the weeds from their dishevelled clothes and returned to their car.

"It must have taken months to decorate that balloon," Frank said.

"Right. Maybe they're entering a contest for the most artistic design. Anyway, whoever was driving deserves an artistic punch on the nose."

Joe got into the driver's seat while Frank slipped in beside him.

"Ow!"

"What's the matter?" Joe asked.

"I didn't get all those confounded thorns out of my trousers!"

They went back by the same route and regained the main road leading towards Krassner's home.

"I guess this is it," Joe said finally.

Dusk had settled now and the lights from their car illuminated a bronze plaque set in a huge boulder announcing the residence of Albert Krassner. A pebbled driveway traversed an acre of lawn extending like a green velvet collar around a sumptuous grey stone mansion.

"I'll say he's rich," Frank commented. "This place must be worth a small fortune."

As the car approached, an ornamental carriage lamp was turned on, casting a pleasant yellow light over a broad band of marble stairs leading to the front door.

Joe parked and they mounted the steps. Frank pushed a button set in the masonry beside the glass-and-wrought-iron door. When chimes sounded inside, a maid in a dark dress and starched white apron answered.

"You're the Hardy boys?"

"Yes, we are," Frank replied.

"Wait a moment, please. I'll see if Mr Krassner is ready to receive you." She led them into a centre hall, then mounted a broad stairway.

Frank and Joe looked around. Suddenly Joe whispered, "Frank! Come over here!"

On a table near the door was an Oriental vase. Frank moved closer. "The serpent design! It's almost like the one on that balloon!"

"Very similar."

Then something else caught Frank's eye. He went to

30

examine a beautiful trophy cup. "Here's something interesting, Joe. Mr Krassner is a chess champion!"

The inscription stated that the cup had been awarded for the regional chess title.

Just then the maid came down. "Mr Krassner will see you now," she said.

She led the boys upstairs and ushered them into the largest bedroom they had ever seen. One side was completely lined with mirrors, reflecting the beautifully appointed interior. At the far side was an immense canopied bed and on it, propped up with large pillows, lay Albert Krassner. He beckoned Frank and Joe to his side.

"First of all," he said, "I want to thank you for helping me when I had that seizure."

"Are you better now?" asked Frank.

"Oh yes. I just wanted to take it easy for a couple of days. The old ticker gives me trouble now and then, but I can afford to have the best doctors."

"You are fortunate," Joe said.

"In that respect, yes. But money isn't everything. Learn that while you're young."

"That's the way we feel, sir," Frank said. "Personally, we prefer mysteries and adventures."

"That's what I wanted to talk to you about," Krassner said. "What's happening to me is a frightful, dark mystery. I need your help!"

Frank tried to ease Krassner's obvious tension and chuckled. "Speaking of frightful things, Mr Krassner, we sure had an odd experience on the way over here."

"That's right," Joe added. "A crazy-looking balloon with a fantastic snake design flew over our heads like a hissing serpent."

"What? You saw it, too?" Krassner's face turned ghastly white against the pillow.

"Are you having another attack?" Frank asked, worried.

The man did not reply. Instead he pressed a small buzzer half concealed beneath the sheet and the maid appeared like a genie.

"Please see the boys out," Krassner murmured. "I don't think I can take any more conversation tonight."

"I'm sorry if we upset you, sir," Joe said.

"No, no. It wasn't you. See you later."

The man waved a pudgy hand and the Hardys were escorted to the front door. When it clicked shut behind them, they were silent for a moment.

Then Joe said, "I don't get it. Every time he wants to tell us what bothers him, he becomes so upset that he can't."

"He must have seen that balloon, too, and for some reason it scared him. I wonder why," Frank mused.

"By the way, is he married? Did Chet ever mention it?"

"No. All he said is that Krassner's rich. And he wasn't kidding."

A crescent moon hung low in the dark sky as the Hardys went to their car. Joe drove to the main road and they hummed along towards Bayport. Suddenly Frank said, "There's that noise again!"

Joe took his foot off the accelerator and listened. They glanced up, but could see no balloon. The sound was coming from the back of their car!

Joe stopped quickly and they hopped out. "Look," Frank said, pointing to the exhaust. Fire was shooting from it, accompanied by a hissing sound.

"Turn the engine off, Joe!"

But before Joe could move—*blam!* An explosion rocked the car and pieces of metal clattered to the roadway.

"What the dickens happened?" Joe blurted out.

"Get the flashlight and you'll see," Frank said.

They slid underneath the car and assessed the damage. The blast had ripped open the exhaust and the silencer.

"They're blown apart," Frank said. "Somebody put a charge into the exhaust!"

The boys picked up some of the metal debris and tossed it into the boot.

"Who could have done it?" Joe asked. "Do you suppose Krassner was involved?"

"It's possible," Frank said. "Or maybe Jervis or his buddies were following us."

"How about the serpent balloon people? They didn't seem too fond of us, either."

"Well," Frank said, "speculation will get us nowhere right now. Let's see if this heap will go."

The engine started up, but the racket it made was fierce.

"It sounds like a machine gun," Joe quipped. "Hop in, Frank. The sooner we get home the better."

The Hardys drove on through the night, hoping to reach Bayport without further incident. Going through the village of Allendale, Joe slowed down in an effort to mute the exhaust.

"Hope we don't wake up everybody," he said as the car picked up speed once more.

Two miles farther on, a siren sounded behind them. Joe glanced into the rear-view mirror to see the revolving roof light of a police car.

"Frank, here comes trouble." He pulled to the side of the road, stopped, and got out.

An officer, hardly older than the Hardys, emerged from the squad car.

Frank and Joe walked up to him. "Is there something wrong, Officer?" Frank asked.

The policeman looked grim. "What were you trying to do?" he said. "Wake up the whole town? You drove through it like gangbusters."

"Oh," Frank said, "we're sorry about the noise. Had trouble with the silencer. In fact, it blew apart. We're heading for Bayport for repairs."

"Don't you know it's against the law, riding without a silencer?"

"We know," Joe said. "But the accident happened only a little while ago. We'll stop at the next garage."

"They're all closed," the policeman said.

"Well, what do you want us to do?"

"I'm taking you to headquarters."

"Officer," Frank said, "we're not lying to you. The silencer blew apart just down the road!"

"Where's your driver's licence?"

Joe handed it to him and the policeman studied it. "Hardy," he said. "The name sounds familiar."

"Our father is Fenton Hardy, the detective," Frank explained.

"That cuts no ice with me. You think that entitles you to privileges?"

"We don't want any privileges. Just give us a break so we can get this silencer fixed."

"Tell it to the magistrate," came the unyielding reply. "And now get in that bomb and follow me!"

Disgusted, the boys returned to their car and drove after the policeman to Allendale. He pulled up in front of an old house which had been converted into head-quarters.

Inside, a small light illuminated the sparse office. The officer motioned for the Hardys to sit down, then made a phone call. Ten minutes later an elderly man arrived.

He was wearing pyjamas under a light coat and looked suspiciously at Frank and Joe. "What's up?" he demanded.

"The charge is disturbing the peace while driving without a silencer," the officer said. To the Hardys he explained, "This is the magistrate."

Without listening to the boys' side of the story, the man declared, "Fine is twenty-five dollars."

"But we don't have that much with us," Frank said.

"Then we'll have to lock you up. Besides, you can't drive that car. It's got to be towed away!"

·5·
Cat Trap

JOE was visibly frustrated. He started to reply, but Frank realized that saying the wrong thing would make matters even worse.

"Cool it," he whispered to his brother. Then he turned to the magistrate. "Don't you think this is a bit much, sir? We haven't got the money to pay the fine and on top of that we can't even drive the car. What do you suggest we do?"

"That's your problem," the judge replied with a curt wave of the hand. "The law's the law. You stay here till that fine is paid." With that he walked out the door.

"Being such a small town," the officer said, "we just have one cell. Get the money up or in you go!"

"May I use the telephone?" Frank asked.

"Sure. Calling your lawyer?" the policeman asked.

"Of course not. I'm going to talk to my father."

Aunt Gertrude answered, and to Frank's dismay told him that Mr Hardy was not home yet. But she detected the frustration in her nephew's tense question.

"Are you in trouble?" she asked, then answered her own question, "Yes, you're in trouble. I can tell by your voice. Laura, get on the extension. The boys are in trouble!"

36

Frank heard a click, then his mother said, "What's the matter, Frank?"

"We've been arrested."

Both women gasped. "What for?" Mrs Hardy asked.

"The silencer broke. The car makes an awful racket and the law says you can't drive like that."

Frank explained where they were and his mother said. "That's a shame. It would only be a short drive home."

"Makes no difference in this place," Frank said quietly. "We need twenty-five dollars to pay the fine and we'll have to get the car towed."

Joe gave his brother a nudge. "Ask Mother to get in touch with Tony Prito. He can pick up the money and rescue us with his father's truck."

Frank nodded and passed on the information.

"I'll call Tony right away," Mrs Hardy promised.

The policeman allowed the boys to sit in the office while they were waiting. An hour later a half-ton truck stopped in front of the building. Out stepped Tony Prito, a handsome boy with black curly hair, whose father owned a construction company.

"Are we glad to see you!" Joe greeted him. "This hasn't been our day!"

"Always call Prito for immediate service," Tony quipped. He handed Frank the money to pay the fine. Then the boys went out, put a tow-line from the truck to the car, and drove back to Bayport.

When they arrived at the Hardy house, Tony said, "Biff and I will help you make the repairs tomorrow, okay?"

"Thanks," Joe said. "We'll go down to the garage first thing in the morning and get the parts."

Mr Hardy had come home half an hour earlier and listened while his sons told about the weird balloon, the strange visit to Krassner, and the explosive charge in their exhaust.

"Krassner sounds like a man in trouble," Mr Hardy said. "Did he give any inkling of what's bothering him?"

"Nothing, Dad," Frank replied.

"Well, boys, it's after midnight. Let's hit the sack and talk about this tomorrow."

The next morning after breakfast Frank and Joe went to a garage and returned with the necessary parts to repair their car.

Biff and Tony were already waiting with a couple of heavy-duty jacks, and soon they were busy at work underneath the automobile.

At lunchtime Mrs Hardy brought out sandwiches. The boys got cleaned up and took a half-hour break, then continued with their installation. By one o'clock they had still not finished.

Joe said, "Frank, why don't you go over to the Snyders', and I'll stay here until the job's done?"

"Good idea," Frank agreed. He washed the grease from his hands, took a shower, and put on clean clothes. He entered the Snyders' house shortly before the salesman was scheduled to arrive.

"I found a good place for you to hide," Mrs Snyder said. "Near the entrance of the living room is a closet with sliding doors. Get in there and peek out when the man comes."

"Thank you," Frank said. "That's just perfect."

The bell rang. "Get inside, hurry!" the woman said and went to answer it.

Frank hid in the closet and closed the doors, leaving only a small crack through which he could observe the living room.

Mrs Snyder walked in with a stocky man. He had a large black moustache and a beard, and introduced himself as Mr Horgan.

Mrs Snyder beckoned him to sit down on the sofa. He did, putting a sample case on the floor. Then he opened the bag and revealed a large selection of costume jewellery.

"Here are your earrings, ma'am," he said. "A present from Associated Jewellers."

Mrs Snyder accepted the gift graciously and put them on.

"They're lovely," Horgan said, beaming. "Now look at these other things, ma'am."

The woman examined the baubles which Horgan showed her. She tried on a necklace, held brooch after brooch to her dress to study the effect, and slipped several rings on to her fingers.

Horgan looked up nervously once in a while. Then he stood up and walked to the window.

"Are you expecting someone?" Mrs Snyder asked.

"No, no. It's just not my nature to sit still." Horgan smiled. "Now which of these beautiful pieces of jewellery would you like to buy?"

At this point Frank became aware of something he had not noticed before. He felt a slight movement in the darkness and reached out. The tail of a cat gently brushed past his leg!

"Good grief!" Frank thought. "Another one. They're even in the closet."

The animal wanted to get out and began scratching

39

on the door. Frank picked up the cat, hoping to keep it quiet, while Horgan went on with his sales spiel.

He would give Mrs Snyder a lovely brooch if she would allow a friend to fit Mr Snyder for a Hong Kong custom-tailored suit.

"You see, ma'am, the cost of labour in Hong Kong is very cheap and the tailors are excellent. My friend can take your husband's measurements, airmail them to Hong Kong, and deliver the suit in about four weeks."

"I'll have to ask Ralph about it," Mrs Snyder said. "Wait a moment. I'll be right back."

When she left the room, Horgan walked to the window again and looked out with a nervous expression.

Frank's mind whirled. "Associated Jewellers must have taken on a new line—Hong Kong suits," he thought. "I wonder if it's legitimate. Maybe it has something to do with that tailoring racket Dad's working on." He felt a tickle in his nose and suppressed a sneeze.

He still held the cat, but now it strained to get free, meowing loudly. Horgan cocked his head to listen.

Frank muffled another sneeze. Suddenly he knew why. The cat's fur! He must be allergic to it.

Horgan turned and stared at the closet. The cat, meanwhile, clawed Frank's arm and yowled. He had to sneeze again. His eyes began to water, and he felt as if he were choking. "It's no use," he thought. "I need air." He opened the doors, sneezing loudly, and the cat flew out, landing in the middle of the living room.

The effect on Horgan was electric. His eyes bulged wide and his jaw dropped open. When he realized he was being spied on, the salesman let out an oath and dashed out of the house!

·6·

A Risky Chance

FRANK watched the man jump into his car and speed away as Mrs Snyder came back into the living room.

"What happened?" she asked. "Why did Mr Horgan run off like that? And he left his case!"

Frank quickly explained and showed Mrs Snyder the scratches on his arm.

"Did Princess do that? Oh dear! I'll get some antiseptic." She returned a few minutes later and daubed Frank's arm.

"What are you going to do with that sample case?" she asked.

"Use it for evidence," Frank replied. "Maybe we can identify that salesman through his fingerprints. I'm sure Horgan uses an alias."

Frank took out his handkerchief and clicked the case shut. "If he comes back for it, tell him it's being delivered to Associated Jewellers. And thanks for your help, Mrs Snyder."

When he arrived home, the repair work on the car was done and Biff and Tony had left. Frank went up to their father's comfortable study, where he found the detective talking to Joe.

"Dad, tell Frank what you found out," Joe urged.

Mr Hardy sat back in his swivel chair and smiled. "The Hong Kong tailoring racket I'm supposed to crack is tied in with various jewellery sales operations. When the jewellery business slacks off, they offer to have their customers measured for a suit.

"After they receive the down payment, the clothing is never delivered. By the time the customers catch on, the swindlers have skipped town."

"What are you grinning at?" Joe asked his brother.

"I found out the same thing."

"At the Snyders'?"

"Right. And here's the sample case of an Associated Jewellers salesman."

"That ought to be a real good clue," Mr Hardy said. "You didn't disturb the fingerprints, I hope."

"No. I was careful about that," Frank replied.

Joe went for their fingerprint kit and set to work dusting the black plastic covering of the sample case. Horgan had provided them with a neat set of prints of both his left and right hands.

"We'll take these down to headquarters. Maybe Chief Collig can find out whether Horgan really is who he says."

"What I don't understand," Frank said, "is why Smith and Jones, who are obviously connected with Associated Jewellers, wanted to bug Greene's phone. I mean, that's out of their line."

"We assumed that they worked for Jervis because he acted so strange when we mentioned their names," Joe said. "Maybe we were wrong."

"But they also wanted to meet Radley at the Treat Hotel, where Associated Jewellers had a sales meeting," Frank said. "It's just too much coincidence."

"And Krassner's an enigma, too," Mr Hardy added. "You said he was a chess player himself. Maybe there's a connection between him and Greene."

Joe sighed. "And where do those crazy balloonists come in? And who blew up our exhaust?"

"Questions and no answers," Frank said. "What do we do next?"

"Take the fingerprints to the police first thing in the morning," the detective said. "And keep Associated Jewellers under surveillance."

"There's a vacant building right across the street," Joe said. "Maybe we could use that to spy on them."

"By the way, Dad, did you warn Conrad Greene about the bug?" Frank asked.

"I tried but no one's home yet."

Just then the doorbell rang. It was Chet. "I have some good news," he said brightly.

"No kidding," Frank said. "Did you get your balloonist's licence?"

"No, not yet. But Mr Krassner feels better and wants to see you."

"When and where?" Joe asked.

"Tomorrow afternoon at the clubhouse. Can you make it?"

"Sure. We'll be there."

The next morning the Hardys took the fingerprints to Chief Collig. He was a heavy-set, slow-talking man, who had co-operated with the Hardys on many cases.

When Frank and Joe told their story, he congratulated them on their detective work. "We'll take the sample case to Associated Jewellers to see Jervis's reaction," Frank said. "Is that okay with you, Chief?"

"Sure. If the prints tell us anything, I'll let you know."

When they arrived at Jervis's office, the receptionist told them that her boss was out.

"Well, we have something that belongs to him," Frank said. "When will he be back?"

"Wait a moment," she said and walked out of the room. A few seconds later she returned. "He's in now," she said.

The boys entered the office and laid the sample case on the man's desk. "We thought you'd like to have this back," Frank said. "It must be valuable."

Jervis opened the kit. "This doesn't belong to us," he said.

"Mr Horgan, who used it, claimed to be a representative of Associated Jewellers," Joe said.

Jervis remained cool. "We have been bothered by impostors lately," he said. "Trying to use our good name."

"And you don't try to sell Hong Kong tailored suits, either?" Frank said.

Jervis's mouth twitched a little. "Of course not. And now, get lost. I'm busy!"

As the boys walked out they could hear him grab the telephone off the cradle.

"Somebody's going to catch it!" Joe said with a grin.

"*Tsk, tsk*. Poor old Horgan," Frank said in mock sympathy as they drove home.

During lunch Chief Collig phoned. "Horgan is an alias," he reported. "The man's real name is Gerard Henry. He has a long record of petty crime."

"I had a hunch he wasn't on the level," Frank said, and told about their visit to Jervis. "We'd like to stake out his place," he concluded. "There's an old building across the street where we could set up some cameras."

44

"Just be careful," the chief warned. "The place is unsafe. Also, we flush out vagrants now and then. Mostly junkies. They stay there at night."

"We'll watch out," Frank promised. "Thanks for your help, Chief."

The boys told their father the latest news and that they were planning to set up surveillance equipment.

"We'd like to start right away," Frank said, "but we have an appointment with Krassner this afternoon."

"I can't pitch in, either," Mr Hardy said. "I have a meeting. But maybe Sam Radley could help us out."

A telephone call brought the detective's sandy-haired operative to the Hardy home. He agreed to begin surveillance immediately.

Frank and Joe loaded film into a movie camera and a still camera with a telescopic lens. They also brought a two-way radio and a folding chair and drove off with Sam.

They parked on a street behind the old building and worked their way through an alley to the rear entrance.

"This place certainly is in bad shape," Sam commented as they entered a broken door leading to a flight of badly tilted stairs.

"It even smells rotten," Joe said, sniffing the musty odour of the interior.

They climbed to the second floor and saw no sign of habitation. Sam checked all the windows until he found a suitable spot. "How about right here?" he suggested.

The boys set up the cameras on tripods and focused clearly on the entrance to the Associated Jewellers office.

"If anyone goes in or leaves, take his picture," Frank said. "We'll join you later.'

"Okay." Radley adjusted the folding chair and waved to the boys as they made their way downstairs and out the back.

When the young sleuths arrived at the balloon club, Krassner and Chet were already there.

"Frank, Joe, I'm glad you came," Krassner greeted them.

"You're looking great today," Frank said.

"That's the way it is. These attacks knock me out for a couple of days, but I bounce right back."

"We thought that snake balloon got you upset," Joe said.

Krassner smiled. "Oh no. That was nothing."

Frank said, "We noticed a similarity in the balloon design and the serpent figure on your vase."

"You mean the one in the hall?"

"That's the one."

"Oh yes. Antique Chinese. They used that pattern a lot. Well, Fearless is going to inflate his father's balloon. Chet, why don't you see if he needs help?"

"Sure thing," Chet replied, and hurried out to the grassy clearing.

Turning to the Hardys, Krassner said, "I want to talk to you alone about my problem. And I don't want to go to the police. Once the newspapers get wind of a thing like this, there's a lot of publicity, even notoriety. And in the investment business—well, you know how it is."

"Just what is the trouble?" Frank asked.

"My life has been threatened," Krassner said. "I'll be killed unless I hand over the Ruby King!"

·7·

Aerial Surprise

"THE Ruby King? What's that?" Frank asked.

"A fabulous chess piece," Krassner replied. "A beautiful work of art made centuries ago in China. It is decorated with Burmese rubies and was part of a set made for an ancient warlord."

"Where are the other pieces?" Joe asked.

"Gone. Vanished in the mists of antiquity," Krassner said poetically. "That's one of the reasons why the Ruby King is so valuable."

"And you're in possession of it?" Frank queried.

"Yes. But it's not really mine." Krassner explained that he was part of a consortium of wealthy chess enthusiasts who had purchased it in China.

"We're going to present it to the winner of the world chess championship. Meanwhile, the prize is in my safe."

Frank and Joe knew about the match, which was to take place in Hong Kong the following month. It would pit the United States champion, Conrad Greene, against the Oriental title holder, a Korean named Chan Loo Duc.

Was there a connection between the valuable Ruby King and the intended wiretap on Greene's telephone?

Obviously someone wanted the chess piece badly.

"Isn't your safe a rather vulnerable place?" Frank asked. "I think a bank vault would be better."

"My safe is very strong," Krassner replied. "Now I want you to keep our conversation in confidence. The whereabouts of the Ruby King is known only to a few people."

"Whoever threatened you must have found out," Joe said.

"That's what worries me. I want both of you to be on call in case of emergency."

Frank felt an uneasy suspicion about the man. Why would a rich banker ask the Hardys to shield him when he could well afford to hire an entire protection service? He put the question to Krassner.

"I'll tell you why," Krassner replied. "Life would be unbearable with an army of bodyguards. The press would be on my back with all kinds of speculations and innuendos." He stopped and smiled. "Besides, Chet Morton tells me you have never failed to carry out your assignments to the fullest satisfaction of your clients."

"You flatter us," Joe said with an embarrassed grin. "We'll do all we can to help you."

"But first," Frank added, "we'd like to see the Ruby King."

"Yes, I'll have you over the house soon. Here comes Chet."

The husky boy strode purposefully over to the three. "How about some ballooning today, Mr Krassner?" he asked.

"That was my plan."

"Great. You can take Frank and Joe, and I'll go with Fearless."

"That'll be great," Joe said.

"You've never been up before?" Krassner asked.

"Only in aeroplanes," Frank replied. Both Hardys were experienced pilots and often flew a plane which their father kept at Bayport Airport.

"I'm sure you'll like this kind of flying," Krassner said. "Come on. Let's get ready."

Everybody helped with the preparations. Krassner telephoned for two trucks while the boys inflated the envelopes. People from the surrounding farms gathered to watch the spectacle of a twin ascension.

"They can hold the ground ropes for us," Fearless said. "It's a great sport."

Between bursts of hot air from the burners, the boys discussed ballooning. Chet proved to be a competent historian on the sport. He said two Frenchmen, the Montgolfier brothers, made the balloon used in the first recorded human flight over Paris. The year was 1783.

"Aeronauts have had plenty of adventures since then," Chet said. "Did you know that Napoleon used balloons to spy on the enemy? They were popular in the Civil War, too. And then there was a guy named Andrée who tried to fly over the North Pole in a giant balloon."

"Did he make it?" Joe asked.

Chet shook his head sadly. "I'm afraid not."

"All right, men," Krassner called out. "We're nearly ready." He and Fearless checked their radios and altimeters. The pyrometers, which measured the heat in the bags, were in working order. So were the variometers, needed to tell the rate of climb.

Just then the two trucks arrived. The crowd cheered as the five stepped into the baskets. They held on tightly to the ground ropes until Fearless bellowed, "Hands off!"

Up went the two craft in perfect weather conditions. There was hardly any wind and a clear blue sky. The huge licence numbers on the rounded sides stood out brightly in the late-afternoon sunshine.

Standing beside Krassner, Frank felt an exhilaration unlike anything he had experienced in an aeroplane. As the ground fell away beneath them in silence, the boy was engulfed in an unreal feeling of total peace.

Below, the waving spectators grew smaller, and the trucks set off on the road, as a gentle fluff of wind sent the balloons on their way.

Krassner and the Hardys watched the other craft behind them as they drifted higher and higher. A farm slid past below them and three dogs looked up and barked furiously. Frank was surprised he could hear them so far off.

"Enjoying yourself?" Krassner asked. He picked up binoculars and scanned the countryside.

"I never had such a good time in my life!" Joe said enthusiastically. "Thanks a million for the ride."

"Don't mention it." Krassner's face looked serene. "Ballooning takes you away from all the world's troubles."

But the flight did not lull Frank's mind. It kept working to find the missing links in the puzzle. Was the Ruby King contraband—perhaps stolen in China? Was that the reason Krassner had shunned the police?

As they sailed on silently, the Hardys studied the uninhabited woodland carefully. It was not at all like the view from a fast-flying aeroplane. Suddenly Frank heard the radio crackle:

"Frank, this is Chet. Do you read me?"

"Roger. What a swell ride!"

"Listen. There's another balloon."

"Where?"

"At three o'clock."

Frank turned around. "I see it."

"Look close," Chet advised, and Frank asked Krassner for the glasses. He trained them on the third craft. *It was the serpent balloon!*

Frank told Krassner, and his face again showed tension and fear.

Chet's voice sounded once more. "Keep an eye on the snake. It's armed!"

Frank focused the binoculars on the other gondola. Three men were in it and one had a rifle. There was a muzzle flash, then a bullet whistled over them.

"They're firing at us!" Krassner screamed.

"Duck!" Joe ordered, "and let's land as fast as possible!"

Frank radioed to Chet, "We're descending. Better come with us."

"Roger."

Krassner had regained his composure, and Frank admired his airmanship. The man pulled open the vent and the craft sank rapidly. Three more shots sounded in the distance, but Krassner's fast-moving balloon made a difficult target. However, two slugs ripped through the balloon.

The wind freshened and the sinking balloon picked up speed. Frank saw that Krassner was heading for a small farm at the edge of the woods. There was a level, cleared area bordered on one side by a pond, on the other by an electric power line.

Fearless and Chet were close behind, but the serpent balloon made no attempt to follow them down. As their attackers flew out of sight, Frank talked to Chet again.

"Did you get a look at the snake's licence number?"

"Affirmative. But Fearless says it's a phony. And listen to this. The snake has a little propeller, probably battery driven. That's how it caught up with us."

"The police should be notified."

"I've already done that," Chet said. "Called the trucks and told them to phone the State Police."

"Good thinking. We're landing now. See you later."

Krassner manoeuvered the craft towards the middle of the field while the farm children ran out of the house to witness the descent. The electric wires seemed a safe distance to their left and the pond far enough to the right.

"You're a great pilot, Mr Krassner," Joe said tersely.

"We're not down yet—oh, oh, trouble!"

An errant gust hit the balloon, carrying it towards the power lines. Frank and Joe were gripped by a sickening feeling as the metal wires loomed ominously closer.

"The blast valve!" Krassner shouted. "It's over your head, Joe. Pull it!"

Joe reached up and grasped the lever, sending hissing flame into the envelope. Nothing happened.

"It's not working!" Frank cried out.

"It will in time," Krassner said. "At least I hope so!"

Several seconds passed, then all at once the balloon lifted. The gondola cleared the power lines with two feet to spare!

Krassner looked limp and Frank sighed with relief. Joe shook his head. "We almost got fried!" he said.

The balloon dropped down once more and landed beside the farmhouse.

In their excitement the Hardys had paid no attention to how Fearless and Chet were fairing. Now they jumped out of the basket, with Krassner on their heels, and ran to avoid the collapsing envelope.

Only then did they notice the other balloon. It was descending rapidly over the pond.

Splash!

Chet and Fearless hit the water like home-coming astronauts!

·8·

A Tough Break

FRANK and Joe raced towards the pond, followed by a
farm boy and his two sisters. When they reached the
water's edge, Fearless was splashing towards shore.

"Where's Chet?" Frank yelled.

Fearless glanced back, reversed his course, and
swam furiously to the spot where the basket had sunk.
The Hardys dived in at the same time and with powerful crawl strokes reached it seconds later. They gulped
in deep breaths of air and aimed for the bottom.

Meanwhile the three youngsters ran for their rowing
boat which was tied to a small dock.

"Jenny, Wendy," the boy shouted, "if we get the
balloon out, maybe we can keep it!"

"Don't be silly, Kurt," the elder girl said as they
pushed the boat into the pond. "Come on, Wendy,
we'll row."

In the clear water, Frank and Joe saw Fearless trying
to free Chet's foot which had become entangled in the
coil of rope lashed to the side of the gondola. Frank
helped give a final tug, and Chet, nearly unconscious,
was whisked to the surface.

He was quickly towed ashore and pulled up on to the
grass, where he lay gasping.

"You took in a lot of water," Frank said. "Just lie still for a while."

In the confusion of the rescue, no one had paid any attention to Krassner. Suddenly they heard a feeble call. "A pill! Give me a pill!"

Joe ran to the man, who was lying helpless on his back and quickly gave him the medicine. Minutes later Krassner sat up shakily. "Someone's out to get me!" he moaned. "My heart can't take this terror much longer!"

"Don't worry, Mr Krassner," Joe said. "We'll get to the bottom of this whole thing yet."

While the farm children were busy retrieving the sunken gondola and the deflated envelope, the balloonists talked about their scary adventure. Joe was of the opinion that the serpent gang was only out to frighten Krassner.

"With a telescopic sight they couldn't have missed," he reasoned. "Besides, they didn't bother to pursue us any farther when we descended."

"You may be right," Frank said.

Krassner turned the situation into a feeble jest. "Well, if they tried to scare me, they certainly succeeded."

"But why, Mr Krassner?" Fearless asked. "What do these men have against you?"

Krassner avoided answering the question, and the boys busied themselves with the balloons. First they folded up Krassner's craft, then set about to help Jenny, Wendy, and Kurt drag the other one up on to the shore.

"I haven't seen your mum and dad," Joe said.

"They're in town with the truck," Kurt said. "Wow,

wait till they hear what happened. Are finders keepers?" he added mischievously.

"Hey, this is no toy!" Fearless chuckled. "But for a reward, how would you like a ride some time next week?"

"Oh, that'd be great!" Wendy's eyes sparkled.

"Look, here come the State Police," Jenny declared.

Two squad cars drove right up to the pond, and a pair of uniformed officers plied the balloonists with questions about the mid-air assault. During the interrogation, the farm children said they had noticed the weird serpent balloon about four or five times in the past month.

But no one could shed any light on its owners, or why they had shot at Krassner. The man himself made no mention of the Ruby King.

A few minutes later the trucks appeared and the equipment was loaded. It was dusk when they reached the balloon club, where the gear was stowed away.

"So long, everybody," Joe said as he and Frank went to their car.

"I'm going to your house first," Chet said. "I want to be in on the discussion with your dad."

"You ought to go home and hit the sack," Joe advised. "You've had quite a day."

"No, really, I feel fine now. I'll phone my folks so they won't worry."

Chet followed the Hardys to their house. When the two cars pulled into the driveway, Mrs Hardy and Aunt Gertrude ran out to meet them.

"You had us worried to death!" Mrs Hardy said. "We heard a radio report that several balloonists had an aerial war!"

"You were in it— yes you were!" Aunt Gertrude stared at them piercingly, then shook a skinny finger. "Now tell us all about it!"

"I guess the State Police released the news," Frank said and reported what happened. "Where's Dad?" he added.

"Out looking for you," Laura Hardy replied.

"Did he talk to Sam over the radio before he left?"

"Yes. It seems Sam had some success in his surveillance."

"Let's get in touch with him right away," Joe said.

They used the set in their car and called Radley. There was no reply. They tried again. Nothing!

"Either his set's out of order or something's happened," Frank declared.

Chet, meanwhile, had wandered into the house looking for food. Aunt Gertrude, who had anticipated their need for sustenance, had ham sandwiches ready for them. Chet phoned home, then called out, "Come on, fellows. Let's eat!"

"Forget it," Joe replied. "Something might be wrong at our surveillance post. We're going over there right away."

"Wait for me!" Chet grabbed a fistful of sandwiches and wriggled into the back seat.

The three boys ate on the way. When they reached the street behind the old building, Frank turned off the lights and they crept cautiously towards the alley leading to the back entrance.

Armed with flashlights, which they used only sparingly, they ascended the crooked, creaking stairs. The rotting rooms smelled damp and unpleasant. All was quiet.

On the third floor Frank's light flashed into the room where Radley was stationed.

The boys gasped. Sam lay unconscious on the floor, a deep gash on the side of his head.

Chet said, "I think he's dead!"

"He's breathing," Frank assured his pal. As the Hardys administered first aid, Frank noticed that blood had congealed around the wound.

"Joe, this must have happened a while ago," he said and ripped off a piece of his shirt. He tore it into strips and fashioned a bandage. As he applied it, Radley moaned and his eyelids fluttered.

"He's coming to," Joe said.

They helped the man gingerly to his feet and Frank said, "Chet, grab my flashlight and round up the equipment while we take Sam back to the car."

"Will you be back?"

"Sure. You can't carry it all yourself."

Chet listened to their creaky footsteps fade away on the stairs. Then he shone the light around the room looking for the cameras.

"Holy crow!" he murmured. "I can't see them anywhere. They've probably been stolen."

He got down on his hands and knees and felt about the wooden floor until he came to an old door. It had been broken down and lay propped against the wall in one corner. Chet lifted it. Underneath was the still camera, its long lens sticking out like a telescope!

"Sam must have had enough time to hide it," he thought as he picked it up. Then he froze. Were those voices drifting up from below?

He did not move a muscle, hardly daring to breathe. Now he could hear voices distinctly. They were not

Frank's and Joe's. There were quiet whispers, interspersed with oaths!

Then everything was silent for a while, until footsteps sounded again. "The Hardys must be coming back!" Chet thought.

All at once angry shouts filled the old house, punctuated by scuffling and banging.

Chet grabbed the camera and raced downstairs. On the second floor landing he found Frank and Joe dazed and sprawled out on the dirty floor.

The Hardys pulled themselves to their feet slowly. "What a blitz!" Frank murmured, rubbing his head.

"How many of them?" Chet asked.

"Four dirty tramps."

Joe grasped his jaw and moved it from side to side. "Nothing broken, I guess," he said. Then he felt in his pockets. "But my wallet's missing. And so's my watch!"

"Mine, too," Frank said. "Those rats. Probably the ones who conked Radley."

"I found one camera under a door," Chet said. "But the movie equipment's gone." He handed the instrument to Frank.

Frank and Joe decided there was no point in chasing the hoodlums in the darkness. They had too much of a head start. The three boys walked down the rickety stairs to go home. Suddenly an ominous rumble filled the old building. The next moment plaster began falling on their heads. One wall of the stairway was moving inward!

"Run, fellows!" Chet yelled and braced himself against the wall. "I'll hold this till you're out!"

The Hardys dashed down to the rear entrance. Then

Chet took his shoulders from the wall and ran. But he did not have enough time. Wood and plaster filled the stairway.

Frank and Joe turned in horror to see their friend imprisoned in the debris! Only his head showed above the rubble!

The dust and dirt made Chet cough, but he managed to shout, "Help! I'm stuck!"

"Hold on. We'll get you out," Joe cried out.

They clawed at the debris but could make little headway. They needed assistance! While Joe stayed with Chet, Frank raced to the car. On the way to the nearest alarm box, about two blocks down the road, he told Radley what had happened.

"I'll call the police, then drop you off at the hospital," Frank said. "How do you feel now?"

"Not too hot," Radley said weakly.

"By the way, the movie camera's gone. The other one was under a door."

"I hid it there."

"Did you take any photos?"

"Quite a few. Hope they're the ones you want."

Minutes later sirens screamed as Chief Collig and the fire department rushed to the dilapidated building. The men carefully worked their way through the rubble.

Frank returned half an hour later. He and Joe helped under the direction of the fire chief. Huge lights illuminated the area.

"It's touch and go," the official said. "One false move and the whole building could come tumbling down."

Chet's good humour began to abate as the work went on painstakingly slowly.

"I've got an awful pain in my arm," he said. "Maybe it's broken. Frank, better call my parents."

Half an hour later Mr and Mrs Morton arrived with Iola, Chet's sister. She was a pretty dark-haired girl who often dated Joe. At the same time, reporters and photographers rushed to the scene where firemen were shoring up the sagging walls with stout beams. Others picked away at the pile of wood, bricks, and plaster.

The Hardys were questioned about the accident. Why were they in the building? Didn't they realize the danger? How did they manage to escape unhurt?

Frank and Joe tried to avoid direct answers, knowing anything they said might tip off their enemies. Joe did, however, tell about Chet's heroic action.

An onlooker, who knew the Hardys, said, "You must be on some detective work. Was it a surveillance?"

"We'd rather not talk about it now," Frank replied. He turned to his brother. "Look, Dad just arrived!"

Mr Hardy came directly to his sons, who briefed him on the frustrating events. Meanwhile, Chet's spirits had been lifted greatly by the appearance of his family, though he looked pale and wan.

It was long after midnight when the rescuers pulled him from his miserable prison. Two attendants arrived in an ambulance and verified Chet's suspicion about a broken arm. They applied a splint before lifting him into the ambulance, then whisked him off to Bayport Hospital.

His family followed and the Hardys hurried home. In their lab they developed the film expertly, then started to make prints.

"Hey, these are just great!" Frank said as Mr Hardy looked over his shoulder. Two persons, photographed entering and leaving the premises of Associated Jewellers, were indeed Smith and Jones!

"Now we know for sure they're all in it together," the detective said.

After a few hours' sleep and a quick breakfast Mr Hardy phoned the hospital and learned that Chet was in a satisfactory condition and Sam would be released about ten o'clock. Then he and his sons took the photographs to Chief Collig. They were compared with photographs of known criminals in the area, but to no avail.

"I'll send copies to the FBI in Washington," Collig said. "Maybe they can identify them."

Then the chief drove with the Hardys to Associated Jewellers. The area across the street had been roped off, while workmen razed the remainder of the structure.

The chief tried the door of the office building. It was locked. Frank and Joe went around to look into the windows. "Holy crow!" Frank exclaimed. "They've cleared out. The place is empty!"

The workmen were questioned but had seen nothing.

"Obviously our friends left through the back door," Frank declared.

"Well, Bayport is lucky to be rid of those scoundrels," Chief Collig said.

"But we still have to keep on their trail," Mr Hardy stated. "I'm sure they'll go to another city, probably even another state, and start all over again with their fraudulent business."

By the time the Hardys returned home, the *Bayport Times* had trumpeted the bravery of Chet Morton all over the front page. Pictures and stories described the disaster and hailed the Hardys' friend as the hero.

"He probably saved our lives," Frank commented.

"And he certainly didn't think about his own safety," Joe added. "Let's hope his arm gets better soon."

The boys notified the Motor Vehicle Bureau of the loss of their driver's licences and Aunt Gertrude drove them to the agency to get new ones.

Mr Hardy, meanwhile, called Conrad Greene and spoke to the chess champion's father. When his sons returned, the detective said, "The senior Greene was rather unfriendly and his son won't talk to anyone!"

"Maybe we'd better drive out there and see him personally," Frank said.

Joe nodded. "But first let's visit Chet in the hospital."

The Hardys were surprised to find Krassner sitting at their pal's bedside.

"Hi, Mr Krassner," Joe greeted him. "What do you think of our hero?"

"He's got plenty of guts," Krassner said admiringly.

"I've also got a cast on my arm that's heavy enough to sink a ship," Chet said. "Here, take a look at this!"

Just then two pretty young nurses entered the room. "Chester, we came to autograph your cast," one of them said.

"Oh sure. Right over here!"

While the girls were inscribing their names, Chet said, "What about the surveillance, fellows? Get any good shots?"

"I'll say so!" Joe replied. "Great close-ups of Smith and Jones!"

At that moment Frank happened to glance at Krassner. At the mention of Smith and Jones, a fearful expression came over his face!

·9·

A Gathering Storm

FRANK gave his brother a nudge. But Joe had already realized that he should not have talked about their case in front of Krassner.

The man's look of concern now turned into a subdued smile. "I'm glad to see Chet's coming along so well," he said, leaning forward to write his name on the plaster cast. Then he turned to the Hardys. "How about setting a date for visiting me, boys? You wanted to see the Ruby King."

"Sure," Frank said. "Is tomorrow okay with you?"

"That'll be fine. Late in the afternoon."

The young detectives said goodbye to their friend, waved to Krassner, then hastened down the hospital corridor. As they were climbing into their car, Frank said, "Krassner must know Smith and Jones. Did you see the look on his face when you mentioned their names?"

Joe nodded. "Sorry I didn't keep my mouth shut."

Frank shrugged. "He seemed to be frightened," he said. "I wonder why."

When they reached home, Fenton Hardy was waiting for them in his study.

"I think we've struck gold," he said. "The FBI has

records on Smith and Jones. Smith's real name is Peter Lee Fong. He comes from Hong Kong."

"And Jones?" Joe asked eagerly.

"He's Cyril Eggleby from Kowloon."

"That's near Hong Kong, isn't it?" asked Frank.

"Yes. Right across the harbour. These two are being sought for smuggling operations."

"Smuggling?" Frank looked amazed. "Seems we're on to a big-time racket."

"And a very disturbing one," Mr Hardy said. "Krassner is a well-known and trusted citizen. How he fits into the picture might prove very embarrassing to him."

"He sure fits in somewhere," Joe said, and mentioned their observation at the hospital.

Mr Hardy was thoughtful. "Let's review what we know so far. Krassner is afraid of Smith and Jones and has been shot at in the air. Were his attackers Smith and Jones? And why do those two want to bug Conrad Greene's phone? Maybe because he might win the Ruby King. Someone threatens Krassner's life unless he gives up the Ruby King—"

"So it stands to reason," Frank put in excitedly, "that Smith and Jones are Krassner's enemies who are after the chess piece!"

"Wow!" Joe said. "That *is* the logical conclusion. But what do Smith and Jones have to do with Associated Jewellers?"

Mr Hardy shrugged. "We don't know. And we're not sure if our deductions are correct. Let's think about our next step."

"I'd say we better see Conrad Greene," Frank said.

"What if he won't talk to us?" Joe asked.

"You've got to make him listen somehow," Mr Hardy said. "Also, I think a surveillance of the area where you saw the serpent balloon is in order."

"Aerial surveillance, Dad?"

"That would be fine. Maybe you can discover its home base. I have to go to New York for a few days. Perhaps I can find out more about Krassner from Wall Street friends while I'm there."

In the interest of speed, it was decided that Frank would go to Ocean Bluffs to see Conrad Greene while Joe would do the surveillance. Frank phoned Biff Hooper, inviting him to come along, and Joe contacted Tony Prito and asked him how he would like to do some flying.

"Sure, when?" Tony asked.

"Tomorrow."

"Something to do with your case?"

"Right. Aerial reconnaissance. I want to look for that serpent balloon."

"What about Frank?"

"He's busy on another angle."

"Okay," Tony said. "When do we meet, and where?"

"At the airport, about ten o'clock."

"I'll be there."

When Tony showed up at the airport the next morning, he found Joe busy reading weather conditions in the communications office.

"Good flying weather," Joe said. "There's a cold front due later this afternoon, but I don't think it'll bother us."

Outside, Tony squinted up at the clear blue sky. "We're going to have fun. I'm glad you asked me along."

"Listen, this is no joy ride," Joe reminded him. "We've got a lot of looking to do—but not at the scenery."

When they were airborne, Joe headed first to the area where he and Frank had seen the serpent balloon land at the old farmhouse.

There was no sign of the craft anywhere. "Now what, skipper?" asked Tony from the right-hand seat.

"We'll go to the spot where the shooting took place. Keep your eyes peeled on the ground."

The two scoured the area, but there was not a trace of the serpent balloon.

Joe crisscrossed back and forth, finally droning over the Morton farm. He flew low and dipped the wings.

"Look, Iola's running out of the house," Tony said.

"I think she knows the sound of our engine," Joe said with a grin as the girl waved up to them. Then he pulled back on the controls and the plane reached for more altitude.

"Hey, I see something!" Tony cried out suddenly.

Far in the distance a balloon-shaped object seemed to be rising up from the trees. Joe made a beeline for it. Coming closer, both boys started to laugh.

"It's a water tower." Joe chuckled. "Tony, you're a great detective."

They lapsed into serious silence once more. "Can't we get a little rest from all this?" Tony asked finally.

"Okay. I'll take her up high for a while."

The plane gained altitude as Joe flew through a gorgeous cloud which had begun to form in the west. In the brilliant sunshine he guided his craft deftly along the cloud's tumbled slopes, following the ridges, then dropping down to gaps in the fluffy walls.

"Boy, this sure is beautiful," Tony said.

Along the cloud edges, small puffed balls had broken away and Joe felt the wind nudging the plane even higher.

It was then that he noticed a warning sign. In the distance the cloud wall had become black.

"Tony, we'd better get out of here," he said.

"It does look like a storm," Tony agreed, "but it's a long way off."

"Not as far as you might think." Joe glanced down. The ground no longer stood out clearly as before. Long streaks of clouds had slid between the plane and the green woodland. "Oh, oh," he said. "We may be headed for trouble!"

The wind had become rather severe. Joe had to apply extra pressure on the stick and rudder to keep it in level flight. Finally he saw a long cloud canyon ahead of him. It looked like a deep, narrow valley and was what he needed to get down safely. He knew the landmarks well, having flown this area many times before.

Joe glanced at Tony, whose mouth now was set tensely. "Don't panic, we'll make it," he said and pulled on a knob.

Warm air flooded the carburettor system. "That's so we won't ice up," Joe explained. He slid the throttle control back and the roar of the engine became a throaty hum. Then he eased the stick forward and slightly to the left, at the same time applying pressure with his left foot to the rudder pedal.

The plane rolled into a wide curving spiral, dropped her nose, and sailed along in a controlled turn towards the earth.

As it rounded the corner of the cloud canyon, Joe

suddenly experienced a sick feeling in the pit of his stomach.

There was no way out! He was boxed in between two mighty thunderheads—giant cumulo-nimbus clouds with howling winds and forked spears of lightning!

"Tighten your seat belt, Tony."

The air heaved and rocked the plane. Joe had to hang on to the wheel with all his might to keep it from tearing from his grasp.

Then came a rattle of hail, followed by sheets of rain. It seemed as if they were flying under a waterfall.

"Joe, do you think we'll make it?" Tony asked.

"Start praying, old buddy."

The plane shuddered.

"Look!" Tony cried out. "The wings are coming off!"

·10·

A Strange Hope

WHILE Joe and Tony struggled for survival in the aerial maelstrom, Frank and Biff drove towards Ocean Bluffs. Halfway there, the same storm which had engulfed the Hardys' plane burst with sudden fury on Biff's car.

First there was a machine-gun rattle of hail, followed by a torrent of rain. The windshield wipers were of little use.

Biff pulled off to the side of the road for a few minutes. "I hope Joe and Tony got back before this storm," he said.

"I wouldn't worry," Frank said. "Joe's a careful pilot."

The thunder and lightning finally subsided and after ten minutes the downpour let up sufficiently for Biff to continue on.

Ocean Bluffs was a small community located on a rocky cove and got its name from cliffs which dropped off quite steeply towards the water. It might have been a popular recreation area if not for the narrow beach. At high tide it was barely more than five feet wide, stony and uneven.

The boys found the home of Conrad Greene close to the ocean, midway between a desolated road and the

70

cliffs. With some difficulty Biff negotiated the muddy driveway and pulled up in front of the house, a low ranch type which sat squat and indistinctive in the driving downpour.

"What an isolated place," Biff said. "It would give me the creeps to live here."

"I guess Conrad likes privacy," Frank said as they made their way over the soggy ground to the front door. There was no bell, so Frank rapped loudly. No answer!

The boy banged again.

"Maybe nobody's home," Biff suggested, turning up his collar to keep the rain from running down his neck.

They were about to leave when the door opened a crack. An elderly man stood behind it.

Frank smiled. "Are you Mr Greene, Senior?"

"Go away. I don't want to buy anything."

"We're not salesmen. I'm Frank Hardy, and this is my friend Biff Hooper. We'd like to talk to you."

"About what?"

"Look, Mr Greene, I can't explain while we're drowning. Please let us in!"

"Okay," the man replied grudgingly. "But I'm telling you, I've got nothing to talk about."

By this time Frank and Biff were dripping wet. At the end of a vestibule which led to a large living room, Greene said, "You can dry off, but then you've got to go."

He shuffled into the living room, with the boys following behind him.

"What I want to talk about concerns your son Conrad," said Frank.

"What about him?"

Just then a medium-sized thin man with jet-black

hair and a gaunt face appeared from a door on the opposite side of the room.

"Who are these people?" he demanded. "I told you not to let anybody in!"

"They're only going to dry off," the older man said.

"We'd like to talk to you, Mr Greene," Frank spoke up.

"And we don't want any autograph, either," Biff added, irked by the unfriendly treatment.

"Somebody wants to tap your telephone," Frank began. "Perhaps it's bugged already."

"What?" Conrad Greene now seemed willing to listen.

Frank told about Fenton Hardy's experience with Fong and Eggleby. "Of course my father wouldn't consider doing such a job," he said, "but someone else might not be so ethical."

Colour rose to Conrad Greene's pale face. "The Ruby King!" he muttered. "They don't want me to win it!"

"What was that?" Frank asked. "Did you say Ruby King?"

"Forget it," Conrad said curtly. "Can you tell me whether my phone is tapped now?"

Frank, who knew a lot about detection equipment, checked around the house, taking apart the telephone and the single extension. The other three looked on, fascinated by his expertise.

"Seems you're clean," Frank said finally.

By this time the chess master's frigid manner had relaxed somewhat. "I'm glad you came to tell me," he said. "And I hope you'll understand how I feel in regard to strangers—their interminable questions about chess. I lecture, but I don't give individual instruction."

Frank nodded. "By the way, do you ever pass confidential information over the telephone?"

"Yes, as a matter of fact," the man replied. "Being a grandmaster, I often discuss chess with other masters all over the United States."

Frank suggested that perhaps Fong was trying to get some of Greene's strategy on behalf of the opposition. "Or maybe he just wants to snoop into your personal business to pysche you out," he added.

Greene's lips curled in a sly smile. "Nobody will psyche me. I'm pretty good at that myself." With that, he said goodbye and left the room. His father escorted the boys to the door.

"I hope my son loses the championship," he said. "I don't want him to win the Ruby King."

"Why not?" asked Frank.

Mr Greene did not answer and shut the door quietly behind the boys. They made their way to the car. Starting down the driveway, Biff asked, "Why do you think old Greene doesn't want his son to win the Ruby King?"

Frank shrugged. "All I can say is that Joe and I intend to find out about the King pretty soon." He told Biff about developments in their case and the husky six-footer was much impressed.

As the boys drove back to Bayport, lacy patterns of lightning were still flickering in the sky far to the west, indicating that the storm had not completely passed.

At that very moment Joe was battling desperately with the storm. The Hardys' plane shuddered with teeth-chattering violence. It lifted like an express elevator, then plunged with a velocity that seemed to turn Joe's stomach inside out. The wheel was wrenched from his hands.

"This is the end," he thought.

Suddenly the miracle happened. The plane dropped down out of the heavy clouds and visibility increased. It was in a spin, heading towards the hazy green earth below. Joe shook his head to dispel the feeling of dizziness. He grasped the wheel and it responded sluggishly.

Glancing over at Tony, whose eyes were shut tight, Joe said, "You can open them now, pal. We're not going to heaven yet."

But Tony was not ready for quips. Glassy-eyed, he looked straight ahead for several minutes, while Joe brought the craft down even lower, skimming above the dark forest land. Finally Tony said, "That was great handling, Joe."

"Thanks. We were lucky."

Joe nursed the damaged controls, hoping they would stay intact until they reached the airport. It was then that Tony's sharp eyes spied a crude cabin in the woods.

"Hey, look down, Joe! Isn't that a flatbed trailer behind the shack over there?"

"Sure is."

"Can you fly lower for a better look? Maybe it's the hideout of the serpent balloon gang!"

"Sorry, I can't," Joe replied. "The plane's not handling very well. I'll need all the altitude I can get if we have to make an emergency landing."

The shack slid from view and Joe made a bee-line for Bayport Airport. He radioed ahead telling the control people he was in trouble.

"Emergency equipment will stand by," came the reply from the tower.

"Hold your hat, Tony," Joe said as they came in for the landing. "I hope this crate sets down in one piece!"

A fire truck and ambulance stood beside the runway, but his skilled handling brought the plane down safely.

Joe and Tony reached the Hardy home minutes before Frank and Biff pulled into the driveway.

Excited conversation ensued for the next hour over sandwiches, then Biff and Tony left and the Hardys arrived at Krassner's place an hour and a half later. They locked the car and walked up to the door.

Krassner met them in the sumptuous foyer, and shook their hands warmly. "Glad you came," he said. "I've taken the Ruby King out of the safe. It's in the library."

Hearing that the valuable antique stood unguarded, Joe frowned.

"I know what you're thinking," Krassner said. "Don't worry. We're alone. I can assure you of that."

He led the way to a wing of the mansion and entered a plush library. Bookshelves extended from the floor to the ceiling, and a dim light filtered through heavy curtains on half-open french doors at the far end of the room.

Suddenly Frank and Joe noticed a shadowy figure standing near the doors!

·11·

Over the Cliff

SUDDEN fear gripped Frank. Had the intruder already raided Krassner's safe? And was he making off with the Ruby King?

Joe's reaction was to dash across the room, but Krassner held him back. "Joe, what are you doing?" he asked. "The King won't run away!"

"Is that the King?" Joe asked in disbelief.

With Frank at his side, he approached the figure cautiously. Now they saw that the chess piece was life-size, intricately carved, and bejewelled with rubies.

"Why—we thought—"

"Yes, that should have occurred to me," Krassner said and chuckled. He parted the curtains, throwing more light on the unusual antique. "You probably assumed the Ruby King was small."

"We did," Frank admitted.

"Yes, we certainly did!" Joe added.

The boys walked around the figure, amazed by the subtlety of its carving and the placement of the precious gems. Two of the larger pieces made up the eyes, giving the King a crafty appearance.

"I never knew there were life-size chess pieces," Frank said.

"Oh yes," Krassner told him. "The ancient nobility prized them highly. In several instances the warlords battled over possession of these figures." He went on to explain that the ancients were known even to use people as chess pieces. "Courtyards were laid out as boards," he said, "and the living pieces, usually slaves, moved from one place to another at the master's bidding."

"You know what threw us off," Frank said. "You mentioned keeping the Ruby King in your safe. It must be quite a large one."

Krassner went to the opposite wall, pulled a tapestry aside, and revealed a steel door. The dial was the size of a kitchen plate, and the handle so bulky that it required two strong hands to turn it.

"That's built like a fortress," Joe remarked.

Krassner nodded and pulled the door open. A light sprang on inside and the Hardys looked into the cavernous vault.

"I'd say this is a safe place, wouldn't you?" Krassner said with a self-satisfied smile.

"Where'd you get the design?" Frank quipped. "From Fort Knox?"

Krassner shrugged. "In my business I need a good vault. Now let's put the King in again. Here, Joe, give me a hand."

The boy helped him carry the prize into the safe and Krassner locked the door. Then he put the tapestry back into place and motioned the boys to sit down.

"Well, now you've seen it," he said. "It would be almost impossible to steal, and equally difficult to cart off."

Mr Hardy had told his sons that no safe ever made

was impervious to clever thieves, but Frank and Joe had to admit that Krassner's set-up looked pretty tight.

"Matter of fact," the banker went on, "the consortium trusted me with the piece because of my unique vault."

"Mr Krassner," Frank asked, "how did you acquire the chess piece?"

"It was purchased in China and shipped to this country via Hong Kong."

"Probably smuggled out," Frank thought to himself. He did not quite trust Krassner, and still suspected that the chess piece might have been stolen.

On the way home the boys mused about the Ruby King.

"That was a real shock, wasn't it, Frank?" Joe asked.

"I'll say. Were you going to tackle that wooden dummy?"

"Okay, don't rub it in. I'll bet you thought it was a thief, too."

Frank nodded. "Hey, we're not far from the Morton farm and Chet's home from the hospital. Let's stop in and say hello."

Joe agreed and soon they arrived at the farmhouse. Chet was sitting in the living room watching television.

"Look at this!" Joe quipped. "He's watching kiddie shows!"

Chet was unhappy. "What else can I do? The doctor told me to take it easy for a few days." He sighed. "What's up? Are you breezing around the countryside looking for trouble?"

"Not exactly," Frank said. "We were looking at a life-size chess king."

Iola had come in and overheard the last sentence.

"What?" she said in surprise. "Is there really such a thing?"

"Yes. And it came all the way from China."

"Tell me more."

"Unfortunately that's all we know."

Iola looked thoughtful. "I might be able to find out more about ancient chess pieces. Would that be of any help to you?"

"Sure. How are you going to do it?"

"Oh, leave it to me," Iola said coyly.

On the way home, Frank said, "I wonder what Iola has in mind."

"She's pretty smart," Joe said. "Don't worry about it."

As they pulled into the driveway, Frank said, "Joe, I've been thinking."

"About what?"

"Conrad Greene's place. Maybe the wiretap is on the outside of the house!"

"You only checked indoors?"

"Yes. It didn't occur to me until just now."

"Then let's take a look tomorrow morning."

"Okay. We'll phone him tonight."

After dinner Frank called the Greene residence. Conrad's father answered, saying it was all right to come the next day and check the outside.

"This time you won't get wet, either." He chuckled. "The weather bureau predicted sunshine."

When Frank asked about Conrad, he learned that the champion was out of town conducting an exhibition tour.

"He plays ten games simultaneously—and blind-folded!" Mr Greene said proudly.

Frank thanked him and hung up. When he told Joe about the grandmaster's exhibition, the boy whistled. "Wow! I've trouble playing one opponent with my eyes open!"

"You're not a genius, Joe. I keep telling you that."

Joe gave his brother a good-natured poke in the ribs. "Well, let's see what kind of a genius you are in solving our new mystery."

The boys waited until ten-thirty the next morning, thinking their father might call from New York, but finally Frank said, "We'd better be on our way. I wanted to tell Dad about the Ruby King, but it'll have to wait."

The day was bright and clear. On the highway a black sedan kept behind them for a while, and Joe became suspicious. A man and a woman were in the car. But it turned off on to a side road before they reached Ocean Bluffs.

The elder Mr Greene let them in and Frank introduced his brother.

"How's that big fellow who was with you? What's his name? Boff?"

"Oh, you mean Biff. He's fine. Mr Greene, may we check in the house again for any bugs? Then we'll investigate outside. It could be they have tapped your line by the pole near the road."

"Sure. Go ahead."

The boys went to work with speedy efficiency. "Nothing here," Joe said finally. As they moved towards the front door, a shrill scream pierced the stillness.

The boys ran outside, followed by the old man. They saw a woman running frantically towards the steeply sloping cliff. A man was chasing her!

Suddenly she whirled about and in a high-pitched voice shouted, "I'll throw myself into the sea if you come one step further!"

The man hesitated, then started his pursuit again.

"Do you think it's a lovers' quarrel?" Joe asked.

"Whatever it is, it could have serious consequences. That woman might kill herself!"

The Hardys raced up to the man. "Hold it!" Frank called out. "Leave her alone!"

"You take care of him," Joe said to his brother. "I'll try to keep the woman from jumping off." He rushed towards the cliff.

"What's going on?" Frank asked the man.

"Don't let her do it!" he panted, throwing up his arms in despair. "She's crazy enough to do anything!"

Joe, meanwhile, had reached the woman, who stood precariously close to the edge of the cliff. He put both arms around her waist and began pulling her back. Suddenly she spun around. Now Joe was at the lip of the cliff himself! The woman tried to shove him over, and in her efforts a wig fell off her head!

"Holy crow!" Joe thought. "It's a man!"

Frank was having his troubles, too. The man, who had pleaded for help a moment before, set upon him and wrestled him towards the cliff. In the distance, Mr Greene wrung his hands in despair. "They're trying to shove you over!" he cried out.

This was painfully evident to the Hardy boys, who had a tough fight on their hands. Frank got the better of his adversary with a karate chop. The man staggered, then ran back towards the driveway.

Frank rushed forward to help his brother. Both Joe

and his adversary were still wrestling at the lip of the cliff. Suddenly, to Frank's horror, both fell over and rolled down the steep embankment, locked together in a bear hug!

As they tumbled down the sandy, rocky slope, Frank saw that the other man was getting the worst of it. His head crashed against one rock, then another. By the time both hit the narrow beach a hundred feet below, they rolled apart and lay motionless.

Frank's adversary had reached his car which was parked down the road and drove off. It was a black sedan! "We were followed after all," Frank thought to himself.

He turned to Mr Greene, who had come up alongside him. "They're hurt," the boy said. "Is there a way to the beach?"

The elderly man pointed to a narrow, rutted lane some distance away, which twisted steeply to the water's edge. "It hasn't been used in years," he said. "Part of it's been washed away by rain."

"I'm going down," Frank said. "Better call an ambulance."

When Frank reached the bottom he raced over to his brother. Joe was just opening his eyes.

"You all right?" Frank asked, his throat dry.

Joe stood up cautiously and moved his arms and legs. "I guess so. Don't think I broke anything. But this other character might not be so well off."

The boys walked over to Joe's adversary. He was lying on his side.

"Better not touch him," Frank warned. "He might be in serious trouble."

They bent down to get a look at the man's face.

"Good grief!" Frank said. "It's Gerard Henry!"

"The jewellery salesman?"

"That's right."

Frank and Joe splashed water on Henry's face, but the man did not revive.

Just then two policemen carrying a stretcher came down the narrow trail.

"I'm Lieutenant Skillman," one of them introduced himself. "And this is Officer Gray. What happened?"

Frank told him quickly. "He's still unconscious," the young detective concluded.

The officers carefully moved the man and put him on the stretcher. Then they carried him up the cliff, while Frank helped Joe, who was still shaky and sore.

A police ambulance stood at the Greenes' house, and Gerard Henry was lifted into it. Joe noticed that one of his ladies' shoes was missing.

"The wig got lost, too," he commented wryly.

Just then the "phony lady" came to. He rolled his eyes and sat up, looking ludicrous in his dress. He shook his head to clear the cobwebs.

Lieutenant Skillman advised the man of his rights and began questioning him, but Henry's jaw was set tight and he refused to say anything. Frank and Joe, who had already told what had happened, filled the officers in on Henry's part in the jewellery racket.

"Will you press charges for assault and battery?" Skillman asked the boys.

"With intent to kill!" Frank declared.

"All right. You'll be called as witnesses." Skillman handcuffed Gerard Henry and made him lie down in the ambulance.

"We only have a small jail in Ocean Bluffs," he said,

"but I think it'll be adequate. As soon as you're released from the hospital, that's where you'll go."

Mr Greene shook his head in disbelief as they walked back towards the house. "You boys sure got into a lot of trouble on our account," he said. "Why do you suppose those men were trying to throw you over the cliff?"

"To get us out of the way for some reason," Joe said.

"Let's take a look at that telephone pole," Frank said. When they reached the end of the drive he climbed partly up the base of the pole. It was covered with creosote and tar.

"What a mess," he grumbled as he climbed higher. At the junction he examined the wires and called down: "Here's the tap, Joe. What'll we do with it?"

"Listen, Frank, I've got an idea," Joe called up. "Why don't we leave it and tell Conrad to pass on false information as to how he would tackle different problems in chess? He can get in touch with his partners on a public telephone and clue them in."

"Not bad," Frank agreed. "It would confuse his enemies."

When he came down, Mr Greene chuckled. "Hey, this is like reading a detective story," he said. "I'm sure Conrad will go along with your strategy."

It was early afternoon when the Hardys arrived home. They were met at the kitchen door by Aunt Gertrude. A look of horror crossed her face when she saw them.

"Oh, Frank, Joe!" she shrieked.

·12·

The King's Curse

FRANK felt the blood drain from his face. "What's happened? Is Dad all right?"

"Nothing's happened to your father," Aunt Gertrude said tartly. "But look at you— you're a mess! Filthy, and your face is scratched, and Joe's clothes are torn and he's bruised all over—"

"Is that all?" Frank interrupted, heaving a sigh of relief. "We thought the sky had fallen in."

Hearing the commotion, Mrs Hardy entered the kitchen. Worriedly she scrutinized the boys, then said, "You do look pretty bad. Are you sure you're not hurt?"

"Frank's dirty because he climbed a telephone pole," Joe said, "and I'm a little sore from fighting a lady that was no lady. But everything's okay, Mother."

"Have crooks been chasing you?" Aunt Gertrude demanded. Without waiting for an answer, she said. "Of course they have. Where were you?"

Frank told their story and finally managed to calm his excited aunt. "Did you hear from Dad?" he asked.

"Yes, we did," Mrs Hardy replied.

"Has he had any luck?"

"He said he was making good headway, that's all."

The boys went up to their room and soon returned with clean clothes. They handed the dirty ones to their mother.

"Let me put some antiseptic on your scratches," Mrs Hardy said.

She went to the bathroom to deposit the clothes in the hamper and returned with the liquid. While she pressed soaked cotton swabs against the boys' injuries, Frank dialled police headquarters.

"Hi, Chief. Frank Hardy. I've got some good news. The Ocean Bluffs police captured Gerard Henry."

"He's a slick operator," the chief replied. "How'd they do it?"

Frank told of their adventure and how they had left the wiretap in place in order to mislead Conrad Greene's enemies.

Collig thanked him for his information. "I'll get in touch with Lieutenant Skillman," he said. "We can tack a few more charges on to that hoodlum."

"Like fraud, you mean?"

"That's right. Let me know if anything further develops, Frank."

The hungry boys had just finished a snack when a youth about eighteen came to the door. He had an envelope marked Bayport Museum for the Hardys.

Frank took it and the messenger hurried off.

"Hey, Joe. I wonder what this is all about," Frank said and slit open the envelope. On a piece of museum stationery was typed:

Frank and Joe Hardy:
    May have some information to help you.
Ruby King.

"Is this some kind of a gag?" Joe asked.

"It may be a trap," Frank said. "We're pretty good at falling into those lately, you know."

"Not this time," Joe said. "Let's call the museum and ask about this Ruby King."

Frank did not like the idea. "It might be like phoning the zoo and asking for Mr Fox," he said. "We'll go over ourselves tomorrow morning."

"But not without bodyguards!"

The Hardys decided to phone their back-up team of Biff Hooper, Tony Prito, and Phil Cohen. The latter was a slight, intense boy with a razor-sharp mind.

The three friends readily agreed to meet the boys next morning and serve as lookouts around the museum.

When they met at nine o'clock, Joe looked at the austere stone building without windows and said, "Not a very inviting place. When I was a little kid, I used to think this was a mausoleum."

Biff, Tony, and Phil stationed themselves on the outside. They would go in if the Hardys were not back in fifteen minutes.

Frank and Joe bounded up the marble steps and opened the heavy bronze door. Inside a young blonde woman sat behind the information desk.

"We're here to see Ruby King," Frank said.

"You'll find Mrs King down the hall in the room marked *Ancient Art.*"

"You mean there really is a Ruby King?" Joe asked.

The receptionist cocked her head and looked at the Hardys quizzically. "What made you think there wasn't?"

"Oh, nothing," Joe muttered. The boys found the

proper door and entered a large high-ceilinged room. In it were plaster façades of ancient buildings, glass cases filled with artifacts, tapestries, and a few paintings.

Their eyes swept the room, finally coming to rest on a small desk in one corner. Behind it sat a buxom, dark-haired woman. She wore a blue dress and eyeglasses. Her hair was piled high on her head. She smiled as the boys approached.

"You must be Frank and Joe Hardy."

"Yes," Joe said, surprised, as the woman continued, "You're detectives, interested in an ancient Chinese chess piece."

Frank laughed. "I think you're the detective, Mrs King. By the way, is that really your name?"

"Of course it is. I was born Ruby Smith, but when I married Mr King, I got the name of the famous chess piece."

Mrs King explained that she had been hired recently from the Museum of Natural History in New York City to become a curator in Bayport. "Oriental art is my field, and I understand you'd like to know more about this particular antique."

Suddenly an idea occurred to Frank. "Did Iola Morton tell you?"

"That's right. She was in yesterday."

"You're very kind to take such an interest," Joe said.

The curator said that the piece had been made in India and carried by caravan to China during the Ming Dynasty. "Of course, it was part of a complete set," she explained.

"So we heard," Frank said.

"But did you hear about the curse?"

"A curse, really?" asked Joe.

"Every person who has come into possession of the Ruby King has died under unusual circumstances," Mrs King went on. "The first warlord who owned the piece was struck by lightning the day after he acquired it. Another owner died from poison a week after he bought the King, a third drowned in a flood which carried the Ruby King all the way down the Yangtze River."

"Then what happened to it?" asked Frank.

"It was found by a poor peasant who was gored to death by a bull the next day."

"Then Mr Krassner had better look out," Joe said. "Do you really believe these fairy tales, Mrs King?"

"Maybe they're only legends," the woman replied. "But I thought you'd like to know about them." She went on to tell the boys about the game of chess, which originated in India. *"Shah mat* means *The king is dead,"* she said. "That's where we get the word checkmate. The German word for it is *Schach matt."*

While the boys listened intently, Tony, Biff, and Phil waited impatiently outside.

"Wonder what's taking them so long," said Biff.

"Maybe they got conked," Tony said.

"Let's go in and take a look," Phil suggested. "The fifteen minutes are almost up."

The three went inside and were greeted with the same hospitality as the Hardys. When they asked about their friends, they were directed to the room of Ancient Art.

"Let's enter one at a time," Biff said. "Phil, you go first. If there's any trouble, whistle."

Phil went in. As he approached the group, Mrs King

was saying, "The curse can be lifted, according to an old story."

"How?" asked Frank, waving to Phil.

"If it's buried."

Joe let out a low whistle. Biff and Tony burst into the room, glancing wildly about. But Phil motioned with his hands. "Calm down, fellows, everything's all right."

"What's going on?" Mrs King asked, surprised.

The three boys were introduced and the whole thing explained. She laughed, and they resumed their conversation.

"If the curse can be lifted, why didn't one of the previous owners bury the King?" Joe asked.

"That's the point," the curator went on. "It must not be buried by the owner, or anyone who knows him."

"How is that possible?" Frank asked.

Mrs King shrugged. "That's all I can tell you about the Ruby King. Has it been of any help?"

"Very much so," Frank said.

They thanked the woman and left, their footsteps echoing along the marble corridor.

Outside, the Hardys discussed what they had just heard, then Frank said, "Are you fellows busy this afternoon? I'd like to check out that cabin in the woods. Want to help?"

The answer was an enthusiastic Yes.

"Good idea," Joe said. "But first, how about some food at our house?"

After lunch of roast-beef sandwiches, topped off with wedges of Aunt Gertrude's apple pie, the boys drove off to look for the shack which Joe and Tony had discovered in their horrendous aerial search.

It took more than an hour before they found the small country road which led to the old cabin. Biff parked and they proceeded on foot, peering out from the trees to observe the solitary building.

"It looks deserted," Joe whispered.

The windows were boarded up. Weeds grew high around the walls, and the cabin gave the appearance of having been abandoned long ago.

As the boys were about to go closer, Phil whispered, "Duck!"

Everyone dropped to the ground, and five pairs of prying eyes watched a man sneak out of the woods.

"He looks like Eggleby," Joe whispered.

The man knocked on the door and said, *"Shah mat!"*

A bolt clicked and he was let in.

The boys conversed in low tones about what to do next.

"If that was really Eggleby, he might know us," Frank said. "Tony, you and Phil go up and knock at the door. Give the password. We'll back you up in case of trouble."

"Okay. Here goes," Tony said. He and Phil crept from their hiding place, walked across a small open area, and knocked on the door. *"Shah mat!"* Phil said.

The door opened and they were admitted into the dark interior. All became quiet—ominously quiet, Frank thought. After ten minutes, neither of the two boys had returned.

"Something fishy's going on in there," Joe said. "I think we'd better take a look-see."

"All right," Frank agreed. "Come on."

The Hardys and Biff went to the door, knocked, and Frank said in a loud voice, *"Shah mat!"*

There was no answer. Joe tried the doorknob. It was locked.

"Stand back," Biff said. He leaped forward and banged his shoulder against the door. It gave way with a cracking sound, and the boys dashed inside. It took a few seconds for their eyes to become adjusted to the dark interior.

"Good grief!" Frank said. "They're all gone!"

·13·

The Third Man

"THEY'VE vanished!" Biff exclaimed. "Disappeared into thin air!"

"There must be another way out," Frank declared, moving around.

"All the windows are barred and there's no back door," Joe observed.

"Maybe there's a trap-door," Biff suggested.

The three got on their hands and knees, probing along the wooden floor with their fingers.

"Here's something," Frank said as he felt a small, countersunk hinge.

In the shaft of light coming through the door, the boys made out the thin outline of a small trap-door, barely large enough to admit a broad-shouldered person. Biff prised it open with his pocketknife and lowered himself into the hole, which was about five feet deep.

He groped about, finally locating an opening into the hard-packed earth. "Hey, guys, it's a tunnel!" Biff said.

"Can you get through?" Frank asked.

"Just about."

"Okay, go ahead. I'll follow you. Joe, better stay topside, just in case."

"Okay," Joe said.

Frank dropped down into the hole, found the opening, and proceeded to wriggle through behind Biff. Bits of dirt fell on top of the boys as they inched forward. The air grew heavy, redolent of musty soil.

Biff stopped momentarily. "Are you coming, Frank?" His muffled words sounded like a voice from a tomb.

"Yes. Go ahead. But don't press against the roof too hard."

While the two continued to mole their way through the dank tunnel, Joe stepped outside the cabin and listened. Except for birds twittering, no sound came from the surrounding woods.

"I wonder where they'll finally exit," the boy mused.

Ten minutes later Biff called back to Frank again, "I see the light up ahead."

"Okay, Biff. I'm right behind you."

Now the tunnel widened considerably and the boys scrambled side by side towards the end. Just before they reached it, they came upon Phil and Tony. They were tied hand and foot and gagged, and trussed up in such a way that the least movement would choke them.

Frank and Biff tore off their gags and cut the ropes. "You okay?" Frank asked anxiously.

Tony nodded, sat up, and said weakly, "They're getting away. Outside—look!"

Frank and Biff rushed from the exit, which proved to be the mouth of a cave, and found themselves in a wide clearing. Suddenly they heard the engine of a car. Through the leafy branches of low-hanging trees they could make out a black sedan as it started along a rutted trail. Three men were in it!

Phil and Tony had followed the boys and staggered towards them.

"Were those the three guys who conked you?" Frank asked, pointing to the car.

"Only two did," Phil said.

"Then the third man must have been a lookout at the end of the tunnel," Frank conjectured.

"Where's Joe?" Tony asked.

"Back at the cabin. I'll have to give him the signal." Frank imitated the cry of a bird.

Joe heard it faintly and repeated it. He started out across the woods, reaching the clearing a few minutes later.

"Those two had weapons," Phil said. "They made us crawl through the tunnel, and when we neared the end, they gagged us and tied us up."

The boys walked back through the woods to make a thorough search of the cabin.

"I guess they cleaned it out completely," Frank said. "Joe, did you look around outside?"

"Yes, but I didn't have time to check in the back."

"Okay, let's do it now," Frank said, and led the others through the door and to the rear of the cabin.

Phil noticed something far off in the weeds. "What's that?" he asked, running towards it. He reached into the tall grass and pulled at a dirty tarpaulin. Beneath it was a neatly packed balloon!

Within minutes, the boys had spread open the envelope. "It's the serpent!" Joe exclaimed.

"What a find!" Tony said.

"We'll take it to the police as evidence," Frank decided. "It's the balloon from which we were shot at!"

As they re-packed the nylon envelope, Tony spied a

piece of paper which apparently had fallen from the folds.

"Frank, Joe, look at this!"

"What is it?" Frank asked.

"A cablegram from Hong Kong!"

The boys crowded around as Tony read the message aloud: " 'Ming Do very ill. Hurry via Queen. Serpents.' "

"What do you suppose that means?" Phil asked.

The Hardys studied the cable carefully and Frank said, "A person named Ming Do wants someone to hurry by the way of Queen something or other."

"And Serpents means the serpent gang," Biff added.

"But what is Queen? Is that some kind of code word?" Joe wondered.

"The balloon won't fit in the car," Tony said. "I'll drive back to town and get our truck."

"Good idea," Frank said and handed him the keys.

Tony returned shortly and the boys loaded up the balloon. On the way back to Bayport, they speculated about the turn of events. The evidence they had found certainly advanced the Hardys' case. Or perhaps, as Frank secretly thought, it had plunged them even deeper into an insoluble mystery!

When they arrived at police headquarters, Chief Collig was amazed to hear their story. He accepted the serpent balloon as evidence and looked at the cable.

"Whoever they're talking about is going to Hong Kong soon," he conjectured. "If only we had a way to stop him. But we don't even know who's involved!"

He shook his head slowly. "I have some news, too," he continued. "Not good, I'm afraid."

"What happened?" Joe asked.

"Gerard Henry escaped from the Ocean Bluffs jail."

"How'd he do that?" Biff asked.

Collig said that Henry had feigned illness and fooled an inexperienced guard. When his cell was opened, he had jumped the officer, disarmed him, and raced right out of the front door.

"Listen," Joe said. "Do you suppose he was that third man in the woods?"

"Might have been," Collig said.

After they had made their report, the Hardys thanked their friends for their help. "We couldn't have pulled this off without you," Frank said.

"You'll make detectives out of us yet," Tony said as he drove them back to his house where he had left the Hardys' car.

Frank and Joe decided to visit Krassner in his office to tell him that his tormentors had apparently fled. And perhaps the man could shed some light on the mysterious cable. On the way they dropped Phil off at his house.

Krassner occupied a suite in Bayport's newest office building and received the boys cordially.

"We've got some exciting news for you," Joe said.

The financier looked pleased, but as the story unfolded, his face clouded with fear and apprehension. When Frank mentioned the contents of the cable, Krassner paled.

"Call my wife!" he ordered his secretary. When she reported that his home phone was dead, Krassner jumped up. "The worst has happened!" he cried and ran outside.

Frank and Joe followed him, trying to find out what had upset him so.

97

"Later," Krassner said. He leaped behind the wheel of his sports car and started the engine. Then he drove off.

Frank and Joe took their own car and followed. "Do you think he's going home?" Joe asked.

"Looks that way," Frank replied. "Funny. We never saw his wife. I didn't think he had one."

"Maybe he feels she's in danger," Joe said.

They pulled into Krassner's driveway directly behind him and the three hurried into the house. The banker called for his wife, but she was not there.

"It's the servants' day off, too," Krassner said, rushing into the library. He tried the handle to his vault. It was locked.

"Maybe the worst hasn't happened after all," Joe said. "That is, if you were talking about the theft of the Ruby King."

Krassner did not reply. With trembling fingers he dialled the combination, turned the handle, and pulled open the steel door. Everyone gasped.

The Ruby King was gone!

·14·

The Oriental Connection

FOOTSTEPS sounded and a woman entered the library. She was slightly built, with a calm and lovely Oriental face.

"Albert! What happened?" She looked at Krassner in alarm. He stood as if in a trance in front of the yawning vault.

His mouth moved, but no words came out.

"The King has disappeared," Joe explained. "Are you Mrs Krassner?"

"Yes. Oh dear!" The woman stepped forward and put an arm around her husband, who finally regained enough composure to talk.

"What'll I do?" he repeated over and over. "What'll I do?"

Frank turned to the woman, who tried to calm her husband. "Did you just come home, Mrs Krassner?"

"Yes. I left this morning to visit a friend."

"Did you see anything unusual when you left?"

The woman thought for a moment, then she said, "Yes, two men. They were in a car near the entrance to our driveway."

"Did you get a good look at them?" Joe asked.

"Their faces were turned away."

"Weren't you suspicious?"

"No. Not really. People often stop to admire our place."

Frank took his brother aside and spoke to him quietly. "Those two men probably were Fong and Eggleby. And the Ruby King might be what Ming Do wants!"

"It wouldn't surprise me!"

Mrs Krassner summoned the Franklin Township Police, and they arrived in a few minutes to look for clues. Fingerprints were found on the safe, but they proved to be those of Krassner, who by now had gone to his bedroom in a virtual state of collapse.

After calling a doctor, Mrs Krassner thanked the boys and ushered them to the door. Outside, they were startled to see their father drive up.

"Dad! When did you get back?" Frank asked.

"About an hour and a half ago. Mother said you had gone to see Mr Krassner. I called his office and was told all three of you had dashed out of there in a hurry because his home phone was dead. It sounded like trouble so I came out." Mr Hardy pointed to the police car. "I take it the Ruby King has been stolen."

Joe nodded. "Dad, we've got an awful lot to tell you."

"I have some news, too," Mr Hardy said. "Let's stop at the next eating place and talk."

Frank and Joe led the way in their car until they came to a restaurant. They pulled into the parking lot and their father followed.

Inside, they found a comfortable isolated booth, where nobody could overhear their conversation. Frank and Joe ordered hamburgers and coke, while Mr Hardy was content with a cup of coffee.

THE CLUE OF THE HISSING SERPENT

"Wait till you hear about Mrs Krassner!" Joe said after a waitress had taken their order. "She's—"

"Chinese," Mr Hardy said.

"How'd you know?"

"I found out in New York. Also learned a few other titbits."

"Come on, Dad, out with it!" Joe urged.

"For one thing, Krassner is originally from Hong Kong. One of his grandmothers was a Chinese, which makes him one fourth Oriental."

"So that's what gives him that odd look," Frank said.

"His wife's family," Mr Hardy went on, "is very prominent in Hong Kong circles. Her father is Moy Chen-Chin, a social big wheel and very rich."

"So now the chop suey thickens," Joe quipped. "What else?"

As the boys munched their hamburgers, Mr Hardy filled them in on Krassner's career. "As a youth, he got involved in a smuggling ring. His father-in-law got him out of that scrape and Krassner came to this country. He's been a citizen of the United States for the past twenty years."

"Funny," Frank said. "I never quite trusted him."

"He's been straight ever since and has a fine record as an investment banker. Much of his work involves Oriental securities," Mr Hardy said.

"And his father-in-law is his Oriental connection," Joe put in. "No doubt an invaluable asset."

"Wait a minute," Frank said. "There was no sign of forced entry in this theft. Maybe Krassner returned to his crooked ways and stole the piece himself! Was it insured?"

"You caught on fast. Yes. He took out a large policy

101

on the Ruby King several weeks ago," Mr Hardy said.

Joe looked dubious. "I can't quite believe that. I have another theory."

"What's that?" Frank asked.

"Krassner was intimidated by Fong and Eggleby. We know that he was afraid of them. Maybe they discovered his past and threatened to expose him unless he handed over the Ruby King!"

"Could be," Frank said. "That would be a better reason for his not wanting to go to the police. I never believed his story that he was afraid of the publicity. After all, he was the official custodian of this valuable antique. Just because someone was after it, Krassner's reputation wouldn't have been ruined!"

Mr Hardy nodded. "Of course anyone buying an expensive object like that would insure it properly. I tend to agree with Joe's reasoning."

"Our next step is to find the King," Frank said. "And we'd better be fast about it or Ming Do will get it."

Mr Hardy looked puzzled, and the boys clued him in on their adventure in the woods, the cable they had found, and Mrs King's information on the old chess piece.

Mr Hardy was thoughtful for a while, then he said, "The most logical way of transporting an item like that would be by sea. Perhaps there's a ship in the harbour named *Queen*!"

"Let's go home and call the harbour master," Frank urged, and stood up.

Mr Hardy paid the bill and soon they were on their way. It was dark when they turned into Elm Street and they were surprised to see their security spotlights casting a dazzling glow all around the house.

"Oh, oh, something's happened," Joe said as Frank drove towards the garage. An alarm bell was ringing.

"Something's definitely wrong," Frank said.

All three jumped out of their cars and raced inside. Joe shut off the electronic alarm system, then followed his father and Frank into the living room, where Mrs Hardy and Aunt Gertrude rose to meet them.

"Laura, what's the matter?" Mr Hardy asked.

"We're a little frightened, Fenton."

"I'm scared to death!" Aunt Gertrude said. "It's on account of those terrible criminals."

"Easy," Frank said. "Just tell us from the beginning."

"We received a package!" Aunt Gertrude pointed to a cardboard shoe box lying on the coffee table. Frank went to open it.

"Don't touch it! You'll get bitten!"

"By what?"

"A snake! A big venomous snake!" Gertrude Hardy cried.

Mrs Hardy spoke up. "It's not really big, and I don't think it's poisonous. But you never can tell."

"How'd you get it?" Joe asked.

Mrs Hardy said it was delivered to the door shortly after dark. "We jumped out of our skin when we opened it," she concluded.

Frank set the box on the floor and took the lid off. Inside lay a small garter snake. He picked it up and it crawled over his hand and up his left arm. "I'll take it out in the yard," he said.

"No doubt it was a warning from the serpent gang," Mr Hardy said.

"Fenton, you'd better drop this case while we're still healthy!" his sister implored him.

"If I dropped my cases because of threats, I'd soon be out of business," Mr Hardy said. "But let's turn the alarm system on again, just to be on the safe side."

"Now that the Serpents have the Ruby King, why are they still bothering us?" Frank asked.

"They know we'll keep after them and might nail them yet," Joe said.

Mr Hardy put in a call to the harbour master's office. "They'll check and let us know," he told his sons after he had finished.

The next morning during breakfast the phone rang. Frank took it, listened tensely for a few seconds, then hung up.

"Guess what!" he said. "There's a Japanese ship in the harbour that's due to sail day after tomorrow at midnight."

"Where to?" Joe asked.

"Hong Kong. And her name's *Queen Maru*!"

·15·

Faked Out!

"THAT'S the *Queen* mentioned in the cablegram!" Joe exclaimed. "It has to be!"

Frank was sceptical. "I doubt that the Serpents would be that obvious about it."

"I'm convinced," Joe said. "I'll bet that Fong and Eggleby are still in the area and they plan to ship the Ruby King on the *Queen Maru*."

"It's a strong possibility," Mr Hardy agreed. "Better drive down to the harbour and take a look at the *Queen Maru*."

Before the boys left, the phone rang again. It was Conrad Greene's father. He told Joe that his son was still on the chess exhibition tour. "He's due to play in Bayport tomorrow night," Mr Greene said, "at the VFW Hall."

"Thanks for letting us know," Joe said. "We'd like to see the match."

Half an hour later, Frank and Joe arrived at the dock and parked near the *Queen Maru*. On her deck giant booms were hoisting heavy machinery into her hold.

The Hardys climbed the gangway, asked for the captain, and were directed to a neat forward cabin. At the door they were greeted by a short, smiling, barrel-chested Japanese named Taro Ono.

105

"May I help you?" he asked cordially.

The boys explained they were detectives and were looking for a wooden box, roughly two-feet-two by six, containing contraband destined for Hong Kong.

"About the size of a coffin," Captain Ono said, stroking his chin. "No. We carry only large crates of machinery, as you can see for yourself."

"Are you sure?"

"I know my cargo well," the captain answered, still maintaining his pleasant look.

"Well, thank you, sir," Frank said and the boys clambered down the steel gangway to the dock.

"Now what?" Joe asked.

"The ship doesn't leave till tomorrow night. We'll have to keep a constant watch on it."

Joe sighed. "Okay. Let's get our reinforcement team for help."

Biff, Phil, Tony, and the Hardys staked out the freighter all day and night. No suspicious box was loaded and nothing unusual happened. Tony had drawn the late-night shift, and Frank and Joe arrived in the morning to take over from him. After a few encouraging words from their tired pal, they settled in a strategic spot and prepared for a long wait.

About ten o'clock an old hearse drove up next to the freighter. At the wheel was a youth not much older than the Hardys. He hopped out, opened the back of the hearse, and began pulling out a pine box.

"Joe! We might have struck gold!" Frank said excitedly.

"Come on, Frank. Let's find out and ask this character a few questions!"

Frank and Joe ran up to the youth. "You work for an

undertaker?" Frank asked.

"No. What's it to you, anyhow?"

"Where'd you get the hack?" Joe asked.

"At the junkyard. Not bad, eh? The girls really like it. Say, who are you guys?"

Frank told him. "And what's your name?"

"Oscar."

"If you don't work for an undertaker, Oscar," Joe said, "what are you doing delivering a coffin?"

"Oh, is this a coffin?" The youth eased it on to the dock.

"Don't try to be funny," Frank said. "We want straight answers."

"Okay, okay. So I'm delivering a coffin," Oscar said. "Some Oriental-looking guy asked me to bring it to this ship. And he paid me twenty-five bucks. That's all I know. Why don't you get off my back?"

"You can't deliver a corpse without a licence," Joe said.

"I'm getting out of here!" Oscar slid in beside the wheel and started off as Frank jotted down his licence number.

Joe sat on the pine box while Frank went to call Chief Collig. When the policeman arrived with another officer, Joe related their suspicion that the Ruby King was hidden in the wooden box.

"We can find out soon enough," Collig said. He ordered the policeman to open the box, the lid of which was fastened by eight screws.

The officer got a screwdriver from the trunk of the squad car and went to work.

Finally he was finished. The Hardys held their breath as the top was removed. Then they groaned!

Inside lay a five-foot log!

Chief Collig turned the piece of wood over and examined it. "This doesn't look like contraband, fellows," he said.

Meanwhile, Captain Ono had noticed the police and came off his ship to investigate. When asked about the box, he denied any knowledge whatsoever of the strange cargo.

"What am I supposed to do?" he asked, puzzled. "I can't load it without papers."

"Don't worry about it," Chief Collig said. "You're not loading it at all. I'm taking it to headquarters." He turned to the boys. "We'll give it the once-over in the lab. I'll let you know if we find any clues."

"Thanks, Chief," Frank said.

Then Frank and Joe discussed the ruse. "When the gang suspected that we had found the cable," Joe said, "they must have figured we'd be watching the ship. So they went to all this trouble to keep us here, meanwhile transporting the Ruby King some other way."

"Such as?"

"Such as by air!"

"We should have thought of that before!" Frank said. "Come on. Let's call the airport!"

At home the boys took turns telephoning all the airlines using the local terminal. One after another the replies were negative. No coffins had been shipped out. No rectangular boxes, nothing to indicate that the Ruby King had been flown away.

"Here's a strictly freight service," Frank said, scanning the phone book. "Premier Airways." He called the number and talked with a friendly agent. Two coffins had been transported to the West Coast the day before.

Both were from local undertakers and had been properly documented.

Frank pressed further. "We're looking for a wooden figure. Very valuable. That's why it was stolen."

"Oh, stolen goods! We'd like to help you, but—hold on. Could it have been hidden in a rug?"

"Sure could! Was a rug part of your cargo?"

"Yes, yesterday. A large one, wrapped in heavy brown paper. One end was torn, and now that you mention it, I saw something wooden showing through."

"Where was the destination?" Frank's heart thumped with excitement.

"Wait a minute, I'll check." The answer came shortly. "We shipped the rug non-stop to San Francisco. Final destination was Hong Kong!"

"Then it's out of the country by now," Frank said.

"Sure. Matter of fact, it must have arrived about half an hour ago."

Frank thanked the clerk and hung up, shaking his head. "Boy, did we get fooled! Now what are we going to do?"

"Call Chief Collig," Joe suggested and dialled headquarters. After he told the chief the bad news, Collig said, "This isn't our day. I just learned that Gerard Henry was seen in town the night before last. But he slipped away before we could apprehend him."

Frank and Joe sat in gloomy silence until Joe suggested they have some lunch. As they were eating their sandwiches, Chet walked in the back door.

"Hi, guys," he said breezily. "What's new with his Majesty?"

"It's in Hong Kong," Joe said.

Chet shook his head when he heard the story. "Tough break," he said. Then he turned to Aunt Gertrude. "You haven't signed my cast. Tell you what. I'll let you autograph it in exchange for a piece of pie."

He offered a pen to Miss Hardy. She signed her name on the white surface, which by now had been crisscrossed by other signatures. "There," she said. "If it weren't for that Ruby King and those cut-throats connected with it, you wouldn't have broken your arm."

"It's all in the line of duty," Chet said with a grin. "Anything for my friends."

At that moment the doorbell rang. Frank answered it. Outside stood a man who introduced himself as Peter Carpenter and presented credentials indicating that he was from the security section of the International Insurance Company.

"I'd like to speak to Fenton Hardy," he said.

"He's not here at the moment," Frank told him. "But won't you come in? Maybe my brother Joe and I can help you. I'm Frank Hardy."

"I've heard of you," Carpenter said. "Yes, I'll talk to you."

Frank led the visitor into the living room where Mrs Hardy, Aunt Gertrude, and Joe joined them. Chet lingered in the kitchen over a slab of peach pie with an ear cocked to the living room.

"We would like either your father or you to accept an assignment for us," the man began.

"Sorry, but we're busy on something else. So is our father," Frank said.

"You mean the Ruby King?"

"How did you know?"

"That's the case I'm referring to. It was insured with

us." Carpenter produced a file and went on, "My company stands to pay a sizeable settlement unless the chess piece is found. We want you to find it!"

"Mr Krassner asked us to do the same thing," Joe said. "Unfortunately we have reason to believe that the Ruby King has been shipped out of the country. It might be in Hong Kong."

"Then you must fly to Hong Kong immediately!"

·16·

A Bold Caper

"YOUR father could join you once your preliminary investigation is underway," Mr Carpenter continued. "Your age also is in your favour. You can pose as students or tourists."

Frank and Joe were dumfounded! They tried to take the proposal calmly, but their hearts raced with excitement at the prospect of a trip to the Orient.

"We'll talk it over with Dad," Frank said. "How can we get in touch with you, Mr Carpenter?"

"I'll be in my office until tomorrow afternoon, and I do hope you'll accept the assignment. All expenses paid and a fee based upon a percentage of the money you save us."

Seconds after the man left, Chet burst into the living room. "What's going on?" he asked. "Did I hear that man say something about going to Hong Kong?"

"You did," Aunt Gertrude said. "And the answer is no!"

"Now, Gertrude," Mrs Hardy said, "it might not be such a bad idea."

"Bad! It'll be a calamity! We'll never see these boys again. They might be kidnapped and taken to an opium den!"

"Don't worry about a thing," Chet spoke up. "With me to help them they'll be perfectly safe!"

"Chet, you've got a broken arm," Joe said. "You couldn't help."

"What do you mean? I can really conk someone with this cast!"

"Look, old buddy," Frank said, and put an arm around his friend's shoulder. "The insurance company will only pay for our expenses, not yours."

"I've got a couple of dollars," Chet said. "And besides, I like Chinese food!"

"No!" Joe said.

"Aw, shucks!" Chet tried to smile as he left the Hardy house. "Will you bring me a souvenir at least? Like a carved dagger?"

"Too dangerous," Frank replied. "How about an incense burner?"

"Phooey!" Chet said, and a minute later his car sputtered off.

Frank and Joe contacted the airport. There were no flights available until two days later, and that plane would leave early in the morning.

"I'm sure Dad'll go along with the idea," Joe said. "Let's get passports and our inoculation jabs."

"Good. Then we'll visit Mrs Krassner. Maybe she'll give us a letter of introduction to her family."

Tingling with excitement, Frank and Joe drove first to the doctor for the necessary injections, then to the banker's estate where Mrs Krassner received them cordially. Her husband was at his office. When she heard that they planned to go to Hong Kong, the Chinese woman's eyebrows raised. "You don't think it would be too dangerous?"

"We've handled risky assignments before," Frank assured her. "Could we meet your family, Mrs Krassner?"

"I'm sure they'd be delighted to help you in any way. Are you certain the Ruby King was taken there?"

"Reasonably certain," Frank said.

Mrs Krassner went into the library, where she penned a note in Chinese. "Give this to my father, Moy Chen-Chin," she said.

"Any directions?" Joe asked.

Mrs Krassner smiled. "Everybody knows Moy Chen-Chin."

On the way home the young detectives exulted over this rare opportunity. "Should we tell Conrad Greene about this tonight?" Joe asked.

"Sure. Why not? After the exhibition," Frank said.

At dinner that night Mrs Hardy said, "Boys, where are your appetites? You're just picking at your food."

"I guess we're too excited," Frank said. "Hurry up, Joe. The chess exhibition starts soon."

The VFW hall, a barn-like auditorium, with wooden folding chairs, was half-filled when the Hardys arrived. On the stage was a long table, where six of Conrad Greene's opponents were already seated.

"Conrad will probably come through the back door," Joe said. "He's not one to rub elbows with the peasantry."

The boys looked about, nodding here and there to friends and neighbours. Suddenly a scuffling sounded from backstage.

"Help! Help!" a man screamed.

"That's Conrad!" Frank cried out.

The Hardys ran forward and vaulted on to the stage.

114

There was a door on either side. Joe took the left, Frank the right. The room behind was empty! They raced out of the back door and looked around. Nobody was there but a boy of about ten.

"I saw him!" the boy volunteered. "I saw everything!"

"Tell us what happened. Hurry!" Joe urged.

The youngster said he was parking his bicycle when he noticed a man enter the building.

"Then two guys jumped from a car and pounced on him. I saw it right through the door there. The man screamed and kicked, but the two bad guys dragged him to the car."

"Where'd they go?" Frank asked.

The boy indicated a side street, which led to the dock area.

Frank and Joe thanked the boy and hurried to a nearby telephone booth, where they called police headquarters. Collig was off duty, but a lieutenant took the report that Conrad Greene had been kidnapped. He said he would dispatch a car to the VFW Hall to check out the incident.

After he hung up, Joe said, "Frank, maybe they took Greene to the *Queen Maru!* I still think Ono's in with the serpent gang!"

"The ship's not due to sail until midnight," Frank said. "We'll have a little time. Let's go down to the dock."

They were just pulling up to the pier when Frank cried out, "Hey! Look!"

The *Queen Maru* was moving slowly away from her berth!

"She's leaving ahead of time," Joe said. "Come on,

Frank. We've got to stop them!"

The boys called headquarters again. Chief Collig had been notified and was there busily organizing a search for the kidnapped man.

"We think he's on the *Queen Maru*!" Frank said. "She's sailing ahead of schedule."

"Good work, boys," the chief said. "I'll send the police launch to intercept them."

"We'll go in the *Sleuth*," Frank said. "Meet you out in the bay!"

The Hardys' sleek speedboat was berthed three blocks away. The boys ran to the boathouse and in minutes were streaking across Barmet Bay, their powerful searchlight skimming over the wave tops.

In a few minutes the grey hulk of the *Queen Maru* loomed on the dark horizon. Joe was at the wheel of the *Sleuth* and circled the slow-moving cargo ship.

"There's not a soul on deck," Frank remarked.

He looked back towards the harbour. The *Queen*, despite her lumbering pace, was putting more and more distance between Bayport and the open sea. Near the three-mile limit, the boys spied a light racing towards them from a distance.

"Here comes the launch," Frank said.

The police boat approached with signal lights blinking. The message was easily translated by the Hardys. "Police. Stop immediately!"

Seconds later the lights blinked again. "Lower a ladder. We are boarding."

The launch pulled alongside the freighter. Three officers scrambled up to the deck. Frank and Joe latched the *Sleuth* on to the launch and climbed up behind them.

116

The party was met by Captain Ono, his face wreathed in a broad smile.

"What can I do for you now?" he asked, fixing the Hardys with a long look.

"There's been a kidnapping," Chief Collig said. "We think the victim may be on your ship."

Ono bowed. "Go ahead and search. I have neither a box nor a prisoner."

The police began a careful search of the holds, galley, crews' quarters, and the captain's cabin as well. Meanwhile, Frank and Joe sauntered over the deck.

"Let's check the lifeboats," Frank suggested.

They looked beneath the canvas cover of each one, but could see nothing suspicious. Just as the police emerged from the holds, they approached the last lifeboat.

At one end of it, the sea breeze fluttered a piece of the covering which had come loose.

"Watch it, Joe," Frank warned. "It might not have been the wind that tore off the canvas!" He signalled Chief Collig. "Over here!" he called.

The officers ran to the lifeboat. One flashed his light under the canvas, then barked a crisp order. "Come out with your hands up!"

The cowering figure of a man emerged above the gunwale.

"Holy crow!" Joe exclaimed. "It's Gerard Henry!"

·17·

The Chinese Note

THE prisoner looked surly as the police pulled him to the deck and snapped on handcuffs. Captain Ono, who came running up, was flabbergasted.

"Is—is this your kidnapped man?" he asked.

"No," Collig replied. "But he's an escaped felon."

"How did you get on my ship?" Ono asked Henry sternly.

The man confessed that he had climbed a rope and reached the deck shortly before the *Queen* sailed. Collig turned to Ono. "Why did you leave ahead of schedule?"

"All was in readiness. So why wait?"

"Did you notify the harbour master?"

"Of course. We adhere to proper procedure."

The prisoner was led down to the police launch and Ono was told he could proceed. Frank and Joe hopped into the *Sleuth* and headed home.

When they arrived they received a phone call from their father. Frank answered it. He told about their proposed trip to Hong Kong and asked, "Is it okay with you, Dad?"

"Sure. I'll follow you as soon as I can. Right now I'm going to Dallas. Seems a branch of the tailoring-jewellery racket has sprung up there."

The next morning at breakfast there was a knock on the back door and Phil Cohen entered.

"Hi, Phil," Frank said. "What brings you over here so early?"

Phil looked serious. "I noticed something funny and wanted to talk to you. It's about Chet."

"What about him?"

"He went into Paul Goo's Chinese Laundry yesterday afternoon."

"Nothing funny about that," Joe said. "Maybe he took his shirts."

"You know his mother does all his laundry. He took nothing and picked nothing up. Before he went in he glanced up and down the street as if he wanted to make sure no one saw him. It looked suspicious to me."

"Hm!" Frank said thoughtfully. "Why would he do that?"

"That's just it. It's not like Chet," Phil said. "Maybe he got mixed up in your Chinese mystery somehow, being that he spends so much time with Krassner—"

"I'll get to the bottom of this right now," Frank broke in. He picked up the telephone and dialled the Morton farm. Chet answered.

"Hey, old buddy," Frank said, "what were you doing in Paul Goo's laundry yesterday?"

There was silence on the other end. Then Chet said, "Who told you?"

"A little Chinese bird. What were you doing there?"

"Nothing much. Just got some lychee nuts."

"Tell me the truth, Chet!"

"I am. Is it against the law to visit a Chinese laundry?" Chet would say nothing more.

119

When he hung up, Frank felt uneasy. "Let's check out the laundry," he suggested.

"Right," Joe agreed. "But first we'd better stop at headquarters. Maybe there's some news on Conrad."

"See you later," Phil said. "Let me know what develops." He left through the back door when giggling voices of girls could be heard in the front. After a brief knock, Joe opened the door and Callie Shaw and Iola Morton breezed in.

Frank grinned at Callie, a pretty blonde girl with brown eyes, whom he often dated. "Hi. What's up?"

"We're selling tickets to a benefit."

"When, where, why?"

"Tonight in our barn," Iola said. "Eight o'clock sharp."

"But for whose benefit?" Joe inquired.

"That's our secret. You're coming, of course." Iola reached into her pocket and pulled out two tickets. She handed them to Joe. "You can pay us later," she said.

Just then Mrs Hardy and Aunt Gertrude came in and greeted the girls. As they chatted, the boys drove off to headquarters. There they learned two pertinent facts. Nothing had been heard from Conrad Greene, and they were told that Paul Goo, the Chinese laundry owner, had an impeccable reputation.

"He's been in this country a long time," Chief Collig said. "A friendly old duck. Likes kids."

Frank and Joe thanked the officer, then drove to Mully Street. It was the main thoroughfare of Bayport's Little Chinatown. They passed two restaurants, a Chinese grocery, and a gift shop before coming to Paul Goo's place. They parked and went in. A tinkling bell announced their presence. The interior of the shop smelled of soap, starch, and steam.

Behind an ironing board stood Paul Goo, a spare, elderly man, whose eyes were shuttered in deep fleshy folds. "Hello," he said with a smile. "You have some shirts?"

"Not today," Frank said. "We want to ask your prices."

"Oh yes. Very reasonable here." Goo handed the boy a small printed paper listing his services.

"Thank you," Frank said. "Do you have lychee nuts?"

The elderly man blinked. "Sure. For my friends." He put a hand beneath the counter, produced two of the thin-shelled nuts so popular with Orientals, and handed one to each boy.

"Thank you," Joe said. "You are very kind."

They turned to go, but Frank hesitated a moment. "Are you from Hong Kong, Mr Goo?"

The laundryman smiled broadly. "Yes. How you guess? Most people in Little Chinatown are from Hong Kong."

Outside, the boys cracked the nuts. "Not bad," Joe said. "What do you think of Goo, Frank?"

"He seems all right. But you never can tell. Let's put a tail on good old Chet and find out what's going on."

Joe snapped his fingers. "Phil Cohen would be a good man for the job!"

The Hardys stopped at Phil's home. The sound of piano playing drifted across the front lawn and the boys found their friend busily composing a song.

"Sorry to disturb your symphony," Joe said, "but do you have time for a surveillance job?"

"I think so. What is it?"

"Follow Chet. See if he goes to that Chinese laundry again. He may be headed for trouble."

"Will do," Phil agreed. "I'll phone Iola. She can tell me when Chet's coming into town again."

"Thanks, pal," Frank said.

As Frank and Joe drove off, they heard Phil picking on the piano keys again. An hour later he called them at home.

"I spoke to Iola, and guess what? Chet's on his way to town!" he reported. "I'm going to Mully Street right away."

"Good. Keep out of sight and let us know what's happening."

While the Hardys ate lunch, Phil hurried off to Mully Street. He stationed himself in a doorway where he had Paul Goo's shop in a clear line of sight. And he did not have to wait long.

Down the street strolled Chet, his lips moving as if he were mumbling to himself.

"The poor guy's gone bananas," Phil thought. He left his hiding place and quietly fell in behind Chet, who seemed oblivious to the whole world.

When he stepped into the laundry, Phil flattened himself against the building and listened. He could not make out any words, but Chet and Goo conversed for about ten minutes in low tones. Then another customer entered. The mumbling ceased and Chet came out, a piece of paper in his hand.

His eyes were so intent upon it that he bumped squarely into Phil. "Oh, hello there," he said.

"Getting more nuts?" Phil asked.

Chet was not the least shaken by the point-blank query. "No. Not today. Well, I have to go now."

Phil watched Chet walk away. Suddenly he noticed the piece of paper fall to the ground. Unaware of it, Chet got into his jalopy and drove off.

Phil ran to the spot and picked it up. His eyes widened in surprise. "Wait till the Hardys see this!" he said to himself. Minutes later he drove up to their home.

"Hey, Frank, Joe!" he called out as he rushed to the door.

"What's the matter?" Frank let him in. "You're all out of breath."

"Look at this!" Phil handed him the paper.

On it were lines of Chinese characters, delicately brush-stroked. Alongside each were phonetic pronunciations written in English.

Joe said, "Maybe Chet's some kind of go-between. It could be a message!"

"And he might have to deliver it verbally, hence the mumbling," Phil remarked, and relayed the information he had gleaned on his surveillance.

"We'll have to take this to an Oriental language expert," Frank said.

"You do that," Phil said. "I'll get back to my song."

He left, and while Frank and Joe were studying the mysterious paper, the telephone rang. Joe answered. It was Conrad Greene's father.

"I have some information for you," he said in a quavering voice.

"What is it?"

"I can't tell you on the phone. Come over here as soon as you can!"

"What a day," Joe said to Frank with a sigh. "Mr Greene wants to see us pronto. Do you suppose he received a ransom demand?"

123

"We'll find out soon. Come on."

The boys went to their car after quickly telling their mother where they were headed. Forty-five minutes later they parked in front of the house on the cliff. They hastened to the door and were flabbergasted when it was opened by the grandmaster himself!

"Conrad Greene!" Frank exclaimed. "How did you get loose? Where were you held? Who kidnapped you?"

"Come in and I'll answer your questions one at a time," Greene said with a grin.

In the living room his story unfolded. He had not seen his captors, because a hood had been clapped over his head. Where he was held was a mystery, too, but the why was perfectly clear.

"My captors warned me not to win the international championship!" he said. "They didn't hurt me, but guaranteed that I would be if I made an attempt to win. They drove me back just a little while ago."

"Have you notified the police?" Frank asked.

"Not yet. I wanted to tell you first."

Frank grabbed the phone and spoke to Chief Collig. Then he said, "Come on, Joe. We'll disconnect that phone tap. I don't think the gang is being fooled by it any longer, if they ever were."

The job was quickly accomplished, and as Joe climbed down from the pole, a police car drove up. It was Lieutenant Skillman from the Ocean Bluffs force.

"Chief Collig notified me," he said. "He also got in touch with the FBI. I'm sure they'll have a lot of questions for Mr Greene."

The boys left as Conrad beckoned Skillman into the house. On the way home, Frank said, "I think this whole caper was done to unnerve Conrad."

"No doubt," Joe agreed.

They mulled over the latest developments. The serpent gang had carried off the Ruby King, and it seemed logical that they also had been the ones who had kidnapped Greene. But why did they want him to lose the championship, now that he could not receive the valuable prize, anyway?

"It just doesn't make sense," Frank said.

"Well, what do we do next?" Joe asked.

Frank looked at his watch. "It's too late to have that Chinese note deciphered now. We'll just be in time for dinner. And the party starts at eight."

When the Hardys reached the Morton farm, the barn behind the house was vibrating with music. Frank and Joe entered to find the place festooned with colourful crêpe paper and balloons. They recognized many of their friends from high school and the Bayport area. Couples were dancing to the rhythmic tunes produced by a three-piece group.

"Wow, what a blast!" Joe said.

When Callie and Iola noticed the boys, they came over, took them by the hand, and led them to a long table. On it stood a punch bowl and a variety of sandwiches.

"Now tell us what this is all about, Iola," Joe urged. "You said the party was for a benefit?"

"Right. Yours, to be exact."

"Wait a minute. What—?"

Iola interrupted him by putting a hand on his arm. At the same time she tapped a spoon on the punch bowl and called out, "Silence, please!"

Everyone became quiet.

"As you all know," Iola began, "our two private eyes

125

are going to Hong Kong on a most dangerous mission. We, their friends, felt they needed a bodyguard—a big one. We are holding this party to raise extra money for that bodyguard."

The Hardys were dumbfounded. "Who is he?" Joe finally asked.

"Who else?" Chet declared, a grin on his face.

Everyone cheered.

"We should have guessed," Joe said. "He *is* the biggest one of our friends—or rather the fattest!"

"But size alone is not enough," Chet said. "I have made myself indispensable in other ways!"

"Such as?" Frank had a hard time keeping a straight face.

"I learned Chinese! Listen: Ho-La-Ma, Mmm Goy, Ngor But Duck Lew Ah-h-h, Gau Miang Ah-h-h, Mau Sot Ah-h-h-h!"

"Those were the words on the paper!" Frank said.

Chet's lips curled in a supercilious smile. "Of course. My gag worked. I dropped it on purpose."

Frank and Joe slapped Chet on the back. "Now tell us what all that means!" Joe asked.

Chet took a deep breath. "Hello—please, I'm in trouble—help—murder!"

·18·

Kim-Kim

AT a signal from Phil Cohen, the group broke out in a catchy tune. Everyone started to sing:

> Frank, Joe, and Chet, farewell to thee,
> Sock 'em, rock 'em
> Till the Ruby King is free.
> Hello, Hong Kong,
> You can't hide Fong
> or the slippery Eggleby.

Joe laughed at the serenade, and Frank recognised the tune Phil had been composing on his piano. Then came a rousing refrain:

> For the Hardys will get you
> Sooner or later,
> So surrender right now while you can.
> They'll give you fits
> With their uncanny wits.
> They always come up with their man!

The merrymaking still rang in the minds of Frank, Joe, and sleepy-eyed Chet when they set off from

Bayport at six o'clock the next morning. After the first two transfers the flight became monotonous and the boys were weary by the time the big plane landed in heavy rain at Kai Tak Airport the following evening. They retrieved their baggage, then went through customs.

"Before we leave the airport," Frank said, "let's check on the rug."

They made their way to the freight terminal and inquired about the shipment. The clerk told them he did not know the name of the man who had picked up the rug but would check it out and call them at the hotel.

"Thank you," Frank said and they left. Outside the terminal they hailed a taxi and gave the driver the address of their hotel, the Star Terminal, in Kowloon.

As they approached the city, Chet said, "Wow, this is a big place!"

"What did you expect?" Frank needled. "A dreamy little fishing village? Take a look across the bay!"

Part way up the Hong Kong hill, white multi-storey flats rose like sentinels, looking down on modern glass-and-steel office buildings in the harbour area.

Finally they arrived at their destination. "Boy, I'm beat," Chet complained.

"We'll hit the sack as soon as we get upstairs," Joe said.

They checked in and half an hour later were sound asleep.

The next morning they woke up refreshed and excited by prospects of adventure in the Orient. Joe pulled open the curtains. "Hey, take in that view!" he said, pointing to ferryboats plying their way back and forth in the harbour among the many junks, sampans, and small fishing boats.

"Give me breakfast before any view," Chet said.

"Not a bad idea," Frank agreed. "After we eat we'll go to visit Mrs Krassner's parents. I'll call them right now and tell them we're coming."

An hour later the boys hastened down to the ferry slip to await the next boat to Hong Kong. They joined the good-natured, jostling crowd that elbowed on to the craft like a colony of ants.

Frank, Joe, and Chet sat on the upper deck and watched as the teeming shore of Hong Kong came closer and closer. The ferry glided smoothly into its slip and the three disembarked.

Frank hailed a taxi and told the Chinese driver to take them to Moy Chen-Chin's house.

"Ah, so." The man nodded and smiled, obviously impressed with the importance of his riders.

The higher the road snaked up the hill, the more luxurious the homes became. Finally they reached the estate of Moy Chen-Chin and were amazed by its opulence.

Formal gardens bordered both sides of the drive and gave the grounds the appearance of a royal park. Men were trimming, pruning, and tending the flower beds.

The taxi stopped in front of a beautiful house with a wide terrace. An elderly couple came out to meet them and introduced themselves as Mr and Mrs Moy.

As they led the boys to the veranda, Chet whispered to Frank, "I thought their name was Chin."

"In Chinese the last name always comes first," Frank replied.

As soon as tea was served, the Moys plied the boys

with questions about their daughter Mrs Krassner and her husband.

After the Americans had told them all about Bayport and their life at home, Mr Moy said seriously, "We know you have come for the Ruby King. Will you take some advice from a wise old man?"

"What is it?" Frank asked.

"Drop your case. It will bring you only misery, even death!"

The awkward silence that followed was broken by Chet, who said *"Daw Jer"* which meant "Thank you."

Mrs Moy smiled. "Oh, you speak our language. Where did you learn it?"

"At Paul Goo's laundry," Chet said and told his story, which the Chinese couple found very amusing.

"You must see all the sights," Mr Moy said. "Spend a week or two and have a good vacation. Then return home."

"We'll tour the area to get our bearings," Frank said. "But really, Mr Moy, we can't take your advice. We have an obligation to Mr Krassner and the insurance company which is paying for our trip."

Mr Moy shrugged slightly. Then he said, "Our chauffeur Daniel will take you on a tour. Shall I send him to the hotel tomorrow, say, at ten o'clock?"

"That would be great!" Joe said.

A few minutes later the boys thanked the cordial couple and went back to their hotel. On the way Frank said, "I wonder why Mr Moy made that remark about the Ruby King. He sounds like Conrad Greene's father!"

"He must know about the curse, too," Joe said.

At the hotel they found a message from the airport.

The name of the man who had picked up the rug was Choy Bok. But there was no address.

"Let's look in the telephone book," Joe suggested.

After thumbing through the directory he was perplexed. "Six people are listed under that name," he said.

"We'd better check out each one," Frank said.

"I don't know if that's such a good idea," Joe countered. "We may tip off the real Choy Bok in the process."

"I'm aware of that," his brother replied. "But we have to start somewhere. If any of these men react to the password *Shah mat*, at least it will give us a lead."

The boys left the hotel again, hired a taxi, and were on their way. The first two Choy Boks lived in the poorest section of town, and neither spoke English. The driver acted as an interpreter while Frank talked to the men. They looked blank when he mentioned the password, and the Hardys were convinced that they were not involved with the serpent gang.

The young detectives were no luckier with the next three, who were also poor, elderly men. The last Choy Bok lived in a multi-storey apartment, seemed reasonably well-to-do, and spoke good English.

He greeted the boys affably, and when Frank mentioned the password, he said, "Oh, you play chess?"

Frank nodded. "We have a chess club in Bayport, where we come from. One of the members is Chinese. Told us to visit his friend Choy Bok in Hong Kong."

"Oh? What's your friend's name?"

"Fong," Frank said. He watched the man intently.

Choy Bok raised his eyebrows. "I don't think I know him."

"Well, he forgot to give us the address. We looked in

the phone book, but must have made a mistake."

"I think you did. But have a cup of tea, anyway."

Mr Choy called his wife and the friendly couple served them a snack. They talked amiably to the Americans for quite some time, then Frank rose. The boys thanked the Choys and left.

Tired and discouraged from the long day's sleuthing, they returned to their hotel.

As they trudged up to their room, Joe said, "I'm afraid the whole thing was a wild goose chase. I'm sure none of the men we talked to is a member of the Serpents."

Frank nodded. "I'm inclined to agree. Whoever comes up with a good idea on what to do next gets a prize."

"Let's have dinner and call it a day," Chet said. "And I'll take the prize."

"That kind of idea doesn't qualify," Frank said. "But we'll follow your advice."

The next morning at ten o'clock sharp Mr Moy's chauffeur arrived. "I'll take you through town and out to Aberdeen," he said. "Then if we have time, to the New Territories, which overlook the Peoples' Republic of China."

For many miles the road led along a barren shoreline. Then they came to a bay with hundreds of sampans lying side by side.

"Do people live on the water like this?" Chet asked.

Daniel, the driver, nodded. "This is Aberdeen. The government is trying to get the sampan dwellers to move into new developments, but their way of life is hard to change." He stopped for a few minutes while the boys took photographs with a pocket camera Frank and Joe had brought along.

As they clicked away, a small boy climbed up a steep embankment to the road. "Me Kim-Kim. I help you," he said.

"I don't think we need you," Frank replied, but the ten-year-old was not to be deterred.

He attached himself to Chet. "I help *you!*" he said. "You big man. I carry your camera."

Kim-Kim wore tattered shorts and a discarded army jacket, its long sleeves hanging down over his hands. As the Americans returned to the car, he slipped in beside Chet before anyone could stop him.

"Out!" Daniel commanded.

But Kim-Kim refused. He kicked and struggled, and clung to Chet's neck.

"Okay," Frank said. "We'll take him back with us, give him a square meal, and turn him over to the police."

The little fellow grinned. "I bring you good luck!" he promised.

After Daniel had been driving a while, Frank noticed a semi-circular wall built into a hillside. He asked about it.

"It's an armchair grave," Daniel replied. He explained that the deceased were buried in such graves for one year. Then their bones were disinterred and placed in earthen jars. He pointed. "There's one now."

In a farm field stood a mud-coloured container about three feet high.

"It looks like my mother's cookie jar," Chet commented.

"A little gruesome, isn't it?" Joe said.

Then suddenly the monsoon rains hit. Water came

down in torrents and the road ahead of them turned into a river.

"This could be dangerous," Daniel said, and turned the car around.

Traffic moved along slowly. As they edged past the hillside, a wall of mud slid down, nearly blocking the road. But Daniel drove skilfully over the sheet of yellow slime, finally guiding the car safely back to Kowloon.

"So that's a monsoon!" Chet said as they entered the hotel.

"Well, Kim-Kim, you got us through that," Joe said, opening the door to their room. "And now into the shower with you!"

By dinner time Kim-Kim, who said he was an orphan, had convinced the boys to let him stay with them as an interpreter as long as they were in Hong Kong. After breakfast the next day, while Chet bought him some new clothes, Frank read about the storm in the morning English newspaper.

"Hey, look at this!" he said suddenly. "Ming Do's obituary!"

The world-famous collector of chess pieces had died two days before. The funeral was to take place the next afternoon. The article said that Ming Do was the oldest member of the Royal Chess Club of Hong Kong.

"Ming Do!" Joe exclaimed. "That cable we found mentioned that a man by that name was very ill!"

"Right. He must have been the customer who wanted the Ruby King!" Frank said.

They told Chet the news when he returned. "Wow!" he said. "Who's going to buy it now?"

Frank shrugged. "Maybe we can learn something at the Royal Chess Club."

They discussed strategy. Chet and Kim-Kim would stay outside the club, which was located not far from their hotel. The Hardys would go in and investigate.

Frank and Joe entered the plush interior thirty minutes later and looked about. A chill of recognition ran down Joe's spine. He nudged his brother.

Sitting at a table at the far end corner was Fong, playing chess with another man!

The Hardys approached as close as they could without being seen. Then they slipped behind a heavy curtain to eavesdrop.

The men talked in low tones, and the name Ruby King could be heard now and then.

"Who do you suppose that other guy is?" Joe asked.

Suddenly the Hardys became aware of a commotion. They peered from their hiding place to see Kim-Kim running into the club with Chet chasing him!

"Frank, Joe!" Kim-Kim cried out.

"Good grief," Frank said. "Now we're in trouble!"

·19·

The Payoff

"COME here, Kim-Kim! Wait!" Chet called as surprised club members looked askance at the intruders.

But the small Chinese boy did not stop. His sharp eyes searched the room until they alighted upon the feet of Frank and Joe showing beneath the curtain. He revealed their hiding place, took both by the hand, and pulled the embarrassed Hardys out into the room.

"What are you doing?" Joe muttered.

"No time to lose!" Kim-Kim said. "Big danger!"

His eyes glinting with anger, Fong rose from his chessboard and confronted the eavesdroppers. He beckoned two attendants and spat out some Chinese, whereupon the men grasped the boys by the arms.

"So! The detective babies have left the Bayport playpen. How quaint! What do you want here?"

"You know!" Joe shot back. "You and your crooked Serpents!"

Fong laughed derisively and the men standing about smiled at the discomfiture of the young Americans. "Play your children's games somewhere else," Fong went on. "But I warn you both—and your fat friend, too—you are not in the United States now. Go home before it's too late!"

136

He spoke more Chinese to the attendants, who promptly hustled the boys and Kim-Kim out into the street. When the bouncers had disappeared, Frank said, "Chet, for heaven's sake, why did you let Kim-Kim blow our cover?"

"I didn't mean to," Chet apologized. "He heard something you should know about, and before I could tell him to wait, he ran in there."

"What is it?"

Kim-Kim turned his head slowly and said in a whisper, "Those two men across the street—in front of store window—no look now—they going to kill you. Say so in Chinese!"

"Okay, Kim-Kim, don't worry about it. We'll take care of it," Joe said, trying to calm the excited child.

The Hardys engaged in casual chatter while Frank took out the tiny camera and unobtrusively snapped a few pictures of the men. Then they walked towards the hotel and stopped at a camera shop to drop off the film. Prints were promised that evening.

"We might never see them," Chet said pessimistically. "I'll bet someone followed us."

"Those two guys didn't, I made sure of that," Joe replied. "Anyway, it might help to learn who they are. If they're really out to get us, maybe the police could arrest them."

Back at the hotel, Chet and Kim-Kim remained in the lobby coffee shop while the Hardys took the elevator to their room. Joe turned the key in the lock and pushed open the door.

There sat Fong, smiling like a welcome guest, his feet resting on a coffee table! "Surprise!" he said.

"How did you get in?" Joe demanded angrily.

"Calm down," Fong said, and beckoned the Hardys to be seated. "How I got in is simple enough. Kowloon is my turf, as you say in the States."

"What do you want?" Frank asked. "You've got the Ruby King!"

"Money. I want money," Fong replied. "You can get it for me and save your necks at the same time. Sound interesting?"

"What do you mean?" Joe asked.

Fong removed his feet and leaned forward intently, gesturing with his long, slender hands. "I will sell the Ruby King to the insurance company you represent," Fong said, "at a depressed figure—say twenty-five thousand dollars. The claim will cost them much more than that."

Frank's mind whirled. Of course the serpent gang must have deduced that their trip to Hong Kong was paid by the insurance company who had to pay for the loss of the King. What a cunning plan!

"And what if they don't accept this offer?"

"They will," Fong said. "It's smart business. Phone me at the chess club when you get a reply from your employer." He rose, went to the door, and turned around. This time his face had a sinister expression.

"By the way, no police involvement, or Mrs Krassner's family will be in big trouble!"

A sudden thought flashed through Frank's mind. "Is that how you got her to leave her husband's safe open?"

The question seemed to jolt Fong but only for a split second. "Let's say Mrs Krassner could be persuaded," he said unctuously. "She knows the power of the Serpents. You should follow her example."

When Fong had left, the boys discussed the strange

offer and Mrs Krassner's part in the disappearance of the chess piece.

"I feel sorry for her," Joe said.

Just then running footsteps sounded in the hall and Chet flung open the door with a bang. Kim-Kim stood, wild-eyed, beside him.

"F-Fong!" Chet said. "He just came off the elevator. I thought maybe he—"

"Had murdered us?" Joe said.

"Yes. I'm sure glad to see you alive."

Joe told Chet what had happened, while Frank composed a message to the insurance company. Then they went downstairs to the desk and sent the cable.

For the rest of the day and through the dinner hour, the Hardys speculated on the outcome of Fong's proposal. Whatever the decision of the insurance company, the boys faced considerable risk.

If the answer was "no deal," their lives certainly would be in jeopardy. Even if the money were sent, there was no telling whether the Serpents would carry out their end of the bargain.

As Chet put it, "Fong might take the twenty-five thousand dollars and keep the Ruby King too. Then what would you do?"

"It wouldn't make any difference," Joe said, "because we probably wouldn't be alive to tell the tale."

Leaving Chet and his Oriental shadow to linger over dessert, Frank and Joe stepped out into the muggy night air and made sure they were not being followed as they walked to the photography shop. The prints were waiting and the Hardys examined them.

"Good clear shots," Joe said. "What next?"

"Let's take them to the police," Frank said. "Maybe we can find out who our charming friends are."

At headquarters the captain in charge, a tall, thin fellow named Hawkins, identified the two men instantly. "They're hit men for the serpent mob," he said.

"A friend of ours heard them say they'll kill us," Frank said.

"Then my advice is to be very careful. Unfortunately this is not enough to press charges and to arrest them. We've been trying to crack that ring for a long time, but without success."

In their hotel again, the three boys and Kim-Kim studied the inscrutable faces of the hit men. "I've a hunch we'll see them again," Joe said.

They were all at breakfast the next morning when a cablegram was delivered for the Hardys by a bellhop. Frank took the envelope and opened it. "From International Insurance," he said. "They accepted the offer!" The message said twenty-five thousand dollars had already been deposited in a Hong Kong bank.

The Hardys were to take it out in cash and buy the Ruby King back. The cable ended, "As much as we dislike this arrangement, it seems feasible at this time. Please be extremely cautious."

The boys hastily finished their meal and telephoned the chess club. Fong was not there and they left a message for him to return the call.

Only ten minutes elapsed before he telephoned.

"Fong speaking. What's the deal?"

"Affirmative," Frank said.

"Ah, good. It will be a cash transaction."

"Of course."

"And no police!"

140

"They haven't been told," Frank said.

"Then here's how we'll do it," Fong said. "Got a pencil and paper?"

"Yes. Go ahead."

Fong spoke slowly while Frank took notes. After the Hardys obtained the cash they were to take a taxi out past Aberdeen and into the countryside. "That Chinese kid with you will show you the way," the man said.

He then mentioned a small settlement of sampans. One mile to the north, on the right-hand side of the road, they would see a bone jar one hundred and fifty yards from a farmer's shack made of corrugated sheet metal.

"You understand what a bone jar is?" Fong asked.

"Yes. I've seen one."

"Put the cash in it. It's empty."

"What about the Ruby King?" Frank asked.

"A note in the jar will tell you where to find it."

The time was set for twelve-thirty that afternoon, and before Fong hung up, he warned that any double-cross would be fatal.

The young detectives were keyed up with almost unbearable excitement. They hastened to the bank, where the manager frowned in disbelief as he counted out the amount in large bills and tied the money in a small package. Joe put it inside his shirt and they returned to the hotel.

"Whew!" Frank said, rubbing the sweat from the palms of his hands. "So far so good."

Carefully following Fong's directions, the four set off by taxi towards the rendezvous. Kim-Kim looked wistfully at the city of junks and sampans as they passed

Aberdeen. All watched for the hut and the bone jar.

"There it is," Chet finally said, pointing to the side of the road.

"Looks like it all right," Frank agreed. "Stop here, driver."

They got out and walked towards the dun-coloured jar. Two farmers, sharpening sickles, watched from the side of the tin shack. Nearing the jar, Chet tripped over a bundle of bamboo poles lying in the tall grass.

"Careful. Don't break your other arm," Joe said.

All this time Kim-Kim kept his eyes on the two men. "They no look happy," he said.

"They probably work for the Serpents," Joe remarked, "and are disguised as farmers."

"No," Kim-Kim said. "They real farmers and they get madder."

The boys had reached the bone jar and Frank boldly removed the lid. He put his hand inside. "Let's get the directions to the Ruby King first," he said. feeling about until his fingers touched something soft and at the same time hard.

Frank pulled out a fistful of matted hair and bones!

"Ugh!" he said in disgust. "Somebody's remains are in here!"

"Yes. I think so too," Kim-Kim said. "Here come farmers. Very mad."

The two men raced towards the trespassers brandishing the sickles, which gleamed in the midday sunshine.

"Holy crow!" Joe exclaimed. "Maybe it's the wrong bone jar!"

"Either that, or it's a booby-trap!" Frank said. "Run!"

142

The boys ran towards the waiting taxi, but Chet, with his arm in the cast, could not keep up.

"Hey, don't let 'em chop me up!" he pleaded.

Frank and Joe stopped to pick up the bamboo poles, and when the irate farmers approached, they warded off the sickle blows, while Kim-Kim ardently apologized in Chinese.

But the enraged farmers could not be mollified. One of them flung his weapon and it came at Frank's head like a spinning boomerang!

·20·

The Beggars of Tai Pak

"DUCK!" Joe's warning sent Frank tumbling into grass, and the sickle sailed harmlessly over him. He regained his feet to see the farmers standing with arms akimbo, glowering at the retreating intruders.

Panting for breath, the boys reached the taxi and piled in on top of one another. When the door slammed shut, the driver sped off and Kim-Kim climbed into the front seat. He grinned back at the Americans.

"Farmers very mad. You disturbed honourable ancestors!"

"We didn't mean to. How did we ever get the wrong place?" Joe wondered.

"I'll tell you how," Frank said. "Look up ahead. There's another shack and another bone jar. This must be it!"

"Please, fellows," Chet begged, "be more careful this time. I'm not quite ready to be cut up for chop suey."

After the taxi had stopped, the Hardys sent Kim-Kim on ahead to reconnoitre the shack. He returned with a big smile. "Nobody home. Okay go see!"

Still somewhat weak-kneed from their narrow escape, Frank, Joe and Chet tramped across the field until they came to the bone jar. It looked older than the first, and a thin crack ran up from the lip to the base.

"You put your hand in this time!" Frank said to Chet.

"Oh no. Not me!"

"I'll do it," Joe volunteered. He reached inside, until his whole arm disappeared. "No bones here," he said, feeling around with his fingers. Finally he pulled out a folded piece of paper. On it was a message. He read it aloud:

> " 'Hardys:
> Leave the cash here and go a thousand yards up the road. On the opposite side behind a row of trees is an armchair grave. The Ruby King is buried in it. Remember, you are being observed. If you pull any tricks with the money, you will not return to Hong Kong alive!' "

"I expected something like that," Frank said. "We'd better leave the cash."

"But what if the King is not where it's supposed to be?" Joe asked.

"We'll have to chance it. Put in the money, Joe."

The boy removed the package from his shirt and dropped it into the bone jar. Then they hurried to the taxi and instructed the driver to proceed slowly until they came to the row of eucalyptus trees, about a hundred yards back from the road.

While the driver waited, the four approached the spot. Suddenly voices drifted towards them from behind the trees.

"*Sh!*" Frank warned. "We've got company. Let's sneak up and see who it is!"

Noiselessly they moved to the trees and peered through the branches. There was the armchair grave as the note had indicated, and two men were pulling something out of it. One had his back turned towards the boys, but Frank and Joe recognized the other! He was the man Frank had wrestled with at Ocean Bluffs, just before Gerard Henry and Joe had rolled off the cliff!

Now the other man let out a string of curses and the Hardys recognized his voice.

"It's Reginald Jervis!" Joe whispered.

Frank nodded. "And they're digging up the Ruby King!"

Jervis was still ranting. "Those crooks! Took all the rubies out! It's worthless now, totally worthless!" The men let the King fall down and Jervis kicked it with his foot. "Let's go," he grumbled.

"Oh, no, you don't!" Frank said. The three boys, followed by Kim-Kim, set upon the men like lightning.

Jervis whirled around when he heard the commotion. He still had the shovel in his hand. Instantly he raised it over his head and whacked Joe.

Frank tackled his erstwhile adversary while Chet came to Joe's help. Before Jervis could raise the shovel again, Chet's plaster cast hit him on the side of the head. He toppled and lay still.

Frank, meanwhile, had subdued the other man. "Chet, see if our driver has some rope so we can tie up our buddies," he said.

"I don't think we need it," Chet said. He pointed towards the trees. "Look who's coming!"

Captain Hawkins and another policeman crashed through the branches. "You young foreigners had us worried," he said, "so we tailed Fong's thugs. Followed them to a bone jar and caught them with a bundle of money. You know anything about it?"

While the police snapped handcuffs on the boys' prisoners, Frank and Joe told about the ransom deal.

Jervis laughed out loud. "So Fong was going to let you have the Ruby King after all. But minus the goodies. I thought he'd send you back to Hong Kong after you had delivered the dough."

"And you figured you could help yourself to the goodies?" Frank asked.

Jervis gritted his teeth. "Fong's a dirty double-crosser! You want him? I'll tell you where he is. Sitting at the Tai Pak Restaurant, waiting for the twenty-five thousand clams!"

"Tai Pak?" Kim-Kim said brightly. "I know. Near where I live. Good place to make money."

Hawkins explained that Tai Pak was a large floating restaurant, famous throughout the Orient. "We'd better go and see if this man is telling the truth," he said.

He ordered the other policeman to take the hand-cuffed prisoners to headquarters. "I'm going to the waterfront with the boys," he added. "Have a squad car meet me there."

Soon they arrived at the harbour, alive with small canopied boats. They were propelled by women, wearing black pyjamas and coolie hats, who sculled the craft along with a long oar.

"Those are water taxies," Hawkins explained. "They take passengers to Tai Pak." He hailed one of the little boats.

The boys noticed that some small open craft were rowed by children. They circled among the fleet of

147

water taxies, begging coins from the more affluent passengers.

"Is that what you meant by a good place to make money?" Chet asked Kim-Kim.

The Chinese nodded and called out to several friends he had recognized.

Just then a squad car arrived with four policemen. While the boys hopped into the water taxi Captain Hawkins had hailed, they took another and soon everyone was headed for the floating restaurant.

The Hardys were amazed at the dexterity of the women, who manoeuvred their boats through the traffic without even the slightest collision.

Finally they reached the huge double-deck eating place, colourfully festooned with lights and lanterns. They went aboard and Hawkins suggested that the boys check topside, while the police scoured the main deck.

The Americans were amazed at the size of the restaurant. Scores of tables occupied every foot of the deck. Waiters, carrying large trays, moved through the guests with acrobatic ease.

A broad centre staircase led up to the second deck, which was equally crowded.

"Let's split up," Frank suggested. "If you spy Fong, don't make a scene. Just run down and call Captain Hawkins."

The clatter of dishes, the laughter of the diners, and the swiftly moving waiters made concentration difficult. In addition, the savoury smell of Chinese cooking made Chet hungry. Nonetheless they spaced out and carefully passed table after table.

Suddenly Joe's eyes fell on Fong. He was seated in a

secluded booth next to the wall, talking with another man. Fong glanced nervously at his watch, while his eyes roved the room.

Joe snatched a handkerchief and held it to his face. Then he edged closer, trying to get a look at Fong's companion.

He turned and Joe recognized him. It was the friendly Choy Bok!

A waiter touched Joe's elbow. "Can I help you find a place?"

"No, thank you. Not now."

At that moment Chet hurried to Joe's side. "I see him!" he whispered, and swung his cast in the direction of the booth.

It hit the back of a chair with a sharp crack. The diner sitting there turned around in surprise. At the same time Joe noticed Fong and Choy Bok rise. They had realized that the boys were after them!

"Run down and get the captain!" Joe told Chet. As he hurried off, Frank and Kim-Kim appeared.

"Come on!" Joe cried. "They're getting away!"

The young detectives raced among the tables, trying not to knock into the annoyed patrons.

"There they go! Up the steps!"

The fugitives fairly flew up a small metal stairway on to the roof of the restaurant, and without a moment's hesitation, dived over the railing into the water below.

The Hardys saw them surface and climb into a water taxi.

"After them!" Frank cried out. He and Joe, followed by Kim-Kim, plunged into the bay. They came up next to a surprised taxi-woman and wriggled into her boat.

Kim-Kim gave orders in Chinese, and the woman set off after Fong's craft.

"We're losing them!" Joe said. "Faster, please!"

"Don't worry, I help," Kim-Kim said.

He called out to his little beggar friends, who responded with excited cries. Rapidly they began to surround the getaway taxi. With much banging and shouting, they had its path blocked within a few minutes.

It was boxed in so tightly that escape was impossible. The police arrived in another boat with Chet to arrest the two stony-faced fugitives.

Meanwhile, the Hardys emptied their pockets of all their change and tossed the coins to the beggar boys, who grinned and cheered.

"Good job, Kim-Kim," Frank praised the little Chinese.

An hour later everyone met at headquarters. The Hardys were congratulated, and as interrogation of Jervis, Fong, and Choy Bok proceeded, loose ends of the mystery were tied up.

A cablegram from Mr Hardy had arrived only minutes before. It said that Eggleby had been caught in the States with Radley's help. He and Jervis had been trying to set up another jewellery operation in Texas, but when Eggleby was caught, Jervis quickly left the country.

Jervis admitted knocking out Mr Hardy at the Treat Hotel and putting the explosive charge in the boys' exhaust on orders of Fong. And it was Jervis who shot at Krassner in the balloon fight. Fong and Eggleby were with him at the time.

"You idiot!" Fong muttered. "Why don't you keep

your mouth shut?" But the angry gang leader could not do anything to stop his former confederate from telling everything. As he and Choy stood by with suppressed anger, Jervis provided the answer to the serpent gang's interest in Conrad Greene.

"They ran a world-wide gambling operation," Jervis said, "and were trying to frighten the American champion into losing the match because they had placed all bets on his Korean opponent. The phone tap was meant to find out Greene's strategy, and when that did not work, he was kidnapped and threatened."

"Was he taken to Bayport Harbour?" Joe asked.

"No. We drove him to Fong's apartment not far from there."

"Why did you want to ship the Ruby King via the *Queen Maru*?" Frank inquired. "Is Captain Ono part of your gang?"

"No he's clean," Jervis said.

"Who went into Krassner's home to steal the King?" Frank asked.

"Fong and Eggleby. They took the antique to the shack in the woods, but when your two buddies arrived, they quickly drove off in Fong's car. Later Gerard Henry had the King wrapped in the rug and took it to Bayport Airport."

"What gave you the idea of using the serpent balloon to harass Krassner?" Joe asked.

"Fong knew Krassner was an avid balloonist," Jervis continued. "He also was well aware that Krassner feared the serpent symbol. The balloon seemed a logical idea to unnerve him."

"But he wouldn't hand over the King, even though you threatened to ruin his reputation," Joe said.

151

"No. He held out. When we put the pressure on Moy Chen-Chin, Mrs Krassner co-operated without her husband's knowledge."

"Well, I'm sure glad Krassner is exonerated," Chet said. "I always liked him."

"I'm just sorry we couldn't retrieve the King undamaged," Joe put in. "Without its jewels the chess piece is probably worthless."

"Fong knows where the rubies are. Ask him!" Jervis said.

"I know nothing," the Oriental said as his face contorted in an arrogant sneer.

"Where does Fong live?" Frank asked Jervis.

The man shrugged. "He's been staying with Choy Bok ever since he arrived."

"Why don't we look in Choy's apartment?" Joe suggested. "We know where it is!"

"Good idea," Captain Hawkins said.

An hour later a search party with a warrant arrived at Choy's multi-storey apartment. There was no sign of Mrs Choy. The police combed the place until one of them yelled, "Captain, come here!" In the pocket of Mrs Choy's dressing gown was a sack of gems!

Captain Hawkins invited the boys and Kim-Kim to dinner that night and thanked them for smashing the serpent gang. "Please return the Ruby King to its rightful owner," he said. "It won't be hard to restore it to its original beauty."

"You go back to United States?" Kim-Kim asked, his eyes sad.

"We'll have to. The case is solved," Joe said. Little did he know then that soon they would be involved in another one, *The Jungle Pyramid*.

Chet put an arm around his little friend. "We must leave. But we have a surprise for you. Frank and Joe have decided that part of their fee rightfully belongs to you because of your help!"

Kim-Kim's eyes lit up. "Me good detective!"

"A friend of ours," Chet went on, "will come to Hong Kong soon for the big chess championship. His name is Conrad Greene. He'll give you your reward. You just tell Captain Hawkins where he can get in touch with you."

"Speaking about the chess match," Joe said, "now that all the pressure is off, Conrad might win it, and with it the Ruby King!"

"And old Mr Greene won't have to worry any more," Frank added with a smile. "The King was buried not by its owner, but by Fong's men. The curse is lifted!"